The Yellow Field

By
Lauren Pickering

Strategic Book Publishing and Rights Co.

Strategic Book Publishing and Rights Co.
12620 FM 1960, Suite A4-507
Houston TX 77065

www.sbpra.com

ISBN: 978-1-62857-974-1

Design: Dedicated Book Services, (www.netdbs.com)

Author's Note

The story is set in present-day Warwickshire, England, and in southwestern France.

Chapter 1

Emma screwed her eyes shut and turned her head to the side on the pillow. "Are you never going to come?" she said. She was sore and feeling nauseous.

He stopped, looked down at her, then grinned sardonically. "Yeah. In a minute. Why?"

"I'm a bit sore—and tired."

He pressed hard into her.

"Ow! No, Charlie."

He stopped. "All right. I'll fuck your mouth then," he said aggressively. He pulled out of her, then brought himself to a kneeling position, his legs either side of her body and his cock just above her face.

She looked up at it, red, hard, and glistening. She opened her mouth timidly and he plunged it inside. At the same time, he took both her hands in his and held them down to the bed.

It felt horrible—and she could smell acrid sweat from his pubic hair. She uttered a muffled cry. His sharp jab to the back of her throat nearly made her choke, so she tipped her head back. She pursed her lips and rubbed it with the flat of her tongue. She didn't want his spunk in her mouth—*but anything to finish it*, she thought.

"Oh . . . that's so fucking good," he whispered.

He was pushing her head into the pillow as he sank into her, and she was grabbing breaths through her nose. The sick feeling was getting worse, and she didn't know how much longer she could stand it.

"There's nothing better than fucking a girl's mouth."

He kept pressing hard into her throat and holding it there for a few seconds before pulling back out. She felt trapped, claustrophobic, desperate for it to be over.

"Oh . . . fuck. Yeah . . . yeah . . . ohhhh. Shit . . ." he mur-mured.

A strong spurt of semen shot to the back of her throat and she felt herself retch. He groaned, fucking her repeatedly, his cock enormous, her mouth filling with the slimy liquid, her stomach turning over and over. She was trying to scream—but couldn't—and thought for one horrific moment that she would choke. With all her strength she freed her hands and snapped her head away. His cock slipped out, and with her arm, she pushed him backwards. Once free, she scrambled off the bed and ran to the bathroom, threw herself down on the floor, and vomited copiously into the pan.

She knelt there for a moment, the blood pounding in her head, the acrid taste of the vomit burning at the back of her throat and up into her nose. She retched again, then felt her stomach calm. She got up and rinsed her mouth out. She caught a glimpse of her face in the mirror. She was pale, and her eyes were slightly red. She brushed her teeth.

When she walked back into the bedroom, he half opened his eyes and smirked at her. "What's the matter—go down the wrong way?"

"I don't know. I've not been feeling very well all evening."

"You're normally so good at it. If there's one thing I'll re-member about you, it's that you're brilliant at giving head."

"Well, there's something to be grateful for." She got into bed.

"You're very rare."

"Why?"

"Most women I know hate it."

"It's an acquired taste."

"Yeah—well, everyone knows you've done a lot of ac-quiring," he said. "When I met you, I think mine was the only prick in the college you hadn't sucked. But I suppose one consolation you get from ending up with the college tart is good sex." He turned away from her onto his side.

She looked at his back, facing her in that arrogant way. He often said cheap things like that, and she hated it.

Anger flared inside her. She turned away from him onto her side and felt tears come to her eyes. She could still sense the strong taste of vomit in her mouth. She lay awake. It had been going wrong for some time, but she just hadn't admitted it to herself. Her friend Susie had warned her and she had ignored it—and now she had paid the price. He had been at her parents' house for a week, and the sex had gotten more and more aggressive and disgusting. Twice he had really hurt her trying to push his cock into her anus.

Once he's gone tomorrow, I'll finish it, she thought.

In the morning she woke, and after a few dizzy moments, the events of the previous night swam into her brain. He was still asleep. As she looked at him, his words cut into her just as sharply as they had the night before.

Her mouth tasted nasty. She got out of bed, went to the bathroom, and brushed her teeth again. Then she slipped on a short T-shirt dress and went to the door. She looked back at the bed. *I hate him,* she thought. She hadn't realised that until now, but she really hated him.

She tripped downstairs. Approaching the kitchen, the lovely, rich aroma of coffee filled her nostrils. Her mother had obviously made some before she went out. She leant on the worktop and breathed in deeply. She felt a bit better now. She had made a decision, and she only had to get over the next few hours.

She glanced out of the window and could see that it was a clear, sunny day. She did a double take and looked back. A girl was coming up to the house—quite tall, with long, blonde hair. She hesitated outside, and their eyes met. *She looks rather pretty,* she thought. The girl sort of smiled, looking slightly embarrassed. Emma left the kitchen, crossed the wide hall of the old house, and went to the front door.

As she opened it, she was struck again by how attractive the girl was, dressed in a pale blouse and tight black trousers.

"Can I help you?"

"Oh. Yes," the girl said, in a soft Birmingham accent. "I'm here for an interview, and I'm a bit early. They said the farm office. Have I come to the right place? I tried ringing the bell, but nobody answered."

"For an interview?"

"Yes."

"What, for the farmhand and office job?"

"Yes." She raised an eyebrow. "Odd, I know . . ."

"Oh no," said Emma. "Not really." Emma was surprised. Not because she was up for this job, but the closer she looked, the prettier the girl appeared—tall, slim, blonde, and with very dark eyes. "Sorry—I'm Emma, by the way. It will be my dad who interviews you."

"Oh, right. I'm Sally—Sally Middleton." She put out her hand and Emma shook it.

"Would you like some coffee while you're waiting?"

"That sounds great."

"Good. Come in." Emma walked back through the entrance hall and Sally followed her.

"Wow," said Sally.

"Yeah. It's nice, isn't it?" said Emma as she turned and cast her eyes over the large medieval vaulted space. "There was an old monastery here, and the house was once the Abbot's lodge. There's not much else left, apart from a few walls in the garden."

"Oh. Cool."

"So, like, you've done farm work before?"

"Yes. I helped out on my uncle's farm last year during the harvest. I really enjoyed it, and they seemed to think I did OK."

"Oh. Didn't they want you to work there again this year?"

"I could have done, I suppose, but I just wanted to go somewhere else."

"Ah—right."

"Anyway, I saw this ad and thought I might give it a try."

Emma poured three mugs of coffee. "Black or white?"

"White, please."

She poured some milk into all three and handed one to Sally. "I had better take one to my father. I'll be back in a moment."

She walked down the hall to her father's study and knocked.

"Come," she heard.

She opened the door. "Coffee."

"Oh, brilliant," said her father. He was sitting at his broad desk in the bay window. The diamond panes were covered at the edges by ivy climbing from the wall. The effect made the room bright lemon-green in the sun.

"Your next one is here."

"Oh, right. Well, I hope he's better than the rest."

"It's a she."

"Really?" He looked at a sheet on his desk. "Oh, yes. Intriguing."

"I think you could say that. I think you'll like her—or like the look of her, anyway. Shall I send her down?"

"No, give me a minute. What do you mean, anyway?"

"You'll see." Emma smiled knowingly at him.

As she walked back to the kitchen, Sally was leaning against the worktop, sipping her coffee.

"Apparently the others were crap, so he has great hopes for you."

"Oh dear," she said, smiling sheepishly. "Should I go through?"

"No—he said to give him a minute."

There was a pause. Emma looked at her. Her eyes were so dark they seemed to draw her in. "So, you enjoy farm work?"

"Yeah, I seemed to take to it. I don't know why."

"Well, I know what you mean—there's something about working on the land."

"So you help out as well?"

"Yeah. Sometimes."

"What, making the coffee and stuff?" Sally had both hands on her mug and was holding it to her mouth, smiling cheekily as she sipped it.

Emma looked up at her, slightly surprised, but instantly saw the twinkle in her eye. She smiled. "Yeah, I mean, that's what the women do around here. Make the coffee and service the blokes. I mean, you didn't think you were being interviewed to go on tractors or anything?"

"So you mean I get my knickers down and let the lads take it in turns?"

"If that's how you like it."

"You bet—two at once."

Emma laughed.

"Well no, actually, sorry to disappoint, but I've given all that up." Sally looked out into the garden, and there was an odd silence.

Emma looked at her more closely. Her smart black trousers were tight-fitting around her narrow waist. Her blouse was semitransparent, and Emma could make out the neat white bra beneath. A small gold chain hung round her neck, and her mass of thick, wavy blonde hair cascaded across her shoulders and down her back. Her face had hardly a trace of makeup. She was a naturally nice-looking girl.

"Nice garden."

"Yeah. We're very lucky. It's been in our family for years."

"Lords of the Manor, then?"

"Of course. We don't like riffraff here, you know."

"You won't like me then."

Emma's father put his head round the door. She saw the momentary surprise on his face at the appearance of his next interviewee. "You must be Sally."

"Yes. Hi." Sally shook his hand.

"Come through."

"Right."

"Good luck," said Emma.

Sally turned and smiled. "Thanks."

Emma wandered into the garden and sat on the bench just outside the kitchen window. It was secluded and hot, out of the breeze. She sipped her coffee and closed her eyes, smiling to herself at how her father would be enjoying talking to this extremely attractive young girl, who would be trying to get him to give her the job.

She was nice: quirky, cheeky—but fun. *If she does get it, it would be nice to have her around*, she thought—a change from the old hands and the monosyllabic, spotty young men.

She pulled up her dress, exposing her legs to the top of her thighs, and undid most of the buttons at the top, letting the sun kiss her breasts. She felt nice sitting practically naked in the sun. She knew she ought to go and wake Charlie, but she decided she didn't really want to face him. She was happy where she was and closed her eyes again. The horrible night had left her feeling sleepy. She yawned and turned her face to the side. She dozed lightly, barely discernible dreams flitting under her eyelids.

"Hello?"

She heard a voice and was instantly awake. She sat up sharply and realised Sally was standing at the kitchen door. She stood up quickly and walked over to her. "Hi. Sorry." She forgot that her dress was open almost to the waist. She saw Sally do a double take and stare at her breasts.

"Sorry," said Emma. "I've been sunbathing." She closed the dress and did up some buttons.

"That's OK. Don't worry on my account." The black eyes flashed. "I just thought I'd tell you that your dad has given me the job."

"Really? That's amazing." After an awkward moment, Emma kissed her on the cheek. A light, sweet scent drifted into her nostrils. "Wow. Well done."

"Yeah—I'm really pleased. He didn't even try me out on a tractor or anything. Said he would train me up on anything I wasn't sure of."

"Yeah, well—of course. Anyway, there's not much to making coffee."

"Oh no—he said you would be doing that," she said, smiling wickedly.

Emma laughed. "Well, that's brilliant. It's going to be nice having a girl my own age around the place for a change."

"Hope so."

Emma didn't know what to say. "Well, would you like me to show you around a bit?"

"Yeah—well, if it's not too much trouble."

They went back through the kitchen, out of the front door, and onto the drive. The yard was through the garages opposite the house, but Emma turned left and went through the small gate at the end of the drive and out onto the track that bordered the home field. "Let's go and see the rapeseed in flower," she said. "It's amazing at this time of year."

"OK."

"So, tell me, where have you come from?"

"Birmingham."

"Have you always lived there?"

"Yeah, I was born there and lived there all my life—with my mum."

"Oh, was she divorced or something?"

"Yeah, my dad left before I knew him."

"Oh, I'm really sorry."

"It's OK. I'm used to it. My mum died as well this year."

Emma stopped. "Oh God. How terrible. I'm so sorry."

"Yeah. It's OK. I think I'm over the worst now. It was cancer."

"Dreadful . . ." Emma was stung with a mixture of shock and embarrassment. She wanted to hug her—just to show something. But she was almost a stranger, and it seemed odd. She could see the hurt in her eyes.

They walked on slowly. Emma felt self-conscious and didn't know what to say.

As though sensing it, Sally took her hand and squeezed it. "Sorry. I shouldn't have mentioned that. People never quite know what to say." They had reached the entrance to the field. Sally let go of her hand and turned to look at the blaze of yellow that was in front of them. "This is amazing. I've never seen this before—I mean, you know, gone into a field when the rape is flowering."

Emma looked at her. *It must be so awful,* she thought, *having to cope with all that grief and loss.* She couldn't imagine what it was like. She couldn't even bear the thought of losing one of her parents.

They walked a short way down one of the tramlines, the plants surrounding them. The intensity of the yellow was dazzling, exaggerated by the sunlight. Every year she always made a point of coming into the field at this time, although she had left it a bit late this year, and she was never disappointed. "I love it. It's just, like, so concentrated—the yellow."

"Yeah. Fantastic. Don't they make margarine out of rapeseed?"

"Yeah—and oil."

Sally plucked a flower and held it to Emma's chin. "Ah—you like margarine," she said, smiling.

Their faces were close and they looked at each other for a moment. *Her eyes are so haunting,* thought Emma, *and her face so beautiful in the reflected yellow light.*

Sally brushed the flower slowly up Emma's cheek and across her mouth. "Oh, sorry—I've put pollen over you. Here." She put her fingers lightly across Emma's lips. Their eyes met and Emma couldn't describe it, but there was a kind of moment between them.

"So—did my dad mention where you are going to live?"

"Er, Farley Cottage? Is that right?" said Sally, casting the flower away.

"Really? Well—that's very nice. It's just been done up—and it's got all mod cons. A bit remote though. Do you mind being on your own?"

"No. I prefer it that way. I've gotten used to it in the last eighteen months."

Emma watched her closely. Her eyes seemed so large in her face, and as she glanced at Emma again, they seemed to see right through her. She had white, even teeth and a wide, full mouth. Her blouse was obviously new and quite expensive. The top few buttons were carefully undone to show some cleavage. There was no doubt that Sally was very sexy—even looking at her as another girl, Emma could see it—and that she knew how to use it. And it had obviously worked on her father.

"Well, it's the ideal place to take someone back to."

"Yeah, well—as I said, I'm not really into that at the moment."

"Oh, right."

"Bit of a long story."

"Been let down?"

"You could say that."

"Sorry—don't want to pry."

Sally flashed her a look and smiled faintly.

"My boyfriend is upstairs in bed," said Emma. "I ought to go and wake him, I suppose." *Stupid*, she thought immediately. *Wrong thing to say.* "It's our last weekend together for a bit. He's off to Brazil, and I'm off to France."

"What are you doing there?"

"A business language course. In a Catholic women-only college." Emma pulled a face.

"Oh—so no playing away. Even if you wanted to."

"No. Just lots of hard work in the language lab."

"Do you speak French, then?"

"Yeah. That's what I'm reading at uni. My mum's French."

A breath of wind caught the top of Emma's dress, and Sally's eyes flashed to her chest.

"You're popping out."

"Sorry." She quickly covered herself and did up another button.

"It's OK."

Their eyes met and Emma felt a strange unaccountable blush fly to her cheek. "I'm always stripping off. You'll get used to it."

Sally looked at her and there was a brief silence.

Sally looked away across the field. "Fantastic day."

"When are you going to move into the cottage, then?"

"Well, your dad said I could see it now. He's going to take me over in a few minutes. Then I'm going to come over on Monday—and we'll take it from there."

"Oh, good."

"How long are you away?"

"Six weeks. Then I'll come back and maybe help on the harvest."

"So I could be working with the boss's daughter?" The black eyes twinkled. "Making your coffee and cleaning your boots."

Emma smiled. "Well—someone has to."

They walked back to the field path and onto the end of the drive. As Emma looked back to the house, she saw Charlie standing in the drive, obviously looking for her. Her heart sank.

"Hi," said Emma, as they came up to him.

"Oh, there you are."

Emma noticed him case Sally from head to toe.

"This is Sally—she's going to be working here."

"Doing what?" he said, still looking impassively at her.

"Working on the harvest."

"God—how bizarre." He turned back to Emma. "I've got to go in half an hour. Fancy a walk or something?"

"OK," she said, embarrassed at his rudeness. She turned to Sally. "You're not rushing off, are you? I'll see you later?"

"Yeah." Sally smiled at her.

"OK, then." She turned back down the track, past where Sally and she had stepped into the field. The wall of the house garden was on their left. "You didn't have to be rude."

"Rude? Was I?"

"You know you were."

"It's just she's a pretty girl—and it's an odd thing to do, work at a place like this."

"Yeah, but . . . oh God, forget it." There was silence for a minute. "Her mother's just died and she's been left on her own."

"Really? Even more bizarre."

"She's lovely," Emma said forcefully.

"Yes. Not bad at all."

"Fancy her, do you?"

"She is quite fanciable—yes."

"I see." She felt a flutter of irritation.

They came to a stile into another field. When she got to it, he came up behind her, and she felt his hand slide up her thigh.

"Well, well, well. Nothing under our dress."

She made to climb over, but he put his arm round her and held her back. She felt his fingers run over her pussy. "Get off," she said sharply.

"No. I want to fuck you—in this position."

"Sorry—don't fancy it," she said firmly.

"You know you do, really." He pushed her dress right up her body until it sat round her neck.

"No, I don't." She tried to pull it down, but he put his arm round her neck, holding her against him.

"You fucking love it—and you know it."

"Stop it, Charlie."

With his other hand, he rubbed her sex roughly. "Don't want your pussy stuffed with a nice hard cock? That'd be the first time."

She tried to wrench herself away, but his grip was too tight. "Look—I've said I don't want to," she shouted.

"And I know you do."

"Are you going to rape me, or what?"

"If that's what turns you on." She felt his hand move to his trousers and undo them. The next moment his hard penis pressed against her buttocks.

"No!"

He pushed her sharply forward, and she caught the stile with her hands just in time. At the same time, she felt his cock head press against her vagina. "Ow!"

"Bit dry outside? Bet you're soaking inside . . . can't wait for it . . ." She heard him spit on his hand, and the next moment she felt him roughly rub around her opening.

"No, please!" She struggled again, feeling tears coming to her eyes, but she couldn't move as he had his arm tightly round her waist.

He pressed his cock there again and came into her sharply. "Ow, fuck!" she cried. He was very hard and it hurt. He began to fuck her roughly. She was still quite sore from the previous night, and her whole body was being jarred by his jabbing into her. Her thighs were quivering and she felt a sense of acute panic and went rigid. It was horrible, disgusting, animal—something that went back thousands of years, with countless women used like objects in a ruthless male game.

She hung her head forward and screwed her eyes shut. *It is no use fighting it,* she thought, *just let it take its course—treat it with the contempt it deserves. Think about something else, ignore what's happening. Think about anything—the girl, Sally—yes, Sally—talking to her in the rape field, feeling sorry for her, holding her hand. That had been so nice. Those deep black eyes, the soft white peach of her cleavage, the little lacy bra, that lovely, cheeky smile. She is such a beautiful girl.* She screwed her mind to the images. *Smelling her perfume, kissing her lightly on the cheek. Oh yes, think of her* . . . and the more she thought of her, the more she felt a warming heat building inside her, flooding her body, lifting her mind, and suddenly she was feeling pleasure, instinctively pushing herself back and forward on the hard flesh inside her, feeding the fantasy, imagining Sally's face close to hers, those lovely, full tempting lips, wanting to run her hands through that long golden hair. "Oh," she whispered as a pure flash of pleasure flooded her. "Oh God . . ."

She heard him gasp, and she was wrenched back to reality. The thrusting stopped and he held inside her, pulled out, then in again, spending himself, leaning heavily against her, grunting.

She steadied herself, breathing deeply.

He let go and pulled out of her. "You're such a randy bitch," he said, doing up his trousers. "You just fucking love it, don't you? Don't fancy it—my arse."

The words cut into her crudely. She stood up, trembling, not looking at him, pulling her dress down sharply. She turned and walked off in the direction of the house.

When he caught up with her she didn't say anything, didn't want to say anything. Her mind was in a whirl, and tears came to her eyes. The feeling of revulsion had returned as soon as he spoke—and she almost felt sick as his semen splashed down her leg.

"You all right?" he asked casually.

"Oh, just fine!" she snapped, the words catching on the lump in her throat.

They reached the house and he hovered for a moment as though he didn't know what to say. "I'll go and get my stuff," he said eventually.

"Good. Yeah. You do that." She stood in the drive, took out a tissue, and dabbed her eyes. She was shaking all over.

Minutes later they were standing at his car and he was saying meaningless goodbyes. She couldn't look at him, and when he tried to kiss her, she averted her mouth.

"In a mood, are we?

"Fuck off, Charlie."

He looked at her for a moment, then sniggered. Without saying any more, he got into his car.

As he drove away, she felt an extraordinary relief. She never wanted to see him again.

Her mind reeling, Emma ran into the house, through the kitchen, and out into the garden. She walked over the lawn, through the medieval arch that was the only remains of the old abbey church, and down towards their swimming pool. It was surrounded by a high yew hedge, and as she ducked through the entrance, the wide, blue expanse of water came into view. It was clear, rippling with a gentle ruffle of the breeze across its surface. It looked so inviting.

She kicked off her shoes, pulled her dress over her head, and dived in. The feel of the water swirling over her naked body was invigorating, and as she lay on her back, slowly kicking her legs, looking up into the pale blue sky, it was as though it was washing everything away. After a while, she stopped at the side of the pool and put her fingers down to her pussy. She parted her vaginal lips and ran a finger round inside. She wanted to get rid of Charlie's filthy, slimy spunk. Normally she was turned on by guys' semen—but today she couldn't think of anything more revolting.

She did another few lengths, powering herself up and down until she was breathless, then decided she'd had enough. She glided to the side, climbed out, and walked to the changing room at the other end. She pulled a towel off the shelf and buried her face in it.

She hated him. She must have known it deep down for some time, but hadn't allowed herself to believe it. They had filled the gaping hole in their relationship with sex. They had been rampantly fucking for days, and she had just done it to please him—like everything else—selfish bastard. And slowly the fucking had turned to abuse. *What happened just now was like being raped,* she thought. She hadn't wanted sex, but he had made her do it, and it had been horrible. This was the kind of thing that can traumatize you—scar you for life. She took the towel away from her face and stared outside. But then she forced herself to think about Sally—and she'd suddenly had a gay fantasy. Her head swam. It was the first gay attraction she'd had for years. She felt better—almost—*but God, what was that all about? I'll make myself another coffee,* she thought.

Her mother was out, and her dad was off with Sally, so she didn't bother putting the dress back on. She walked back up to the house, and as she entered the kitchen, threw it onto a chair by the door.

"Oh—hello."

She jumped. Sally was standing there. "Oh. Sorry . . ."

Sally's eyes flashed up and down Emma's body. She flushed a little. "It's OK. Your dad's having trouble finding the key to the cottage."

"Oh. Right." Emma put her hand nervously through her hair. "I've just had a swim."

Sally smiled. "Oh. I see. I was beginning to think you were allergic to clothes."

There was a brief silence, then Emma heard her father coming down the corridor. "Shit," she whispered, smiling at her. She quickly ducked out of the doorway, grabbed the dress, and spread it across her front. "Hi, Daddy. I've just had a swim."

"Oh yes. Well, I'm just going to take Sally to the cottage. Do you want to join us for lunch?"

"Yeah, that would be great."

"Good. I'll give you a call later."

As they left, Sally turned and looked at Emma again. "See you in a bit."

Back in her bedroom, she started filling a suitcase and sorting herself out for France, but she couldn't stop thinking about what had just happened: Sally's beautiful dark eyes scanning her body. She had a quick shower, blow dried her hair roughly, then went to her cupboard for some clothes. As she stood there thinking what to put on, her phone rang. It was her father. He suggested she join them in a pub in the village in about half an hour. She thought for a moment, then put on a white blouse, short skirt, and a cashmere cardigan. She checked herself in the mirror: She wasn't wearing a bra. She undid another button.

In the car on the way, excitement seemed to bubble up inside her.

When she got to the pub, Sally and her father were sitting by the window. She could see her father was engrossed.

"Hi," she said, and sat down near to Sally. "Had a good look around?"

"Yeah. It's a lovely cottage."

"You had better order your food from the bar. We've ordered already," said her father.

"Oh. OK." Emma went to the bar, scanned the menu, and decided on a salad. As she glanced back at their table after a few moments, her eyes met Sally staring intensely at her—a gaze that was turned immediately and rather self-consciously into a smile. Emma smiled back.

When she sat down again, she found herself looking at Sally. The sun from the window was catching her hair, and she was sure another button had come undone on the blouse, revealing a little more of the smooth mound of her breasts. As they talked, Emma looked at her wide, full mouth, her lovely smile, and even, white teeth.

They chatted about the farm, the house, the people who worked for them, and how they thought Sally would fit in.

"I'll give you my real thoughts later," said Emma, smiling at her father.

"And probably be very rude about everyone, including me," he said. "Anyway, I'll go and pay the bill."

"So you like the cottage?" Emma said when he had gone.

"Yeah, it's amazing. I mean, like, really lovely—far too good for me."

"He did it up for holiday lets, but then he realised he was going to be short of accommodation—so it's all yours."

"Yeah. He was saying."

"Bit remote though."

"No . . . it'll be fine."

"No trouble nude sunbathing there."

"Don't suppose I'll have time. Don't let me stop you coming round, though."

Emma looked at her and again saw a flash of that strange, penetrating look. "You bet." Their eyes held each other until Emma looked away.

"So, has Charlie gone?"

"Yeah."

"Nice walk?" She smiled slightly, wickedly.

"Yeah—yeah . . . OK. Bit obvious, weren't we?"

"Well, you had a nice day for it," she said.

Emma could see the twinkle in her eye again. "Yeah. Fantastic in the pool."

"Swimming without a cozzie?"

"Yeah, I like that."

"Well, I don't know. Shagging al fresco and skinny-dipping in the pool. What am I getting myself into on this farm?"

"Well, we're not boring, you have to admit that."

"No, you're not."

She met Sally's eyes and felt a flutter in her stomach.

Her father returned. "Well—we'll see you later, Emma," he said.

"Yeah. OK. I'll see you back at the house." She smiled at Sally. "See ya."

"Yeah—OK." Her look lingered.

Emma whiled away the afternoon trying to pack but somehow had no enthusiasm for it. She rather wished she had asked to go with Sally and her father. In the end, she decided to put on her bikini and take a book and some sun cream and go down into the orchard.

"I'm going to sunbathe, Mummy," she said as she walked into the kitchen. Her mother was busy tidying the kitchen, looking crisply elegant as she always did. "Could you rub some cream into my back? Just in case someone is looking for me, I'm going to be topless." She took off her top and turned her back.

"Do you like this new young girl?" her mother said, rubbing in copious amounts of coconut-smelling oil.

"Yes. She seems lovely—and fun."

"I haven't seen her yet. Is she pretty?"

"Yes—very. You'll have to watch Papa, Mummy."

"Oh, I gave that up a long time ago. He likes young girls. Most men do. As long as he doesn't get silly about it—which I'm sure he won't."

"So you don't mind him looking?"

"Of course not. I like to look too."

"Very French," said Emma, pecking her on the cheek.

She made her way down to the bottom of the orchard, laid out a rug on the grass, and lay on her stomach to read.

It was hard going, keeping her mind on the book. The nastiness of what had happened with Charlie—her stupidity in letting the relationship drag on despite the fact that neither her family nor Susie had liked him. The shock of his behaviour—the violence of it. Time and again she read and reread paragraphs of her novel without taking a word of it in.

Then Sally—what was this attraction she felt? Maybe it was just a reaction to what had happened—some kind of psychological refuge—nothing more.

She gave up and discarded her book, coated her front in cream, turned over and lay on her back, soaking up the warm sun. She dozed again—that sweet half-sleep of a daytime nap . . .

She heard some steps in the grass. She looked up and saw Sally walking towards her. She felt a little flutter in her stomach—and wondered momentarily whether she should cover up. She decided not to. She'd seen everything earlier anyway. "Hiya," she said brightly as the girl approached. She propped herself up on her elbows.

"Hi," said Sally, looking rather intently at Emma's breasts. "Sorry—only I'm off back to Birmingham, so I thought I'd come and say good-bye."

"Oh—so soon? That's a pity. Well look—don't rush off—sit down for a minute."

"If you're sure I'm not in the way? Don't want to muscle in on the nude sunbathing." She sat down next to her.

"Sorry. Starting my tan," said Emma.

"That's OK. Good idea. Do I have to strip off too?" She pushed her hands through her hair, a cheeky smile on her face.

"Only if you want to." There was a sort of pregnant pause.

"I've just met your mum—she's lovely."

"Yeah—she's great. We're very close."

"You're lucky."

"Yeah. . . . So, did you like the farm?"

"Yeah, there's so much of it. I still haven't seen it all."

"Oh well—there's plenty of time for that. So you start on Monday?"

"Yeah. I'm going to come over and do some stuff in the office, meet the other guys—you know."

"Great."

"I can't believe I'm actually going to be living here."

"You sure you're not going to be lonely in that cottage?"

"I think I need a bit of that at the moment—besides, what I like about farmwork is that you're always busy."

"I suppose . . . but . . ."

"Anyway, you'll come and visit me?"

"Yeah . . . course." Emma looked at her, then suddenly feeling self-conscious, looked away, letting the comment hang in the air. The attraction was there again, making her feel awkward and self-conscious.

"God—it is hot here," said Sally, after a moment.

"Sorry—do you want to go inside?"

"No, I wouldn't want to make you feel uncomfortable."

"Sorry?"

"Having to wear clothes."

Emma chuckled. "You'll have to join the club, then."

"Someone might come. I've only just got the job. I don't want to give the wrong impression."

"Oh, don't worry."

"I can blame you, can't I? The boss's daughter told me to take my clothes off." She undid the buttons on the white cotton blouse and slipped it off, her long golden hair cascading round her delicate shoulders. She kicked off her shoes, undid her trousers, and pushed them off her legs. They were long, pale, and slim.

She reached behind to her bra and fumbled, trying to undo the clip.

Without thinking, Emma sat up. "Here, let me." Sally's skin was warm and soft against her fingers as she freed the little fastening. Sally took it off and laid it beside her. Emma saw that it had left a red mark. "It was cutting into you a bit," she said and ran her hand gently over it to smooth it away. "There."

Sally looked round at her. "Thanks," she said, her dark eyes suddenly fathomless.

Emma tingled. She noticed how perfectly round Sally's breasts were, not large, but naturally shaped, tipped with small, pert nipples. She swallowed hard and tried to think of something to say. "So you didn't go to college or anything?"

"Nope. Had enough of all that—institutions. Wanted to get out into the fresh air."

"Did you do A levels?" Emma said, lying back down. She scanned the long expanse of Sally's back. It was a light honey colour and contrasted with the brown of her arms.

"Oh yeah. Got three straight As."

"But you didn't want to go to university?"

"No. My mum was ill . . . and there was other stuff going on. It was a bit of a bizarre time. I guess I knew my mum was dying, and I just wanted to get my A levels for her. Everything else was just out of the window."

Emma felt a wave of gentle emotion. "God, you poor thing. However did you cope?"

"I don't know. You just do. I got strength from somewhere."

Sally lay down, so Emma turned on her side, leaning her head on her arm, looking down at her. Lying back, Sally's breasts were two low, perfect mounds, topped by the small rose-pink nipples. Her skin, rippling over her rib cage and descending into the toned flat of her stomach, shone in the sun. A brief, lacy pair of panties sat sexily across her hips.

"So what did you do—you know—after your mum died?"

"Worked in a supermarket. Went a bit crazy."

"Crazy? Doing what?"

"Oh . . . getting pissed. Shagging around." Sally's deep, dark eyes scanned hers, but they were distant, as though dredging up memories. "I'm afraid I'm a bit of a tart sometimes."

"Oh well—you and me both. I've spent a year at university drinking and fucking far too much. It's time I got serious about my life."

Sally smiled, still looking at her intently. "Are you a bit of a heartbreaker, Emma?"

"Yeah, I suppose so, sometimes. Why do you say that?"

"I don't know," Sally said lightly. "You're very beautiful. Men must fall for you all the time."

"But you're lovely looking too." Emma saw a vulnerable flash in Sally's eyes, and there was that charge between them again.

Sally sat up abruptly and looked away into the garden. "I fall in love too easily," she said. "That's why I've just spent a year away from it all."

There was a brief silence.

"Emma?" It was her mother, calling from the house.

"Yeah?"

"We're going soon."

"Oh. OK—we'll come back up." Emma sat up and reached for her bikini top. "Look, why don't you have supper and stay over?"

"Oh no, I couldn't," said Sally.

"Why not?"

"I don't want to put you to any trouble—and I mean, I'm going to be an employee. Isn't that a bit . . ."

Emma laughed. "You're so sweet. Honestly, we're not like that. It'll be fine."

"Well, if you're sure."

"Anyway, my parents are out tonight. It'll just be you and me eating leftovers and watching the telly—yeah?"

"Sounds great—if it's OK with your parents?"

"Of course it will be."

"Good." Sally took her blouse and put it back on, then stood up and pulled on her trousers. Emma noticed she stuffed her bra in her handbag.

Emma picked up the rug and sun cream, and they walked through the trees back up to the house. She took Sally's hand. It seemed the natural thing to do for some reason. It was soft . . . nice.

"Mummy—I've persuaded Sally to stay the night. It seems silly for her to rush back now."

"If that's all right?" added Sally hastily.

"It's a lovely idea," said her mother, smiling at Sally. "The spare rooms are made up. Or you can sleep with Emma—she has a double bed."

"OK. Thank you."

Mr. Pascoe appeared at the kitchen door.

"Bill, go and get changed. We have to go in five minutes. We're out for the evening," she said to Sally, then turned and went into the hall.

"You might as well sleep with me," said Emma. "I changed the sheets this morning. Part of getting Charlie out of my life."

"Oh really?"

Emma took a bottle of white wine from the fridge. "Yeah. We split this morning—after we left you. I just wasn't interested anymore and—well, anyway . . ." There was a sudden lump in her throat. "The more I think about it, I really wasn't enjoying it—him, I mean. The sex was . . . frantic—well, horrible might be a better word." She shuddered, and tears pricked her eyes. "Sorry."

"It's OK." Sally put her hand gently on Emma's back. "Are you all right?"

"Yeah. Yeah—no. I'm fine."

Sally looked at her, the lovely dark eyes seeming to draw her in.

"Sorry—would you prefer beer?"

"No, this is great."

Half an hour later they sat at the kitchen table eating the remains of a *chili con carne*.

"So is your thing with Charlie completely over?" said Sally. "I mean—you don't have to say if you don't want to."

"No, it's OK. He's just so bloody arrogant, for one thing. You saw the way he talked about you this morning without even introducing himself."

"Oh—that was OK."

"No it wasn't. He was sort of looking down on you—that's appalling."

"Well, I am just a hired hand," she said, smiling knowingly.

"No, it's just his bloody attitude. He's a bastard, really."

"He's quite good-looking."

"That's what he said about you."

Sally looked at her incredulously. "Really?"

"Yeah. He's also a *randy* bastard."

"Well, I suppose they have their uses."

"Mmm. Well—I don't have a use for him. And—by the sound of it—you wouldn't either."

"What?"

"Well, you said you'd given all that up—sex and stuff."

"Oh—I had some bad experiences and got upset."

"Well, you must have been through a lot recently."

"Yeah. You could say that."

There was a silence. Emma poured her another glass of wine. "Shall we go through into the drawing room? We could watch a DVD."

"Sounds great."

"I'll light the fire. It's a bit chilly—of course Dad has turned off the heating."

They walked through the vaulted entrance hall, through a long passage and into the drawing room. Emma loved this room. It was very large, with a beamed ceiling. Blocked-up stone arches on the walls showed its history—smaller leaded windows had been put in at a later date. The large, medieval fireplace had a basket of logs. Emma took some matches from a side cupboard and lit the kindling. The room was so long that her father had put a grand piano at one end and a snooker table at the other—and there was still enough room in the middle for three spacious sofas surrounding the fireplace.

Emma glanced at Sally.

"God—it's amazing."

"Yeah, it's lovely. It was fantastic growing up here."

Sally sat at the sofa that faced the widescreen TV that stood to the side of the fireplace. Having lit the fire, Emma came and sat next to her.

"This is a wonderful house."

"Yeah. We're really lucky."

"Bit different to where I was brought up."

"Are you still living—you know—in the family home?"

"Yeah, but I'm going to sell it. It's really good getting this job. I can get on with it now. I just want to be away from all the memories."

"Sure. Well, you'll be able to work here until October at least—longer if you want to."

"Your dad said I could probably work over the winter, helping out in the office."

"Oh yeah. Well, Molly's on maternity leave and might stay off—I don't know."

"You can't get rid of me that easily."

The black eyes bored into her again. Emma looked away, then back at her. "I really don't see how you coped—you know—with all that's happened to you. I mean, is there anyone else in your family?"

"Just an uncle and aunt. They were really good over Mum dying—sorted out everything. It was all just a blur to me. They've said I can live with them if I want to, but I don't fancy it. I might go there at Christmas, I guess."

"I can't imagine what it was like."

"It was horrible." She paused. "Makes me think that I don't want to get close to anyone any more—just in case I lose them."

There was a silence. Emma didn't know what to say.

"Anyway. Tell me about the farm."

"OK."

Sally fired questions at her. Emma sensed it was as much to divert attention from herself as to find out anything, but she had fun talking about her family and the other workers. As they talked, she found herself looking at Sally closely—at her eyes and lips—at how the long blonde hair brushed the fine skin of her neck. Another button had worked loose on her blouse, and Emma's attention wandered constantly to the curve of the pale, bare breasts sitting behind the near see-through material. She was puzzled by her attraction, and somehow she sensed that Sally knew. As the light outside faded, the firelight flickered on Sally's face and tinged the blonde hair a reddish gold.

"Can we play some snooker?"

"What? Yes. Of course."

Sally leapt up and walked over to the table. "Where's the light?"

"Oh. Here." Emma went over to the switch on the wall. The sudden brightness cast over the green baize dazzled her for a moment.

"Hey—great. Are you sure your dad won't mind?"

"No—of course not."

"Brill."

"Have you played before?"

"Yeah, loads. I'm not that good, though."

"Well, Dad will like it that you play. He's always grumbling about how bad Mum and I are."

After a few minutes it was obvious that Sally knew how to play. It was only a three-quarter table, but her shots were very accurate, and she left Emma a long way behind.

Emma's mobile rang. She picked it up and glanced at the screen. It was Charlie. She pressed the off button and put it down.

"Aren't you going to answer it?"

"No. It was Charlie. I've said all I want to say to him."

"Right. Plenty of fish in the sea. Anyway—you're going to be celibate for a few weeks now."

"Yeah. Good thing too."

"Really?"

Sally leaned down across the table and lined up a shot. Emma could see the neat breasts and the round curve of her cleavage.

"It's just his attitude to sex has put me off, I think. I mean, don't misunderstand me—I love sex, but he was just . . ."

She broke off. A sudden lump had come in her throat, and tears were welling up again.

Sally looked up.

"I'm sorry . . ."

Sally put down her cue and walked round the table. She took Emma in her arms. "Hey . . . come here."

Emma began to cry. "He . . . he was just such a bastard. I didn't want to do it—you know, this morning—and he just made me do it. Forced himself on me." She squeezed Sally tightly. She was so soft; her lovely golden hair smelled so nice.

"You poor thing." Emma felt Sally kiss her cheek and her hands rub her back. "How dare he treat you like that."

"No, it's my fault. I should have ended it weeks ago. I didn't love him or feel much for him. The sex just became animal . . . disgusting."

Sally put her hands on Emma's face and brought it close to hers. "No. It's not your fault. The last thing you should do is blame yourself. Women are different. We're more emotional about stuff."

There was a warm throb in Emma's stomach as she looked into the huge dark eyes. "Yeah . . . yeah, you're right. I'm just being a bit pathetic. Only that's never happened to me before—you know, someone almost raping you, just taking what they want. I don't want it to put me off sex. People can become scarred for life by that sort of thing."

"Don't be silly. You're a warm, lovely person—and you're so beautiful." Another kiss on the cheek and Sally hugged Emma tightly. Emma could sense the warm skin of her back as she touched the thin blouse.

Sally eased her arms off her after a few moments and brought her face close to Emma's. "Now. No more silly thoughts, OK?"

"Yeah," whispered Emma. Sally's face so close to hers was mesmerising.

"Good," she said—and kissed her lightly on the mouth.

Emma was stunned. It was so soft, so unexpected. It tingled on her lips. She smiled sheepishly.

Sally stroked her face and kissed her again. This time she held her lips on Emma's. It was such a tender sensation, so new, so extraordinary.

When their lips finally parted, Sally smiled and rubbed her nose on Emma's. She stared into her eyes for a moment—then let her go and turned back to the snooker table. "Men are such jerks sometimes." She went and picked up her cue. She leaned down, took another shot, and sank the black.

"Yeah." It was slightly odd. Sally was behaving as though nothing had happened. "Thanks. Thanks for the hug. I feel so much better now."

Sally looked up and smiled cheekily. "Sorry—just beaten you."

"Well done. Sorry I was crap."

"You're fine. Just need more practice."

"That's not what my dad says."

Sally yawned.

"Would you like a shower before we go to bed?"

"Yes. That would be nice."

"OK. There's a bathroom in my room."

"En suite?"

"Oh yeah. We don't slum it here, you know."

They walked back into the hall and up the wide staircase that split at the half-landing. Emma led her down a long corridor that led to her room. "These are the only two bedrooms on this side of the house," she said. "The other one is a spare one."

"So nice and private," said Sally.

"Yeah. Just the way I like it." Emma opened the door.

"Blimey," said Sally. "It's amazingly big. And God—look at the size of that bed."

"Yes. All for little me."

"Big enough for a gang bang."

Emma chuckled. "I haven't—but I suppose there's always a first time."

Sally stood in the middle of the room looking admiringly around her.

"Have you ever done it?" said Emma.

"What?"

"A gang bang."

"Well, I've done three in a bed—but I'm not sure if that counts."

"Three? What was that? Two blokes and you?"

"No—it was with a girlfriend of mine. We both fancied the same bloke, so we both had him. We thought it would be better that way." She said it quite casually, at the same time picking up a DVD from the side table and looking at it.

"Oh. Was it nice?"

"Yeah. It was. Lovely combination." She looked at Emma rather intensely.

Emma felt herself flush.

"Is that the bathroom?"

"Yeah." Emma opened the door for her. "There are clean towels in there," she said, pointing to a cupboard. "I'll, er . . . put you out a T-shirt."

Sally frowned.

"You know—to wear in bed."

"Oh. OK. You mean bed is the only place you actually wear something?" she said, with a cheeky smile.

"Well no, I never wear anything."

"Nor do I."

"Oh . . . OK." Emma felt herself flush again. "Let's not bother then."

"OK," said Sally brightly.

Emma left the door open, then turned back into the bedroom and undressed. As she stood with nothing on, putting her clothes away, she felt strange. She had only ever slept naked with lovers—with guys. She lay down on the bed and switched on the TV.

A few minutes later, Sally emerged with a towel around her, holding her clothes. She laid them on a chair. "All right if I put these here?" Her eyes swept Emma's naked body, just as they had in the kitchen earlier.

"Yeah—sure. Oh, and I forgot to tell you—there's a new toothbrush in the wall cupboard, the one with the mirror on it. You can use that."

"Oh, thanks."

She disappeared back into the bathroom. After a while, Emma got off the bed and went to the bathroom door. Sally had taken off the towel and was naked, bent over the sink, brushing her teeth. *She is very beautiful,* thought Emma, *pale, slim, with a boyish figure.* She had seen plenty of girls nude before at school—but suddenly this was different.

Sally turned to her, the toothbrush still in her mouth.

"Sorry," said Emma.

"It's OK," she said, spitting the toothpaste out. As she picked up a towel and wiped her mouth, Emma caught a full view of her body—of the small, pure-blonde bush and firm, natural tits.

"You're a real blonde, I see," said Emma with a smile.

"Too right," said Sally, smiling knowingly. "All yours," she said and went into the bedroom.

"Thanks."

Emma peed, had a brief wash, and brushed her teeth. When she came back into the bedroom, Sally was sitting up in bed watching the TV.

"Am I OK on this side of the bed?" she said.

"Yeah, sure. I mean, I normally sleep wherever I end up after a shag."

"Oh—so I've got to shag you, have I?" Sally said, her eyes twinkling with mischief.

Emma felt herself catch a breath. She laughed nervously, but couldn't think of a witty reply.

"Suit yourself—but don't say I didn't offer," she said playfully. "Anyway, I'm pretty shagged out myself." She slid down the bed and turned onto her side facing Emma, the deep dark eyes looking at her almost impassively. "Lovely, comfy bed."

"Yeah, it's good. You happy to turn off the light?"

"Sure."

"OK." Emma slid into the bed. She felt an impulse to embrace her—hug her or something—but immediately checked herself. "Night."

"Night."

She took the remote control and clicked off the TV—then hesitated before switching off the reading lamp. Her heart was racing and she almost felt breathless. "Thanks for giving me a cuddle earlier. I really needed that."

"That's OK." Sally shifted closer. "It was a horrible thing to happen." She stretched out her hand and stroked Emma's shoulder gently. "Sure you feel better now?"

"Yeah." Emma was mesmerised. "I mean . . . It's been lovely having you here."

"Good." The hand drifted across Emma's shoulder, traced the line of her neck, then stroked her face. Sally's eyes dropped to focus for a moment on Emma's mouth—then she leaned across and kissed her lightly on the lips.

Emma felt as though she would melt. Her lips were so soft, tender, different. Without thinking, Emma returned the kiss, pecking Sally's lips softly. There was a moment's hesitation, and Emma could feel Sally's breath on her mouth. Then they kissed again, lingering a little more this time, their lips moving sensuously together. She was kissing another girl, but it felt wonderful. She felt Sally's tongue tentatively probe her mouth. It was an electric sensation, and she touched it with her own. Their bodies intertwined, their legs rubbing deliciously together. Emma's hands roamed down over the rich, smooth skin to her buttocks—tight, boyish, and round.

Emma felt her heart thumping, her body warming with desire. They paused for a moment, planting light kisses on each other before kissing deeply again. It was long, but when their lips parted, they stayed close.

Emma felt a wonderful sexual thrill at the touch of the bare, soft, female body. Sally kissed Emma's neck and shoulders. She brought her mouth back to Emma's and kissed her again, her hand stroking Emma's breast.

"Ohhh . . . Sally . . ."

Sally looked at her anxiously. "Are you OK with this?"

"Yeah . . . God, it's so lovely."

"But you're not sure?"

"Yeah—no. I mean, it's just that it's so incredible; it's a bit overwhelming."

"Maybe we should go to sleep?"

"No, please—not just yet." Emma kissed her again and felt her body glow wonderfully. She wanted to feel Sally's body all over. It was so sexy, so gorgeous. She massaged Sally's breast with her hand. It felt so arousing—firm and perfectly round, the nipple pert and hard.

Sally took Emma's face in her hands. "You're so beautiful."

Emma stroked her hair, her shoulder. "So are you."

Sally smiled widely and laughed softly.

"What?"

"You're an amazing kisser."

"So are you . . . God . . . fantastic." Emma laughed nervously as well.

They kissed again and Emma felt her pussy burn with the touch and feel of the other girl. She kissed Sally's cheek and pushed her tongue into her ear.

Sally sighed and started rubbing herself against Emma's leg. She could feel Sally's pussy, hot, wet, and slippery against her skin.

Emma kissed all round her neck, moving her body to Sally's rhythm. She found her mouth and they kissed passionately, wrestling their mouths together.

The gyrations of Sally's body became quicker and more urgent—then suddenly she lifted her head and cried out. She tensed, her voice shrill, then she seemed to spasm several times as though an electric shock was going through her.

Emma held her tightly, kissing her face and hair until she relaxed and fell limp in her arms.

Sally looked up, her eyes dreamy and soft in the light. "Oh . . . that was lovely. I'm sorry, I just haven't been this close to anyone for so long. I couldn't stop myself."

"Did you come?"

"Oh God, yeah. Sorry."

"That's OK. It was lovely to feel you."

"That was amazing."

Emma kissed the soft, passive mouth.

"Can I do it for you?"

"N-no. Really. I'm OK," said Emma.

"Are you sure?" Sally lowered her head and kissed one of Emma's breasts. It scattered sensation all over her—so soft, so different. At the same time Emma felt Sally's hand trace down to her pussy and caress her there gently. Emma gasped, a wave of emotion flowing through her. She was unbelievably aroused—after everything that had happened that morning, she had thought she would never feel like this again.

"You're lovely and wet. But I won't if you're still sore from—you know."

"No, don't worry . . . I feel wonderful."

She felt Sally's fingers explore and then a finger push inside her. An incredible thrill shot through her, shimmering all over her body. "Oh God . . . Sally . . . so lovely . . ." The finger was moving so subtly in and out, and she could feel Sally's thumb roving over her clitoris. She pushed her hands through the long, silky, fair hair and stroked the soft delicate shoulders. She put her hands on Sally's face, pulled it up to her own, and kissed her tenderly. "Oh my God . . . this is so amazing . . . I've never wanted anyone so much." For so long she had just been a receptacle for someone else's pleasure, but now she knew she was on an equal journey with a lover who wanted to give to her.

"When I first saw you this morning, I don't think I'd ever seen anyone so gorgeous looking," whispered Sally. "I couldn't believe my eyes. I just wanted to snog you right there. Then when I saw you starkers in the kitchen, I knew I just had to make love with you."

"Oh—and you," said Emma. "I kept thinking about you all day. Standing in that field. Your lovely eyes." She sighed again, as another tremor from Sally's fingers shimmered through her body. They kissed again.

"When I kissed you downstairs—I couldn't stop myself. I was so afraid you might react badly."

Emma smiled. "You behaved as though nothing happened. But I was overwhelmed. It felt so lovely." Suddenly, her body seemed to freeze for a moment as the tension built sharply. She cried out at as a sudden thrill of acute pleasure shot through her. "Oh, Sally," she gasped. But quickly it dispersed, and a wonderful sensation of relaxation followed, making her feel light and serene.

"Are you OK?"

"Yeah . . . yeah."

"Did you come?"

"I don't know. But it was so lovely. I mean . . . I've never come in my life before, but . . . oh, Sally . . . what's happening to me?" She kissed her deeply again, wanting to eat her lovely mouth. She touched Sally's face with her fingers, running them lightly over her cheeks, forehead, and lips. "God . . . fuck."

"Are you OK?"

"Yeah . . . yeah, oh yeah. It's just . . . this is all so new."

"Yeah, I'm sorry. Maybe it's a bit soon." Sally withdrew her finger slowly from Emma's pussy.

Emma immediately felt a huge longing and hugged the girl to her. "Oh God, no, don't be sorry."

They looked at each other for a few more seconds before Sally kissed her lightly. "Maybe it's time to go to sleep."

"Yeah." She hesitated for a moment, not wanting it to end—then turned, switched off the light, and lay back down again.

Sally laid her head against Emma's chest. "I had such a lovely orgasm. It was just what I needed," she whispered. "I feel so good now." Her body was half spread over Emma's and she felt her relax, her hand cupping Emma's breast. "Good night."

Emma kissed the top of her head. "Night."

Emma lay in the darkness. She could still feel the touch of Sally's lips. She felt light and sexy, almost as though she had taken some sort of drug. Sally's body was warm, wrapped around her, and she felt a sense of joy that she realised had just not been there with any other lover. She didn't know what was happening to her, but at that moment she didn't particularly care. It was incredible . . . just amazing. She closed her eyes.

Chapter 2

When she woke in the morning, she was still on her back, and Sally was lying cuddled up next to her, her arm across Emma's stomach. She glanced down at the pretty face, her long dark eyelashes and her mouth slightly open, her breath warm on Emma's skin. The long blonde hair was tumbled and sticking up in places, not neat and ordered as it had been the day before. She kissed it gently and ran her hand through it. She could still sense that wonderful feeling from a few hours back. She slid her hand down under the duvet, ran it down Sally's body to the smooth ridge of her hips. She fondled her buttocks. So sexy, so nice.

She needed to pee, and her other arm was going to sleep, trapped under Sally. She gently disentangled herself, trying not to wake her. As she slid out from their cuddle, Sally stirred.

"Sorry. I didn't mean to wake you. I need to pee."

Sally sat up slowly, still half asleep, and pushed her hair away from her face. She looked at Emma. "It's OK."

"Be back in a minute."

Emma stepped into the bathroom, sat on the loo, and blissfully emptied her bladder. Daylight was seeping through the blind, and she blinked. What had happened in the night seemed like a vivid dream in the light of the morning. In one sense it was almost as though it had never happened, but in another she also knew that her life had changed—and changed wonderfully.

She washed her hands, splashed some water on her pussy in the bidet, then walked back into the bedroom. She opened the curtains, and sunlight flooded into the room.

Sally blinked, and as she walked back to the bed, Emma could see her eyes scan her naked body. Emma felt uninhibited, nice, just like she felt when she was with any other lover.

She sat on the bed next to Sally. "Did you sleep all right?"

"Yeah." Sally ran her hands through her hair. She looked flushed, vulnerable.

Emma smiled at her—then slightly awkwardly leant over and kissed her lightly. She felt rather self-conscious and put her hand up and stroked her own hair. "Your hair's gone a bit spiky."

"I know. It does that."

"OK, well, you have a doze. Tea or coffee?"

"What, in bed?"

"Yup," said Emma gaily, as she slid off the bed and took her dressing gown from the back of the door.

"Tea, please."

"Good choice. Back in a minute." She blew her a kiss.

She flew happily down the stairs, through the hall and into the kitchen. She felt light, almost delirious—so alive, so different from the day before. Her mother sat at the table, drinking coffee and reading the paper.

"Hello, Mummy."

"Hello. You're very bright. Sleep well?"

"Blissful."

"Was Sally all right?"

"Yeah, brilliant. She's really great. I'm going to make her some tea."

"Good. It will be nice for you to have her around. Company when you come back, I mean."

Emma put on the kettle and took out the teapot. She leaned on the worktop and looked at her mother. "She's amazing, you know. She was telling me she has lost both her parents. Her dad walked out on them when she was very young, and her mum died a year ago. Did you know that?"

Her mother looked up and took her glasses off. She was always so elegant, thought Emma, so refined, in that way French women were. "Why, that's awful. Poor thing. Has she got anyone else?"

"An uncle and aunt—but she doesn't really feel close to them."

"How terrible." She thought for a moment. "Why does she want to work here, do you think?"

Emma poured the boiling water into the pot. "I'm not sure. It's certainly an odd thing to do. She says she really loves working on the land. But she's got good exam results. She could go to university easily if she wanted. I don't quite understand it. It's almost as though she wants to be away from everyone. She thinks the cottage is really cool, even though it's miles from anywhere."

"Yes. I said to Bill, I have reservations about that. A young girl shouldn't be living in a remote place on her own without anyone else around."

"No. I said I'd spend time with her there when I come back."

"Yes, of course."

"I'd better take her some tea." She poured out a cup and a cup of coffee for herself. She smiled at her mother and waved. She couldn't wait to get back upstairs.

Sally sat up in bed as Emma came, her long golden hair splayed over her pale breasts.

"There. Tea for you. Coffee for me."

"Brilliant. Thanks."

Emma took off her dressing gown and climbed back into bed.

Sally's dark eyes studied her as she took a long drink from her cup. "This is such a lovely room."

"Yeah. I love it. You can see for miles—and it gets the sun in the morning." Emma looked at her. The tousled blonde hair was a bit more ordered now. Emma scanned the little snub nose, the wide, sexy lips, and pure, white teeth. What had happened between them had been a revelation—but at the same time sort of lay unsaid.

"It was lovely last night." The words had come out before she had even thought about it.

Sally looked at her wide-eyed. "Yeah. Fantastic." She looked down at her cup, took a sip, then looked back up at her.

"I've never done anything like that before. It was so different. Different to what's been happening in my life," she said, trying to make it sound as light as possible. She could feel her heart thumping in her chest. She looked at Sally, nervously pushing her hand through her hair.

"I mean, like—are we going to be all right with it?" said Sally.

"Yeah . . . why not?"

"Good . . . I mean, we can take it—you know—as it comes."

As Emma looked at her, she realised she desperately wanted to hold her again.

Sally smiled. "You're going away, anyway."

"Yeah." Emma put her cup down on the side table. "Er . . ." She felt herself blushing. "I just . . . could we do it again?"

Sally looked up at her, her eyes so huge. "Sure," she whispered.

"Oh God—that sounded so stupid."

She looked at her cup of tea, then put it down as well. She turned back to Emma and smiled knowingly. "No it didn't. Come here."

Emma lay down in the bed and put her arm along the pillow. Sally lay down close to her, her legs touching Emma's, put her hand on Emma's face, and kissed her.

As they came together, Emma felt herself fill with a sexy warmth. Their tongues played together, and Sally seemed to massage Emma's mouth with her own. She could feel Sally's sex pressing against her hip as she pulled herself closer. Emma wrapped her arms around her, her hands searching the golden skin. They kissed deeply and intensely, moving their bodies together—that wonderful exploring play of first-time lovers.

Emma broke from the kiss. She squeezed Sally's buttocks gently, ran her hand up the long, firm back, then stroked Sally's forehead, cheeks, and lips delicately with her fingers.

"When you said that you had that threesome—did you mean that you made love to them both?"

Sally's eyes scanned Emma's face. "Yes," she whispered.

"You had sex with the girl as well?"

"Yeah. I like girls. You may have noticed."

Emma looked into the dark eyes. "God . . . you really turn me on. I've never felt anything like this with another girl. Apart from schoolgirl crushes—you know."

Sally kissed her gently. "You really turn me on as well. Here." Sally took Emma's hand and put it between her legs.

The smooth lips of Sally's pussy were slippery, oozing fluid. She ran her fingers down them, from the soft down of her pubic bush to the little line of flesh that linked to her anus, then back up to the nub of her clitoris. It was so strange to feel another girl in this way, to know exactly what it felt like, how to please. Only once before had she ever touched and kissed another girl—pathetic fumblings, years ago now, when she was very young. It must have lived with her at the back of her mind, because doing it now felt like the most natural thing in the world.

Sally turned onto her back and sighed, and Emma cuddled up to her, kissing her face, cheeks, forehead, nose, and finally her willing mouth. She pushed her finger down between the folds, found the entrance, and without hesitation slid it into the tight tunnel.

Sally moaned and her mouth broke away, her hands running keenly over Emma's stomach, breasts, and face. "Ohhh, you're going to make me come again."

"Good, I want you to come. It's so nice to feel you there." She put another finger alongside and pushed them back in. "Is that OK?"

"Ohhh yes . . ."

Emma put her thumb on the little hillock of her clitoris, and as she pushed her fingers in and out, she could feel the hard little point slip and slide beneath it.

Sally breathed in deeply and shuddered. The lids of her dark eyes were half closed as her chest rose and fell, her small pink nipples tight across her breasts. Emma lowered her head and took first one, then the other into her mouth, sucking on them gently.

Sally took Emma's head in her hands, pulled it up, and kissed her hotly, her tongue strong in Emma's mouth. Emma pumped her harder and deeper, feeling the lust build wonderfully in her own abdomen.

Sally turned her head away and gasped, her body rising, then subsiding. "Oh God, I'm so close . . ." Her hands massaged Emma's breasts as she brought her mouth back close to Emma's, her breath fast and hot on Emma's face. "Ohhh, Emma, you're so gorgeous." Her mouth opened, she cried out, and then she threw her head back as her body went rigid. She breathed in sharply and relaxed, only to tense again, and Emma felt her pussy muscles clench on her fingers.

"Oh yes . . . darling."

Sally finally drew in a long breath and fell limp, pulling Emma into a long, soft kiss. She looked at Emma, the pupils of her eyes huge, the lips of her wide mouth slightly parted. "Fuck, that was amazing."

Emma smiled and kissed her softly. "I loved it."

"I can't believe you've never made love to a girl before."

"No—never." As she withdrew her fingers, Emma could feel that Sally's sex was running with juice and the sheet was wet. She felt a pang of lust deep inside herself as she brought her fingers to her mouth and licked them. The taste was sweeter than a man's cum, but still strong and strangely intense. She put them to Sally's mouth, and Sally licked them.

Emma lay her head down next to Sally's, kissing her cheek. "I don't know what all this means," she said, "but yesterday, when Charlie and I went for that walk and he fucked me—well, raped is a better description. I hated it so much. He was fucking me like some animal, fucking me from behind. It hurt, and it just felt horrible. He was gripping me so tightly—I couldn't get away. So I just tried to wrench my mind away from what was happening to me. I started to think of you, of us standing in that field."

"Really?" Sally stroked her face.

"Yeah. And the more I thought of you, the better it felt."

Sally kissed her softly. "That's lovely."

"So you can see why I'm a bit confused."

"Yeah."

They lay there looking at each other, kissing, their hands roaming each other's bodies. Sally's hand found its way to Emma vagina.

"Your turn."

Emma rolled on her back and took the mass of Sally's long blonde hair in her hands, bringing the lovely mouth to a deep and luscious French kiss. Pleasure scattered like a hot rash all over her as Sally's fingers caressed her clitoris, their mouths wrestling together, their tongues playing deliciously.

Sally pushed a finger inside her and Emma broke the kiss sharply. It was as though an electric current had suddenly passed through her veins. "Sally . . . Sally . . . oh God, Sally . . ." She felt the same tension gather inside herself that she was sure she had felt the night before, that feeling that her body could achieve any height of pleasure. This was so different, so beautiful, almost too much.

"Are you OK?" whispered Sally, kissing her cheek and neck.

"Oh yeah . . . so lovely." Emma looked down at Sally's finger moving in and out of her. She couldn't believe that such slow, gentle lovemaking could make her feel so wonderful. So many men had been inside her, so many had fucked her so many times, but nothing felt like this slim, subtle invasion. Her vagina seemed to suck it inside her, the tissue tingling as it was pushed slowly and deeper into her. The kisses on her neck were so tender, shimmering delight across her shoulders. The feel of Sally's skin was so soft and feminine.

Sally's light kisses travelled slowly across her shoulder blades and on down to her breast. She kissed round the areola, then traced with her tongue round again, finally taking the nipple into her mouth, suckling and gently biting.

Emma sighed at the acute pang of pleasure that resonated from her breast to the longing building so wonderfully in her pussy. She stretched herself, feeling every muscle tense with the sublime resonance that Sally's loving fingers and mouth was exciting in her. She wanted this to go on forever—this was the kind of love she had wanted for so long. It was almost as though Sally was some kind of purifying angel sent to heal her by showing her how gentle and profound sex could be.

She moved her head to Emma's other breast, eking out the most wonderful sensations. Emma put her hands on her head and pulled Sally up to her, kissing her passionately, more passionately than she had ever kissed anyone else before.

"I'm sorry he hurt you," said Sally. "Men don't think of how delicate a woman is down there." She kissed her way over her stomach until Emma felt the warmth of her breath among her pubic hair. "Let me kiss it better."

Immediately she cried out as she felt Sally's tongue caress her. Her stomach lurched as though Sally had made contact with something inside her that had lain hidden for so long, something she had longed for but that had always eluded her. She found it almost difficult to breathe. She gasped with a rush of sensation as she felt Sally pull her finger out and then push it back inside. Then suddenly she knew that she had put another finger alongside, and her vaginal walls were expanding. She wanted more and more—and the tension returned to an unbearable level in her loins, as though the pleasure coursing through her was unsustainable—the nerves, muscles, and flesh couldn't contain it any longer.

Sally's hot mouth engorged Emma's clitoris, and immediately Emma screamed. "Oh my God, Sally—I'm going to . . . oh God . . ." It was as though the tiny, tortured little nub was the fuse that set the purging fire of relief through Emma's veins. "Sally—I love you, I love you . . . OOOOOOHHHH!" The whole of her body seemed to suddenly burn at a height of pleasure she had never imagined, the tension screwing itself to a pitch that seemed to mount and mount. She could hear her own cries and feel her seizing muscles and knew that her whole frame was being wracked with unbelievable sensation where it was held for a burning moment before engulfing itself in a sweet, raging fire . . .

Her lungs were so starved of breath she thought she would never recover—and as she came to, her chest heaving to regain composure, she knew she was crying tears of pure joy—the joy of having just had her first orgasm. She pulled Sally to her and hugged her, crushing her head to her chest. Then she brought the lovely mouth to hers and wanted to weld it there forever.

She lay with her eyes closed, a sublime, almost paralysing sense of relaxation in every muscle of her body. She sensed Sally move and looked up to see her lovely face close.

"Oh God . . . God, Sally, I love you. That was wonderful—thank you. That was so amazing." She kissed Sally's face and hair uncontrollably, something pouring out of her that she had never known before. She felt the tears flood her eyes.

"Are you OK?" said Sally.

Emma stroked her face and kissed her softly. "I think you just gave me the first orgasm of my life."

"Oh, have you never had one before?"

"No—never. It was so quick and sudden, but so incredible."

Sally put her arms around Emma's neck and hugged her. "I'm glad it was me."

"Ohhh, I never want to get out of this bed."

They lay there holding each other for several minutes. Emma thought she had never in her life felt so at peace, or so happy.

"Your dad never mentioned this bit when he described the job," Sally said, in her mild Birmingham drawl.

Emma giggled—then sat up and looked down at Sally, the deep dark eyes smiling up at her. "Yeah, well, servicing other members of the family is really important."

She was not just pretty, but profoundly beautiful, thought Emma. She had seen so many girls naked before, but had never looked at their bodies in this way.

Sally grinned. "Should we get dressed? I mean—what's your mum imagining we're up to?"

"Dunno. Don't care. Do we have to? I suppose we do." She thought for a minute, then leapt off the bed. She picked up her phone from the dressing table. "Lie there—I want a record of this." She clicked on the camera and pointed it at the bed.

Sally stretched out on top of the duvet. "You better be careful who you lend your phone to."

"I'm going to need someone to fantasise about in France."

"Bet you won't."

She took three full-length, then closed in on Sally's face. "There."

As they sat over breakfast, Emma couldn't take her eyes off the blonde-haired girl. She was feeling that first flush of a new relationship, that incredible excitement, making her light-headed and happy. And when their eyes met, she could see a glint deep in those dark eyes.

Emma's mother kept reminding her that she had to go and pack, or else she would be late for her flight—but Emma insisted on one last walk with Sally. "We're going into the garden, Mummy."

"OK. But don't be too long."

They strolled out through the kitchen door and over the sunlit lawn.

"Ohhh, there's so much to say, and you're leaving, and I'm going away," said Emma, putting her arm round Sally's shoulders.

"Plenty of time when you get back."

"Yeah. But I want to stay with you now."

You're going to have an exciting time in France." Sally's eyes were soft but also suddenly distant.

"Mmmm . . ." They had reached the long hedge that surrounded the pool area. "Come and have a look at the pool. We could have a swim if you like?"

"I don't have a costume. And anyway, your mum says you've got to get ready."

"Oh, there's plenty of spare costumes in the pool room. I can find you some slinky little pair of bottoms, just in case somebody comes, but I don't expect they will. Come on." She took Sally by the hand and led her through the archway. The pure blue water lay nearly still, the surface gently ruffling with the breeze.

"God—amazing."

"Yeah, come on."

Emma led her to the other end of the pool and into the changing hut. She opened a small cupboard and rifled inside. "There should be some of mine here." She pulled out a small pair of bikini bottoms. "There. Try those."

"Just the bottoms? What if your mum comes in?"

"If she does, which is unlikely, she's a lady of the world—and you're not exactly a sight for sore eyes."

"OK." Sally pushed her trousers and panties to the floor, undoing her blouse and unclipping her bra.

Emma watched her, her eyes drinking in Sally's nude body. She could feel in her stomach that excitement again.

"God, it's so nice to be cool," said Sally, running her hands over her breasts. She seemed to know that Emma was looking at her and wanting her. She took the little pair of bikini pants, bent over, put both feet in, and pulled them on. "OK. Ready."

"Good. Now—these should do for me." Emma pulled on a tiny pair of briefs.

They walked out to the pool and Emma dived in. The water was colder than she thought it would be, and she shivered as she surfaced. She swam briskly to the other end and back again several times to warm herself, then rested on the side. Sally was standing on the edge, watching. "Come on, it's lovely."

Sally dived in and swam up to her.

"Feel better?"

"Yeah. Great. But I feel a bit nervous with your family around."

"Don't worry." She put her hand to Sally's face and brushed away a wet lock of hair. I'm sure my dad would love it if he saw you topless. Quite get him going, I think."

"Your dad? Lusting after me? Well—I suppose. He's very attractive for a man his age."

She swam away, then stopped for a moment and waited for Emma to catch up.

"Oh—have you got a thing for older men?"

"In the right situation, yeah."

"Well, I'm sure he admired your lovely tits in that blouse. I watched him at lunch yesterday."

Sally launched herself forward again, only for Emma to come up behind her, reach round, and put both hands on her breasts.

"He might have a tiny crush on you," she said.

"Do you think so?" laughed Sally.

"Mmm."

"Well, that's OK—it's in my contract. As is his daughter feeling up my tits."

"They feel lovely."

"Well, please take your pleasure with your serf." Emma pressed close behind her and kissed her neck. Sally turned her head and rubbed her cheek against Emma's.

"Just now was fantastic," said Emma. "I can't stop thinking about it."

"Oh shit. I've really done it now."

"What?"

"I turned the boss's daughter into a lesbian," said Sally, breaking away.

She glided to the side of the pool and leaned against it, stretching her arms either side of her.

Emma came up and stood close. "You've got fantastic eyes—you know that?"

"You're beautiful all over." Sally put her hands on Emma's breasts.

Emma bent forward and kissed her. She felt the slightest touch of Sally's tongue against her lips and searched for it with her own. She suddenly felt Sally's fingers on her pussy, feeling the full lips beneath the skimpy costume. The fingers slid up and down, then pushed the little string aside.

"Oh yeah," whispered Emma and wrapped her arms around Sally's neck.

"Emma, darling, are you there?" came a voice.

They broke apart and Sally dived under the water, surfacing at the other side of the pool.

Emma's mother appeared at the side of the pool. "Darling, you really ought to get ready. It's only two hours before you need to leave."

"OK, Mummy." Emma swam to the side of the pool and got out.

"Oh, hello, Sally. Cooling off?"

"Er . . . yeah."

"Well I'm glad to see the pool used. Most of the year it just sits there. Well, don't be long, Emma." She turned and went.

Sally climbed out of the pool and walked to the sun loungers, picked up a towel, and began to dry herself.

"That was a bit close," said Emma. "But I wouldn't have cared if she had seen us."

Sally turned round to face her, holding the towel to her chest, smiling. "I don't know—you give a girl a job one day, then the next morning she's standing in your pool with her tits hanging out."

"Oh, don't worry about that." She kissed her lightly.

"Oh shit!"

"What?"

"I've got to go—and I don't want to."

"Well, I should really go as well."

"OK. Let's go and get dressed."

They strolled back to the changing room. Once inside, Emma closed the door. She slipped her briefs off and threw them onto the bench.

"What shall I do with mine?" said Sally.

"Oh, just put them here with mine. I'll take them back to the house."

"Do you want me to dry your back?" said Sally.

"Mmm." Emma turned her back to her.

She shivered with delight as she felt the soft material caress her skin.

"I think I'm going to like this part of the job," said Sally.

"What part?"

"Servicing the boss's daughter."

Emma felt Sally's soft lips kiss between her shoulders.

"Turn round."

Emma turned to face her, and Sally brushed the towel over Emma's breasts. "I can be your lady's maid." She gently moved the towel down and rubbed it between Emma's legs. "Get you nice and dry, my lady."

"If you do that, you'll get me nice and wet," whispered Emma.

Sally leant forward and kissed her tenderly. "Will I? I better feel . . ." Her beautiful eyes were wicked and smiling. Her slight shoulders looked so delicate, and Emma brushed her hands across them.

Emma sighed as she felt Sally's fingers explore her pussy and her mouth descend and suckle one of her nipples. "Oh God, Sally, you turn me on so much."

"All part of the job," she whispered, as she licked her way across to the other breast.

"Kiss me."

Their lips massaged together. *Sally's lips are so full and sexy*, she thought, as she put her arms around her. Emma whimpered beneath their kiss, and she moved her hips to meet the caresses of Sally's fingers, still circling her clitoris.

Emma thrust her tongue deep into Sally's mouth and felt her suck on it. She pushed it in and out gently and heard Sally purr with pleasure.

She felt Sally's finger search among the thick folds of her pussy and slide inside her. A delicious tremor ran across her skin and a deep throb pulsed in her groin. Emma hugged her tightly. "Oh shit, I just want you to make me come again."

"Well, you're a greedy girl."

"Please . . ."

Sally gently pulled her finger out and stepped back from Emma. She brought it to her mouth and licked it. "Sit down on the bench."

Sally reached for the wet towels lying on the floor, knelt on them, then took hold of Emma's legs and opened them wide. "Now where were we?" She adjusted her kneeling position and leaned down so that her head was just above Emma's vagina. Then she brought her fingers to the lips and peeled them apart, revealing the little hillock of her clitoris.

Emma jerked at the contact and uttered a little cry.

Sally put her lips round the little mound, then sucked it into her mouth.

Emma felt a rich pulse shiver through her. "Oh fuck, that's gorgeous." Sally did it again more slowly, then began to do it repeatedly, sometimes pulling it hard so that the skin stretched up from its hood. Emma took Sally's head in her hands, running her fingers through the silky blonde hair. She hung her head back and closed her eyes, moaning softly.

She felt Sally release her clitoris and then run her tongue around it lovingly. She circled it again and again, her fingers pulling away the little hood and pushing the clitoris upwards.

"Oh, Sally, fucking hell."

Her tongue dropped down and probed Emma's vagina, sliding a little way in.

"OOOOH . . ."

After a few seconds she pressed her face closer and searched deeper, rubbing her tongue along the roof of Emma's passage, then probed again, this time moving in and out in a slow rhythm. Emma screwed her eyes tight shut as she felt that same wonderful ache deep in her groin.

Sally lifted off and Emma looked down. She was putting her fingers in her mouth, that same wicked smile on her face. She leaned forward and kissed Emma's lips tenderly, running her tongue sexily along the line of Emma's teeth. Suddenly Emma felt Sally's finger on her anus, rubbing there softly. Emma broke the kiss and gasped. It was a strange and intense feeling that seemed to tighten the tension even more. After a few more moments, the fingers slid upwards and into Emma's vagina.

Emma cried out again, turning her head from side to side, her hands grasping the front of the bench.

Sally moved her fingers in and out quickly now, kissing her way slowly down Emma's neck, chest, breasts, and stomach on a slow, tortuous journey to her waiting clitoris. Emma could feel it throbbing, gorged and hard, the aching trigger to her orgasm.

Sally attacked it with her tongue, catching the underside, flicking it mercilessly.

"SALLY...YES, YES, YES...YESSSSSSSSSSSSS!!!!!!!!!" Emma screamed as the incredible sensation came again, her body rigid, her hands returning to the beautiful blonde head, pushing it hard against her pussy, wanting it to be part of her forever.

When Emma was able to finally relax, she opened her eyes to see Sally smiling up at her. Her mouth was wet.

"Get off all right?"

Emma sat up and took Sally's face in her hands. "That was so lovely. God, I just came again—so easily and so hard."

"All part of the service."

Emma kissed her deeply and lovingly. She wouldn't let Sally go, massaging her mouth. "Ohhh, I love you."

Sally sat next to her on the bench and they hugged tightly.

"This is so big for me," whispered Emma. "Just meeting you—in the last twenty-four hours—it feels like the biggest thing in my life. And now we're both leaving and it's . . . oh, I don't know."

"Just take it easy," said Sally, her eyes wide and dark.

As they stood beside Sally's car, Emma didn't know what to say. She kept fiddling with her hair and saying inane things, and not what she felt, which was that now she really didn't want to go away. She so desperately wanted to stay here and see Sally again.

"So I'll see you as soon as I get back," she said. "I hope everything goes OK here on the farm, you know."

"Yeah. Thanks."

"I've got your number—so I'll ring you."

"Yeah. But you have a good time as well. Don't think about what's going on here."

"No—but of course I will."

When Sally finally got into the car, Emma leaned in and kissed her on the lips, not caring if anyone saw her.

Sally looked at her, smiling, but Emma couldn't tell what she was thinking—then she reached up, pulled Emma's face to hers, and kissed her firmly. "Bye. And . . ."

"What?"

"Think about whether this is what you really want—you know, with me—or another girl."

"Yeah. I will."

"Cos you're going to a place full of girls. Maybe play around a bit."

"I can't even think about that."

"You should."

"OK. But—I love you."

Sally smiled warmly. "Yeah. Love you too."

"Bye."

Sally closed the door. Quickly, she started the engine and drove out of the yard.

Emma watched the car till it was out of sight, then closed her eyes and sighed.

A moment later, she skipped back into the house and into the kitchen. "Mummy, don't you think she's great? I really love her. We had such a great evening together. It's brilliant she's going to be working here."

"Yes, she seems very nice. Very pretty."

"Yeah, gorgeous. It's really good that she'll be working on the harvest. It'll be so much more fun than normal. She's really funny. I'm a bit sad I won't be seeing her for a few weeks."

"Yes. So did Charlie get off all right?"

"What? Oh—yeah. I'm finished with him. I've decided I really don't like him—you know? He's so bloody arrogant. He was unbelievably rude to Sally. Prick."

"I'm glad you've said that."

"Why?"

"I'm afraid I didn't like him from the first moment I met him."

"Really? Yeah, I'm sorry, Mummy. It's funny, when you suddenly meet someone like Sally, you just realise how amazing a relationship can be—you know, a friendship. Just being with her those few hours made me realise that the thing with Charlie was just awful. Anyway, all he ever wanted to do was have sex."

"And you didn't enjoy that?"

"Not as much as . . ." She stopped herself. "No, not as much as I normally do. He's so self-absorbed. Just after his own pleasure."

"Ah. Not so good."

"No."

"So you're glad your father gave Sally the job?"

"Yeah—amazing."

"Good. I'm glad too. I think she's going to be lovely to have around."

Chapter 3

During the drive back home, Sally went over and over the last twenty-four hours. *God, she's gorgeous*, she thought. *I've never seen anyone so amazing looking.*

She was in the slow lane, taking it easy, and the motorway was pretty empty. She put her fingers down, opened her legs slightly, and rubbed her pussy. She sighed and felt an immediate thrill. She took her hand away sharply. "Don't be an idiot."

As soon as she got back to the house, she went upstairs to her bedroom and threw off her clothes. She folded the duvet to one side and lay naked on the cool sheet. She went over and over in her mind what had happened. She slid her hand down over her stomach, through the small thatch of her pubic hair, and ran her fingers over the smooth lips of her pussy. Almost instantly, she felt herself becoming moist. She slid her middle finger inside, and as she moved it slowly in and out, she recalled the scene in the bedroom, holding Emma naked in her arms. *God, so beautiful . . . irresistible.*

She wanted something inside her. She leapt off the bed, ran naked down the stairs and into the kitchen. She noticed a couple of courgettes sitting in her basket of vegetables on the worktop. She smiled to herself and took one.

She ran back upstairs and lay back on the bed. She took the courgette and put the round end in her mouth. It tasted strange, slightly bitter and cold, but as she sucked on it, saliva gathered and coated it thickly. Quickly she took it out and positioned it at the entrance to her pussy. She moved it around her lips, then pushed it gently inside. She caught her breath sharply—it felt good, oh so good. She closed her eyes and imagined Emma lying naked beside her, pushing it in and out of her, kissing her breasts. She pumped herself sharply, feeling her juice seep from her pussy, pulses of pleasure resonating around her.

"Ohhh . . . Emma . . . yes . . ."

She remembered pushing her hands through the fine, silky hair, kissing her warm, fragrant mouth, their breath and saliva mixing, their tongues playing together.

"Ahhh . . . Emma . . . yes, yes, YEEESSS! Oh fuck, it's so good . . . I want you . . ."

She came quickly and sharply—and it possessed her for a long time, flowing all over her, right through her, and as she lay there it was as though she had the gorgeous girl in her arms.

She turned onto her stomach. *Fuck. Let's get a bit of reality here. What will happen when she gets back? She's the boss's daughter, for God's sake. Maybe I'm misinterpreting. Maybe she will just forget all about it. There was something about the way Emma had been, though. And each time I have fallen in love with a girl it has been so intense, so heady, so wonderful. But she's away in France for six weeks. She'll get off with someone else—and when she comes back it will probably just not be a problem. We'll just be friends.*

She got up off the bed and looked around the room. God, so many memories. She'd been away from the house for nearly a year—and since she'd been back she hadn't allowed herself time to remember.

This room: She had made love with Maddie in this bed, and with Lou, and lost her virginity with Jamie, her stepbrother.

The memory was so intense, she felt randy again. She glanced at her naked self in the full-length mirror. Sex. It was back in her life. For a whole year she had avoided even thinking about it. But now—with what had happened the previous day and here, now—there was no escaping it.

She put on her dressing gown and wandered out onto the landing. She glanced into her mother's old room. When her mum had married Jamie's dad, she had hated them being in that room together. The sounds she sometimes heard. But after Jamie and his dad left and her mother got ill and died and she was on her own, she started using that bed for casual sex, fucking people like crazy, just for the sake of it. One night she brought three guys back and told them to tie her up. She lay there, spread-eagled, high on booze and dope—and they fucked her, one by one, then all together, and she was screaming her head off. *Then I told them to turn me over and fuck me in the arse.*

Her head swam for a moment when she recalled what she had wanted them to do. Then the next morning there had been the disgust at herself at what she'd done, desperation, and tears.

She went down to the kitchen and made some tea. She sat at the table and almost instantly she could feel the loneliness that had finally driven her out of this house, the sort of loneliness that no amount of sex and drink can take away. She had left. She went away to her uncle's, away from sex and booze, away from people desiring her, wanting her.

She felt tears come to her eyes. She wanted her mum, so desperately, and all she had was the image of her wasting away, terrified of the disease that was wracking her with pain, eating her from inside. *"I'm going to die, Sal . . . I can feel it. There's nothing they can do."*

The tears poured down her face and she cried bitterly. It was no good trying to keep this place. She had to get rid of it.

After lunch, she'd just come out of the shower and was pottering, still naked, in her bedroom, when her mobile rang. "Emma" showed on the screen. "Oh my God," she murmured. She pressed the green key. "Hello?"

"Sally. Hi, it's Emma. Hope I'm not disturbing you?"

"Hi. No—I've just come out of the shower."

"Oh. Right. I'm just at the airport waiting. Thought I'd give you a call."

"Sure." Sally didn't know what to say. "So, what time's your flight?"

"Ten past three."

"And where are you flying to?"

"Carcassonne. Then I've hired a car."

"Oh—so you'll be able to get around a bit."

"Yeah, I hope so. My gran lives in that part of France, so maybe I'll be able to go and see her, but I'm not sure."

There was a silence and Sally tried to think of something to say.

"Look," said Emma, "I just wanted to say how amazing last night and this morning was. I can't stop thinking about it."

"Yeah—it was lovely."

"I've never made love with a girl before, and it was just so amazing."

"Can anyone hear this conversation?"

"What? No—I'm standing on my own by the window."

"Oh—OK. It's just you sounded as though you were broadcasting to the world that you had a gay fling."

"No, no," she laughed. "Though I don't think I'd care, the way I feel at the moment." Another pause. "So you've just come out of the shower?"

"Yeah. Lying on my bed."

"With nothing on?"

"Yeah. Starkers."

"That sounds nice. I wish I were there with you."

"Yeah, well, as soon as you get to France, you'll be so busy with all the beautiful people over there you'll soon forget about me."

"I don't think so."

"And there'll be loads of girls if you fancy experimenting a bit further."

There was another silence, and Sally wondered if she had said too much.

"Have you always been gay?" said Emma.

"I've had both—but my first affair was with a girl."

"So you're bi?"

"Yeah. I guess."

"Yeah . . ." Her voice trailed off. "God—this is such a big thing for me. Like . . . everything has changed suddenly."

"Yeah, but, you know, whatever happens between us, you've got to work out for yourself whether you're gay, bi, or whatever. I suppose I've never had an issue with—you know—the fact that I have gay affairs. It's always seemed really natural either way. It's the falling in love bit I'm so crap at."

"Why?"

"Because I go head over heels and get hurt."

"Oh God, I just want to be there with you and hold you and kiss you."

"Yeah. Me too. But have a lovely time in France, and we'll talk—you know, about everything—when you get back."

"Yeah, sure."

"Six weeks is a long time."

"Yeah, but I certainly won't forget about you."

"I know."

"Anyway, look—I'm sorry to go on, but I'll see you when I get back—and I'll ring you sometime to see how you are."

"Yeah. That'll be good."

"Right, well I hope everything will be all right. Don't take any crap from my dad. He's a pushover, really."

"He's great."

Another pause. "OK. Speak soon. Lots of love."

"And you."

Sally rolled onto her back and looked at the ceiling. Just the sound of Emma's voice brought it all back so vividly. She felt so randy just thinking about it.

God, I feel just the way I did with Maddie—the first time.

Maddie. She was the school bad girl: rebellious, loud, constantly bending the rules, hanging around with boys, outrageously dressed, always smoking. She was actually very attractive—but dyed her hair, had a ring through her nose, and wore Goth-type makeup. I got on OK with her, but always kept my distance. I was the shy type, anyway, but I also looked up to her in a strange way. She was attractive and very confident—and I suppose sexy in a way I wanted to be.

She amazed everyone—and annoyed the school—when she got a raft of top results and came back to the sixth form. She wanted to do textiles, she said, and music technology. So she did—and went on being outrageous.

Although she had always paid a lot of attention to me—she called me "Goldie" because of my hair—I had never thought anything of it. I just humoured her and talked to her when she wanted me to, but I could never think of her as a friend, because I suppose I was a bit afraid of her. I did catch her looking at me a lot—and I suppose if I'm truthful I quite liked it. But I don't think I ever seriously thought that she fancied me. Up to that point I'd never had sex, but I did think about it a lot. I masturbated regularly, thinking about girls as well as boys. I thought about my best friend, Lou—and I definitely thought about Maddie, but only in a passive way, thinking about the way she looked. Maybe I should have known. I don't know—but I was just eighteen at the time, so that day when it happened it came as a complete shock.

It was on the playing field during a free period. It was a hot day in May and no one was around. I was lying on the grass reading a book for my English course when suddenly she was there.

"Hello, Goldie." She lay down beside me.

"Oh. Hi."

"What you doing then? Reading? You're such a swot, you know that?" She was smiling at me, her head supported by her hand.

"I've got to read it for next week."

"So do it next week."

She looked at me for a minute. I didn't know what to say—I didn't know what she wanted. "You ought to get out more, you know? You're such a pretty little thing—why haven't you got a boyfriend?"

"I don't know."

"Don't fancy them?"

"It's never sort of happened, really."

"Don't blame you—most guys are such jerks."

I put my book down, turned over on my back, supported myself on my elbows, and smiled back at her.

"I'm sure they're all desperate to slip between your legs— get your knickers off," she said. "You've got gorgeous legs . . . bound to get them going. Has no bloke ever tried it on with you?"

"No. Not really."

"So who do you fancy in school?"

"I don't know. No one particularly."

"Yeah well, best not. Pity though, if a pretty girl like you didn't want to have some fun. What a waste."

Then suddenly she put her hand on my thigh. I had a short summer dress on, which had pulled up slightly. "You never fancied mucking around a bit?"

She gently stroked my right thigh, then brushed the back of her hand on the inside of my left one. I instantly felt a sense of panic—this wasn't right. No one had ever touched me like that, least of all another girl. Not that I didn't like it—it was nice . . . very nice.

I looked down at her hand and then at her and could feel myself blushing. She just smiled at me and kept stroking, getting higher each time. Her hand disappeared under my dress. "Are you still a virgin?"

"Y—yes."

"Haven"t you ever wanted to do it? Have sex?"

"Well . . . I don't know, I . . . I." Her fingers touched my panties. I felt a shock of pleasure. Now she was rubbing me through them—the feeling was incredible and I could feel myself getting wet.

"Look, I've—I've got to go." I put my hand on hers, but she resisted.

"Why, when you are enjoying yourself?" She pushed my panties aside and touched the lips of my pussy. "Well . . . somebody's pleased to see me. You're so wet."

I was so aroused by now I couldn't get my breath. I wanted her to do it forever—but I also knew I shouldn't. "I'm—I'm sorry, I've really got to go."

I pushed her hand sharply off and somehow scrambled to my feet. Grabbing my book and my bag, I walked away as quickly as I could, almost running, my whole body on fire.

"Bye then," I heard her call after me.

I couldn't stop thinking about it all the way home, turning it over in my mind again and again. What had happened to me? Was I gay? Another girl had touched me up, and it had felt incredible. I wasn't meant to feel that. As I sat on the bus I kept thinking that everyone knew, that they were looking at me, that I had this guilty secret.

When I finally put the key in the door of the house, I was relieved to find no one at home. I rushed up to my bedroom and threw myself on the bed. As I buried my head in the pillow, I knew only one thing: I wished I hadn't left like that. I wished I'd stayed. I wished I'd let her go on doing it. Already I wanted her to do it again. Nothing else mattered.

I sat up and pulled my dress over my head, unclipped my bra, and took it off. I lay back down again and put my hand into my panties. The moment I touched myself it was like my whole body caught fire again. As the memory replayed in my head, I was flooded with gorgeous feelings. I thought of her hand exploring me, her fingers pushing inside me. I rubbed my breasts with my other hand. They were incredibly firm, my nipples so hard. I was building to an orgasm quicker than ever before. My pussy was dripping as I ran my fingers up and down the lips, then up to my clitoris. My body erupted as I came. I pushed my fingers deep and hard into my pussy again and again. I cried out as it seemed to go on forever and ever, my heart beating so fast, almost suffocating.

When I finally lay still, I worried that someone next door had heard me. Surely I had screamed loudly enough. I lay there for what seemed like a long time, thinking about her—wanting her.

I was nervous the next day at school. I desperately wanted to see her, but at the same time I didn't. How would I react? On the bus, I decided the best thing was to try and avoid her. What would all the other kids say if they knew? It would be awful. I didn't want to be thought of as gay, so all morning I avoided those places where she would ordinarily hang out. When I did see her from a distance, she didn't see me. I stood transfixed for a moment looking at her. She was with a group of boys and was larking about. I turned and walked the other way.

Then, inevitably, I ran slap bang into her at lunchtime.

"Hello, Goldie, all right?"

"Hi. Yeah."

"Recovered?" She was grinning in that sort of provocative way she had about her.

"What? Er . . ." I stammered, trying not to look her in the eye.

"Dried out your knickers yet?"

I couldn't suppress a smile, but then panicked. "Sorry—I'm late. I've got to go."

"Always off somewhere . . ."

As I walked sharply away, my heart was thumping again, my throat felt dry, and I'm sure I was trembling.

The next day, I tried harder to make sure I didn't even see her and succeeded all day. By the end of the afternoon, it was pouring down with rain. As I left to go home, it was coming down in torrents. I ran to the far school gate because it was nearest to the bus stop, but as I got there it was coming down so hard I ducked into a doorway. It was a small flat-roofed building, standing on its own, a store for the playing field. The door was locked, but there was a small porch in front I could shelter in. I stood there for a few minutes, but it showed no sign of letting up. The porch looked directly over the football fields, and there was nothing for a long way. I sighed and resigned myself to staying there for a bit. It looked so grey and miserable.

Suddenly, I was aware of someone running up and pushing in next to me. It was her.

"Can't avoid me forever, you know." Her red spiky hair was dripping with rain, and I could smell the soaking wool of her coat. "I don't know why you're running away from me," she said.

"I'm not," I said. I didn't know what else to say. I just stared out at the rain, my heart thumping.

"I've been looking for you all over the place," she said.

I looked at her briefly, then turned away. "Sorry. I didn't know." Her eyes looked so bright as she smiled at me intently.

"Bit different from the other day, isn't it?" She paused, but I knew she was still looking at me. "Did I freak you out touching you up like that? You're not trying to tell me you didn't like it, 'cos I know you did."

I was frozen to the spot, unable either to look at her or move away. My stomach was churning with a strange mixture of panic and excitement. Then suddenly she was touching me. Her hand was under my skirt again and moving ever so lightly upwards. Then it was on my pussy, and she was rubbing me just like the last time. I felt the same hot rush of pleasure. "You can't. Not here . . ."

"Why not? There's no one around. Everybody's keeping out of the rain, aren't they?"

She kissed me on the side of my head and nuzzled her mouth into my hair. I could feel her hot breath against my ear, then her tongue pushed inside my ear lobe and massaged all round it.

Goose pimples shot all over me and I felt a burning in my groin. I moaned softly and closed my eyes. Then I felt her kissing my neck, slowly working her way round to my cheek. The next thing I knew her mouth was on mine and she was kissing me—softly at first, then deeply, the deepest kiss I had ever had with anyone. Her mouth felt so sweet, so different. I didn't care that we were there in the open. As that wonderful feeling coursed through my body, I knew she was going to make me come, and I was not going to run away this time. I felt her finger feeling for my entrance. Then suddenly, it was up inside me. My pussy burned with pleasure and I pushed down against it, wanting her to go further and further into me, to fill me. The feeling was overwhelming, and just as I thought I couldn't bear it anymore, I felt myself begin to come.

"Oh God . . . ohhhhh . . ."

"Is that good?"

"Yeah . . . I'm going to . . . ."

"Yeah . . . come on, Goldie, come for me. Yeah . . . that's good, go on, let it go . . . ."

I felt my whole body tense as the orgasm welled up and burst through me. I buried my head in her neck, gasping and screaming, as that incredible pleasure just took me away.

I tried to calm my breath and thumping heart as the feeling subsided. I reached up and brought her face to mine and kissed her softly. I felt her gently remove her finger. Then as our lips parted, she brought it to her mouth and licked it. "Mmmm. So was it good for you, then?"

"Oh yeah. It was fantastic." I looked at her and smiled. Suddenly, it was nice not to be scared of her anymore. I glanced around nervously at the playing field, but no one was in sight. "Do you want me to do it for you?"

"Yeah, I'm fucking bursting. Quick."

She also looked out across the field, then fumbled under her skirt and pushed her panties down a short way. I felt between her legs and found the warm wetness of her vagina.

"Oh yeah, just rub my clit."

It was so strange feeling another girl like that, but I wanted to please her in the same way she had pleased me. I moved my fingers around until I could sense the stiff little mound of her clitoris and worked at it, gently.

She breathed in sharply, put her hands to my face, and kissed me again, her tongue invading my mouth. "You're so gorgeous. I've wanted to do this for such a long time."

"Yeah. I think you're lovely too."

"Oh, yeah, that's right. Do it like that. Oh fuck, you make me feel so horny. Oh shit, I'm going to come," she whispered.

I increased my working at her clit and kissed her neck and ears. Her skin was so pale and creamy.

"Oh . . . yeah . . . yeah . . . ohhhhhh."

She screwed her eyes shut and I saw her face flush in a long groan as her thighs crushed against my hand.

"Ohhhhh . . . fuuuuck. Oh fuck, that's great. Ohh . . . yeah." She pushed my hand hard against her sex as her body tensed. She cried out and went tense again, gasping, uttering little cries. Then after a few moments she relaxed, breathing heavily. She turned to me and kissed me for a long time.

"That was fucking great." She looked at me intently for a few moments, then laughed. "We'll do it somewhere better next time. Right now we better get going." She started to pull her clothes together.

I did the same, putting my panties back in place as best I could. Looking out at the field, the rain was still coming down heavily and nobody appeared to be around.

"I'll see you tomorrow," she said, once she had finished rearranging herself. She quickly looked around, kissed me lightly, and was gone. I stayed for a few minutes, trying to collect myself, my eyes closed. Such a short time—just a few minutes—but it felt like it had changed my life.

As I sat on the bus home, soaking wet from the rain, my underclothes still twisted uncomfortably, I felt wonderful. The only thing I could think about was seeing her again.

Chapter 4

Sitting in the airport lounge, Emma couldn't shake what had happened. Another girl had made love to her and given her her first orgasm, and it felt so natural. And just now she had loved the thrill of just talking to Sally on the phone—her wonderful new lover.

She glanced around—was she really a lesbian? Had someone flicked a switch in her head? She looked at several girls and young women, but none of them seemed to interest her. Emma frowned to herself and opened her phone. She brought up the three pictures she had taken of Sally. Her tummy seemed to twinge as she looked at the smiling, rosy-cheeked face.

She snapped the phone shut. Was it the thing with Beth Dorsington at school? It had seemed a really big thing at the time, but after a while she had just dismissed it from her mind as the sort of thing adolescent girls do. Beth was eighteen and about to leave the school. Emma had just turned fifteen and had a wild crush on her. Emma adored her from afar, but never dared speak to her, and she assumed that Beth had no idea how she felt and wouldn't have cared anyway. She could still feel that amazing attraction—a heady, passionate love.

Beth was captain of the first hockey team, and as Emma was a promising hockey player, she would often be asked to help out on match days at the school. One particular day, she helped put the equipment away after the match and was late getting back to the changing rooms. By the time she got there, everyone had gone, so she undressed and got into the showers on her own. After a little while, she heard someone else come into the shower room but thought nothing of it.

But when she turned and looked, it was Beth—naked, gorgeous, and smiling at her.

"Hi, Emma," she said.

Emma's head swam. "Er . . . hi," Emma said, swallowing hard, suds pouring down her face. She felt her heart begin to race.

Beth began to wash her hair. Emma rinsed hers and began to wash all over, trying not to look at the girl next to her.

"Could you wash my back?"

Emma looked at her, stunned. "Y-yes," she said. Beth turned her long, lovely back to her, and Emma swallowed hard. She ran the soap all over the warm, wet skin with her hands. She tingled all over and her hands were trembling. She'd held hands with other girls, hugged them and kissed them on the cheek, but nothing felt like this. This was pure paradise.

"Do you want me to do yours?" said Beth, when Emma had finished.

"Yeah," she whispered, hardly able to utter a sound. She handed Beth the soap and turned round. The next moment she felt the soft hands roam over her. She closed her eyes and sighed as her whole body seemed to glow.

Suddenly she felt Beth kiss her on the shoulder and her hands run down and over her buttocks. "You're so pretty," she said, squeezing Emma's bum cheeks gently. "I've seen you look at me a lot."

Emma's heart leapt. She turned her head slightly towards her. "Yeah . . . sorry."

"Why are you saying sorry? I love it. It's nice." She pressed herself against Emma's back, moved her hands up to her breasts, and kissed her neck.

Emma gasped. She had never been touched or kissed like this before. It was hot between her legs, and she could feel that her nipples were so sensitive as Beth fondled her breasts. She felt herself being turned, and seconds later, Beth's lovely face was close to hers and she was being hugged tightly.

Beth smiled and put her mouth on Emma's in the gentlest of kisses. Her first ever kiss . . . so soft, so lovely. "Let's dry off," said Beth. She turned off the showers and they walked through into the changing room. The room was L shaped, and Beth took her hand and pulled her round the corner away from the door. "Let's go here."

They stood together and rubbed the towels over each other. After a moment, Beth took both towels and dropped them on the floor. She put her arms around Emma and kissed her again lightly. Emma felt as though her skin was hypersensitive to every touch and she thought she could gaze into the other girl's misty blue eyes forever. "Open your mouth," Beth said, as she leaned to kiss her again.

Emma parted her lips. The next instant she felt Beth's tongue slide along them, then push into her mouth. She felt as though she was lifting off the floor, floating in heavenly sensation.

At that moment, there was a noise of someone approaching, and two other girls burst through the door. Beth pushed her away and pretended as though nothing had happened.

"Come on, Beth, what are you doing?" said one girl.

"Sorry—let me just get dressed." She had her back to Emma as she quickly put her clothes on and chatted to the others. Emma sat down on the bench, terrified, her body stinging. She didn't dare get up, but just sat there rigid.

They never saw her, and all three left after a couple of minutes. She sat on the bench for a few minutes longer, bereft emotionally, but also feeling something new to her—an intense sexual frustration.

Emma's head swam for a moment at the vividness of the memory. She felt hot—randy. She suddenly knew that, although nothing had happened all those years ago in that changing room, she'd had her first real sexual experience—with another girl.

She became conscious that her eyes were resting on a girl sitting opposite her. She had short, curly black hair and that tanned Mediterranean complexion of the south of France. She was wearing a matching khaki top and trousers and was reading a magazine. As Emma studied her, she looked up, her dark brown eyes looking quizzically in Emma's direction. She was young and pretty and Emma could sense her attractiveness. Emma looked away.

When she looked back, the girl was looking at her again. Emma held her gaze and there was an odd sort of moment— the sort of look that she had exchanged hundreds of times with guys.

Later, she climbed the steps to the aircraft and found her seat. She pushed her hand luggage into the overhead compartment, then sat down. She supposed there had been other times as well. On her gap year with Susie, bumming round Greece and Turkey, they had been really close physically. They had spent a lot of time nude on some of the beaches, swimming, sunbathing, rubbing oil into each other's bodies—or those times in the mountains when it was so cold at night that they had zipped their sleeping bags together and cuddled up, their bare legs entwined. Emma remembered waking once in the night and feeling Susie cuddle her. Their faces were close, and she kissed her lightly on the forehead. She could still recall the glow of wellbeing as they drifted back into sleep. She could see now that, at the time, she had felt something more than the intensity of their friendship— it was the trace of sexuality, the smell and feel of Susie that had seemed to get right inside her. She was sure it had meant nothing to her friend, but to her—she could see now it had meant a lot. And one morning, early, she had secretly watched Susie masturbate and give herself an orgasm, her friend's lovely nubile body stretched out on top of the sleeping bag.

Emma had an aisle seat, and she came to as the girl from the airport lounge took the other aisle seat across from her. They smiled at each other. The girl stretched up and pushed her luggage into the overhead locker. Emma watched as her buttocks pushed against the thin material and her top pulled out to expose her creamy brown hips and back. When she sat down, Emma studied her delicate neck, the dark curls sitting just above the soft down of the hairline.

Once the aircraft had taken off, they got talking. The girl's name was Marie, and she had been staying with her boyfriend, who was doing a PhD at an English university. Emma was struck by how the whites of her eyes set off the deep brown of her pupils. After a while the conversation petered out and Emma closed her eyes and snoozed. Later, when she looked at the girl, she somehow knew that she had been watching her.

And in the destination airport, waiting for their baggage, their eyes met several times, sometimes a smile, sometimes not. It was like Emma had suddenly come across an undercurrent of female sexuality possibilities beneath the surface.

It was close to 7:30 local time when Emma walked out of Carcassonne Airport and went to the car rental agency. The sun was setting, the air was warm, and the French countryside looked lush and beautiful in the evening light. The journey to the chateau took about an hour and ten minutes, and it was dark by the time she drove up the long drive and saw the imposing house. It was huge in scale, with large round towers topped by conical roofs at either end and tall, slim windows marching in strict order across the front.

She parked at the side of the building, following the directions, then walked back round to the entrance. The large gothic door opened into a vast reception hall. Its bare stone walls were interrupted at various intervals with tapestries depicting what looked like mythological scenes. The high ceiling was coffered at its centre with a large circular painting. Immediately in front of her a huge stone staircase rose to a half landing and then doubled back either side and out of sight.

A smartly dressed woman sat behind a desk isolated on its own to the left. It appeared to be the only piece of furniture in the whole bare edifice, and a simple wooden crucifix was placed on the wall just above it.

Emma walked up to her and announced in French who she was.

"Ah yes," the woman replied in English, "you are sharing with Sophie Baddleshaw in room fifty-four. Take the lift to the first floor, and it is the corridor on the left as you come out." She indicated a wooden door to the right of the staircase. It matched a similar one on the other side.

"Thank you," said Emma. A single stainless steel button sat in the stonework at the side of the door. She pressed it. The door slid open and revealed a mirror-lined lift. She went inside and pressed the button for the first floor. It moved quickly and noiselessly upward. *Baddleshaw—that's odd, sounds really English,* she thought. She was supposed to be put in a room with a French girl. That was the whole point.

When it opened, she was greeted by a long, high corridor stretching to the left, and to the right, she could see a gallery with arcading that opened on the entrance hall below. The corridor was lined with paintings of ecclesiastical figures and the odd ornate chair. A series of doors opened off the corridor on both sides, and a sign directly opposite said "*Les chambres 26—55.*" She walked down the dimly lit corridor, wheeling her suitcase behind her and found number 54, the last one on the left. She thought the girl Sophie might already have arrived, so she knocked softly before opening the door gingerly. As it swung back, she heard a sound—and froze. She pulled the door closed quickly and felt the blood rush to her face. She looked down the corridor. It was deserted. She leaned against the door and listened. She felt rather silly just standing there, but couldn't think of what else to do.

Slowly, she pushed the door open a little again and peered inside. On a bed to the left, a naked girl was moaning softly and moving up and down on top of someone else. Emma's first instinct was to pull the door shut again, but she couldn't take her eyes off the girl's long, elegant back, her gyrating hips and buttocks, and the lush black, shoulder-length curly hair. She stood transfixed as the girl's cries mounted and she pounded up and down on her lover. She could see a man's penis disappearing inside her, with small, tight balls clearly visible at its base, nestling between his thighs.

"Oui . . . oui, oh . . . OOOOOOHHHHHHHHH!!!"

Emma quickly pulled the door closed again to try and stop the girl's high-pitched cries being heard down the corridor. Eventually, the room went quiet. She waited for a few moments but heard nothing more. She pushed the door open again a crack. They were still making love. They had switched positions, and the man was now on top of her, his buttocks thrusting urgently. She felt a pang in her stomach as she watched the strong contortions of his body. It was hypnotic—and rather beautiful. Suddenly he moaned loudly, jabbed into her several times, then relaxed.

Emma swallowed hard. She would give them a couple of minutes, then knock louder and pretend she had only just arrived. She swung the door back—but it closed a bit too quickly and the latch clicked loudly. "Shit," she whispered. She stepped back—and her foot caught the suitcase, knocking it onto its side with a bang, echoing round the cavernous building. "Fuck!"

She retrieved it quickly, the blood running to her face, and her heart pounding. She heard talking from inside the room and the rustle of clothes. Seconds later, the door opened and the girl appeared, hastily pulling a dressing gown around her shoulders. She had a strange but very attractive face, with dazzling green eyes.

"Ah," the girl said in a slight French accent, "you must be Emma."

"Yes . . . I'm sorry if I disturbed you, I . . ."

"It's OK. Antoine and I were just saying our good-byes." She rolled her eyes and giggled softly. "Come in."

Emma picked up her case and followed her into the room. It was large, now that she could see all of it. There were two beds—one on either side—and a door near to her led into what looked like a bathroom. A tall, wide, shuttered window was at the end.

The boy—Antoine—was fastening his trousers. He was quite tall and good looking. Emma was conscious that she let her eyes rest on his face and torso rather a long time before speaking.

"Bonjour. Je m'appelle Emma."

"Bonjour. Ca va?" His eyes scanned her. Undressed her.

"Oui."

"I am Sophie," said the girl. Her eyes were extraordinary, thought Emma—mesmerizing.

"Bonjour."

"Hello." She put out her hand and Emma shook it. Her dressing gown fell open, revealing her nude body.

Antoine had put his shirt on now and was smiling at her in a rather strange way.

"You're half French, is that right?" said Sophie.

"Yes," said Emma.

"Good. I am half English. So we match," she said, squeezing her hand. She leant forward and kissed Emma on the cheek, her eyes staring at her intently. "Antoine, you'd better go," she said in French, not taking her eyes off Emma.

"OK," he said. He reached over and kissed her, then said in halting English, "Good-bye. Maybe you come for the weekend, no?"

"Er . . . yes. That would be nice," said Emma.

"Bon. A bientot." He smiled, then left.

Sophie closed the door behind him. "I'm sorry about that, but you understand—yes?"

"Yes. Yes, of course." Emma couldn't stop her eyes flashing down to the girl's dark, neat bush of pubic hair.

"Good. Come. Let's have a shower. You must want to freshen up? And I think I need one." She winked. "It's—how you call it in English—a wet room? We can have one together. I'll turn it on. You get undressed."

"Oh. OK," said Emma. She stood for a moment feeling slightly nonplussed. She heard the sound of the shower running. Gingerly, she took off her clothes and laid them on the opposite bed to Sophie's.

She hesitated a moment, then walked through the door into the bathroom. A small cubicle with a door was on the right and a sink to the left—and directly ahead was a large tiled area with a showerhead. Sophie was standing under it. Emma tried not to stare at her tall, slim body with small neat breasts and a light olive skin tone.

Sophie smiled at her, her eyes blatantly scanning Emma's body. "Would you like to wash your hair?" She held out a bottle of shampoo.

"Yes, thanks." Emma took the bottle and Sophie moved out of the shower stream. The water was hot and felt good. "Mmm, nice."

"It feels good—yes?"

"Yes." Emma wet her hair thoroughly and applied the shampoo. As she rubbed it in to her hair, she felt Sophie rub her back with her hand.

"You have a beautiful body."

Emma froze. "What? Oh. Thank you. Well, so have you."

"Here. Let me." Sophie stepped towards Emma and put her hands into Emma's head and massaged her scalp.

Emma tingled all over. "Ohhh. That's lovely."

Sophie gently used her fingernails, moving all over Emma's head. Although she had her eyes tight shut, Emma could feel that Sophie's face was very close—and she felt their bodies touch.

"Now rinse," she said.

Emma stood under the jet of water and let the soap run out of her hair.

"There," said Sophie, and just as Emma opened her eyes, Sophie placed a wet kiss on her cheek. "Now you can wash my back. Use your nails like I did. I love that."

Emma took the soap from the holder and washed the girl's back. Sophie's skin was smooth with the odd tiniest freckle. Emma scratched very lightly.

Sophie sighed. "Ohhhh, that is very good."

"Am I doing all right?"

"Mmm. Wonderful." Sophie stood under the shower, showing no signs that she wanted her to stop.

"There," Emma said, patting her gently.

Sophie turned, put her arms round Emma's neck, and hugged her. Emma could feel her nipples were hard, pressing against her own breasts. Sophie brought her face close to Emma's. "I think we're going to be very good friends," she said. She paused and smiled, her eyes drifting seductively down to Emma's lips. "Come on." She turned away quickly and stopped the shower.

Emma felt shocked. Sally, the girl on the plane—what on earth was going on?

They dried themselves, then returned to the room. Sophie flopped onto her bed and lay back, her legs apart. Emma couldn't help staring at her for a moment.

She took her suitcase, put it on the bed, opened it, and searched for a pair of panties.

"I'm sorry if we embarrassed you just now," Sophie said. "But we just couldn't resist it. We both got carried away."

Emma turned to look at her, panties in hand. "Wasn't it a bit risky? I mean, like, this is a Catholic college."

Sophie smirked. "It gives it spice—the danger. Makes it more intense. Don't you think?"

"Yeah. Maybe." Emma put on her panties. They were small, scanty, and see-through, and as soon as she had pulled them up, she wondered why she had chosen them.

"You look very sexy in those."

She turned and looked at her. "Thank you."

Sophie's eyes were smiling in a suggestive, penetrating way. Emma felt herself flush very slightly and turned back to her case. She pulled out her nightie and laid it on the bed.

"You're not going to wear that, are you? It's very warm at night. I don't wear anything."

"N-no, probably not. I brought it just in case I was sharing with someone a bit more prudish. But I wouldn't describe you like that." Emma grinned at her in a cheeky way.

Sophie leapt up. "No. No, I'm not," she said, excitedly. "I'm completely outrageous, as you might have noticed." She did a sort of elegant pirouette, finishing in a ballet pose. "Come on—I'll get dressed and then I'll show you the house and the village. You'll love it."

They sat in the little cafe in the village square. Even though it was nearly ten o'clock, it was still warm, and Emma sighed with contentment as she sipped her glass of the house *vin rouge* they had ordered with their meal. The village was very pretty, as Sophie had said, a tumble of medieval buildings within a fortified wall. A lot of the castellated remains had been built into and smart new interiors graced the old houses. At the centre of the village was a charming square bounded on one side with the church, the front of which was directly opposite them.

Sophie had asked Emma to tell her everything about her and listened intently for a long time, the haunting eyes scanning her face. The food was every bit as good as Sophie had promised, and now Emma was enjoyably tired from the journey, but also from having talked incessantly for the last hour. She couldn't remember being so closely interrogated ever before. As she talked, she thought that Sophie was beautiful in a rather strange way. Her face had sharp cheekbones, and her mouth was wide with lips that were full and pronounced. Her nose was aquiline, but ended in an upturn, making the whole effect of her face impish and sexy. And those eyes . . .

"So, I've told you everything there is to tell about me. Why don't you tell me about yourself," she said finally.

"Oh, nothing much to tell. I live with my family near the Pyrenees. I go to university in Paris. I like swimming, and I love my boyfriend and girlfriends. And I like making love, as you saw. That's me."

"What does your father do?"

"He is an artist."

"Oh, really? What sort of artist?"

"He paints nudes. People pose for him. Or sometimes he paints from photographs."

"Oh."

"Are you shocked?"

"No, I don't suppose I am." Emma smiled. That her father was some kind of erotic artist—no, that didn't surprise her. Not at all.

They chatted some more, then paid the bill and set off back to the chateau.

As they walked back, Sophie took Emma's hand. It felt nice, but unexpected. "Tomorrow is registration, so we need to do that early," said Sophie as they strolled up the dark stretch of road to the gates. "Then we can have a look round the garden and the park. If it is nice, we can sunbathe."

"Good. That sounds fun. You're looking after me very well."

Sophie squeezed her hand. "I like looking after you."

As they walked up the long drive to the chateau, the grounds were in darkness, but Emma suddenly saw to the left what looked like a Greek temple on a hill. It was floodlit, with a fountain in front of it.

"What's that?"

"That is what I want to show you tomorrow. It is a lovely fountain. We used to have a lot of fun last summer fooling around in it."

"You were here last year?"

"Yes. The temple was one of our favourite places." She paused, then stopped, bringing her face close to Emma's: "I had sex in the fountain once."

"What? Who with? Antoine?"

"No. Someone else." She laughed and walked on, taking Emma's hand again.

An unexpected tingle crept up Emma's back. She felt a little squeeze from the long fingers entwined with hers.

Back in the room, the first thing Sophie did was take off her clothes, then sit on her bed, naked. Her complexion was flawless, and the light olive skin tone was uniform all over—and Emma was very conscious that she kept wanting to look at her. She took all her own clothes off except her panties.

"You have very nice breasts," said Sophie.

"Really? I suppose they're all right," said Emma, smiling at her and feeling herself flush slightly.

"They are bigger than mine, which are very small."

"I've never thought about it," said Emma. She put her hands on her breasts. They weren't large, but were full, round, and quite perky. "I suppose they are quite nice."

"I bet men love them."

"I haven't had any complaints," said Emma, turning away to open the wardrobe beside her bed.

"I wish I had tits like yours."

"Why? Yours are lovely as well."

She heard Sophie get up and step over to her. The next moment, she pressed herself gently against Emma's back and put her hands round to rest on her breasts. Emma was taken off guard again and tensed. Sophie fondled them very gently. "They feel so nice. Maybe I'll have mine enlarged."

Emma turned her head back. "Don't have anything done to them. They're really lovely as they are."

"OK. As long as you like them."

She laughed nervously. "It doesn't matter about me. What does Antoine think? Does he like them as they are?"

"Oh, he doesn't seem to care. He just loves fucking me."

"As all men do."

Sophie kissed the back of Emma's head and let go of her. She went into the bathroom.

Emma felt a twinge of excited panic in her groin. She could feel her nipples were stiff. She finished packing her clothes away.

A few minutes later, Sophie emerged from the bathroom, came up to Emma, and kissed her on the cheek. "Goodnight," she said casually, as though nothing had happened. "Remember, bright and early in the morning."

"Goodnight." Emma went to the bathroom, sat on the loo, and peed. She couldn't quite believe this was happening. This girl was coming on to her—fondling her tits, kissing her. What on earth was going on? Was she suddenly sending out gay signals? She unpacked her toilet bag and brushed her teeth.

When she came back into the bedroom a little while later, Sophie was lying in bed and appeared to be asleep. She was on her side facing the wall, barely covered by the sheet on top of her. Emma stood for a moment staring at the other girl's nakedness. She could still sense the touch of Sophie's body against hers a moment ago.

She slipped out of her panties and got into bed, turning off the light. She was incredibly tired—but for a while she couldn't get to sleep. She went over in her mind the day that had just passed. Twenty-four hours ago she was naked in bed with Sally—the girl with the golden hair—making love to her. And now Sophie. This was all so new—and strange.

Chapter 5

Sally lifted her head off the pillow, and immediately the memories of the previous day came flooding back as though some sluice gate had been opened. Emma. God, Emma. Amazing. Sex back in her life. Well, it was obvious it was going to happen sometime. But the boss's daughter—well, that might be tricky.

But actually, thinking about it today, she didn't care. Why should she? Emma had gone away, and who knows how she would feel about it when she came back. Might just be embarrassed and never mention it again. She smiled to herself, then got out of bed and stretched. She pulled aside the curtain and looked out on the day. Sunny again. Good.

She went downstairs and put the kettle on. Funny how what had happened at the farm had brought all the stuff about Maddie back. In some ways that was so long ago—but then, not really—two and bit years. But lying there thinking about it—it had all seemed so vivid. Maybe because it was so important. Her first real love. Amazing.

The following day, I left home for school feeling on top of the world. I didn't care about anything except being with her and doing it again. As soon as I arrived, I looked round the school precinct trying to find her. I didn't know what I would say—we couldn't say anything if we were with other people—but I just needed to be with her or near her.

In the event, I hadn't been there for many minutes when she walked past me and pushed a slip of paper into my hand.

"Hi, Goldie—all right?"

"Yeah, you?"

"Yeah, good. See ya."

I stood there, the piece of paper crushed in my hand, not daring to look at it. Finally, I went to the toilet, locked myself in a cubicle, and read what she had written. "School theatre wardrobe, top floor, old building. 12:45." Just that.

I knew where it was, though I had never been in. It was a dark, dingy door that looked as though no one ever went inside. I flushed the paper down the loo and went to class. The morning dragged impossibly, but when lunch came, I made my way to the old building, trying to look as unobtrusive as possible.

Fortunately there was no one around when I arrived. My heart was beating fast. I knocked softly. It opened almost instantly and I was pulled inside. It was Maddie. She closed the door behind me, pushed me up against it, and kissed me. It felt wonderful to have her mouth on mine, our tongues playing together. She put her arms around my neck and hugged herself against me as she kissed me more intensely. I could feel her breasts pressing on mine—and she was pushing her groin hard against me. I ran my hands down her back and under her short skirt. She was wearing nothing underneath.

"You've got no knickers on." I squeezed the bare round cheeks gently.

"All ready for you," she said.

"Are we OK in here?" I asked nervously. The room was long and very narrow with racks of costumes down either side. There appeared to be a space at the far end with a light on.

"Course," she said and reached down beside me and turned the key in the lock. "No one ever comes here."

"Oh. Right. You sure?"

"Yeah, don't worry," she said and began to undo the buttons of my top. "Now I want to see your tits." She undid them all, pushed my top off my shoulders, then reached behind and unhooked my bra. She looked down at my breasts and put her hands on them.

"They're gorgeous."

"Not very big." Her hands felt warm and nice and I could sense my nipples stiffen at her touch.

"Only men care about that." She bent her head and kissed my left nipple. It sent shivers through me.

"Oh, that's lovely."

She looked up at me and smiled wickedly. She sucked my whole breast into her mouth, while massaging my other one with her hand. My stomach lurched. I had never been kissed on my breasts before—they suddenly felt so incredibly sensitive. I fondled her hair and stroked her face as she moved to my other breast, licking, kissing, and teasing it. I was in heaven, my heart racing, my pussy throbbing and hot. She carried on for several minutes, moving from one to the other, teasing and caressing them. I was breathing so deeply and moaning with pleasure and could feel that delicious tension in my stomach grow.

Then I felt her hand touch my thigh and move to my pussy, rubbing me through my panties. I could feel they were so wet now. She pushed them aside and inserted her finger, pushing quickly up into me.

"Oh God," I gasped.

"You like me fucking you?" she said, moving her mouth from my breasts to kiss me lightly.

"Yes. Yes, oh God, it feels so good." I put my hands on her head and kissed her hard. I wanted to eat her mouth.

She pushed my panties down my legs, and they dropped to my feet. "How about some more," she whispered as I felt another of her fingers join the first. "Does that feel OK?"

"Yes, oh yes."

"And this?"

I looked down and saw her push three fingers into me. I felt a slight pain as my pussy stretched, but after a while my muscles began to relax and the pain was replaced by a warm rush of pleasure. I could see my juices coating her hand. It was so intense I couldn't believe it. I wanted her whole hand inside me, going deeper and deeper. My knees felt weak as I stood there, her hand pumping in and out of me, her mouth kissing all over my breasts and neck.

Almost immediately I felt myself coming. It almost seemed to start at my breasts—her caresses sending a shiver that ignited my pussy and burst through the whole of me. I heard myself cry out again and felt my head being pushed into her neck. She kept pumping into me and I kept coming in wave after wave. I remember biting into her shoulder and hearing her squeal. I don't know how long it lasted, but finally I grasped her hand and made her stop.

"Oh God. No more . . . please."

"Had enough?"

I put my head against the back of the door and tried to regain my breath. "Oh God . . . brilliant."

"And to think two days ago you ran away from me. You better come and sit down. I want some now."

I stepped out of my panties and picked them up, then we went down to where the costume racks ended and the room opened out. There was an old battered sofa on one side and a sewing machine on a small table on the other with a window above it. I glanced out and could see the playground below, but it was high up so nobody could see in.

My top and bra were still hanging off me, so I took them off. Maddie sat down on the sofa and undid a few buttons of the battered shirt she was wearing. I could see her breasts underneath. They were larger and more round than mine, with bigger nipples.

I sat down beside her and we kissed. She fondled my breasts and ran her hands all over my back and shoulders. We kissed for a long time. Her tongue played round my mouth. She kissed me so deeply and for so long sometimes I could hardly catch my breath.

I put my hand down between her legs and began to play with her pussy, running my fingers up and down the full wet lips. I found her clit in the midst of her thick bush and rubbed it gently and she started to moan.

"Oh fuck . . . yeah . . . do that."

I took my mouth down to her breasts and ran my tongue round her nipples, then sucked on them like she had done to me. She ran her fingers through my hair and pushed me onto them.

She was very wet now, so I ran my finger down and tried to put it inside her. Immediately she jumped and grabbed my hand.

"No. Not inside. I don't like that," she said sharply. I felt shocked. Her eyes were suddenly full of anger.

"OK. Sorry, I was only trying to . . ."

"It's OK. Just play with my clit like you were."

I moved my fingers across her vaginal lips, massaging them gently, and she seemed to like that. I sucked on her nipples and bit them gently, running my tongue round the areolas then round the whole of her breasts. I began to feel excited again. I felt a dry hunger in my throat. It was as if I wanted to take the whole of each breast into my mouth.

I found her clit again and worked at it harder, pinching it between my fingers.

"Ohhhh fuck . . . yeah."

I kept doing it repeatedly and she began to cry louder and louder. It was as though I had suddenly found the key to bringing her off. She shut her eyes and threw her head back, her face screwed up in concentration. I kissed her hard and pushed my tongue deep into her mouth. I felt really aroused again and I held her with my mouth and hand and played her until she jerked and crushed my hand to her pussy, uttering short, sharp muffled cries, her whole frame in spasms.

She pulled away from my mouth, but I kept my hand teasing her until I thought her climax had finished.

"Fuck . . . fuck . . ." she said as she relaxed and regained herself. "Fucking hell, Goldie, you are fucking amazing."

"I'm sorry about, you know, my finger, but I didn't realise you didn't like it."

"It's OK. It just doesn't turn me on, that's all."

"OK." I put my leg between hers and lay down on top of her and kissed her. "Just doing it for you makes me feel turned on again." We were more or less naked apart from our skirts pulled around our waists. We kissed, open mouthed, our tongues melting together. I could feel her nipples hard against my breasts. I looked down and rubbed mine against them, feeling little flashes of pleasure as they touched. I was beginning to feel very excited and instinctively began to rub my bare pussy against her right leg.

"You horny little bitch. You're getting yourself off on my leg."

"Sorry. I can't help it."

"It's OK. Come on then." She grasped my bum cheeks and moved her leg against me. The friction was fantastic and immediately I felt another climax coming. I let my body submit to her rhythm, gyrating myself in little circles to stimulate my clit, sometimes pressing it hard and feeling the sparks scatter all over me. I was very wet again and her leg became slippery with my juice so that I could slide blissfully up and down. She leant up and kissed my nipples, biting and teasing them, winding me up into a fury.

"Are you going to come again?" she whispered, licking her way across my chest and up to my neck.

"Yeah . . . yeah, oh shit, yeah . . ."

"I can feel you're so wet. Give me all your cum juice. Come on . . . soak me in it."

I uttered a silent scream as the orgasm hit me, the blood pumping to my screwed-up face. It was as though her leg had suddenly ignited my pussy, lit a fire I could never put out. I writhed and jerked on her for what seemed ages, until I finally collapsed.

"Oh God . . . I don't believe it." I lay on top of her, regaining my breath.

"Plenty more where that came from. You're so fucking randy . . . it's brilliant. And you get so fucking wet . . . good job, I like that too."

She moved to push me off. Her leg was dribbling with my juice.

"Do you want me to do you again?"

"No, you better go. It's getting near to the end of the lunch break. Just remember, you owe me one."

I lay back on the sofa for a minute, trembling all over, then I got up and put my clothes back on. When we were both dressed, she kissed me.

"Same time tomorrow?"

I nodded.

"After that we better vary it a bit. Can't have anyone finding out, can we?"

"No."

"Good. See ya tomorrow then?"

"Yeah. Bye."

We went on doing it every day for weeks. Outside of that room, she largely ignored me and I her—just text messages, quick murmured words about what time to meet. But once we were in there together, it was a lovers' paradise. We just let our hormonal teenage instincts rip.

Eventually, when I knew I was going to see her, I would deliberately not wear any underwear. I would sit in tutorials feeling nude under my clothes, relishing the anticipation so much—then once inside the room, I would let her take me completely naked. And she taught me so much about sex and how we could please each other. She said she had first had sex when she was fifteen. I didn't ask her much about it, but from what I could gather, she'd had both boys and girls.

I remember one day I had been playing netball just before lunch, and I turned up at the room, having just showered. When she opened the door, I walked straight over to the sofa and pulled my dress over my head. As usual now, I had nothing on underneath.

I sat down and looked at her cheekily.

"Want me?" I said.

She looked at me for a moment, then said: "Your hair's wet. What have you been doing?"

"I've been playing netball."

"Have you just come out of the shower then?"

"Yeah," I replied.

She gave me a wry smile, then knelt down in front of me, put her hands on my ankles, and lifted my legs so that my knees were bent and my feet were either side of me on the cushion. She looked down at my exposed pussy and then back up at me, and said, "I'm going to give you a real treat today, Goldie."

With that, she began to kiss her way down my thighs.

I sighed as a shudder of goose pimples went all over me. She had never kissed me there before, and I felt myself gush with wetness as I realised what she was about to do. She bent towards my pussy and hesitated. She looked up at me and licked her lips provocatively. There was a moment of unbelievable anticipation, then her tongue licked from the bottom to the top of my slit. I cried out at the electric shock it sent through me. "Ssshh," she said, grinning. "I won't do this unless you shut up."

I felt breathless. "God . . . that was so nice . . . shit . . ."

Her mouth was back, her strong tongue massaging my lips, running up and down my slit, sending waves of hot pleasure I didn't think possible. I put one hand over my mouth and the other on the top of her head, stroking her thick, spiky hair.

"Oh God, oh God . . ." I spluttered.

I could feel rivers of juice pouring out of me and dribbling down between the cheeks of my bum. Her tongue worked at my pussy relentlessly. I built incredibly quickly—but just as she was close to making me come she pulled away, leaving me a hopeless wreck, gagging for more. She seemed to love doing it as much I did getting it, and it was as though she didn't want to stop teasing me. I found myself wondering what it was like, what it tasted like—just longing to do it to her.

After a while I couldn't bear it any longer. "Please let me come . . . please."

She looked up at me. I could see the wickedness in her eyes as she paused for a moment—then she leant forward again and kissed my clitoris. It was the trigger I had been waiting for. A bolt of lightning tore through me and my whole body was wracked with orgasm. It seemed to freeze every muscle—I couldn't utter a sound. The only parts of me that still moved were my hips, pushing relentlessly against that teasing mouth.

I don't know how long I was locked in this silent scream, but eventually I grabbed her head and pushed it away. I was totally breathless. "Oh God . . . God . . . fuck. Amazing."

She looked at me grinning, her face covered in my wetness. "You taste fucking gorgeous, Goldie. You know that? You just pour with juice, and I fucking love it." She kissed my pussy again, lightly. Another shiver went through me. "And look at that tight little arsehole . . . all rosy and pink." She put a finger between my bum cheeks and I felt it touch my bumhole. "And you're wet there too . . ." She began to massage all round it. I felt a tingle of pleasure spark all the way up my back passage and finish like a firework rocket with a burst in my pussy.

"Mmmmm . . ." I moaned. I had never thought that you could get a thrill from there, but my body seemed completely switched on to anything at that moment. She bent her head again and licked my pussy gently, her finger still teasing the ring of my bum. I gasped and felt another rush of liquid squirt from me.

She uttered a small cry and lapped harder, as though trying to catch all my juice in her mouth. But now she was pushing up into the centre of my bumhole and her finger went a little way inside.

"Oh yes . . . yes . . . oh fuck . . ." I cried as immediately I started coming again. "Oh fuck, I don't believe it . . ."

She intensified her licking and thrust her finger right up into me. A small spear of hot pleasure shot up my bum. Somehow, I was coming there as well and as she lapped my clit my whole groin seemed to erupt and take me over the edge.

I was moaning and snatching for breath and thrusting my bum down on her finger and could feel her moving it around inside. And I couldn't stop coming. As soon as one climax seemed about to subside another came, tensing and releasing me in an endless stream of ecstasy.

In the end it was Maddie who brought me down, calming me, taking her finger away, gently kissing my pussy as the climax melted.

She took my feet back to the floor and then put my legs up onto the sofa so that I was laying on it lengthways. It was long enough to take us both stretched out, and we had often had sex that way. I felt exhausted, breathless, my heart thumping in my chest. I lay my head back and watched as she slowly took off her clothes.

"That's what's called a multiple orgasm, Goldie," she said. "Good, isn't it?"

She lay down on top of me and I wrapped my arms around her. I loved the feel of her skin on mine. She was slim, but still had a bit of puppy fat that I loved. It made her seem so soft and cuddly—very sexy as well. She kissed me, our tongues dancing in each other's mouths.

"I've never known a girl who produces so much come. You actually squirted into my mouth just then."

"Sorry."

"What for? I fucking love it."

She put her leg between mine and started to rub against me. I could feel her clitoris was pushing down on my hip. She kissed me passionately again. I felt like she was a man and I was the submissive female. I liked that, lying back, being taken and used. I stretched my hand down and tried to find her bum. I wanted so much to give her the same sensation she had given me. I couldn't stretch that far, only managing to cup the top of her bum cheeks, but she somehow knew what I was trying to do and shifted herself upwards, without losing that essential contact with my hip. Then suddenly I found it. I wet my middle finger in my mouth, put both arms down, parted her cheeks, and pushed the finger around her ring. She gasped.

"OHHHH . . . fuck . . ."

I circled the little bud, rimming her, trying the soft centre for signs that she would let me penetrate. She kissed me hard, forcing her tongue to the back of my mouth so that I thought I might choke. Then she broke the kiss, her flushed face hovered above mine, her eyes rolling in their sockets. Her pussy was crushed hard against me, so I pushed my finger more firmly around her bum. She began to gasp for breath, uttering long moans. She screwed her eyes tightly shut then grunted again. She seemed to stay like that for several seconds, then let out a final groan. Then I felt her relax.

She opened her eyes, looked down at me, and smiled. "Fuck . . . that was good."

I felt light-headed as I crept out of the room a few minutes later. When I met some friends in the schoolyard I could barely keep my mind on what I was saying. The glow in my body kept bringing me back to what had just happened and how amazing it had felt.

The next day I found out that I was to spend the Friday night of the coming weekend alone. My stepfather was away on business, and my mum was going to take my stepbrother, Jamie, to a football tournament and stay overnight with relatives. This had happened before, but not since I had gotten together with Maddie. I immediately began planning how she could come to stay. I wanted to be alone with her, really alone, with no risk of any kind, in a proper bed. I wanted to sleep with her.

When we were alone together the next day, I asked her whether she would come. She was a bit reluctant at first and took some persuading, but in the end she agreed. On the Friday evening, I waited till everyone had gone and phoned her that it was all clear. Then I had a bath and waited for her to arrive. I walked around the house naked, feeling excited and unbelievably randy. When she finally rang the doorbell, I opened it, pulled her inside, and threw my arms around her neck. I kissed her passionately and for a long time.

"Hi," I said eventually, grinning at her.

She ran her hands all over my nude body. "Fuck, you're gorgeous."

"You're gorgeous too. Do you want anything, or shall we go to bed?"

"Can I have a shower?" she said. "I'm a bit sticky."

There was a bit of a glint in her eye. I knew what she meant. I had never gone down on her like she had on me, and tonight I wanted so badly to do it. It was strange. She was slightly off-guard like she wasn't on her territory and so was a bit unsure of herself. Maybe I would get closer to the real her tonight, I thought.

I showed her the bathroom and left her to it. I went to my room, pulled the covers off the bed, and lay down on it. I can still remember that feeling: laying there with nothing on . . . the delicious anticipation.

I heard her come out of the bathroom.

"In here," I called.

She came in and stood at the end of the bed, naked. She looked lovely. I had seen her without any clothes, of course, but not like this. In the frenetic sex we had at school, we both always had something left on—like a sock or a skirt tangled around our legs. Now we were completely bare with each other, and as I took her in my arms and we kissed and felt each other's bodies, it was so different.

As she kissed my breasts, I ran my hands over the lovely texture of her shoulders and back. Her skin was pale, with a milky tone. I found it so sexy. Maybe it was because she was my first lover, but I have always been able to think of her since and feel that same excitement. We kissed for a long time, feeling each other's bodies, taking our time. It was so nice not to have that pressure of quick, passionate sex we always had at school. But all the time I could feel a hunger growing inside me.

I pushed her onto her back and kissed my way down to her breasts. I always loved doing that. She liked me to suck them hard, drawing her nipples right into my mouth and gently biting them. Once I made her come just from that. But today I was anxious to move down. The hunger I felt was like a chasm opening up inside me that I needed to fill. I kissed into the bush of her pubic hair and could smell her sexy arousal. I wanted to get my head directly between her legs, so I slid off the bed and knelt on the floor. I looked at the moist, glistening folds of her vagina and felt a surge of lust. I was ravenous now and I could sense saliva gathering in my mouth. I put my tongue on her pussy and licked up and down. The taste and smell was so exciting. It was a totally new sensation that seemed to pull me in, and I found myself lapping strongly all round her sex, drinking in her juices, finding my way around this new, delicious territory.

I heard her sighing with pleasure, and found myself trying different things to please her. I knew she loved her clitoris being played with, so I lavished it with attention. I licked round it gently, flicked it with my tongue, then sucked it right into my mouth. She cried out and began to buck against my face and I knew she was coming. I teased her clitoris harder, exciting it in every possible way I could. She grabbed my hair and held me in a vicelike grip, but still I forced my mouth onto her little button, caressing it, massaging it, as she came for a long time.

She relaxed and stroked my hair. I looked up at her and smiled, my face covered with her juice.

"I'm still thirsty," I said.

"OK by me," she said.

Very gently, I placed my pointed tongue at the bottom of her vagina and probed gently. I wanted to be inside her, to love her in that most intimate of places. I knew perhaps I shouldn't, because she had never allowed me to go inside her, but I couldn't resist. I brought my fingers to either side of her pussy and pulled the lips apart, then put my tongue there and pushed ever so gently. It slid in and was met by a dribble of strong tasting juice. I heard her gasp, but she did nothing to stop me, and inclining my head and stretching my tongue, I pushed farther in and moved it around inside, gently caressing the roof and walls. I heard her whimper.

"Yeah . . . yeah . . . oh yeah," she whispered. "Oh fuck, Sally . . . yeah . . ."

It was the first time she had used my name and not called me Goldie. I felt thrilled. I pressed inside her pussy and worked my tongue more strongly. It was hurting from stretching so much, but the sensation of eating her was so good. From my stomach to my groin I seemed so full of the most wonderful lust. Shivers ran round my mouth from the taste of her cum. I curved my tongue to lick the roof of her pussy, trying to find her G spot. She shuddered and uttered a strange cry. It wasn't like the usual noise she made when she was about to come; it was kind of like a wail of emotion. My tongue was aching even more, but I carried on relentlessly, wanting to bring her over the top. She carried on louder and louder until she suddenly clenched my head between her thighs, and I knew she was coming.

But then suddenly she sharply pushed me away, turned on her side, and I realised she was crying.

I knelt before her for a moment, not knowing what to do. Then I climbed on the bed beside her and held her in my arms. She grasped me and clung to me for what seemed a long time, her sobbing gradually subsiding. All of a sudden she seemed like a very young, vulnerable girl—not the brash, confident rebel I had known before.

She lay still, clinging to me for several minutes, then looked up at me through tear-stained eyes.

"Sorry," she whispered.

"Don't be silly . . . did I upset you?"

"No. No. It was brilliant . . . but it's the first time anyone has been inside me since—since I was raped."

"Raped?"

"Yeah, two years ago now."

"Fuck, how awful." I stroked her hair and kissed her softly. "Who was it? I mean, you don't have to tell me."

"No, it's OK." She lay with her head beside mine for a few moments then looked up at me. "Me and my mates met three boys in the park one night. My mates went home, but I stayed with them till quite late. We were drinking beer, and I was pretty pissed—you know what I'm like. Then they tried it on, saying they wanted to do it with me. And I didn't want to. Anyway, though I refused, they just did it anyway, all three of them. Two of them held me down while the third one fucked me—and they didn't stop until they had all done it. It was horrible. Their fucking horrible cocks inside me, their spit all over me, their revolting spunk dribbling out of me."

"God, I'm so sorry. It sounds terrible."

"Yeah. I was sixteen. I didn't say anything when I got home, just went straight to bed. I had a bath the next morning and went to school—then just broke down. I told that twat Vincent, and she called the police, but I didn't even know what their names were. I gave descriptions and they found out who they were, but there was not enough evidence. And Vincent made it really clear that she thought that it had happened because of the way I behaved. You know, the way I dressed and stuff. Bitch."

Mrs. Vincent was the school principal—none of us liked her. I was shocked at Maddie's story. I was so sorry that this had happened. I wanted our night together to be so good. But it didn't matter. The important thing was for her to feel better. I just hugged her and after a while we fell asleep.

When I woke up about an hour later, she was smiling at me and seemed perfectly normal.

"I've been watching you for about half an hour. You're something special—you know that?"

"So are you. Do you feel better?"

"Yeah."

"Do you want to get something to eat and go to a movie or something?"

"You're joking. Let's ring for a takeaway—then we can stay like this. I feel better now, better than I've felt for ages. And I'm very randy . . ."

And we made love for ages. It was amazing.

Sally sighed at the delicious feeling flowing round her. She hadn't been able to resist frigging and getting herself off while she thought about that time.

She leapt off the bed. There was stuff to do, now that she was going to be living at the farm.

She phoned the estate agent and then the solicitor. She wanted the house sold as soon as possible. That would give her financial security, and maybe later on she could buy another place. She set about deciding what to do with all the furniture. She thought about what to keep and what to sell, but then came to the conclusion that there was nothing she wanted. A new start. That was essential. She could take most of her personal stuff—clothes, CDs, DVDs, telly—and the rest she would just get someone to take away.

After a couple of hours, she felt pretty tired, but delighted with what she had achieved. She could take the rest of her stuff over in the car, move out the following week, and let the estate agent organise the rest.

Chapter 6

"Wake up, sleepy head."

Emma opened her eyes to see Sophie's face very close to hers, smiling. She kissed Emma lightly on the lips. "Get dressed. We have to have breakfast and then register."

Emma sat up, the softness of the other girl's lips tingling on hers. "I'm sorry. I must have been really tired."

"That's OK."

Sophie was wearing a white mini dress that was close-fitting at the top and splayed out to form a frilly skirt. Her rich, pale brown skin stood out against the whiteness of the fabric. Emma got out of bed, opened a drawer, and pulled out some clothes. As she pulled on a pair of panties, she felt Sophie stroke her back. She shivered.

"It's OK—don't hurry."

They ate in the stone-vaulted basement restaurant, as grand in size as the rest of the sprawling chateau. A few more students had gathered—all girls—and she noticed Sophie wave at one or two of them. Emma had put on some shorts and a T-shirt: with a bra—unlike Sophie. She was still conscious that this was a Catholic institution. As they sat eating croissant and good strong coffee, Emma felt excited and had a warm feeling: This was France—her other home.

Registration took place back in the entrance hall. Emma's father had paid the fees in advance and thus hers was completed quickly. Sophie's took a little longer with much discussion in fast French.

"They are so stupid," she said as they left to go outside. "My mother faxed all the information weeks ago, and now they have no record. Anyway, it is OK. Let's go to the chapel first."

"The chapel?"

"Yes. You must see the chapel. It is lovely. Anyway, I want to say a prayer."

"You do?"

"Yes. Why?"

"No, it's OK. That's fine."

The chapel stood apart from the chateau and was reached by a gravel track to the side of the house. Like everything else at Montrichet, it was big, but unlike the house, it had been built in the Gothic style.

Entrance was by the side door. Inside, it was dark and cool. Tall stained glass windows soared to the vault on all sides, and their footsteps echoed. Shafts of coloured sunlight streamed down and splayed across the paved floor.

Sophie went to the altar rail and knelt down, crossing herself. Emma was Catholic, because her mother was, but they had never been a religious family particularly. Her father read the lesson in the local parish church now and again, but he wasn't that regular. She smiled to herself at the kneeling figure, remembering Sophie the day before—naked, fornicating with complete abandon. Now praying, there appeared to be no contradiction; she knew Sophie wouldn't feel one anyway.

"Were you praying for forgiveness?" said Emma, as they left the chapel and walked towards the garden.

"For what?"

"I don't know. For having sex with your boyfriend in a Catholic college?"

"Why? Sex is not wrong. It is an act of love." She put her arm round Emma's neck and kissed her on the cheek. "What is wrong with giving pleasure to someone? Loving them?"

"I suppose . . . but that's not the accepted view, is it? The church condemns sex outside marriage. Fornication."

"I think orgasm is a spiritual experience. Some of my lovers have sent me to heaven while making love to me."

Emma said nothing. Her mind flashed to the night with Sally.

"Don't you ever feel so fantastic when you have sex that you are kind of . . . I don't know . . . in another place?"

"Yeah. I do."

They walked through a gate in a high wall and into an ornamental garden. A sculpture in the middle was surrounded by a maze of symmetrically patterned hedges.

"You must know what I mean? You have had a lot of lovers," said Sophie.

"What makes you say that?"

"Because you are so beautiful."

Emma felt herself flush a little. She put her own arm around Sophie's waist so that they were locked into each other. "I haven't had that many. Although I did go a bit wild in my first year at university."

"I bet everyone wanted you."

Emma laughed. "Not quite everyone."

"Anyway, I don't see anything wrong with sex—whoever you do it with. I think God wants us to enjoy life, and he made sex for us to enjoy as well."

"But the church says sex is only OK inside marriage, and is really only for procreation."

"When I make love I feel divine. It's about what is beautiful and good. And two people making love is the most beautiful thing you can think of."

Emma laughed. She looked at her. She had an earnest innocence that was so bewitching. She looked away. "Come on. Show me the temple."

They walked on to the end of the ornamental garden where another door led through to a long series of stone steps. Roses lined the walls on either side, and a heady perfume wafted over them, combined with the sweet smell of old stone. It was warm in the sunshine and the air was full of birdsong. They stumbled up the steps—larking around and pretending to be stuck to each other—and were breathless when they reached the top of the flight. Emma suddenly thought how happy she was. She really loved being here.

Sophie, with her off-the-wall, slightly outrageous manner, was such fun.

"I just want to say—this is such a lovely place. And I'm so glad I'm here."

Sophie stopped, turned to her, and took her other hand in her own. "Yes, it is," she said. "And I think the people are good, too—don't you think?"

Her big green eyes made her smile so intense somehow, thought Emma. She squeezed Sophie's hand. "Yes. The people are lovely—one in particular."

"I am so glad we are roommates. It's good, isn't it?"

"Yes, it is."

"Can I kiss you?"

"What? Sure." Emma gave an embarrassed laugh.

Sophie hesitated for a moment, then kissed her lightly on the lips.

Another girl's mouth—so soft, tender . . . lovely.

"You don't mind me kissing you?"

"No. I like it."

"Some girls think it is unnatural. Have you kissed girls before?"

"Yes—a few times."

"Good, because I think I will want to kiss you a lot."

"That's OK. I mean . . . I like it." Without thinking, she kissed Sophie back. "There." There was a brief moment between them. Emma felt goose pimples shoot all over her body. "Let's go to the top," she said. "I want to see the view." She wanted to kiss her again. *This is almost too strange to be a coincidence,* she thought.

They climbed the next set of steps, and when they reached the top, they came to a paved area dominated by the imposing stone fountain. It was circular, with a tall male figure at its centre, standing on a rock from which jets of water sprayed into the surrounding pool. At its feet were carved several female figures, together with exotic-looking sea creatures.

"It is supposed to represent Neptune," said Sophie. "Don't you think it is beautiful?"

"Yeah . . . amazing."

Sophie's hand found its way under Emma's blouse and stroked the bare skin of her back.

"And you made love actually in the fountain?" she said without thinking.

"Mmm. It was after midnight, and the jets had been turned off. But we bathed together in the water naked. I remember lying back on that stone ledge, watching the stars, and being given the most amazing orgasm."

Emma laughed nervously. "You're outrageous," she said. She felt slightly stunned. The implication of what Sophie had said was so obvious; it was like she was challenging her.

"I know I'm outrageous—but that's what you love about me." She brought her face close to Emma's and kissed her. Emma felt the tip of her tongue lightly graze her lips.

Emma smiled, catching her breath. "Yeah, I guess I do."

Sophie broke away, got up on the ledge of the fountain, and stepped down into the pool. "Come on, let's paddle."

"What? We'll get drenched."

"So? Come on, it's nice."

Sophie's dress was instantly wet from the various jets of water. It clung to her body, and Emma could see the small hillocks of her breasts with their dark nipples at the centre.

Emma climbed on to the ledge and stepped in. It was deeper than she thought, and as she tried to find her balance on the slippery bottom, she fell forward. She put out her hands, but was almost completely immersed. She heard Sophie laugh, and, looking up, burst into giggles herself. Her shorts were clinging to her, and her blouse and bra were almost completely see-through. Sophie looked pointedly at her breasts.

"Let's walk all the way round."

She followed Sophie, treading gingerly on the slippery stones that lined the pool. They shrieked and giggled as they went round, trying to dodge the many jets that hit them at different angles. The water was warm and refreshing and Emma relished the feeling.

When they had walked all the way round, Sophie jumped out and Emma followed her. She could see a farther flight of steps leading up to an imitation of a Roman temple, with a pediment and pillars of coloured stone standing imposingly at its front. Sophie ran up the steps, and when she reached the top, started to take off her dress.

"What are you doing?" said Emma.

"We must dry our clothes."

"But I haven't got much on underneath. Nor have you."

"So? There is no one around, and we can see if anyone comes." Sophie slipped her dress off. She was wearing a small thong underneath and quickly removed that as well.

Emma looked around. There was a wood all round the back of the temple, and it fell away on either side, stretching down to the massive chateau at the bottom of the hill. "Can't they see us from the chateau?"

"Of course not. It's too far away."

"Well . . . OK." She undid her blouse and slipped it off, took off her bra, then pushed her shorts down and stepped out of them. She kept her panties on. Then she sat down quickly on the smooth marble and leaned against one of the pillars.

Naked, Sophie took her dress and laid it out on the steps leading up to the temple. She put her thong beside it. She turned and smiled at Emma, running her hands through her thick black hair.

"You're such an exhibitionist," said Emma, looking at her lithe nude body. "You almost want people to see you."

"I think I have a nice body. I don't mind if people see it— especially if it gives them pleasure."

"You could be a model. You have that look."

Sophie mimicked model poses and pouted her lips. Emma giggled.

"I don't think I want that kind of life," said Sophie. "And anyway, my tits aren't big enough."

"Yes they are. The natural look is all the rage now."

"I told you, I need tits like yours. They are perfect."

"I don't know about that."

Sophie came and sat beside her. She leant her head on Emma's shoulder. "Mmm. It's nice here. Warm."

"We might burn."

"Mmm."

"I have some lotion in my bag. It's by the fountain."

"Oh, but don't move. I am really enjoying your shoulder. I feel sleepy."

"Be back in a minute." Emma walked down the steps, tentatively looking around. There didn't appear to be anybody about, and the chateau was a long way off. She picked up her bag and found the lotion. As she came back up the steps, she could see Sophie was laying back, eyes closed, her long body stretched out on the marble ledge. Her breasts were the slightest of smooth mounds with the dark nipples like little points. Her small thatch of pubic hair barely covered the pink gash of her vagina nestling between her slim thighs. Her skin was the palest brown in the bright sun. Emma could feel herself being attracted. "Here. Want some?"

Sophie didn't look up or open her eyes. "Just rub some into my tits, will you? The rest of me should be all right."

Emma hesitated and felt a flash of embarrassment. Then she smiled to herself and squeezed some lotion onto her hand. She smoothed it into Sophie's chest, rubbing gently all around her breasts. Sophie's skin was hot from the sun, and the smell and slippery feel of the lotion made Emma swallow involuntarily. Sophie's nipples stiffened under her palms and, unmistakably, she was conscious of a gentle warmth building inside herself.

"There," she said.

Sophie opened her eyes and looked at her. "Mmm . . . that was lovely. Can I do yours for you?"

"No—it's OK."

"Oh. Please . . ."

Emma hesitated again. "All right. Thanks." She handed her the lotion and lay down. "I know you have a thing about my tits."

Sophie sat up and put lotion on her hand. "Yes, I do. I love them." She began to caress Emma's breasts, softly running her palms all over them. "I think I have shocked you."

"Why?"

"Because of what I said about making love in the fountain."

"Oh, no. Not really."

"I was making love with another girl."

"Yeah . . . well, I guessed that was what . . . you know . . . happened."

Sophie grazed her thumb provocatively over Emma's nipple. "Does that put you off me?"

Emma opened her eyes and looked at her. "No, of course not."

"I'm bisexual."

"Yeah. Well—that's fine."

Sophie's hand stopped on Emma's right breast and massaged it. "You will be a bit worried about me now."

"Why?"

"You won't want to kiss me in case I misinterpret things."

Emma looked at her again. Shaded from the sun, Sophie's full lips were so appealing. "It's OK. Like I said, I like kissing you."

"Even though I find you very attractive?"

"Yeah, I like that."

"Can I kiss you again?"

"Sure."

Sophie bent down and put her mouth on Emma's. The feeling was so sweet and soft, their mouths seemed to melt together. She felt her breasts become tender under Sophie's touch, and a sense of arousal stirred in her groin. As the kiss broke naturally, she turned her head slightly away, but Sophie found it again, kissing her more passionately this time, her lips searching and moving on Emma's mouth. Emma shivered as their lips finally parted.

"You must tell me if I am too much," said Sophie.

Emma breathed deeply, putting up her hand to stroke the dark mass of Sophie's hair. "No, you're a really good kisser," she said, trying to sound as casual as she could.

"Have you ever had sex with another girl?"

"No." Why was she lying? She had made love with Sally only two nights before.

"I first did it when I was fourteen. It felt very natural."

"That's very young."

"Yes, but it was incredible."

"So when did you first have sex with a boy?"

"When I was sixteen. I found I liked it just as much. I like sex whichever way it comes."

Her eyes were mesmerising, and Emma felt herself wanting to kiss her again. As if reading her thoughts, Sophie bent down and kissed her neck, her fingers gently rubbing and pinching the nipple of her breast.

Emma sighed. She sat up. "We'd better get back. We've got this reception thing soon." Her head reeled. It was as if her whole sexuality was being turned inside out.

"I'm sorry. Am I too much?"

Emma looked at her and smiled. "No, it's me. I'm not that way—you know? But it's funny—I really like you, and you are lovely . . . and . . ." She hesitated, feeling her heart pump in her chest, fuelled by this unfamiliar desire. "I don't know . . . you're just so bloody French!"

They laughed. Sophie stroked her face. "I would love to make love to you, but if that is not your way, that's OK. Just tell me to lay off."

Emma paused, looking at her. "Come on. We'd better go."

"Our clothes are soaking."

"They'll dry quicker if we wear them."

As they walked back through the rose garden, Sophie stopped. "Oh. Hello, Father."

Emma turned to see a young priest coming towards them. He was dressed casually, but with the Roman Catholic clerical collar.

"Sophie—how lovely to see you," he said, in a very English accent. He was smiling, with a slightly knowing expression.

Sophie took Emma's hand. "It's nice to see you again. This is Emma—she's English as well."

"Hello," said Emma. She thought he looked rather nice. He had reddish, slightly long—for a priest—wavy hair that went into curls at the back. His face was intelligent looking, with rather piercing eyes offset by a mouth that seemed to want to smile all the time.

"So you are here again this year?" said Sophie.

"Yes. I'm very lucky to be able to be chaplain again. And you're back too?"

"Yes." She turned to Emma. "Father Maurice was chaplain here last year." She turned back to him. "Maybe we can meet up again sometime?"

He paused for a moment, his smile broadening. "I was hoping you'd say that. Yes, that would be good." He glanced at Emma, before looking back at Sophie. "Will I see you at mass on Sunday?"

Emma thought that there was an amused glint in his eye.

"Of course. I always go."

"Good. Well, I look forward to seeing you there. Maybe you could bring Emma."

"Yes," said Emma quickly. "Yes. That would be nice."

"Excellent. See you both there, then." He hesitated, his eyes dropping momentarily to Emma's breasts, then smiled slightly knowingly and walked on.

Sophie watched him go, then turned to Emma. "I thought you said you don't go to church?"

"No, I don't. But I think he's quite nice, and anyway, I'll go to keep you company."

"That's nice."

"Doesn't he get tempted here, with all these pretty young girls?"

"Yes, I'm sure he does." Sophie giggled to herself. They started to walk towards the chateau. "He probably finds it a bit of a turn on."

"He's not supposed to think about sex."

"Ah, but in his lonely bed at night, he fantasises, I'm sure. Anyway, priests take an oath of celibacy, not chastity."

"So, the church would be happy if he jumped into bed with any one of us? I don't think so."

"Or both of us."

"Fancy that, do you?"

"You said he was nice-looking."

"He is, but he's still a priest."

"Don't you wonder what it would be like to have a man of God put his cock inside you and fuck you?"

"What—no!"

"All that holy spunk lighting you up inside?" Sophie laughed.

When they got to their room, Sophie took off her clothes. "I think I want to wash after that fountain," she said. She went into the bathroom and turned on the shower.

"Yeah," said Emma. "You're probably right."

After what had happened, she felt slightly awkward, but she undressed and joined Sophie in the wet room.

It was Emma this time who found herself looking at the other girl's naked body—and experiencing an unmistakable attraction. *This has never happened to me before,* she thought. *But somehow I like the way I'm feeling.*

"Don't worry, I'm not going to pounce on you," said Sophie, as they began to wash themselves.

Emma smiled. "Do you want me to wash your back, or is that a silly question?"

"Yes please, and it is a silly question."

Emma ran her hands over the soft sheen of flesh. It was so smooth it was like soft marble.

"Are you missing your boyfriend?" said Sophie.

"Yes, a bit." *Not,* she thought.

"Only a bit?"

"Well, yeah. It wasn't very good, you know, when I left."

"Don't you miss the sex?"

"Yeah, of course."

"You don't sound very sure. I miss it terribly if I haven't had it for a day or two."

"I've noticed. There." She patted her on the back. "Now me." She turned her back and Sophie began to rub the suds into her skin. "Mmm. That's good."

"I can't go without an orgasm for very long."

Emma felt herself flush slightly. "Yeah. Well . . ."

"Well what?"

"Oh, nothing."

"No. Come on, tell me."

"It's just the way I am."

"What is?"

"I find it difficult to have orgasms." Emma felt a strong pang of guilt. She couldn't bring herself to say what she wanted.

"What? Guys don't make you come?"

"Well . . ." Emma smiled at the horrified look on Sophie's face. "I guess I can count the number of times I've come on the finger of one hand."

"But that's terrible. Everyone can come—of course they can."

"As I said, it's just the way I'm made. Of course I get excited, but most times it never comes to anything."

Sophie's face was almost comically ablaze with outrage. "That's rubbish. Your lovers must have been very selfish. Taking their own pleasure but not bothering about yours. I would kick a man out who didn't make me come."

"It doesn't matter really. I still enjoy it. I mean—I love it."

"You poor thing." She put her hands on Emma's face and kissed her, lightly at first, then a deep French kiss, her tongue wrestling inside Emma's mouth.

Emma felt arousal rise sharply. She couldn't resist putting her arms lightly around Sophie and stroking her back.

Sophie broke the kiss and looked at her intently. She ran her hands down to Emma's breasts and fondled them gently, then she kissed her way down Emma's neck to her chest, finally putting her mouth over Emma's right breast and suckling the nipple.

The pleasure was so acute, Emma recoiled. "Sophie . . . I. Look, I don't know. I'm not that way, please . . ."

Sophie raised her head and licked Emma's nose, taking the drops of water on her tongue. Then she kissed her lightly again. "I can make you come. I know I can. I want to make love to you and give you an orgasm. I want to be your lover."

She felt Sophie's hand trail down and reach between her legs. As her fingers touched Emma's pussy the shock made her cry out. Impulsively, she pushed the girl gently away, took a towel from the rail, walked out, and began to dry herself. Her head was reeling.

"Are you OK?" Sophie came up behind her and stroked her back.

"Yeah. Yeah." Her body was at a fever pitch, her heart pumping hard, her mind racing. It had felt so good, so natural. Her head was swimming. "You've just given me a lot to think about."

"You must think less and do more."

Emma felt her stomach lurch. "We'd better get dressed; we'll be late."

The reception was held in the chateau's ballroom—a huge baroque space with soaring windows and a fine plastered ceiling. Suddenly, from nowhere it seemed, dozens of girls had arrived from all parts of the world. They had mingled and introduced themselves as best they could, and after a while, Sophie had recognised some students she knew from the previous year, so she left Emma on her own. Emma chatted to a Swedish girl called Hannah and to several other students. Everyone seemed to speak English or French, and after a while she relaxed and began to enjoy herself.

An hour later, when the reception was over, she glanced around the room for Sophie. She was standing by one of the windows, and Emma was somehow aware she had been looking at her for some time. It was a long, intense stare. Emma smiled quickly, feeling herself flush.

Sophie came across. "Sorry, my darling—was I neglecting you?"

"No. I was fine."

"Good, only I was chatting with some friends I met last year. I am going to their room for a drink. Did you want to come?"

"No—I think I'm still tired from yesterday. I'll go to bed."

"Are you sure?"

"Yeah, I'll see you later."

"OK, my lovely." Sophie kissed her lightly on the lips and then joined her friends.

Emma blushed. One of the girls waiting for Sophie seemed to look at her in a knowing way, smiling.

Emma left to go to their room.

In her sleep, she heard a sound. It was unmistakable, just as before. She slowly opened her eyes. Sophie was back, her reading light was on, and she could see her lying on the top of her bed. She was naked and had one hand between her legs and was moaning softly, her breathing excited. Her hips were gyrating and with her other hand she was squeezing her breasts and pinching her nipples. Emma watched, fascinated. She remembered when she had secretly watched Susie do it two years ago. Suddenly, Sophie turned and looked straight at her.

"I'm sorry. I didn't mean to wake you," she said breathlessly.

"It's—it's OK," Emma stammered.

"When I get carried away I make a lot of noise."

"No. I mean . . . I didn't mean to look."

"That's all right. You can watch me if you want to."

"No. It's . . . I mean—I'm all right."

Sophie sighed again and rolled her head on the pillow. "Ohhh . . . it feels so good . . ."

Emma turned onto her stomach and put her face into the pillow. She pressed her pelvis against the sheet, her pulse quickening.

"Emma."

She looked across at Sophie. "Yes?"

"Let me see you. Take the sheet off you."

"What?"

"Let me see you naked. I want to come looking at you."

Emma froze for a moment—and she felt blood pump to her face. Slowly, without thinking, she pushed the sheet off herself. Then, keeping her eyes on Sophie, she sat up, leaned against the wall, pulled one of her legs up and let the other trail across the bed, bringing her pussy blatantly into full view. The wall was cold against her skin, but as though in a trance, she put a hand down and played with herself. She trailed her other hand through her hair, her mouth slightly open.

Sophie sat up as well. Emma could see her eyes drinking in her body. She frigged herself faster and began to sigh and moan louder, her breathing jagged and uneven. "Ohhh . . . Emma . . . you are so beautiful . . . OH YES . . . YES! . . . YEEESSS." Her mouth opened in a silent scream, her face reddening. She gasped, then gulped a breath before crying out again, her eyes tight shut now, her whole body lurching with the spasms wracking her. Her body was still for a moment, as though hanging in the air.

Finally she relaxed and opened her eyes. She smiled. "That was so good."

Emma was suddenly conscious of how acutely aroused she was. Feeling embarrassed, she laughed softly. "I've never done anything like that before. You're amazing."

Sophie got up from the bed, walked over and leant over Emma, then kissed her softly. Emma could smell the strong scent of her sex—of female arousal. Without thinking, she stroked Sophie's face. They kissed again. Their tongues entwined. It was not only the wonderful soft feel of her mouth, but the taste, the sense of their saliva blending together.

Sophie kissed all over Emma's face lightly. "There's a lot I can do for you."

Suddenly Emma felt Sophie's hand touch her pussy, sliding her fingers up and down. She sat up sharply, seized by

a mixture of acute pleasure and a sort of panic. "Sophie—I
. . ."

She withdrew her hand. "Sorry."

"I'm not sure I'm ready."

"It's OK. Don't worry." She brought her hand to her mouth
and licked her finger, smiling. "You taste sweet."

"I'm sorry."

"Only when you're ready. Goodnight, my darling." She
brushed her lips softly against Emma's, then turned and got
back into bed, switching off her light.

Emma sat for a few minutes in the dark, her eyes shut,
her body pounding, her confused thoughts flying round her
mind. It was not only the intensity of the pleasure when Sophie had touched her, but the incredible sight of her having
an orgasm. Only twice had she felt her body take off and
take her away, in that brief, magical time with Sally. So many
times she had lain next to boyfriends and watched them go
to sleep, her body still raging. Lain there frustrated feeling
the fruits of their climax dribbling out of her pussy. Maybe
Sophie could do it for her again—but somehow she didn't
want to do it with another girl. She wanted to save herself
until she saw Sally again . . . maybe. She raised her head and
looked across at Sophie. She was breathing evenly and had
gone to sleep. In the moonlight streaming through the window, Emma could see that she had turned onto her stomach,
her arm across the pillow above her head, her long beautiful
body still uncovered.

Quietly, Emma got out of bed, walked across, and sat on
the side of Sophie's bed. She put out her hand and gently
touched her. Her skin felt like warm satin, and the feel of it
as she spread out her palm tingled up her arm to her armpit
and down her back. Tentatively, she moved her hand across
Sophie's shoulders and down the furrow of her back to the
rising mound of her buttock. Warmth grew in Emma's pussy
and her nipples stiffened. She put her other hand onto her
own breasts and fondled them, feeling how firm they were
and how the touch of her hand made them feel so sensitive.

Gingerly, she lay down and delicately wrapped herself around the sleeping girl, feeling the contact between them in every part of her body. She kissed Sophie's outstretched arm and shoulders, licking the rich, warm flesh. Sophie stirred and moved farther into the bed, allowing Emma more room, but she didn't wake. She felt the same sharpness of arousal she had that night with Sally, holding that slim body in her arms, kissing that lovely, sensuous mouth.

I want this, thought Emma. *I want this so much. I want to give myself to this.*

The sound of her alarm shot through Emma's brain like a pneumatic drill. She sat up—and suddenly realised she was in Sophie's bed. Quickly, she climbed out, just as she heard Sophie stirring. She felt foolish. She stood not knowing what to do for a moment, looking at the other girl, her hand playing nervously with her hair.

Sophie opened her eyes and looked at her. "Hi."

"Hi."

"You slept with me. That was nice."

"Yeah." She didn't know what to say. "I felt like a cuddle. I couldn't get to sleep after, you know."

Sophie smiled at her and turned onto her back. "Come here."

"I've got to go. I've got a class in the language lab."

"Just a quick kiss."

"OK." She hesitated, then stepped towards the bed, leant down, and kissed Sophie lightly on the lips. Then she turned away quickly and went to her drawers and started to dress.

"Are you busy in classes all day?" said Sophie.

"No, just this morning."

"Good. So I can see you this afternoon?"

"Yeah—sure."

Sophie said nothing as Emma finished dressing and then went to the bathroom.

When she came out, Sophie was sitting up in bed, the covers thrown off and the fingers of one hand playing in her pubic hair. She looked so seductive, the whites of her eyes so pure, the pupils vividly green, her complexion clear, that soft brown skin almost translucent over her delicate shoulders, and the small buds of her breasts.

"I'm just going to grab some coffee and go straight there. I'll see you later."

"OK."

Emma walked to the door.

"It was so lovely last night," said Sophie. "I had such a wonderful orgasm looking at you."

Emma turned. "Yeah. It was nice." She looked into the beautiful eyes for a moment then looked away. "Look, I'm sorry. I can't do this. I really can't. I have someone else at home and—you know—I find you really lovely. I do, believe me, but they come first. So . . . I mean I love sharing a room with you, but can we just be friends?" She couldn't think of anything more to say. She looked at Sophie. Her beautiful green eyes were hypnotic, like X-rays piercing right through her.

Sophie got up and walked towards her.

The sight of her lithe, naked body caused an unexpectedly sharp twinge of lust deep in Emma's groin. "Of course . . . I'm sorry. I shouldn't have come on to you in the way I have. Oh, you poor thing. Come here." She took Emma's hands in hers and pulled her into a hug.

Emma hugged her tightly, pressing her lips to her cheek. "Sorry. Let's just take it easy—yeah?"

"Sure." Sophie loosened herself from Emma's grasp and kissed her very lightly on the lips. "We'll talk about it. You have a lovely day."

"Yeah, I better go." Emma turned quickly and opened the door, passing through and shutting it behind her. Her heart pounding, she made for the restaurant.

She sat in the cafe on her own sipping fresh coffee, the luscious, bitter taste sharp in her mouth. She ate a croissant hungrily. Her mind was in overdrive. She wanted sex with Sophie—she knew she did. Just at the point of telling her that she didn't want it to go any further, she'd felt it all the more strongly. It had only been three days since she had finished with Charlie and got it on with Sally and discovered she was lesbian. Everything had happened so fast—and now this. For five years, all the time she had been sexually active, she had been straight sexually—and happy with it. But now?

When she had finished, she went outside and speed-dialed a number on her mobile phone. There was no answer for a long time, but finally a sleepy voice answered.

"Susie?"

"Oh God . . . Emma. What time is it?"

"What? I don't know, eight o'clock or something?"

"Yeah, in France. That's seven here."

"Sorry. Had a debauched evening?"

"Mmm. Rather."

"Oh, right."

"So how are you?"

"Fine."

"Behaving yourself?"

Emma could hear her yawning.

"Look, I've got to tell you. I'm sharing a room with this girl."

"Yeah?"

"Yeah—and, well . . ." She paused. How do you say those things? "She's sort of coming on to me."

"Oh God—urgghh. Have you told her to piss off?"

"Well . . . I sort of . . . I don't know how to explain this, but I quite like it."

There was a pause. "What? What do you mean? I didn't know you were like that," said Susie sharply.

"No, I know, but I just really like her and . . . well, she's really lovely and . . ."

"What? Are you going to have sex with her?"

"I don't know. No, I've said I won't . . ." Emma stopped and sighed. "But, the trouble is, I think I might."

"Emma! Have you suddenly discovered you're a dyke or something?"

"No, but . . . it's just really weird. I'm sort of mesmerised by her."

"But you've only been there two days!"

"Yeah, I know, I know . . . it's weird. But it's just like she's opened something up in me. When she touches me, it's . . ."

"Touches you? So what have you done?"

"Oh nothing . . . nothing. I mean, just kissed and stuff."

"You've snogged her?"

"Yeah."

"And what was that like?"

"Nice. Really nice."

"So is there anyone else sharing your room?"

"No, just the two of us."

"So I take it she's a dyke?"

"No, she's bi. She was fucking the arse off her boyfriend when I arrived on Saturday evening."

"Then she started coming on to you?"

"Yeah, straightaway after he was gone."

"And does she turn you on?"

"Yeah, she does actually. I mean it surprises me as much as it does you."

"But you haven't actually had sex?"

"No . . . we nearly did last night."

"Nearly did?"

"Yeah, I chickened out."

"But you wanted to?"

"Yeah. A lot."

There was a silence from the other end. Emma felt a slight sense of panic.

"Are you appalled?"

"What? No, not really. I mean, you know, go for it, I suppose. I just never thought for a moment you were like that."

"Nor did I."

"I certainly can't imagine doing it—I don't think anyway."

"Well, I just think, what the hell, I mean, so I'm suddenly fancying someone of my own sex—so what? And she's really up front and relaxed about it. Why not—it might be fun."

"Yeah . . . well. I mean, if that's what you really want."

"Yeah. I think it is what I want." She paused. "Look, I've got to go. You don't think I'm awful if I do? I mean, you won't go off me or anything?"

"Of course not. Don't be idiotic. Just don't expect *me* to shag you."

Emma laughed. "I love you . . . still love me?"

"Yeah, yeah, yeah. Go on—bugger off."

Feeling better, she scampered down to the language laboratory, located in the vast basement of the building.

Work in the lab was hard. Emma thought her French was good, but the speed and complexity of some of the business language left her floundering. By the time she had gone through that and a conversation class, she felt mentally exhausted. And, in any case, she knew the work was not the only thing occupying her mind.

She had tried to keep the beautiful, sexy French girl at the back of her mind all morning, but later, as she mounted the steps to go back to their room, she felt her stomach fluttering with a mix of anxiety and mounting excitement.

Just as she reached the door, Sophie came out and they nearly collided.

"Sorry," she said. "I am late for a lesson."

"Oh, OK. I'll see you later, then."

"Yes. Listen—I have arranged to go to the village tonight with some friends. Will you come?"

"Yeah—why not? That would be lovely."

"Good." She put out her hand and pulled Emma's face to hers. She kissed her softly. "You are so beautiful."

Emma felt a melting sensation down her spine. She patted Sophie's bum. "Go on. You'll be late."

Emma watched her as she went down the corridor, smiling to herself. She was so sexy. She was wearing a short mini dress that clung tightly to her slim, swaying buttocks, but exposed her long model's legs to maximum effect. Emma had also noticed how the thin material had displayed her nipples, braless underneath.

As they sat in the village square later, Emma watched Sophie talking animatedly to some other students. She looked at her wide, full mouth, her incredible eyes, black curly hair, and long elegant neck. She was overwhelming, so packed with energy.

Sophie glanced over in Emma's direction and smiled. Emma smiled back and held her gaze for a moment. She didn't know how much wine she had drunk, but she knew she had refilled her glass several times. She so wanted to have sex with her. *Why not,* she thought. *She is beautiful, sexy—fun. What's wrong with playing around with your own sex? I loved it with Sally.* For a fleeting moment she remembered holding Sally naked in her arms in her bed at home— then she had an image of her and Sophie making love in their room, naked on Emma's bed. She shivered and turned away. She remembered Sally saying that she should try it out with other girls, see if that was what she really wanted.

As they got up from their table to leave, Sophie linked arms with her friends and walked on ahead. Emma followed, casually chatting to Hannah, with whom she had walked down to the village. Emma felt her eyes flick constantly to Sophie. She was thinking back to that afternoon when they had rubbed oil into one another's breasts.

"So you are at university in London?"

"What? Oh, yes." Emma struggled to drag her mind back to the conversation she was having with Hannah.

"That must be exciting?"

"Yes. It is. It's great being in the capital city."

"But you live in the country?"

"Yes. Near Stratford—you know, Shakespeare and all that." She looked at Sophie again. She had her arm round one of the friends she was with.

"Do you play the tennis?"

"Yes, I do."

"Good—I will give you the game if you like. In the to-morrow afternoon?"

"Yes. I'd enjoy that. Are there courts here?"

"Yes. Round by the stable block."

"Oh yes. I know."

"Shall we say four o'clock?"

"Yes. Shall I meet you there?"

"No—I will come to your room. Number fifty-four, is that right?"

"Yes."

"Good."

They were nearing the gates to the chateau and Sophie looked back and stopped. She said something to her friends and turned back towards Emma.

Coming up to her she took hold of Emma's hand. "Hold on to me for a minute. I have something in my shoe."

"Oh. OK." Hannah lingered with them, but Emma turned pointedly to her. "I'll catch you up."

Hannah smiled and walked on. Sophie took off her shoe, balancing on one foot, then she glanced ahead as the other students disappeared through the gate. "Good," she said. "I have nothing in my shoe. I just wanted to be alone with you." She put her shoe on, then took Emma's arm and walked them both just inside the gate, away from the glare of the street lamp.

The wine had made Emma's inhibitions disappear and she stopped and relaxed against the gate. "That's nice."

"What?"

"That you wanted to be with me."

Sophie took both her hands in hers, brought her face close to Emma's, then kissed her on the mouth. "I want to be with you all the time."

Emma felt desire light up her body. They kissed again and she felt Sophie's tongue probe her mouth and met it with her own, making the kiss deeper. She ran her hands lovingly up Sophie's back and round to her breasts. She touched them through the thin material, small and firm. She moved her thumbs over the tiny nipples. First Sally—now this. Part of her still couldn't believe she could become so aroused by another woman. "I love kissing you," she whispered as their lips parted.

"I love kissing you too." Sophie kissed her again lightly. "You are feeling my tits."

"They feel nice."

"Can I feel yours?"

"Sure."

Sophie kissed her ear, and at the same time, her hands found their way to Emma's breasts.

"Here," Emma whispered. She lifted her shirt so that Sophie could touch the bare flesh—and at once she sighed with the sensation scattering all over her body.

"Sophie!" A voice came out of the darkness ahead. It was obviously one of Sophie's friends, and Emma could hear footsteps coming back their way.

They disentangled, and Emma quickly pulled down her shirt.

"Sorry, Madeleine. Emma was just helping me get something out of my shoe."

The other girl joined them. "We are going to have a drink in Anna's room. She has the photos we were talking about. Are you coming?"

"OK. That sounds fun. Emma, will you come too?"

"No. I am tired—and anyway, I have an early class. You go on." Emma thought Sophie looked a little surprised and disappointed.

"OK. I will be quiet when I come in." She kissed Emma on the cheek and squeezed her hand tightly.

As she walked back up to their room, Emma felt a strange, heady mixture of happiness, excitement, and apprehension bubbling inside her. *I want to make love with her,* she thought. *I'm not sure if I'm a lesbian, but the way I feel is just amazing.*

Back in their room, she undressed and went to bed. Lying naked between the sheets, she put her hand between her legs and rubbed her vaginal lips, feeling them become quickly moist. Her mind swiftly moved to Sophie. Being together that first afternoon, touching each other, kissing, rubbing oil into their breasts. She pushed a finger inside her pussy and was surprised how wet she was. She moved it around, causing little heights of pleasure to come and go. She so wanted to satisfy the tight knot of lust in her abdomen. She stimulated and played with herself for a few minutes, loving the light sexy feel of her body. Maybe she should keep herself awake until Sophie came back.

Eventually, tiredness overtook her, and she was unable to resist the warm blanket of sleep.

When she woke the next morning, Sophie was still asleep, curled under a single sheet. Emma slipped out of bed and went over to her. She leant down and kissed her lightly on the cheek. She looked at her for a moment. She looked so lovely, her eyes closed, her breathing so slow and even.

She showered and dressed quickly. As she was about to leave, Sophie stirred. "Sorry—didn't mean to wake you."

"That's OK. What's the time?"

"Nearly eight."

"Will I see you later?"

"Yes—I will come back after lunch."

"OK, my darling."

Emma wanted to kiss her again. Instead, she opened the door and left.

She forced herself to listen hard during the tutorial, although her mind wanted to slip constantly back to the girl in her room. She had back-to-back classes through to mid-afternoon, with only half an hour for lunch, so she wouldn't be able to get back to see Sophie. It seemed so long and frustrating.

When school finally ended, she rushed back. Sophie was on her bed, reading. She was naked, lying on her stomach, her hair tousled and wet looking.

Emma felt her pulse leap. "Just had a shower?"

"Yes. And now I am trying to read this book in English, and it's hard."

"Oh dear." She went to her own bed and began taking off her clothes.

"What are you doing?"

"Getting ready to play tennis." Emma pushed her shorts to the floor and pulled her shirt over her head.

"You're mad."

"Why?"

"It's too hot."

Emma was naked now apart from her panties. She put her hand out to take down her tennis skirt from the wardrobe, then stopped. She swallowed. She put her things down and strolled over to Sophie's bed. "It *is* a bit hot. Is that why you are not intending to put any clothes on today?" She sat on the edge of the bed, reached over, and lightly scratched Sophie's back.

"No, I'm not. Oh yes, that feels good."

Emma spread out her hand and caressed the lovely skin. The touch brought dryness to her throat. "You must have been a cat in a former life."

"Mmmm. Use both hands."

Emma swallowed hard. "I'll have to sit on your legs."

"OK."

Emma climbed on the bed, sat astride Sophie's thighs, and moved both her hands up and down the girl's back. She felt goose pimples scatter across her at the touch. "You have such a lovely back." She could feel her pulse quickening and chuckled nervously. "It's the first part of you I saw."

"When?"

"The day I arrived and you were making love to Antoine." As she leant forward to rub her shoulders, she could feel her pussy press against the soft mounds of Sophie's buttocks through the thin slip of her panties. Instinctively, she spread her legs farther outwards to make closer contact, feeling gentle waves of pleasure as she gently rocked herself back and forth.

"Ohhh," Sophie purred. "That feels so good. You must be a wonderful lover."

"I try to be." She could feel her wetness seeping into the thin material of her panties. "Listen," she said. "When I said I had never had sex with another girl, that wasn't strictly true."

"Why?"

"I had a thing with a girl on my father's farm, just before I left to come here. She had come for an interview and stayed over with us. She slept in my bed—and well—we ended up making love."

"And how did you react?"

"I loved it. It was wonderful."

"Was she pretty?"

"Yes, she was—I mean, is. Very."

"Did she seduce you?"

"Yes, she did. I mean, we weren't wearing anything, and she kissed me. We cuddled and—and—she came from just being with me and rubbing up against me. Then she played with me—and it felt incredible. In the morning, I wanted to do it again, so we kissed and cuddled and I made her come. And—and the other thing I said—about me never having orgasms. She made me come for the first time that morning—and again later. It was just—oh God—all this was only three days ago. And now I've met you, and—she said to me that I ought to try it with other girls just to make sure it was right for me . . . and . . ."

"And?"

Impulsively, Emma lay down on top of Sophie's back. The contact of their bodies made her shudder with randy excitement. "I want to make love with you. I know that now." She kissed the side of Sophie's face, neck, shoulders, then rolled her tongue into her ear lobe.

Sophie uttered a little cry. "Wait," she said. She felt Sophie trying to turn over beneath her so she raised herself slightly. Once she had turned onto her back, Emma lowered herself once more so they were lying face to face.

They kissed deeply. Emma felt a wonderful sense of relief. All her misgivings were gone; she just wanted this so much.

Sophie's hands ran down Emma's back and pushed her panties off her buttocks.

"Ohhhh, Sophie. I want you."

There was a knock at the door.

Emma looked up. "Fuck," she said. "That will be Hannah. Fuck. Fuck her and her fucking tennis."

Sophie kissed her lightly. "You'd better answer it," she giggled. "The door is open; she might come in."

Emma clambered off the bed, pulling her panties back up, and strode to the door, feeling irritated and frustrated. She opened it—and saw Hannah's immediate surprise at her near nakedness. "Sorry, Hannah, I won't be a minute."

She pushed the door to and walked to her wardrobe, pulling out her sports bra, tennis skirt, and T-shirt. She started to quickly put them on, turning to look at Sophie. "I'm sorry," she whispered.

Sophie smiled at her with a seductive glint in her eye. "You've got me so excited."

Emma felt saliva gather in her mouth. "I'll be back within an hour," she said, finishing dressing, then she walked over to the bed. She took Sophie's head between her hands and kissed her. "Stay here—and don't put any clothes on." She stood up, her body pumping. Quickly she pulled on her socks and trainers and did them up, blew a kiss at Sophie, then turned and walked towards the door.

"I'll be waiting for you," called Sophie.

As she walked to the tennis courts with Hannah, she could feel her panties sticking to her pussy—and all she could think of was what would happen in an hour's time. She was going to make love with Sophie—just as she had with Sally—and every fibre in her being wanted it.

"Are you OK?" said Hannah.

"Yes, I'm fine. I'm just a little tired, I think. Could we just play one set? It's a bit hot to do any more."

"Sure."

Emma did her best to concentrate on the game, but kept missing shots she would normally have found easy. Sometimes she hit the ball hard out of sheer frustration. Several times she found herself looking at Hannah. She was an attractive though not beautiful girl: athletic, slim, and tanned with pure blonde Scandinavian hair. Emma looked at her long legs, her full breasts beneath the bra and T-shirt, and her elegant neck. She wasn't sure if she was sexually attracted; all her mind could dwell on was the naked girl back in their room waiting for her.

After half an hour, Hannah had beaten her six-love. Sweat was trickling down Emma's back, and she felt tired and frustrated. "OK—shall we stop now?"

"Yes," said Hannah. "Maybe it is a bit hot."

"Yes, it is." As they walked off the court, Emma put her arm round her and kissed her on the cheek. The warm, damp touch of female skin—the taste of salty sweat. She licked her lips.

"Thanks. I'll play better next time."

Emma half ran back to the chateau. She felt the same nervous excitement as before as she went up the stairs and along the corridor. By the time she reached their room, she could feel her heart racing. She opened the door. "Hi, I'm back."

The room was empty. Emma felt the disappointment hang on her. She looked around, seeking for some clue as to where Sophie had gone. Realising it had only been half an hour since she had left, she thought maybe Sophie had just popped out to get something or see someone.

She undressed, put her clothes away, and went and turned on the shower. The hot water felt good, and slowly she began to feel it calm and relax her. She washed her hair, rinsed it, washed herself, and turned off the shower. Sophie still hadn't come.

She toweled herself dry, then blow-dried her hair. She stopped and listened but could hear no one walking in the corridor.

She went and stood in front of her long mirror and brushed her hair. After a moment, she heard approaching steps and the door opened. She suddenly felt awkward. "Hi." She saw Sophie in the reflection in the mirror walk up behind her. Her eyes were mesmerising.

Sophie hugged her from behind, kissing her on the shoulder. "Did you have a good match?"

"No. You were right; it was too hot. Anyway, my mind was on other things."

Sophie's hands, sitting lightly on Emma's hips, moved up to her breasts and fondled them. She kissed Emma's neck and cheek. "And what was that?"

Emma caught her breath. "That I want you to make love to me."

Sophie gently turned Emma to face her and kissed her deeply.

Emma put her hands to the blouse Sophie was wearing and tried to undo the little buttons. Sophie chuckled softly and took her hands gently away. "Wait, darling, wait." She kissed her softly on the lips, stroking her hair. "You are so beautiful." Then she started to kiss her way across Emma's neck, chest, and shoulders. Emma felt goose pimples scatter across her chest and could see her nipples standing out like little bullets. Sophie looked down at them and smiled. Looking up at Emma, she licked her way to both breasts, sucking the nipples into her mouth, kissing and loving them. Emma sighed. Sophie traced her way down her smooth, flat stomach, curling her tongue into Emma's navel and down to the small light brown thatch of pubic hair. She blew a long hot breath, casting the flat of her tongue across Emma's swollen clitoris. Emma gasped.

Sophie looked up as she kissed her way back up to Emma's mouth, sucking on Emma's tongue. "I'm going to make you come," she said. "We will lock the door so that no one can disturb us, and we will take each other to heaven. Lie down on your bed."

Emma did as she was told, trembling with anticipation. She lay on her back, her body feeling so alive. She watched as Sophie went to the door, locked it, then walked back, slowly undoing the buttons on her blouse.

"You're so gorgeous too," Emma said, as she looked at the clothes fall off the slim, light brown body.

Sophie lay down on the bed next to her and kissed her tenderly. Emma ran her hands over the clear, smooth skin, feeling her neck, back, and buttocks. For several minutes, their mouths just melted into each other, their tongues playing, their saliva sweet. Gradually, Sophie's kisses found their way to Emma's neck, pressing gently on the sensitive muscles, scattering sensation across her body—and she felt Sophie's hands stroke the inner parts of her thighs, awaking a deep longing in her abdomen.

Still kissing and licking her, she traced her way to Emma's left breast. She opened her mouth and seemed to suck the whole breast in, her tongue teasing the little nipple. She raised her head and smiled at Emma. "I love your tits. They are so perfect. I could kiss them forever."

Sophie moved to the other breast, teasing and caressing it, arousing pleasure that Emma didn't think possible. "Ohhh, Sophie, that's so lovely. Oh, I love you."

Sophie engulfed her mouth again, kissing her more passionately, shifting her body against Emma, her eyes almost fierce with intensity. She looked at her for a moment, then slid her body down so that her face was level with Emma's vagina. She paused, looking down at the little bush, then, looking back up at Emma, slid farther down and began kissing the insides of Emma's thigh.

Emma ached for her vagina to be touched. She could feel the air cool on her wetness—but she was content to wait. She knew that Sophie would love her there when the time was right.

Sophie kissed her way over the sensitive skin, taking time to lick behind her knee and down her calf to the sides of her foot. Then she rose into a kneeling position, and licking the sole of Emma's foot, rubbed it gently over the small buds of her breasts, closing her eyes and sighing.

Emma could feel the erect nipples topping the firm cushions of the little hillocks. It was so intimate; Sophie's skin was so warm and smooth touching her feet.

Sophie opened her eyes and, looking at Emma as though in a trance, moved Emma's foot up to her face and took her toes one by one into her mouth. She sucked each one and licked between them.

Emma sighed at the incredible sensuousness. She looked at the dark bush of pubic hair nestling between Sophie's legs. She felt a dryness in her throat—and a longing to touch her there.

As though knowing what she was thinking, Sophie put her leg gently down on the sheet, then opened her own legs farther, lowering her body towards the bed. She moved Emma's big toe over her clitoris several times, then searched among the folds of her wet lips and pushed it inside her.

Emma uttered a little cry as she felt Sophie's intimate, warm wetness close round her toe. Her eyes glazed, Sophie began to move up and down on top of it. "I could come like this," she said.

"Yes," said Emma. "I want to watch you come, like we did before."

Sophie rolled her head, her breathing deep and uneven.

Emma could feel Sophie's slippery tunnel opening wider as more of her toes sank inside. She could see Sophie's breasts were so smooth, round, and firm, her nipples tiny, hard points. She thought how sexy she looked, her flat stomach giving way to the hip bones and the slim, taut thighs thrusting out at an angle either side.

Sophie put her other hand onto her clitoris and began to frig herself. Emma thought how she wanted to do that for her, wanted to touch and feel her so much.

"Oh yes . . . I'm coming . . . oh, it is so good . . ." moaned Sophie. "Yes—yes, OHHHH YEEEEEEEEES!" Her body tensed and the blood shot to her face, then she gasped for a breath only to force Emma's foot deep inside herself again and cry out.

"Yes . . . come for me . . . feel me inside you."

"Aaaaaaaaah," Sophie screamed, the noise echoing around the room as her finger frigged herself again furiously, her body in a wild ecstatic fit. For a moment she didn't move and was silent, as though the climax would not let her go, but then she took in fast breaths, crying and whimpering as she relaxed and her head fell forward.

She lifted herself off Emma's foot and looked down at her, a dazed, satisfied smile on her face. Then she lifted Emma's leg again and brought Emma's toes to her mouth and licked them. Her eyes were wicked, piercing.

"Was it good?" said Emma.

Sophie lowered Emma's leg to the sheet and lay down beside her and kissed her. "It was wonderful."

Emma put her arms around her and pulled her close. "I want to touch you. Can I feel you there?"

"It should be me touching you."

"No—please."

Sophie took Emma's hand, kissed it, then brought it between her legs. She gave a little gasp as Emma's hand made contact.

Emma ran her hand round the soft wet folds of flesh. It felt so exhilarating, so different. She moved her fingers to Sophie's clitoris, teasing it gently, rubbing in the way she herself liked, knowing how to please and excite her. Then she moved down and found the opening, and easing the delicate lips apart, pushed her finger inside.

Sophie uttered a little cry. She took Emma's head and pulled her into a kiss. "I'm going to come again so quickly," she said.

"Good, I love it when you come." Emma kissed her again for a long time, and as she worked her finger in and out, could hear Sophie making little crying noises under the kiss. She added another finger and pushed deeper in. Sophie's vagina was tight and hot and she could sense the walls sucking in around her fingers. She ran her thumb up to Sophie's clitoris, rolling it around the stiff, sticky little mound. She broke the kiss and ran her tongue down Sophie's neck to her shoulders and then on to one of her small, taut breasts. She sucked the little nipple into her mouth and massaged it with her tongue.

"Oh . . . yes, yes . . ." whispered Sophie.

For several minutes, their little cries of pleasure were the only thing that broke the quiet intensity of the room. The more she made love to Sophie, the more she could feel the knot of her own desire tighten and grow. The mounting feeling of lust was like a profound ache and she could sense her pussy and breasts almost hurting with acute arousal.

Sophie pulled Emma's head towards her and kissed her, wrestling her mouth over Emma's and thrusting her tongue inside. Her hands fondled Emma's breasts, sending shivers down Emma's spine.

"Let me kiss your breasts. I need to kiss them."

Emma shifted and Sophie's mouth engulfed her left breast. She felt a pang of pleasure from her nipple that scattered sensation to every nerve ending in her body. "Oh . . . so lovely. Ohhhh . . ." She slipped a third finger into Sophie and pumped them in and out quicker and deeper.

Sophie opened her legs as wide as she could. "Fuck me, Emma, fuck me, please . . . OHHHHHHHHHHH YES! YES! YES! AHHHHHHHHHH . . ."

She thrust her groin down onto Emma's hand repeatedly. Suddenly, she seemed to spasm, lifting her back off the bed and closing her legs tightly. She tensed repeatedly, crying in between each shock of her climax.

Finally she relaxed and released Emma's hand from between the tight, clenching thighs. Dreamily, she looked up and smiled, her chest heaving, making its way back to normality. "Mmm . . . so good."

Emma kissed her tenderly, easing her fingers out of her pussy. Keeping her eyes locked on Sophie's, she brought her fingers to her mouth and licked them clean. The taste was strong, strange, and seemed to create a wonderful sensation in her mouth that echoed with something deep in her abdomen.

Sophie pushed her onto her back. "Now it's my turn," she said. "I'm going to taste you. I can feel the longing inside you. You need release. I want you to relax now and let your body respond."

Emma stroked her face, losing herself in the beautiful eyes. Sophie kissed her and it felt as if she was pouring desire into her, as if the sweetness of her saliva was like some kind of drug raising her to a different level. At the same time, Sophie was stroking and caressing her gently, the feather-light touch of her fingers drifting all over her body.

Emma's hands searched through the glossy, dark hair as their kiss parted and a long string of saliva extended between them.

Sophie kissed Emma's chin and down to the nape of her neck. Emma closed her eyes and sighed as the caresses journeyed to her breasts.

"Ohhh . . . God, it's so nice." As the hot wet mouth engulfed her nipples again, it was the sweetest torture. A deep throb of pleasure pulsed through her pussy and up into her vulva. A few days ago, she would never have thought it possible that love with her own sex could bring this degree of excitement, this intense longing.

Sophie played with both breasts, licking round them, drawing her tongue up between them, flicking the nipples, sucking them, drawing her teeth gently across them, loving them, teasing. She put her hands on one and then kissed the other, but the stimulation never stopped until Emma wanted to cry out. Once or twice she thought her body would erupt; she didn't know why or how or when, but the pleasure kept mounting and the tension in her stomach became almost unbearable.

She jumped as she felt Sophie's fingers touch her pussy.

Sophie looked up at her and smiled. She began to rub her fingers over Emma's vaginal lips, spreading her juice up and down and from side to side. "Does that feel nice?"

"Ohhh . . . amazing."

"Is it as good as a guy does to you?"

"Ohhh, better, so much better."

"And do you like me kissing your tits?"

"Oh I love it. I love it so much."

"And what about lower?" Sophie lowered her head and kissed her way across her stomach—and Emma felt her skin go tender to the point of ultra sensitivity. Sophie's fingers were probing her now, searching her vagina for entry. "Oh, Sophie, come into me, please."

She felt Sophie's fingers push inside her, and then suddenly the hot embrace of her mouth on her vagina. She could feel Sophie's tongue exploring, caressing her clitoris—but it was so gentle, so subtle, that Emma's whole groin seemed to become energized. Sophie's fingers plunged back in, wider, deeper. Emma opened her legs, wanting her whole hand inside, that clever tongue to torture her forever. The tension seemed suddenly to build in her stomach until she felt her whole body seizing. She was crying out as a sweet, intense flash of acute pleasure swept through her and she was suspended for a sublime aching moment, crushing Sophie's face to her pussy, her fingers blindly pawing at the lush, dark hair, until she felt a wave of the sweetest relief searching and purging her body . . .

Sophie kissed each of her eyes tenderly.

"Lovely Sophie . . . thank you . . . it was unbelievable. So amazing."

She kissed Emma again and they wrapped themselves around each other.

After a few minutes, Emma stroked Sophie's hair and looked excitedly into her eyes. "Let's go to the village. I want champagne!"

As they sat at the restaurant table, Emma could still feel the warm glow of her orgasm. She couldn't stop looking at the girl next to her, her long, smooth neck with its milky skin, her wide, sexy mouth, aquiline nose, and alluring green eyes. She kept reaching across and stroking her arm and found herself constantly wanting to kiss her. Occasionally, she would brush her lips across her cheek, sneaking her tongue to lightly touch Sophie's ear.

They were so engrossed in each other, that they hardly noticed the fizz of the champagne or the food they had ordered. Every sense seemed to be saturated with her lover. She could smell, even taste, her and her body cried out to touch her all over again. "I was so afraid that I wouldn't be able to come with anyone else. I had come for the first time with Sally—but sort of felt that maybe it was a one-off."

"No, of course not. She showed you what your true sexuality was."

"Yeah, it's funny. She said to me that I should experiment with other girls to see if I really liked it."

"And you do . . ."

"Mmm . . ." She kissed Sophie on the cheek again.

"So," said Sophie. "Is she still at your father's farm?"

"Yes."

"So she'll be there when you get back?"

"Yeah."

"What will you do about it?"

"I don't know."

"I bet you will fling yourself at her."

"Right now I have someone else to think about." Emma put her arm around her. "And I think I want to go back to our room right now," she whispered.

"That sounds nice," said Sophie, her huge green eyes scanning her face. Emma felt Sophie's hand trace up her leg and rub her panties.

Emma drew in a deep breath, savouring the tremulous little flurries of pleasure. "Oh yes, let's go back now."

They walked hand in hand up the road, deliriously happy in the warm, sultry night.

"So, you were telling me you had a crush on a girl at school?"

"Yes, when I was fifteen."

"Did she know?"

"Oh yes."

"So did anything happen?"

"Yes—sort of."

"Really?"

"I was alone in the shower block one day after games when she came in. I was so embarrassed when I saw it was her. I had nothing on, and you know how sensitive you are when you're that age."

"Mmm. I don't think I was embarrassed at that age."

"Anyway, I started washing and she came in. She stood next to me for a few moments and then asked me to wash her back. I was totally overwhelmed. I mean, I was so in love with her—you know—from afar. She was eighteen and very beautiful—and knew it, of course. As I touched her, I remember thinking how lovely it felt. Then she washed my back and I was in seventh heaven.

"Anyway, when we came out of the shower, she suggested we dry each other. She said she had noticed me looking at her—and that she liked it. She said she thought I was very pretty. She stroked my face and then she kissed me on the lips. I couldn't believe it—it was so amazing. She kissed me again, pressing our bodies together—then said that I mustn't tell anyone. I said of course not. I remember feeling that I wanted to tell her how much I loved her, but didn't dare."

"Then what happened?"

"We were interrupted by two of her friends looking for her. She just leapt up and pretended as though nothing had happened. That was in May, and by the end of June she had left the school. I never saw her again."

"And she never said anything to you before she left?"

"No, she totally ignored me from then on. I was heartbroken—for a while, anyway. I soon got over it, and the next year I was like everyone else—madly into boys. But that was my first-ever sexual experience."

"I think that was more important than you think—that little encounter. Maybe you have had some kind of fantasy about making it want to happen again, lurking in your sub-conscious."

They had reached the entrance gates to the chateau. "Maybe you're right," said Emma, giggling. She pushed Sophie against the gates and pulled up her blouse. "Maybe you and Sally are the fulfillment of my secret desires." She leant down and took one of Sophie's nipples in her mouth and sucked on it greedily.

"Maybe that night with Sally changed everything for you."

Emma put her hand on the crotch of Sophie's jeans and rubbed gently. "I think it did. I'm a lesbian—and I love it." She kissed her deeply and long. Sophie whimpered beneath the kiss and her hands moved under Emma's dress and explored her bum.

"Maybe you're in love with her," said Sophie as their mouths parted.

"I . . . I don't know," said Emma.

"It doesn't matter. Come on, let's go to our room."

"OK," said Emma.

They tripped along the path to the entrance to the chateau and Emma glanced up the hill, where she could see the floodlighting of the fountain was still on. She checked her watch. It was half past ten—half past nine in England. Strange guilty feelings about Sally suddenly flooded her mind—and an acute desire to speak to her.

She stopped just as they reached the entrance. "I need to call home. I couldn't get them earlier. The signal's better outside."

"OK, *cheri*. I'll be waiting for you upstairs . . . naked," said Sophie, and she kissed her sexily.

"OK. Love you."

The light above the door cast a pool of illumination for several yards, but beyond that the park was dark. She flipped through the numbers on her phone and found Sally's mobile. She looked at it for a second and wondered why she was doing this. She pressed the call button and put it to her ear.

"Hello?"

"Sally? It's Emma. From France."

There was a short silence.

"Oh . . . hi. How are you?"

Emma thought she sounded genuinely pleased.

"Yeah—I'm fine. Not keeping you up or anything?"

"No, it's only nine thirty."

Her voice brought her face vividly back to her mind. Emma suddenly ached to see her. "So how's everything? I suppose you haven't started yet?"

"I went to the farm this morning, just to meet everyone. They were all really nice."

"I bet they were. Can't believe their luck, having a gorgeous young girl around. Did you see my dad?"

"Yeah. He was fine. And how about you?"

"Yeah, it's great. Hard work, but good."

"Good. Nice weather?"

"Yeah, warm. Not that sunny, but I guess it's in the mid-twenties."

There was a brief silence.

"Well, it's nice of you to call," said Sally.

"Well . . . I was just wondering if everything was going OK." She hesitated for a second. "I miss you, actually. I know we were only together for a day, but it was pretty intense, you know, when it happened." She paused. There was so much to say that she couldn't say anything. "I think about you a lot—and what happened."

"Yeah. It was lovely." Sally paused. "Are you still OK with it?"

"Yeah. The more I think about it, I'm really OK with it. I don't know whether that means I'm gay or not. I certainly get all hot when I think of you."

"What am I like? You invite me to stay, and I turn you into a dyke."

Emma laughed. "It was amazing."

"Anyway—are you having any luck on that front?" said Sally after a moment.

Emma felt a pang of guilt. She swallowed. "I'm not really thinking about that. Anyway, I bet everyone will try and get into your knickers."

"Maybe—but I'm not really interested, you know."

"I'd make you interested. God, it seems like forever till I come home."

"Anyway, as I said before, you'll get shagged by someone and forget all about me."

"No, I mean, even if I did have a shag, I wouldn't forget about you."

"Planning it, are you?"

"No, not at all . . . but, you know, I suppose you never know." Silence again. Emma was sure she'd said the wrong thing. "Anyway—better go. God knows what this is costing me. Give yourself a big kiss from me."

"I'll give myself a bit more than that."

"Hmmm. So will I. Love you."

"Yeah, you too."

"Night—and lots of kisses."

"Night."

Emma switched off the phone and breathed in deeply. She felt sad, happy, hypocritical, in love, bereft, a heel. Not bad for a few days.

She felt better with herself as she climbed the long flight of stone stairs. She had spoken to her—bridged the gap. What happened here was off-limits—experimentation— they both knew that.

She wasn't going to feel guilty about it, she told herself, as she walked down the corridor to their room. She opened the door to see Sophie lying totally naked, seductive, and gorgeous on her bed . . .

Chapter 7

Sally put the phone down and looked at it. That was a guilt call; she could sense it instinctively. She had made love to someone else, probably another girl. Well, that was what she should have expected. And she was glad in some ways. Maybe. She brought up the photos she had taken on her phone of them in the pool house. Emma, naked, her lovely grey eyes so wide and full of disbelief as Sally made love to her. Her lovely soft skin and gorgeous body.

She sat down at the kitchen table and sighed. When she had first set eyes on her, walking out of that house, that light dress flowing over her bare breasts, she knew she would never be able to resist her if anything happened. And, of course, Sally had done everything she could to make it happen.

She lay back on the bed. She had been unbelievably promiscuous for several months following her mother's death, and after a brush with a nasty infection, she'd fled to her uncle's farm. She'd had a year celibate—not even a kiss and a cuddle—kept herself away from it. And she'd really thought she'd cracked it, had got a lever on sex and stuff—relationships. Then this, meeting Emma, she just hadn't been able to stop herself.

She had been over to the farm that morning. She got there early at eight o'clock and was taken to meet the rest of the farmworkers. They were a strange bunch, and she smiled to herself at how accurate Emma's description had been. They were shy and a bit sullen and stared at her.

She went into the house with Mr. Pascoe so he could talk to her about some office duties. When she followed him into that huge, old hallway, she had felt a mixture of excitement, but also a flash of regret. That amazing night just a few days before seemed such a long time ago somehow, and as she walked through the house, God, she knew this had to be a one-off. She could never have a relationship within this family; she wasn't their class. Emma was a girl with a public school education, a slightly plummy accent, all that charm and confidence. Sally was a working-class girl with a fucked up head.

It was so weird being there in that office again. In one way it was like the thing with Emma had never happened, but at the same time she was so acutely aware that it had. She sat down opposite Mr. Pascoe at his large desk. Her eyes roamed round the room as he booted up his computer. It was a cluttered, comfortable room lined with shelves and filing cabinets. The large bay window looked out onto the garden, and there was a fireplace to the side with the remains of some burnt logs in the grate. A painting was lit above the mantelpiece.

Glancing back at the desk, she saw a photograph of Emma. She was laughing, her hands in her hair, her white teeth shining from that wide, sexy mouth. Sally stared at it. She was so stunning—why was she even thinking anything could come of it?

"If you come round here, I'll show you what to do," said Mr. Pascoe, jolting her out of her reverie.

"Oh. Right. Sorry." She went and stood behind his large leather chair. He explained how to input figures into the computer from a pile of invoices to the side of the desk. He went through it painstakingly, making sure she understood, then they swapped seats so that he could watch her do the first few. "I did a bit of this for my uncle," she said.

"Oh, right."

"Not too difficult."

She entered them painstakingly, making sure she didn't miss anything.

"Good," he said, after a few minutes. "That looks fine. Well, I'll leave you to it."

"OK. I think I'll be all right." She glanced up at him and saw his eyes flash from her cleavage. She smiled to herself. Men could never help themselves. Anyway, that kind of stuff had never bothered her—and he was a very attractive man in some ways. "Can I have your mobile number, just in case?"

"Yes, of course," he said.

Once he had disappeared out of the door, Sally looked at Emma's photograph again, then she leaned back and closed her eyes. The sun coming in through the window made the room warm, and she undid a couple of buttons on her blouse. She'd had a lot of sex with a lot of partners, but that night—that had been just amazing. It wasn't just that she hadn't had sex for a year, it was that Emma had the looks and body of a supermodel and was just so irresistible.

She snapped her eyes open and looked at the photo. The only trouble was Sally wasn't any good at the love bit. She fell too easily and hurt too deeply, and she didn't want that again. Too many times it had left her reeling. Even if they ended up getting together and Emma did love her for a while it would be like all the rest. It would be like Maddie. That had been amazing, then came to an end—just like that, she thought.

Mind you, we had been really stupid that day. We had decided we couldn't meet in the wardrobe room and would have to leave it until the next day. Then I found I had left my phone in one of the sixth form rooms, so went back to get it. By chance she saw me go in and followed me.

"Hi, Goldie."

"Hi, you all right?"

She came up to me, glanced round to see if there was anyone there, then kissed me.

"Hey, not here."

"Sorry—couldn't resist it."

I giggled and we kissed again. Then she saw the cupboard door open at the back of the room and suggested we go in.

"No, it's too dodgy."

"Come on, I just want a snog."

Reluctantly, I agreed. We went in and she closed the door.

"Can't fucking wait until tomorrow," she said, pushing me up against the wall and kissing me again. I tried to stop her, but she undid a few buttons of my blouse and kissed her way round my chest and neck.

I ran my hands through her hair, feeling instantly randy.

"How's that little pussy, getting nice and wet?"

"What normally happens when you touch me?"

"Let's have a feel, then." She put her hand under my skirt, pushed my panties aside, and ran a finger around my wet lips.

"Ohhh . . ."

"It's no good, I've got to have a taste."

"Maddie, no . . ."

But before I could stop her she had pulled my panties down my thighs, knelt down, and begun to lick my fanny.

Instantly I no longer cared where we were. I ran my hands through her hair, closed my eyes, and gave myself to the delicious feeling.

What happened next is etched on my mind forever. The door opened and there was a short, horrendous silence. Then a sharp voice rapped out— "What the hell are you doing?"

After that I remember being completely dazed. At some point I was summoned to the principal's office. As soon as I arrived I could hear shouting. It was Maddie, screaming abuse. A few minutes later, the door flung open and she emerged.

"Fuck you and fuck your school!" she shouted and stormed past me.

That was the last I ever saw of her.

I went into the principal's office and sat down. The deputy was there, and their faces were angry and hard. I couldn't look at them. Instead I remember staring at the edge of the desk—at a stain in the wood. Staring at it but not seeing it. Nor do I really remember what was said. Only a few phrases stuck in my mind.

"Of course, we do not hold your sexual orientation against you. The school has policies on equality, but it was gross indecency—abuse of school property."

It seemed Maddie in her fury had told them everything. The sessions in the wardrobe, how long we had been lovers—everything.

They decided to suspend but not expel me.

But they told my mum. I remember her shock. "I didn't know you were like that."

Like what? I was just a kid.

"I don't understand," she said. "Aren't there any boys you like? Why are you like that?"

"I don't know," I said. "It just happened—and I found I liked it. And now she's gone. You don't seem to care about that." Then I burst into tears and ran out of the room.

I was suspended for a week, which I spent sitting on my own in my room. I rang and texted Maddie endlessly but with no response. Finally I got a message: "Forget me, I'm no good for you. I'm going away." And that was it. I cried. Endlessly.

Sally stared out of the office window. It had hurt her a lot, and the worse thing was that from then on it kept on happening. No sooner had she recovered from one relationship, had another fling, than it would all break up and she would feel devastated.

She reached over and turned Emma's photo at an angle so she couldn't see it. She pressed on with the invoices, determined not to think about anything anymore.

It was fun sitting in Mr. Pascoe's comfy leather office chair working behind his desk. By the time she finished the invoices, she felt in a good frame of mind. She rang him and told him she had nothing more to do.

"Wow, that was quick. OK, I'll be there in a minute."

He genuinely seemed pleased with what she had done when he came back in, and they agreed that she would start full-time on the following Monday. He also gave her the keys to the cottage and said she could move in when she wanted. As she got up to leave, she noticed him glancing at her breasts. She hadn't done the buttons on her blouse back up. She blushed, and they smiled at each other. He was quite like Alan, she thought, her sixth form tutor.

As she bounced across the driveway to her car, she felt really happy. Everything was going to be OK. The thing with Emma would resolve itself, and she was going to love it here. She was going to go back to Birmingham, pick up some bedding and stuff, and start moving things over. There was time enough today to do that.

Just then, Gernie, one of the farmhands she had met that morning, came into the yard. When he saw her, he came up, looking a bit shy.

"Hi, Sal. Listen, I don't know if you're interested, but we're all going to a party tonight at a farm near here. Maybe you might want to come along—you know. Get to know everyone."

"Er . . . OK. Yeah, that would be fun. I can stay over at the cottage. First time." She smiled, instantly regretting what she had just said.

"Great. OK, we're meeting at eight at the Cock—the pub in the village. We'll run you over."

"OK. Great. See you later."

Now, a few hours later, Emma had rung her and things didn't seem so simple, and she definitely didn't want to go to this party. *But there we are,* she thought. *You agreed to it. Nothing to be done. Can't give the wrong impression first time out.*

She lay back on her bed and trailed a finger between her legs. Maybe it would be fun.

She packed up some stuff in her car—clothes, her telly, CD player, and bedding—and drove back to the farm. By the time she got to the cottage and moved the stuff in, it was nearly time to go and meet the rest of the gang. She sighed.

She still didn't really want to go, but she knew she had to make herself.

"Are you all right, Sal?"

"Yeah. Fine." Sally smiled at Gernie. She wasn't really all right—she felt out of place, not knowing many people. There were plenty of guys eyeing her up, but she wasn't in the mood.

She had dressed sexily in a short denim skirt and T-shirt with a thin, see-through bra and had put some plaits in her hair. She thought the effect was good—but thought maybe it was a mistake when she'd walked into the pub. Everyone hadn't been able to stop themselves from looking at her. She had drunk a couple of pints there and played some pool, but was nervous, and they seemed a bit intimidated by her.

The party was at a large farm in the next village in one of their barns. The place was decked out really well, the booze was flowing, and it was just swimming with people.

She had a bop with some of the guys. The trouble was they just weren't very exciting—you quickly ran out of conversation, even if you could make yourself heard over the pumping music.

She took another beer from the bar and wandered outside. There were some really pretty girls coming and going, and she found herself wondering if Emma would have come to something like this. She rested her gaze on a striking girl with long brown hair who was chatting to another blonde.

So what is Emma doing right now? Probably in bed with someone.

Somebody bumped into her—she was knocked sideways and nearly fell over. "Sorry," came a voice. It was a young boy with blond curly hair and an attractive face.

"That's OK," she said as she steadied herself—but then felt wetness all down her front. She was soaked in beer. "Shit—oh no."

The boy was staring at her chest without being able to help himself. Sally looked down and saw that her nipples and the outline of her tits were clearly visible through the wringing wet material. She pulled the T-shirt away from her flimsy bra. "Urgh. God—I'm soaked."

"Oh no—I'm really sorry."

She felt a rush of irritation. "Oh fuck." She could sense the people around her staring—it wasn't as though she had her car here and could go and get a change of clothes. She was stuck here, effectively half naked. She looked at him. He had gone very red in the face and looked completely gutted. She thought he looked so upset it made her laugh. "I guess you'd better spend the rest of the evening standing in front of me."

"Oh shit."

"You got any other ideas?"

"Er . . . I dunno."

She tried to wring out the T-shirt. "Well, that's really helpful."

"Er . . . well . . . I mean—why don't you come over to the house?" he said hesitantly. "Maybe I could borrow one of my sister's T-shirts or something."

"You live here?"

"Yeah. My name's Danny. Youngest brother of Ed."

"Ed?"

"Yeah, it's his party."

"Oh, right."

His voice was slightly plummy and public school, a bit like Emma's, she thought. "So—er . . ."

"Right. Sounds like a good idea." She looked over at some blokes who were sniggering to themselves. "Well—stare, why don't you?" she said, pointedly.

"Er . . . right. It's this way," said Danny, looking anxiously at them.

They walked across the garden to a wide barred gate on the other side of the lawn. They went through it, and as they walked along by a tall hedge, Sally saw the house loom into sight. "Sorry, I didn't mean to snap just now."

"That's OK."

"Only, I, like, sort of tagged along to this party. I work at Abbey Farm," she said.

"Oh. What, in the office?"

"Yeah, and as a farmhand."

He looked nonplussed. "Wow . . . OK."

Sally laughed. "I know how to do it, though I guess it's a bit weird."

"No, not really. Enjoying the party?"

"Yeah—well, not really actually, I'm not in the mood. And—well apart from the guys who work with me, I don't know anyone."

"I've been watching the telly in the house for most of the evening."

"Oh, right. That sounds good."

"Yeah. My parents are away and only allowed the party as long as the house was out of bounds, so Ed said I had to stay in and make sure no one got in. Did you come with someone then?"

"Yeah—so I'm sort of stuck until they go."

"Right. Through here." They went through a small gate that led into the garden of the house. "My parents have a place in Croatia and are there for a couple of weeks. I'm flying out in a couple of days. My sister's with them, so my brother and I are on our own."

The house was about two hundred metres from the barn. It looked quite old. As he unlocked a door that led into a low, heavily beamed kitchen, she could see it was older than it looked outside.

"Er—shall I go and see what there is in my sister's room?" He still couldn't help himself glancing at her breasts.

"Yeah—or maybe one of yours would do?"

"Yeah—OK. Right—er, do you want to come upstairs?"

They went down a long passageway and, at the end, up a twisted narrow staircase. At the top, they walked down a corridor a short distance and finally into his room. It was large, cluttered with books, clothes, wall posters of medieval cathedrals, and classical looking prints. It wasn't the normal stuff you would expect a boy of his age to have, she thought, but it was untidy, as any kid's room would be. There was a single bed in the middle of the room and a television standing directly opposite.

"I'll see what I have that's clean," he said, pulling a drawer open. He rummaged around and finally pulled a white T-shirt out that looked quite big. It said "Beer Festival" on the front.

"Seems appropriate," said Sally, smiling at him. "Can I have a quick shower? I reek of beer."

"Yeah . . . yeah, sure. It's here."

He led her out back into the corridor and pushed open a door on the left. It was a large, slightly old-fashioned bathroom, with a shower curtain round the bath. "Great." He was standing looking awkward—but, she thought, so innocently sweet. "Er—towel?"

"Oh right." He went to a cupboard and pulled a large, clean towel out and gave it to her.

"OK. See you in a minute."

"Yeah." He left and she closed the door behind her.

As she undressed, she looked around. There were bottles of shampoo, conditioner, and perfume that obviously belonged to the sister. She ran the taps and managed to get the shower to work, then got in. *Danny is quite sweet,* she thought, as she washed herself, *and very pretty looking for a boy of his age.*

She dried herself quickly, then climbed back into the clean T-shirt, her panties, and skirt. The bra was soaking so she left it off. Moments later she was back in his room.

He was lying on the bed watching the television.

"Oh, that looks good," said Sally, flopping onto it next to him and kicking off her sandals. "May I?"

"Sure." He shifted over.

She put her head on the pillow. "Oh, feels so nice. Makes me feel quite sleepy."

"Yeah . . ."

"Really comfy bed. I could drift off."

"Well—I mean—you can kip there if you want to and someone can take you back in the morning. I can sleep on the floor. The spare room's taken, I'm afraid."

"No, no. It's OK. Sorry. It's that nice warm shower making me feel dozy. But I might take you up on your offer." She watched for a few minutes, thinking how odd this was. Here was this boy she didn't know from Adam, and here she was on his bed falling asleep. Bizarre. She yawned and closed her eyes . . .

She sat up.

"Sorry. I was trying not to wake you." He was standing next to the bed in a pair of boxer shorts. "I'm going to sleep on the floor." The TV was off and there was just a light on above the bed. She thought his bony, rather immature body looked sweet.

"No, no, sorry, I must have fallen asleep."

"Yeah, you did. But that's OK. Will you be all right?"

"Yeah—but look—don't be silly. You can sleep here. We can cuddle up together. Come on." She lifted her bum off the bed and slipped off her skirt.

"Oh, OK."

She pulled back the duvet and slipped into bed and he got in beside her. The bed was narrow and they were pushed together.

He put off the light. "All right?"

"Mmm," she murmured. "Good night, and thanks for this—invading your bed."

"That's OK."

She shifted around to try and make herself comfortable. The bed was narrower than she thought, and she ended up really close to the edge. Shifting back into the centre, she cuddled behind him and wrapped her arm round him. "Is that OK?" she said, feeling their bare legs touch.

"Yeah . . . yeah. Fine."

"Good." She hadn't been in a bed with anyone since that night with Emma. His skin was warm and soft—a bit like a girl's.

They lay silent for a few minutes. "Have you ever shared your bed with a girl before?" she whispered.

"No."

"Have you got a girlfriend?"

"No."

"Have you ever had?"

"No. Not really."

"I'm sure you will soon."

Without being able to help herself, she was suddenly feeling mildly randy. She pressed closer to him and gently stroked his stomach. He shifted nervously. "Sorry," she said softly.

"It's OK." He moved again and her hand brushed against his boxers. She froze. There was a long, hard pole stretching upwards, taut against the material. "Oh—wow," she whispered.

"I'm sorry. It just happened. It's . . ."

"That's OK. It's natural. I'm flattered." She hesitated for a moment, then touched it very gently. "Oh—it's big."

"Is it? I dunno . . ."

She ran her fingers round it a bit more. "Mmm . . . nice." Her stomach fluttered. "Can I feel it?"

"Yeah," he whispered, breathlessly.

She slid her hand under his boxers, closed her hand round it. It was hot—and so hard. She moved it up and down. "Is that good?"

"Yeah."

"Do you want me to carry on?"

"What?"

"I've done it for boys before."

"Er . . . OK."

"Put the light on."

"What?"

"Put the light on."

He reached up and switched the reading light on.

She looked at him. His face was flushed, but his eyes were wild with excitement. "Now what have we got here?" She suddenly saw herself and what she was doing. *Don't do this,* she thought—then put her hands on his boxers and pulled them down. His cock sprang up, rigid and straight at a forty-five degree angle. It was slim, but extended a good six or seven inches. "Mmmm . . . impressive." She lay down beside him and took it in her hand.

"Oh God . . ."

"Now." She tossed him slowly. "You're lovely and hard."

"Yeah . . ."

"And nice and long—there's a few girls going to enjoy that."

"Oh shit . . . oh God . . . ohhhhhh . . ." A long streak of semen shot out of the end and splashed across his stomach and neck. It was followed by another and another, covering him in droplets of pearly white.

"God—so quick." She kept pumping him and was amazed at how much came out. It was a good ten seconds before it stopped. "So much cum. Nice?"

"Yeah . . . amazing." His big eyes stared at her, his cheeks flushed.

The smell of his cum was really strong and seemed to fill the whole room, like some kind of church incense. Some had dribbled on her hand. She looked at it, then scooped it up with her tongue. "Mmm—tastes really sweet." She leant down and licked up some more of the thick, white jism on his stomach and rolled it around her mouth. She jerked him a bit more. "Is that the first time someone's done it for you?"

"Yeah. Fantastic."

"I didn't really do anything. You came so quickly."

"Sorry."

"Don't be silly." She put her hand round his cock again. "Mmm. He's not gone soft at all. Still nice and hard. Maybe he wants to come again?"

"Er . . . yeah—I mean, if you don't mind."

"Course I don't. I mean—I hardly did anything the first time." Her nipples were stiff and her pussy warm. She smiled at him. "Have you ever seen a girl naked?"

"N-no."

"Never?"

"No."

"Would you like to?"

"Yeah."

"Wait a moment." She sat up, pulled the T-shirt over her head, then got out of bed and went and laid it carefully over a chair. Then turning round and looking at him, she pushed her panties to the floor.

His eyes looked as though they were about to pop out of his head. "You're really beautiful."

"Thank you," she said, kneeling on the bed. "And you've made me feel really randy." She lay down beside him. "Have you ever kissed a girl before?"

"Yeah, once or twice."

She leant over and kissed him lightly. He was passive, as though he didn't quite know what to do. She wanted to giggle, but moved her mouth on his, slowly coaxing him to open his mouth. She slid her hand down and wrapped her fingers around his cock. It was still amazingly hard. She worked up and down it, feeling its steely core slip under the silky covering of skin. "I'm going to give him a little suck." She leaned down and took it in her mouth. It was the first prick she'd tasted for over a year—that lovely warm, fleshy hardness. She sucked it gently, closing her lips around it and stroking it with her tongue.

She lay back next to him and kissed him again. She slid her hand over his diminutive chest and stomach. Jamie hadn't been that much older, but he was more of a sporty type. Danny's torso was very immature—but she thought quite cute.

"You've got a really big cock for your age."

"Have I?"

"Yeah . . . I mean, I've seen a few, and I can tell you that there are plenty of guys who wouldn't mind one this size."

"I've seen other guys in the showers, but never hard—you know."

"Well, I can tell you—you've got a good one. It's not very thick—but lovely and long." She put her hand down again and gripped him harder. "Do you like the skin pulled back?"

"Yeah—I like doing that."

"What—when you do it yourself?"

"Yeah."

"Do you do it often?"

"Yeah. Most days."

She pulled the foreskin right back until he was one long pole, ruddy pink and glistening. It was very clean. "Did you like me sucking it?"

"Yeah . . . fantastic." His hand roamed her tits, feeling and gently squeezing them.

"Do you like my tits?"

"Yeah . . ."

She looked at his hands exploring a female body for the first time. She smiled and kissed him again, pushing her tongue forcefully into his mouth. It was young, innocent, girlish.

She kissed down to his stomach, licking the remains of his semen. It had turned runny and tasted saltier. "I want another suck," she said, sliding the long, hard shaft to the back of her throat. She pressed farther, seeing how much she could get in before she gagged.

He moaned. *He's getting a real treat,* she thought. *His first time and already being sucked off.* His hands were roaming her back and she felt herself shudder. Rather puny though his body was, she could almost imagine impaling herself on him. She quickly dismissed it from her mind. She wasn't on the pill anymore, and she didn't want to risk getting pregnant. She didn't know how old he was, anyway. Just tossing him and sucking him off was fun for them both, but she would draw the line at letting him come inside her.

She circled her head in a rolling motion, feeling his prick revolve in her mouth, touching the sides and rubbing against her tongue. He moaned again, so she did it a bit more, before lifting her head and licking her lips. She looked at his body.

His legs were spindly and hairy and his balls were cupped quite tightly in their sac. So cute, she thought. She turned and smiled at him. "Nice?"

"Oh God . . . yeah."

"Are you close to coming again?"

"Yeah . . ."

"Good. Come in my mouth."

"OK."

She pulled the foreskin right back again and held it back with her hand wrapped around it. She lowered her head, took him deep into her mouth, and pursed her lips around his shaft, then she began to move up and down. It was a long time since she had done this. Lust pulsed in her groin and saliva gathered in her mouth.

It only took three or four more pumps before she heard him gasp and felt the warm gush. She held her breath, closed her throat, and just let it gather, more and more of it until it was leaking from the corner of her lips. She waited till he had finished, holding it swimming around, then she lifted, swallowed a bit, and savoured the taste of what was left. She closed her eyes. It tasted so different from an adult, a warm, sweet saltiness that was so strong.

She lay back down beside him, swallowing the rest. "Feel better now?"

"Yeah. That was fantastic."

"Good." She cuddled up to him, hugging their naked bodies together and kissed him. Her body was gently rippling with desire and she still had the sexy taste of his sperm in her mouth. She put her arms around him. "How old are you?" she asked.

"Eighteen. I mean . . . just eighteen. My birthday was two days ago."

"God—but that's OK. I'm only twenty."

She ran her hands over his back, kissing him lightly on the lips. She felt his hands roaming her back and buttocks. She smiled to herself at his wild-eyed puppyish look. She ran her tongue teasingly over his mouth, then kissed him harder. He was better this time, playing his tongue on hers and the kiss became long and deep.

He moved on top of her and she instantly felt the long hard pole of flesh against her groin. "God—it's still hard. That's amazing." She moved from kissing his mouth to his ear, gently biting it and pressing her tongue into his earlobe. Her stomach throbbed. *Don't be fucking ridiculous,* she thought, but somehow the itch in her pussy was so strong she couldn't stop herself. "Do you want to fuck me?" she whispered.

"What?"

"Do you want to fuck me?"

"Er . . . do you want me to?"

"Yeah—I do. Treat it as my birthday present for you. I don't suppose you've got a condom?"

"No. Sorry."

"OK. But try not to come inside me because I'm not protected. Fuck me for a bit, and then if you want to come again, I'll finish you off in my mouth. OK?"

"OK."

He pushed his penis against her pussy. She giggled—she could tell he didn't know what to do. "Wait," she whispered. She opened her legs, reached down and took his cock in her hand, then guided it to her opening. She rubbed it over her wetness. "Now push inside."

She felt a wonderful hot thrust and then a pang of pain. It had been over a year.

"Oh God . . ." he gasped.

It was crazy, she knew, but she just wanted to do it for him. He could flood her with semen at any second, but she'd already made him come twice, so she thought maybe he could hold himself. If not, she would just have to deal with it. Right now, with the discomfort fading, she was amazed at how this young boy could feel so good inside her. He was long and so hard, churning her abdomen. "Oh . . . you feel so lovely."

His face was hovering above her, and it was as though he simply couldn't believe what was happening to him.

She put her hand on his buttock and squeezed it. "Oh yeah . . . fuck me. Don't stop. Keep fucking me until you make me come. You've got such a lovely hard prick. I know you can make me come with it."

"Yeah . . ."

"Go really deep into me . . . oh shit, yeah. YEAH! That's so nice." This innocent young boy with his naïve, young face and his immature body somehow only turned her on more. He was ploughing her insides, using that incredible prick to dig deep in her, find the beginnings of her climax so quickly.

He pumped her wildly, grazing her clitoris deliciously. "Oh fuck, Danny—that's so good." She pulled his face down to hers and kissed him, clawing his lovely, thick yellow hair. The rhythm of that long slim organ pulsing inside had her shimmering. The sweetness of his young boy's mouth was just like a girl's, that insistent probing, reaching right to her cervix, was sending her mind into a spin.

Uncontrollably, she thrust herself down on his invading prick as her climax built. It was coming so suddenly and she wrenched her mouth away and cried out, clasping his head to hers. "Danny . . . yeah, yeah, YEAAAAAAAAAAAAAAAAAHHHHHH . . . OH FUCK ME, FUCK MEEEEEEEEEEEEE!!!!" She dug her nails into his back as she came, screaming out his name, every extremity of her body screaming with her . . .

When she came to, she looked into his astonished eyes and giggled. She was panting, still revelling in that gorgeous post-orgasmic sensation. "Wow, you've just fucked your first girl and made her come." She stroked his face. "And it was a lovely fuck."

"It was amazing . . ."

"Have you come again?" she said anxiously.

"No."

"Good boy." She kissed him gently as she regained her breath. "So sweet. Here." She pushed him upwards, and he lifted himself slightly. She took his penis in her hand, and pulled it gently out of her. "Better take him out—just in case."

She had squirted when she came and both his cock and her pussy were dribbling with juice. She felt it run like a river between her legs, and there was a little twinge from her anus. Her whole groin was glowing. Why not, she thought. He was nice and slim—and in any case, she felt so relaxed, it wouldn't hurt. With her finger she rubbed her cum around her tight star and pushed a finger inside, lubricating the strong, thick muscle of her sphincter. She smiled up at his pretty boy's face and kissed him lightly. "Let's put you somewhere where you can let yourself go." She tilted her pelvis upwards, then took the head of his penis between her fingers. She brought it to her anus and circled it around her ring. She shivered at the little flurries of pleasure. "Now push."

She felt a little pressure on her sphincter. "Harder." She pulled her legs up so that her feet were in the air and hooked them over his shoulders.

He grunted as he came into her, and she cried out at the initial sharp pain. He stopped.

"No—no, go on, in me . . . push." This time she felt herself give and he slid deep inside in one long thrust. She gasped and grabbed him again. It was painful, but with a pure intensity, a fullness edged with a sharp ring of fire.

"OHHHHH . . ." he gasped. "Shit . . ."

"Oh yeah . . . in my bum."

He groaned and began to thrust in and out. She could feel how tight she was around his cock—and could see from his eyes that he wouldn't last long. She pulled his face to hers and kissed him. She held his soft, girl-like mouth on hers, clasped the slight feminine body to her as she was taken by the insistent throbbing in her rectum.

Suddenly he lifted his head and groaned.

She was sure she could feel the hot jets of cum inside her bum, as he pushed and stayed deep inside her. His eyes were almost bulging out of his head, his face was flushed, and his thrusts urgent and random as he spent himself over the next few seconds.

"Yeah, yeah . . . come in me . . . come in my bum . . . fill it with your spunk . . ."

She smiled at him and kissed him.

"Was that good?"

"Fuck . . . incredible."

"That's the third time. Can you keep fucking me?"

"Yeah," he whispered, with that same look of disbelief.

He started moving in her again and her rectum seemed to heat up, pleasure slowly banishing the discomfort. "Oh yeah. Fuck me in my arse. I'm going to come again."

She frigged herself quickly, flicking her fingers across her little stiff clitoris, pressing and squeezing it between her fingers, rubbing it to a frenzy. Suddenly an intense pleasure flashed from her clit to her pussy and into her bum, her sphincter relaxing totally and her whole groin going into spasm. Her head became dizzy and blood seemed to rush into her vision as she threw her head back and screamed. "OH YEAH, DANNY . . . FUCK ME . . . YEAAAAHHH . . ." Her lungs were tearing at the air as she thought it would never end, and at the pitch she thought she would faint, her muscles tensing so hard they might convulse . . .

She lay gasping for a few moments, her breathing and heart still pumping, her eyes closed.

"Do you want me to keep going?" he said.

She looked up at him. He was watching her with that same look of innocence.

"Yeah," she said. "Take me round again, just keep fucking me with that wonderful cock. My bum is so relaxed."

He slid in and out of her again and again and she could feel that her sphincter was putting up no resistance. The nerve endings just seemed to tingle at the friction all the way up inside her and her ring buzzed. She slipped her legs down, crossing her feet across his back, then she lay there passive, loving the sensation of being taken, putting her arms around his neck.

The movement of his torso against her clit was giving her enough stimulation, and she could feel another orgasm building—and it was in her bum as well this time, so different yet no less intense. The tissue around her anus and buttocks glowed with pleasure each time he thrust against her. She had never known that anal sex could be this good. It was a whole new experience. All the times she had done it before, it had been extreme and desperate, but now it was so natural, so relaxed.

She lay there for several minutes, feeling it build, but in no hurry to let it come. She held on to him, sighing as the waves of sensation came and went. She held this soft, girlish boy. He was so innocent. It wasn't like sex with a guy. It was sort of androgynous, a soft young body fucking her with a strong, slim organ that never seemed to tire.

Suddenly she felt him quicken his movements and his cock swell. He gasped and tensed and it was as though she'd been waiting for him to squirt inside her again. The heat in her bum seemed to come to near searing point, an itch deep inside that suddenly connected to her whole groin and erupted in orgasm. "Oh fuck, Danny–yes, yes, YESSS!" She almost strangled him as she cried out, wanting him to go on forever and burn her out . . . .

As she slowly came back to awareness, she knew that she would not be able to believe what she had done in the morning—but she pushed it from her mind. She was glowing and relaxed in a way that only three amazing orgasms could give. She opened her eyes and kissed him lightly. "I don't take it up the bum very often—so count yourself as privileged," she said. She pushed a lock of his floppy gold hair away from his eyes. "And not many girls like it, so don't get too used to the idea."

"OK."

"Ohhh . . ." He was withdrawing and her bum was sucking back on him almost painfully. She felt a little flood of semen splash out of her before her sphincter closed up.

His puppy-dog face was staring at her as though he was totally obsessed. "You've fucked me in every orifice. Not a bad way to lose your virginity."

"Yeah. Fantastic."

"Better get some sleep now."

"OK."

She put her arms around him, kissed him again, and felt sleep descend.

When she woke in the morning, she opened her eyes to see Danny's pretty, boyish face staring down at her. Oh my God, he was so young. "Hi," she said.

"Hi. OK?"

"Yeah . . . you?" She grinned at him, knowingly.

"Yeah. Do you want some tea or something?"

"Sounds great." She stretched and turned her face back into the pillow.

"OK. I'll er . . . go and get it then."

"OK."

She closed her eyes and dozed. His single bed was very comfortable, she decided.

It must have been a few minutes later when he came back holding two mugs. He handed one to her, so she sat up. She saw his eyes flash to her boobs. He sat on the bed in his boxer shorts, nervously looking at her. She smiled and sipped hers, feeling the hot liquid slip down satisfyingly.

When she had finished it, she lay down again. She thought how young, how cute he looked. "You don't have to sit there. Come and have a cuddle."

He put his cup down and got into bed beside her. She drew him to her and kissed him. His mouth was tentative, but so soft. As their kiss deepened, he rolled on top of her and she felt his thin, hard penis press against her stomach.

"I can feel something."

He grinned sheepishly.

"What's the time?"

"Ten past nine."

"Oh shit!"

She pushed him off and sat up abruptly. All the other farm hands would be wondering where she had got to. "I'm late. Can somebody run me back to the pub? My car's there."

"I don't know. Everyone's asleep."

"Isn't there anyone around?" She got out of bed, suddenly sensing soreness in her bum.

He got out as well. "I could go down to the barn. I know they are coming to take away the lights and stuff."

"Yeah. Do that."

Twenty minutes later, she was sitting in the low, heavily beamed kitchen sipping a cup of coffee he had made for her. He opened the outside door and came in looking wet and bedraggled. It was pouring with rain. "It's OK. There's a guy with a van-load of stuff going to Stratford who said he'd drop you off."

"Great."

"He's driving up here in a minute."

"Good." She looked at him and smiled—but didn't know quite what to say.

"Can I see you again?" he said, sheepishly.

"Well—I'm sort of in a relationship, you know?"

"Oh. Right." He looked crestfallen.

"But look. Give me your mobile number."

"Yeah." He spelt it out and she tapped it into her phone and saved it. She then pressed her green button. "Now I'm ringing you, and you'll get my number. OK? Call me sometime. We'll have a chat."

"Yeah—that'd be great. Got it," he said, after a few moments.

She got up and went to the window. The sky was hung over with thick cloud. She looked back at him. "This was fun—yeah? But it was just a one-night stand."

"Yeah. Sure." He looked down at the table.

She felt a heel. Fortunately, there was a noise of a van driving up outside. "Is that him?"

"Yeah."

"Right. You needn't come out. Don't want you getting too wet." She went over to him, took his face in her hands, and kissed him. "Bye."

"Yeah—bye."

She felt tired and slightly irritable sitting in the waiting room at the doctor's surgery. She had told the po-faced receptionist that she needed an urgent appointment. The guy that had taken her to her car was quite old and talked incessantly during the few minutes it took to get to the pub—much to her relief. Then she had driven back to Birmingham, had a quick shower before coming here, where she had now sat for forty minutes.

The doctor was young and kind when she finally got in to see her. She gave her a prescription for the morning-after pill, just in case, and suggested she go back on the contraceptive pill regularly. She took her blood pressure and a blood test. She was about thirty-five, Sally guessed, and attractive—slim, but with that plumpness around the bum that young mothers have. She decided she quite fancied her.

Back home, she sat in the lounge, staring at the wall. So, she was back on the old routine—casual sex—the addiction she had gotten into after her mother died. She was worried about what to say to Gernie and the others. She had simply disappeared with Danny and not said where she was going. But then she was hardly in a fit state, with a beer-soaked T-shirt and her tits fully visible. She wouldn't have wanted them to see that—not the best start to a working relationship.

Chapter 8

Emma laid her head back on the pillow and sighed. "That was amazing." She stroked Sophie's hair and kissed her lightly. "But then it's always amazing." They had just made love—as they did every morning when they woke up. They had made love the night before and twice during the day before that. Two weeks had passed—but their appetite for each other seemed insatiable.

"Will you come to mass with me again this morning?" said Sophie, sitting up.

"Yes, sure. I enjoyed it last time."

"I think Maurice was very pleased that you came."

"The priest? Have you seen him since?"

"Yes," she said lightly. "We meet up occasionally."

"Do you? I didn't know that."

"Yes." She paused—then the look on her face became sheepish. "I do things for him."

Emma felt shocked. "What things?"

"I relieve him. He has a very high sex drive, and as a priest, he finds that difficult."

Emma was taken aback. "So what do you do? You don't fuck him," she said, sharply.

"No. He doesn't want that. And anyway I wouldn't—not while you and I are lovers. I masturbate him."

"Get him off?"

"Yes. And he likes me to do it naked."

Emma almost felt she should feel angry—but she just laughed. "God, that's amazing. So when do you do it?"

"Every few days. I did it yesterday. When you were in class."

"What? You went to his room?"

"Yes."

"And took your clothes off and tossed him off?"

"Yes. He doesn't touch me, or kiss me. He says that would make him want more. But it helps him to come regularly. It clears his mind."

"Can't he do it himself?"

"It's not the same."

Emma smiled. "No, it's not."

"You're not angry or anything?"

Emma looked at her with incredulity. She knew she should be really shocked—but she wasn't. She couldn't stop grinning. She leaned in and kissed her. "No. I don't blame him—or you. You're so gorgeous—he must find it very satisfying."

"Yes, he does. I like doing it for him. He is a scholar, you know, and he is doing research for the Vatican. He spends a lot of his time here looking at archives."

"Did you do it for him last year?"

"Yes."

"But you hadn't seen him since?"

"No."

Emma hugged her. "You're amazing. You never cease to surprise me."

Sophie brought their mouths together and kissed her deeply. "Anyway—after church we are going somewhere special."

"OK? Where?" said Emma.

"You'll see."

As they sat in the quiet chapel with the sun pouring through the coloured glass windows, Emma recalled how it had struck her that the young priest had been gently familiar with Sophie when the three of them had met. At the time she had thought nothing of it, but now she could see why.

As the two of them knelt at the rail to receive communion, she saw fleetingly a little glance between Maurice and Sophie as he placed the host onto her tongue. She couldn't help picturing them both naked, his prick in Sophie's hand. *How bizarre the world is,* she thought. When he offered her the wafer, she looked directly into his eyes—and thought she could see the faintest trace of a smile.

"He is very young. I can understand he must find sex really difficult to deal with," she said as they strolled back to their room.

"Yes, and it's hard for him to find an arrangement like he has with me. He says that some young girls have fallen head over heels in love with him, and that's hopeless for someone in his position."

"God, yes. So isn't he lucky he's got you at the moment." She put her arm around Sophie's neck and kissed her cheek. "Has he got a nice prick?"

"Yes—quite big."

They giggled—and Emma kissed her warmly. "I ought to be so shocked, but I'm not. You're amazing." She kissed her. "But look, where are we going?"

"Put on some trainers," Sophie said when they were back in their room. "Oh, and bring a towel. You can put it in my bag."

"A towel? Are we going swimming?"

"Yes."

"So do I need my bikini?"

"No, no. There's never anyone there."

"We're going to swim nude?"

"Of course."

"But where are we going?"

"You'll see. We have to walk through the village," said Sophie as they left the chateau. "There is a path from the back of the church."

The chateau sat on one side of a steep valley, just at the point where it was joined by another smaller ravine. Two rivers came together at the centre of the village. As they walked past the church, a narrow road appeared that led up the ravine. It was wide at this point, with some houses fronting onto it, but Emma could see that it turned into a track ahead and the cliffs on either side became higher and closer together. The river was fast and noisy, and they were soon climbing up away from the village, walking through the trees that lined the riverbed.

"What did you think of Antoine?" said Sophie, as they walked.

"Very nice. I mean, like, I hardly met him, and it was two and a half weeks ago."

"Did you think he was good-looking?"

"Yes, very."

"Did you fancy him?"

"I don't think I had time. Anyway, you were too busy having sex with him." She put her arm around Sophie and kissed her cheek.

"I could tell he fancied you."

"Really?"

"Oh yes. I always know."

"Did you mind?"

"Of course not. Why should I? Especially as it was you."

"But you didn't know me then."

"No, but I could see instantly that I wanted you." She stopped, pulled Emma to her, and kissed her. "I couldn't believe how beautiful you were."

"Have you told Antoine—about you and me?"

"Yes."

"And what did he say?"

"That he envied me."

"Is he used to his girlfriend having sex with other girls?"

"Yes, of course. Sometimes he joins in."

Emma felt herself blush slightly. "Really?"

"Does that shock you?"

"Knowing you, not at all."

"Did you find it sexy, when you watched us?"

"Yes. Very."

"Would you like it if he joined us for sex?"

"What—the three of us together?"

"Yes."

"Would *you*?"

"Yes. I would love it."

"I'm not sure. I don't know . . . as you know, I had a really bad experience with the last guy I was with."

Emma became conscious that her hands were wandering all over Sophie's body, feeling her beneath the thin material of her clothing. She couldn't stop looking at her mesmerising face. They were quite alone in this isolated spot with just the sound of the rushing water of the river and the wind gently stirring the trees. Emma kissed her, the rush of intense lust making her want to almost eat Sophie's mouth. She pulled Sophie's blouse right up to her neck and ran her hands across the warm flesh of her back, arms, and breasts. "I want to make love. Now."

She felt Sophie's hand rub the gusset of her shorts and her hot mouth kiss her neck. "We're nearly there . . . we'll make love in the pool." She broke free and grasped Emma's hand. "Come on."

They walked on and came into a clearing, the sun suddenly warm on Emma's skin.

"You see," said Sophie. "The path is wider from here."

"I mean . . . I suppose in some ways I should find out whether I'm still turned on by sex with guys. I think I'm a bit confused. Sex with you is so amazing—and it was wonderful with Sally. I guess I haven't really thought I've been missing anything."

"I'm going to invite you to my parents' house. If Antoine can join us there—then maybe we'll see."

"OK. That would be nice."

The sheer cliff of rock had been close to their right for some time, but now it gave way to a space where a small field had been cultivated. The short stubble was all that remained of a wheat crop. To the left, some buildings and a small house hugged the riverbank.

"Fancy living here."

"I would love it," said Sophie.

"As long as you had a steady stream of girls and boys making love to you."

Sophie giggled. "Maybe."

At the other side of the field, the ravine closed in again and the banks of the river were overgrown with trees, the path snaking over their roots. Once again they were plunged into shade.

Looking up ahead, it seemed to Emma that the cliffs joined and the river disappeared. Then suddenly, she heard the rush of water take on a different sound, and as they got closer, she could see that the river fell over the cliff face in a waterfall and plunged into a deep blue pool.

"Here we are," said Sophie.

"It's lovely." As they reached the edge of the pool, Emma could see that it was deep and that the river escaped on its way to the village by seeping out of the pool to her left. The area around the pool was wide enough for the sun to beam down on them again, its rays plunging deep into the clear water.

"Would you like to swim?"

"Are you sure there's no one around?"

"Can you see anyone?"

"But do people come here? I mean, they might just turn up."

"Relax. I have never seen anyone here."

"OK. If you're sure."

Sophie quickly took off her clothes and walked to the edge of the pool. Emma looked lustfully at the slim, gorgeous figure of her friend. *Her back*, she thought, *I particularly love her back.* Glancing round once more to be sure, she also removed her clothes and joined Sophie at the edge. She gingerly put her toe in.

"It's freezing!"

"You get used to it—honestly, it will only feel cold for a minute."

"Ohhh . . . no, I can't."

"Yes, you can."

Emma suddenly felt herself being pulled forward—she lost her balance and was engulfed by an intense, numbing cold. She shrieked.

The bottom of the pool fell sharply away and she was forced to swim, gasping at the shock of the cold water. She swam towards the centre and looked back, treading water, her heartbeat racing, desperately trying to accustom her body temperature. Sophie was following her, seemingly unperturbed by the cold.

"It's nice—yes?"

"Yes—but it's still bloody freezing!"

Sophie laughed and dived under. Emma swam close to the waterfall, and as she got near it could feel the strong force of the water under the surface plunging down into the depths of the pool.

Gradually, her skin became accustomed to the cold and she began to enjoy the feel of the water. She reached the other side and held on to a ledge of rock. Sophie swam towards her.

"Good—yes?"

"Yeah. Now."

"There, I told you." She put her hands on Emma's hips and leaned forward to kiss her. "Are you glad I brought you here?"

Emma smiled and pulled her close, pressing their loins together. She wrapped her arms around her cold, wet body and kissed her again. Locked together, they fell forward and broke apart, laughing and giggling.

"I am going to dive," said Sophie as she swam back to the rock.

Emma glided across to the shallows where they had first gotten in and lay on the smooth cobbles, a ray of sun warming her body, the water lapping over her feet.

Sophie slowly and carefully climbed out onto the rock ledge and made her way higher up the cliff.

Emma watched her. "Careful!"

Sophie reached a narrow ledge across the cliff face about ten or fifteen feet up and stood poised, then dived and cut cleanly into the water. Emma watched the water, and it seemed a long time before Sophie broke to the surface and glided towards her.

"That was fun."

As she came close, Sophie reached forward and opened Emma's legs. She kissed her way up her thigh until her mouth was within an inch of Emma's pussy.

Emma felt her stomach churn as the hypnotic eyes fixed wickedly on hers. Then she gasped as Sophie's tongue searched her vagina.

Emma stretched her arms above her head. She looked up into the pale blue of the sky, the leaves of the trees glistening gold in the sunlight. She luxuriated in the sensation of Sophie lapping her clitoris, running that strong tongue restlessly up and down. Every time she made love to her, Sophie could bring her effortlessly to an intense orgasm. Lesbian sex was the most wonderful thing she had ever known. She'd had a fleeting brush with it at school, all those years ago, and then Sally had come as if from nowhere and shown her how wonderful it could be . . . oh God, she loved her so much for that.

The tension built sharply, and she put her hands down to ruffle the wet, thick black hair. The small pointed tongue was inside her now, massaging the roof of her vaginal passage. Instinctively, she shifted downwards to get her deeper. Her thighs were trembling. She was rolling her head back and forth, moaning uncontrollably. So many years with so many lovers she had worked at trying to find the gate into the enchanted garden and now, so easily, so lovingly, the caresses of that expert tongue were bringing her home. It was as though the hot sun on her skin was being echoed in the aching in her groin.

Sophie seemed to sense how close she was and eased her teasing, removing her tongue, and inserting her fingers, exploring her gently, stretching her walls, bringing a different kind of pleasure. Emma massaged her breasts, squeezing them, feeling the sensitivity and arousal. She wanted to enjoy the journey, to savour her body tingling and shivering at different sensations in so many places.

Sophie kissed around her vagina, caressing her inner thighs, her mound of pubic hair, and up across her stomach. Her fingers slid lusciously in and out of her, but Emma's expectant clitoris was left waiting, the blood pumping within it, making it hard with anticipation.

Emma gazed upwards, the sun dazzling her eyes. She drew a deep lungful of the pure, moist air. Every muscle seemed to shift within her to meet Sophie's playing with her. It was as though her body was an instrument that for years had waited for this sweet music to be drawn out—and now every time the harmonies became more complex, surprising, unexpected. "Ohhh . . . Sophie . . ."

The wicked eyes flashed up to Emma's, then quickly down again as her head lowered. Emma's tortured clitoris seemed to swell with expectation, then instantly ignited as Sophie's mouth closed on it.

"Ohhhh, my darling, so good—ahhh . . . please. Ohhh yessss . . ."

Sophie sucked it into her mouth, her tongue flicking over it.

"AHHHHHHHHHHH!" Emma cried, as her orgasm took her, the pure sound echoing around the lonely glade. She felt complete abandon, her body lifting off the ground, light exploding in her eyes, the sun purging her body and her mind.

She lay still, exhausted, her body in spasm. Her climax had cleaned her so completely, it felt as though she were floating. As if from a long way away the light kisses of her lover made their way across her stomach and breasts to her face. She sensed the shadow across her eyes and opened them to see the beautiful green pupils gazing down at her. She sighed at the touch of the soft, succulent mouth. She felt the cold, wet skin of her lover against her own, hot from the sun. She held her tightly. "I love what you do to me."

"I love doing it." Sophie chuckled, then drifted off back into the water, diving down and disappearing beneath the surface.

Emma stood up and walked over to the side of the pool where the bare face of the rock was in the full sun. She leant against it, closed her eyes, and relished the warmth seeping into her. She heard Sophie splashing in the water, then her feet pad across the flat stones towards her. The sun was blocked, and she shivered as she felt Sophie's cold torso press against her own. Her mouth touched Emma's and kissed her lightly. Emma kept her eyes closed as Sophie pecked lightly all over her face. She kissed her cheeks, forehead, and nose, before making her way to Emma's ears and neck.

Emma sighed and ran her hand down the wet expanse of Sophie's back to grasp the round cheek of her bum, spreading her palm across and squeezing gently. She breathed in deeply and found Sophie's mouth, kissing her with passion.

As their lips parted, she turned her friend round so that now Sophie had her back against the rock. She moved her hand down to Sophie's stomach, then to her pubic mound, her fingers tracing across Sophie's vagina. The outer lips were cold from the pool, but as Emma's forefinger slipped inside the folds, she felt the warm slippery fluid of her arousal. Gently, she soaked her finger in it and moved it to the little mound of her clitoris.

Sophie whimpered and broke the kiss. "Oh yes . . ." She moved her feet farther apart, allowing Emma to find her opening.

Emma's index finger pushed into her, sinking right up to her knuckle. She withdrew, added her middle finger, and slid back in, fucking her slowly and deeply. Sophie's tunnel was hot and slippery, hugging her fingers.

Sophie stretched out her arms to the rock face and leant her head back.

Emma dropped her head down and sucked on Sophie's nipples, tracing the tip of her tongue around first one, then the other. She sucked on each of them, pulling them into her mouth, then letting them go, only to lick and caress them again.

She reached up and kissed Sophie's mouth, and they rubbed their tongues together as though they were two separate parts of their bodies making love on their own.

Pumping her fingers rhythmically in and out of Sophie's vagina, she kissed her way down to Sophie's breasts again, then crouched in front of her, continuing her journey down her stomach to the little dark bush of hair and the waiting clitoris.

Sophie gasped.

Emma worked the stiff little mound, flicking it, then bringing the flat of her tongue across it in long strokes. That little hill of flesh seemed so succulent, she seemed to want to eat it forever, rolling it around her mouth, playing with it with her tongue. She lapped up the love juice seeping from Sophie's sex, and as her friend began to utter short little cries, she increased the pace of her fingers and her tongue, driving her towards orgasm, loving her relentlessly.

Sophie screamed and her body jerked, but still Emma wouldn't stop. The noise was echoing around the ravine, and anyone within a mile could hear it, but she wanted to hear more cries of joy from Sophie and their act of love never to stop.

Sophie grasped Emma's head and pushed it hard against her groin. She sighed as Emma continued to snake her tongue all round the soft wet crevices, bringing her down, her face covered in the wetness. She glanced upwards and smiled.

"Nice?"

"Mmm . . ."

Emma stood up and they hugged together and kissed deeply.

She heard a twig snap and the unmistakable sound of footsteps. They broke apart and looked across to the path. A girl was making her way towards them.

"It's Hannah!" Sophie whispered to Emma.

"Oh shit," said Emma. "You said no one ever came here."

"They don't." She giggled. "Anyway, it doesn't matter." She walked across the clearing to the path. "Hello, Hannah. Have you come for a swim like us?"

Hannah stared at them both, clearly embarrassed at the sight of both of them with nothing on. "Yes, that's right."

"Hi, Hannah," said Emma. She went over to where their towels were lying on the ground and picked one up. She put it across herself, then walked over to them.

Hannah's cheeks were flushed. "Hello."

"Emma and I had a lovely swim together," said Sophie, slipping her arm round Emma. "Then we made love."

Emma almost gasped. "It's lovely—but a bit cold," she said quickly.

"Yes—it usually is," said Hannah, smiling shyly. "Yes—very cold, but I am liking that." She pulled the dress she was wearing over her head to reveal a pink bikini.

"I thought Swedish people always swam naked," said Sophie.

Hannah blushed. "Yes, I do sometimes with my friends. Only I thought that here in France this was not the way."

"Well, we are your friends."

"Leave Hannah alone. Maybe she doesn't want to. Anyway, we are going."

"No, she is right," said Hannah, reaching behind to unclip her top. "I like to be naked." She slipped the little top off and then pushed down her bikini bottoms. She stepped out of them and then looked rather intensely at Emma.

Emma smiled, trying not to look at the medium to large-sized breasts and small thatch of blonde hair between her legs.

"You have a lovely body," said Sophie.

"Thank you," said Hannah, smiling self-consciously.

"Come on," said Emma. "Let's get dressed. We have to get back." She let the towel drop and began to dry herself. She saw Hannah's eyes flash across her body, then the girl turned and walked to the edge of the water. A moment later, she plunged in.

"Oh God," whispered Emma. "We really embarrassed her."

"She loved it."

Two minutes later they were ready to go.

"Good-bye, Hannah. Enjoy your swim," said Sophie. She put out her hand to Emma and kissed her on the cheek.

As Emma waved, she was conscious of Hannah treading water and looking at her rather intently.

They walked in silence until they were out of earshot—and then Sophie burst out laughing. "The poor thing. She must have heard us making love, so I thought I would tell her."

"You made it rather obvious that we are together—like, an item."

"So?"

"Well, now she knows I'm a lesbian."

"Does that bother you?"

"No. I guess not. In fact, I like it."

"Do you fancy her?"

"Quite. She's attractive, and as you said—very embarrassingly—has a nice body."

"She is shy. She needs bringing out of herself. Did you see the way she looked at you? I think she fancies you."

"Honestly. You're outrageous."

"Perhaps we should invite her to our room, get her drunk, and seduce her. For you."

"And not for you?"

"Of course for me."

Emma nuzzled her mouth into Sophie's hair and kissed her.

"Do you really tell Antoine about everything you do?" Emma said as they walked down the path.

"Oh yes."

"And doesn't he mind?"

"No. He has far too good a time with me to mind if I share myself a bit."

"And does he share himself?"

"Yes. We compare notes." Sophie looked at her. "I think you are shocked."

"No, not really."

Sophie stopped and pulled Emma to her. "I want to share him with you."

Emma ran her hand over Sophie's blouse, sensing the bare skin beneath. She looked at her and hesitated. "I don't know . . . we'll see."

"Are you a bit afraid of sex with men now—because of what happened?"

"Yes." Emma looked away then back at her. "Yes, I think maybe I am."

"But you love sex with guys normally?"

"Oh yes—I used to love it. But I have only ever come with you—and Sally."

"OK. If I arrange a weekend can you see how you feel? I want you to meet my parents anyway—they're fantastic!"

Chapter 9

Sally stood in the kitchen of the cottage. It had been five weeks, and she still couldn't believe she was living here. It was so pretty and tastefully done up by Emma's parents, and it was hers to use. Her home—for the next few months anyway. She had wanted this for so long: somewhere she could call her own, that she maintained herself, where she could feel centred again.

When she had escaped and lived with her uncle it was their place, not hers. They loved having her there, but she had to live in *their* house, and although she had her own room, it was not the same as this. She somehow didn't mind being on her own here. She didn't know what would happen when Emma came back, but it didn't matter for the time being. Now she was enjoying the work in the office and out on the farm and coming back and being domestic. And thinking—she'd been doing a lot of that, going over the past three years to try and understand what had happened and make some sense of it.

She flopped down in one of the garden chairs. She'd had a bath and eaten some supper, then thrown on a skirt and a blouse with a cardigan. She didn't bother with underwear. She liked that. She could wander round in the house in the nude, or wear very little. Feeling sexy was good, she thought, after a year where she just wouldn't let herself feel anything in particular.

It was about eight-thirty, still light, but with a slight chill in the air. She looked round the pretty little garden. The house was surrounded by fields, and the garden was private, lined by tall trees. She let her mind drift into the past again.

I was really upset about Maddie—but thinking about it, I got over it pretty quickly really. That was down to Jamie and Lou.

Jamie had come to live with us when his father and my mother got married. I was eleven at the time and hated the whole idea. My own father had never been part of our life, and although I never knew him, I didn't want anyone else stepping in and trying to take his place. I'd done without a father, and I didn't want some kind of substitute now.

Anyway, it happened, and I just had to put up with it. I wasn't a tear away, and I didn't throw tantrums. I just went into myself. I had nothing to do with either of them for months—years even. I answered more or less politely when spoken to, but never really wanted to know them. My mother used to tell me off, say that I ought to be nicer with them, that was the only way we were going to be a family. But I would just be quiet and not say anything.

When puberty happened, I began to notice Jamie, how he was nice-looking—but he didn't really take any notice of me and was always off with his mates playing football, and so I kept to my small group of friends, especially Lou.

Lou was my best friend. She was a mousy brunette, slightly smaller than me—really bubbly—and she got into sex and boys before I did. She was really open about what she did with her boyfriends, and we had giggly sessions talking about it. She tried to get me off with several blokes, but I wasn't ready, and so although I snogged off with a few, nothing happened.

And anyway, I was a bit confused sexually. I found myself fancying some girls—and I knew that I fancied Lou. It made it a bit difficult sometimes. She would come round and we would lie on my bed together—and when she slept over, we would cuddle up in my single bed in our pyjamas. It was nice in one way, but I also found it frustrating—because I didn't dare suggest anything. I guess I thought having gay feelings was something that I would grow out of.

I often wondered whether Lou guessed I fancied her, because sometimes she was a bit provocative, as though she wanted to flaunt herself in front of me. There was one day when I was round at hers. We had just been shopping. We were trying on some clothes we bought, and she deliberately took off her bra. She stood there with nothing on apart from her panties. She looked gorgeous. From that day on I fantasized about her a lot.

But then because she was always round our house, Jamie started getting friendly with her and ended up going out with her. For a few weeks I was a bit screwed up about it. Some days when our parents were out, they would be in his room having sex. I remember several times sitting in my room, turning up the music to make sure I couldn't hear anything. I went through lots of different moods: sometimes really worrying about being left out, feeling jealous—but also fantasizing about them at night. I suppose because I was so screwed up, that was one of the reasons I got it on with Maddie. Once that happened, I felt so much better about them. I had my own sex life—hidden and secret, but amazing.

Jamie was great when Maddie and I split up and I was suspended. He said I shouldn't worry and that he didn't understand what all the fuss was about—and he thought it was really hypocritical, given the emphasis we had at school on understanding single-sex relationships.

"I guess it's the fact that we did it in the open," I said. "That was really out of order."

"Yeah . . . but not that much." He put his arm around me. "Well, anyway, I'm on your side, and so is Lou."

"Yeah, she rang me. I was really relieved; I thought she might have gone off me."

"Course not. She wanted to talk to me first."

That evening, Lou came round. We went up to my room, and she gave me a hug. "Listen," she said. "I'm really fine with it. So what if it was another girl? I mean, girls are really physical with each other anyway. We're a lot more, like, into touching each other—you know."

"Yeah. So you don't hate me then?" We sat on the bed next to each other.

"No, why should I?" She put her arm round me and kissed me on the cheek. "You're my best pal—take a lot more than that to put me off you."

"Thanks." I felt tears welling up again. "It's been horrible here, because my mum's not cool with it. She seemed really disgusted. But Jamie's been great. I'm just terrified that everyone at school will know and be talking about me behind my back."

"Well, I guess a few will, but most won't even know about it. And you're not the only one. I know at least three who've done it with other girls."

"Really?"

"Yeah."

"I'm just not looking forward to going back in and everyone staring at me and whispering behind my back. Catcalling—that kind of stuff."

"Don't worry—Jamie and I will be there with you, standing up for you. I'll give them a mouthful if anyone says anything."

I looked up and smiled at her, tears running down my face. "Thanks . . ."

"Oh, come here." She pulled me to her and hugged me again. I put my arms around her and squeezed her tight. I felt so relieved.

Then she sat back and took my hands in hers. She looked at me sort of coyly and said. "Can I ask you something?"

"What?"

"You know—when we were younger—and we thought we'd try out kissing?"

"Yeah."

We were just sixteen at the time, and I was staying over at Lou's. We were in our pyjamas and had a giggly session talking about kissing boys and what you had to do. We decided to experiment with each other—kissing on the lips. Then Lou insisted we did it with tongues—so we kissed on the lips at first, then I felt Lou open her mouth and her tongue play with mine. It was electric. I remember shivers going all through me—and a hot feeling between my legs. Our mouths parted, and I remember we giggled, but I knew I was blushing.

"That was fun," she said at the time. "Shall we do it again?"

So we did—and the second time I felt the same way. I put my hand through her hair and our mouths and tongues moved sexily together for quite a long time.

"Better not get too used to it," she said. "We might turn into lesbians."

And that was it. We didn't do it again—but I often thought about it and fantasized when I was touching myself.

"And you remember that day when we were at mine trying on dresses and stuff?"

"Yeah."

"And I had no bra on and was just in my panties?"

"Yeah?"

She squeezed my hands. "I mean . . . did it sort of . . . turn you on? Seeing me like that?"

I felt the blood rush to my cheeks. I looked down at our hands. "Well . . . you know I think you're lovely . . ."

"But did it make you fancy me—you know, sexually?"

"Lou, I . . ."

"Cause if it did, that's really nice."

I looked up at her. She was smiling shyly and her eyes were really shining.

"Because . . . I remember thinking at the time . . . it was, you know . . . actually quite sexy, the two of us without much on."

I hesitated, then said, "Yeah, I did too. I really fancied you."

"You always have, haven't you?"

I felt myself blush. "Yeah."

She giggled nervously. "I had a little fantasy . . . in bed. That we made out and stuff."

"Really?" I was gob smacked. Didn't know what to say.

"Yeah. I imagined we kissed again, and had a bit of fun . . ."

I felt my heart pound. "I've done that too."

We both blushed and there was a silence. We looked at each other for a moment, then I saw her eyes drop to my mouth and slowly she leant in and kissed me on the lips. It was magical—the kiss lasted several seconds, and as our lips parted, I shuddered.

"Lou . . . look, you didn't do that just to make me feel better, did you?"

"No, really. Ever since, I've been wondering what it would be like. Not because I'm a lesbian or anything. I mean, I don't fancy anyone else—but I guess you and I are so close that . . ." She put her hand on my face. "Can I do it again?"

"Yeah . . . I mean, if you enjoyed it."

"I loved it. Did you?"

"Yeah." We kissed again, and this time I could feel her lips searching mine and her tongue probing my mouth.

A door slammed downstairs and we broke apart. We looked at each other for a moment, then she laughed again. "Wow!" she said and stood up. "I better go."

I heard steps on the stairs and a moment later Jamie put his head round the door. "Hi. OK? All right. Sal?"

"Yeah."

Lou immediately went over and kissed him. "Hi, gorgeous," she said. "I was just going." As she went out of the door, she turned to me and winked.

The following day, Lou came round at lunchtime. Everyone else was out, and I was still in my pyjamas. It was nice to see her, but I felt a bit strange about what had happened the day before. I had been thinking about it a lot. We went into the kitchen and I made some coffee. She chatted about what was going on at school, but all the while I could sense we were a bit hesitant with each other. It wasn't the same easy relationship we normally had.

We went up to my room and we sat on the bed—and I knew she wanted to say something.

"About what we did yesterday," she said. "That was OK, wasn't it?"

"Yeah—it was nice. I mean . . ."

"What?"

"I don't know . . ." I giggled nervously.

She touched my hand, then leant across and kissed me again. It was so nice, kind of melting. Her lips were like Maddie's, only different. I nearly spilt my coffee, and we broke apart and laughed.

We both put our mugs down and shifted together. We kissed again, and I felt her tongue push into my mouth. I responded and we French kissed for a long time. It was wonderful. I ran my hands through her lovely hair, then down across her back and round to her breasts. They were soft and I could tell she wasn't wearing a bra. I wondered whether she had done that deliberately.

Our lips parted and we smiled at each other. I kissed her cheek, then pecked my way down to her neck, where I opened my mouth and licked the warm flesh. I felt quite emotional—and very turned on. This was Lou, my best friend, with her lovely, sexy smell. I had been feeling so low, and now suddenly I wanted this so much.

She sighed and I felt her hands push up my pyjama top. It was loose fitting, and I was bare underneath. She fondled my tits.

I straightened up and pulled it over my head.

"You've got lovely boobs," she said.

"So have you." I pushed her cardigan off her shoulders, then began to undo the buttons of her blouse. My fingers were trembling as I finally opened the front and pushed it off onto the bed. I looked at her small, pert tits and put my hands on them, rubbing my thumbs across her nipples. "They are as nice as I remember them." I pushed her onto her back and lay on top of her, tingling as I felt her soft, bare torso touch mine. I kissed her passionately, and I heard her whimper softly. I parted my legs slightly so that my pussy was touching her leg through the material and rubbed gently. All thoughts of Maddie had gone.

I lifted my head and looked at her. She was so pretty. "Look, how far do you want to go with this? I mean, you're going out with Jamie, and . . ."

"Yeah . . ." She looked shamefaced for a moment, but then looked at me intensely. "But this is different. This is about you and me."

I stroked her thigh and ran my hand up to her pussy.

"Oh fuck yeah—take me all the way."

I smiled at her and kissed her neck and shoulders, then took her tits one by one into my mouth, kissing and licking them. I looked up at her and could see she was really turned on. I continued downwards, kissing across her skirt, then down to her thighs, licking close to her pussy. She was gently sighing now and she jumped slightly as I blew hot breath onto her panties. I looked wickedly at her and pulled them aside. Her sweet little pink pussy sat there looking so inviting.

Quickly, I got hold of either side of her panties and pulled them off, then I spread her legs and slipped off the bed so I could bring my head close to her pussy. I put my fingers to the lips and pulled them wide. She cried out quietly as I ran my tongue from the bottom to the top near her clit. She smelt clean, but also strongly of sex. The more I licked, the more juice began to seep from her and I found myself rolling it round my mouth, mixing it with my saliva, sucking on her strongly.

I pushed my tongue deep inside her a few times, then ran the flat of my tongue upwards, flicking her clit with the tip. She seemed to love that, so I repeated it, teasing her as much as I could. I raised my head and smiled at her, licking my lips. "You taste so good," I said.

"Oh please don't stop," she whispered. "I'm so close to coming."

"You like me licking your clit?"

"Yeah, yeah—I love that."

I slid a finger into her pussy. She was really wet, and I moved it around inside as I brought my tongue back to her clitoris. I licked it a few times, then started really flicking it, teasing it from the underside in the way that I really liked Maddie to do to me. She was uttering a little cry with each panting breath now, and I thought to myself how nice it felt. I had known her such a long time. We had played together and been best pals for years, and now we were lovers.

My breasts felt so sensitive, my nipples tingling and my pussy had a lovely warm glow. I could feel her thighs quivering as she built to her orgasm. She was pressing her sex against me, and the touch and taste of it was causing lots of saliva to gather in my mouth, dribbling out, mixing with her juice. Her cries mounted, and I increased the speed of my tongue, pushing my finger in and out. I could feel her vagina really sucking on it, and I suddenly wondered what it must be like to have a penis and push it into that lovely warm, wet sheath.

"Oh fuck, Sal . . . .YEAAAAHHHHHHH . . ."

Her body lurched as she came—she froze then cried out, her thighs clenching round my head. I always loved when Maddie came, I remembered, trying to keep on licking when my head was held so tight.

When she relaxed, she stroked my hair, her eyes closed, still sighing heavily. After a few moments, she raised her head and smiled at me.

"Good?" I said.

"Fantastic—you're a genius at that."

I lay back up on the bed and she cuddled next to me. We kissed tenderly for a few minutes.

"Are you OK with us doing it together?" I said. "I mean, it doesn't mean you're gay or anything."

"Yeah . . . I mean, it felt a bit odd coming round today, and me thinking, are we going to have sex—you know? I mean, like, I don't think I am gay—but I do like you. It just feels natural—but I don't really fancy other girls. It's weird."

"Maybe it's because we're such good friends and have been for a long time."

"Yeah. Aren't you going to take your bottoms off?" she said, kissing me again.

I pushed them off my legs, and she took off her skirt that was still wrapped around her waist. When we were both naked, she put her arm around me and her other hand down to my pussy. She stroked it softly. "Your turn," she said.

I lay there, kissing her while she played with my pussy. It felt fantastic.

"I love you licking my pussy—but I don't know how I feel about kissing yours," she said eventually.

"That's OK. I mean, I'm gay, so I really like it—but if you're not, then what you're doing is really nice."

"Do you want me to suck your tits?"

"Oh yeah . . ."

She put her head down and licked around my left nipple. It felt great—and I sighed as she slid a finger into me as well. I knew I could come anytime, but I didn't want to. I just wanted to lie there, loving what she was doing to me. I wanted to get to the destination but enjoy the journey along the way. I ran my hands over her soft, silky hair and the smooth skin of her back.

"This feels amazing," I whispered.

"Yeah. But that's because we're really close friends—and that's love," she said, leaning up and kissing me.

"Yeah. Yeah, it is." I kissed her more forcefully and instantly felt the heat in my groin surge. It was like what she had said made every bit of feeling in my body shoot to my pussy. My clit burned with intense pleasure—it was so emotional, like all that I had felt for her all my life suddenly boiling over. "Oh yeah, Lou . . . yeah, yeah, yeah . . ." I jumped with a sweet and intense orgasm, holding her to me.

"Oh—that was so lovely," I said, trying to catch my breath.

"You came so suddenly."

"Yeah. It's because of what you said. We do love each other, don't we?"

"Yeah, of course." She looked down at me, and her eyes were so blue and her face so gorgeous. "I need the loo," she said, and bounced off the bed.

When she came back, she stood by the bed and looked at me. "I want to try it," she said.

"What?"

"Cunnilingus."

"OK. I mean—if you decide you don't like it and want to stop, that's OK." I couldn't quite believe what was happening as I spread my legs and watched my friend kneel in front of me.

Lou stroked my thighs and looked at me shyly. "You're gorgeous, and you're my best friend. That's why I sort of want to do it for you." She leant down and quickly ran her tongue over my pussy lips, then looked up again, running her tongue around her mouth. "Tastes funny. It's quite nice though."

"Haven't you ever tasted your own cum?"

"Yeah." She started licking me again, very gently. Pleasure just shimmered around my body. I closed my eyes and moaned softly at every little wave that hit me.

"Am I doing it all right?"

"Yeah, it's great."

She tried putting her tongue inside me, but couldn't get it in very far. It was nice, but felt a bit frustrating. "Lick my clit again," I whispered.

"OK. Sorry."

"No, no. It's fantastic."

She ran her tongue gingerly around my clit again. I breathed deeply, squirming on the bed, loving the sensations she was giving me, but she kept stopping. After a while, when she stopped again, I took hold of her head and pushed her down. "Sorry—I'm just so close."

"Sorry."

She licked again, but I could tell somehow she wasn't enjoying it. Maddie had always loved it, being really clever, licking me in just the way that would bring me off quickly. This was nice, but I wasn't getting there.

She ran a finger down to my bum and touched my ring— then I felt a sudden spark of pleasure that brought me close. "Oh God . . ."

"Like it there, do you?"

"Yeah. Come here and kiss me."

She quickly got up and lay beside me.

"Keep your finger on my bum." I kissed her, and with my left hand, frigged myself. I felt the heat build. Her tongue was playing with mine in our mouths, and I felt myself uncontrollably pushing down onto her finger. I would have liked her inside, but knew that she might not want to do that. I could feel my cum trickling between my legs, and I gathered it on my fingers and rubbed it around my clit.

As the tension built, I had to break away from her kiss to shriek my head off. I was rubbing my clit really hard and knew I would come off at any moment. "Oh fuck, Lou, I'm going to come. Stick it in me. Stick it in my arse . . ."

A second later, I felt her push her finger inside. I was so wet it just slid in. She pushed it in deep and moved it around inside. "Oh Lou, YESSSS, LOU, LOU, AAHHHH . . ." My body exploded and I came really hard, screaming out her name, the blood rushing to my head . . .

As I came down from the orgasm, I kissed her tenderly.

"Sorry . . . I don't think I was very good going down on you. It felt a bit weird."

"That's OK. It was just brilliant."

"I liked putting my finger up your bum, though."

"That was really amazing."

"And I watched you squirt. I never knew girls could do that."

"Yeah. I do that quite a lot."

"God . . . incredible."

I kissed her softly. "Are we going to tell Jamie about this?"

"I don't know. Not yet maybe. What do you think?"

"I don't know. Let's think about it."

"I mean . . . you won't mind if he—you know—fucks me and stuff?"

"No—course not."

"Sure?"

"Yeah."

After she left, I felt dizzy with what had happened. From having been totally miserable a couple of days before, I now felt amazing. But I felt a bit funny when Jamie came back that evening. He was really nice to me, and I suppose I felt a bit of a hypocrite.

He started talking about his dad and my mum, how they weren't getting on very well. I had noticed it too, but I suppose I had been too wrapped up in myself to really think about it.

"This has happened before," he said, "with my mum in Australia. He sort of gets bored with people. And he's started drinking a lot."

"Yeah, I noticed he came back pissed the other day—and I heard them rowing."

"Trouble is, I don't know what to do. I don't want them to split up—do you?"

"No. Course not. It's weird, but I . . . like, feel this is the first time I've got to know you." I put my hand on his knee and stroked it. "I know that's a crazy thing to say, but we were never really close before. And now you and Lou have been really good about what happened with me and Maddie."

"Well, you and Lou have always been really close, haven't you?"

I felt myself blush a bit. "Yeah, I really like her."

He was silent for a moment. "Did you ever fancy her?"

"What?" I felt the blood really rush to my face. "Well, hey, you've made me blush!"

"So you did?"

"Yeah . . . yeah, I did. She's lovely. It'd be hard not to." I desperately wanted to change the subject. "So what do we do about your dad and my mum?"

"There's nothing we can do. I might talk to him, I suppose. He does listen to me sometimes."

I didn't see Lou for the next couple of days, but she rang me to say that she wanted all three of us to go to a party at the weekend. She thought it would be a good way for me to sort of "put a brave face" on what had happened. Then it would be easier going back to school the next week. I said I wasn't sure, but later I talked to Jamie and he persuaded me.

I remember dolling myself up for the party, and when I came downstairs ready to go, I saw my mum. She looked a bit drawn and preoccupied.

"Are you going out?" she said.

"You know I am," I said coldly. We still hadn't really talked since we had the row about Maddie.

"Don't be too late."

"We won't. I'm going with Jamie and Lou."

"All right." She sat down at the kitchen table and just sat there, running her hand over the surface.

"Mum—are you all right? Has Ray been upsetting you?"

"Oh, it's nothing. Ray . . . and—oh, nothing."

The party was really good. I felt a bit strange at first and saw a few people looking at me, but after a while I just got on and enjoyed myself—bopping and drinking and having a laugh. At one point, I went to the loo, and as I opened the door, Lou pushed in with me. She pushed me up against the wall and kissed me. She was really pissed.

"I need some lezzie," she said. "I want a good lezzie kiss." She kissed me again, messily.

I hugged her, running my hands all over her. She felt amazing. I lifted her blouse and felt her tits.

"Are you OK with everything?" she said.

"Yeah—I'm really glad you persuaded me to come."

"I really want to go to bed with you again. The last time was so fantastic."

"Me too."

"Come round tomorrow."

"OK."

There was a banging on the door, so we both quickly had a piss. As we were coming out, another girl was outside waiting.

"Oh, it's the dykey Sally," she said. "And—oh my God— the dykey Louise."

"Yeah, it is," said Lou. "We'll fuck you too if you like."

"Fuck off," said the girl, going in and slamming the door.

Lou looked at me wild-eyed and giggled. "Let's find Jamie," she said.

On the way home in the taxi, Lou sat in the back in between me and Jamie, one on either side. She put her arms round both of us, and we all cuddled up together. When we got to her house and the taxi stopped for her to get out, she pulled my face close to hers. "Goodnight, lovely girlfriend," she said, then kissed me full on the mouth. She tongued me for ages. I was gob smacked she'd done it so blatantly in front of Jamie—but she just turned to him and did the same. "Good night, lovely boyfriend." She threw her head back. "I've got one of each!" She shrieked with laughter, then suddenly pushed Jamie's and my faces together. "Go on—snog," she said, giggling. We both pulled back, but she pushed us harder. "Go on," she said.

I felt Jamie's mouth on mine—quite rough—but I also felt his tongue, and I touched it with mine. It was nice, exciting.

She laughed hysterically, let us go, and got up. She clambered out, and as the taxi pulled away, she staggered on the kerb, blowing us kisses.

Neither Jamie nor I said anything. I felt stunned because the kiss with him had been quite intense. We just looked at each other and smiled. When we got to our house, he paid the taxi, and I let us in.

"Do you want some tea?" I said.

"Yeah . . . yeah, why not?"

The house was silent. My mum was doing a night shift and presumably Ray was in bed.

"She's well pissed," I said as I came into the lounge with two mugs. "God—she's anyone's when she's like that."

"Well—she certainly seemed into you," he said, smiling. "Just as well you fancy her."

"Yeah, I do. It was nice. You didn't mind, did you?"

"I didn't mind any of it," he said, looking at me knowingly.

"No, nor did I," I said, smiling at him shyly.

He took my mug out of my hand, leant into me, and kissed me. I was almost paralysed. I didn't know how to react except to just return the kiss. It was different, but lovely. I was kissing a bloke, and feeling very turned on.

We became more passionate, put our arms around each other, and he pushed me down onto the sofa. Then I felt something I had never experienced before. His penis. It was hard and pressing into me. "What's that?" I said, giving him a knowing smile.

"Sorry," he said. "It's just, well, you know."

"You couldn't get your evil way with Lou tonight."

"No."

"It feels so big."

"Yeah."

"Well—what are we going to do about that?"

"I don't know."

I shifted from under him, then put my hand on it. "Can I see it? I mean—this is the first time I've been with a guy. I've never seen one before."

He blushed a bit. "OK . . ."

He turned over and laid back. I undid his trousers and pulled down his boxers—and there it was, long, hard, and laying along his stomach.

"Can I touch it?"

"Yeah. OK."

I took it in my hand. It was amazing. It was so hard. I ran my hand up and down, and I could feel the skin sheath moving over the stiff stalk inside.

He moaned softly. "Oh shit, that's really nice."

I laughed nervously. I felt a bit embarrassed. "Is it?"

"Yeah."

So I continued pumping it up and down, and he started closing his eyes and sighing. I kissed him again.

"Am I doing it all right?"

"Yeah . . . oh fuck, I'm going to come."

And suddenly, long spurts of white, creamy fluid shot out of the end—and he was moaning, his body tense. It splattered all over his stomach and shirt. Some of it splashed onto my hand.

I was really amazed.

"Was that nice?"

"Yeah . . . amazing."

"It happened so quickly."

"I was really excited."

I pulled a tissue out of my pocket and wiped my hand. "I liked doing it for you." I thought about Lou and felt guilty." Listen—like—there's something I've got to tell you."

"What?"

"Me and Lou . . . I mean, the reason she snogged me tonight was . . . well—fuck—I don't know how to tell you this."

"What?"

"We got it on together a couple of days ago."

He looked gob smacked. "What? Had sex?"

"Yeah."

"Wow."

"She . . . well, she said she kind of fancied me—only me, mind—and wanted to try it."

"And she liked it?"

"Yeah, a lot." I couldn't help myself smiling, but also blushed deeply. "I suppose it was something she wouldn't have suggested if she didn't know I was gay—you know."

"Yeah."

"I mean I felt a bit bad—because you didn't know." I looked at him. I wasn't sure what he was thinking. "You're not upset, are you? I mean, do you mind?"

Suddenly he smiled. "I think it's amazing. God . . . so sexy."

I laughed and kissed him.

I lay in bed that night thinking about it. It was all right, I told myself. He wasn't my real brother. And I knew that when he cuddled me I had felt a bit more than brotherly love. Somehow that was quite exciting. I fancied a guy, and that hadn't really happened before. But I had to tell Lou before anything else happened.

In the morning, I woke early and I crept to Jamie's room. He woke as soon as I went in and sat up in bed.

"Hi," I said.

"Hi. You all right?"

"Yeah. I woke early."

"Yeah. So did I. I've got to go to footie in a minute."

"But not just yet?"

"No. Come here."

He lifted the duvet and I slipped in next to him. I was wearing the same pyjamas as I had been with Lou just a couple of days before.

We wrapped our arms around each other and kissed passionately. He just had a pair of boxers on and it was lovely to feel his bare skin underneath my hands. His male torso was taut and different, his tongue really strong in my mouth. We kissed like that for a long time, and I was happy to let him lead—do what he wanted. It was just so amazing to feel myself so randy with a bloke.

He kissed my neck and pushed my top up. I quickly pulled it over my head and threw it off. He looked at my tits. "Do you like them?" I said.

"They're fantastic. Bigger than Lou's."

"Hers are different but lovely. Very suckable."

He put his hand on them and felt them. "You like sucking her tits, then?"

"Mmm. Her nipples are gorgeous."

He kissed me hard again. "God—it's so sexy to think of you and her together."

"Turns you on, does it?"

He rolled on top of me and pushed his legs between mine, his prick hard against my pussy. I moved my pelvis slowly, grinding my clitoris against it, only separated by the two sets of thin material. "I want you," he whispered. "I know I shouldn't, but I do."

"So do I," I said. "But not yet. I'm not going to cheat on Lou—not unless she's cool with it—OK?"

"All right."

"I'll give you a hand job. Take your boxers off."

He smiled and pushed his boxers down to his ankles.

I took his cock back into my hand. He put his arm around me and cuddled me to him as I began to slide my hand up and down. It was nice, him being naked. He had a good body. His chest and muscles were well developed. His was the first boy's body I had been close to. I kissed his shoulder, then laid my head on it. His cock felt amazing in my hand. It was hot and hard and there was a little bead of liquid coming out of the top. I pulled his foreskin back a bit further. He sighed. "Is that all right?"

"Yeah. You can pull it right back each time."

I tossed him longer and a little bit faster, my hand travelling right up and down, the red bulbous head appearing then disappearing beneath his foreskin. He began to moan.

"Yeah . . . fuck, that's so good. Oh, yeah. I'm coming . . . oh shit . . ."

"Oh yeah . . . I love it when you come."

He groaned loudly and jerked his hips as a long spurt shot out of the end. Then another came quickly, and another, scattering white droplets all over him. I pumped him hard, wanting to get every drop I could out of him.

After a few seconds he relaxed and I took my hand away. A little bit was on my fingers. I looked at it, then licked it off. The taste was strange again, but somehow really sexy.

He watched me. "Do you like the taste?"

"Yeah. I could get used to it. It tastes different to a girl."

"Do girls taste nice?"

"Haven't you been down on Lou?"

"No."

"You ought to try it. She tastes lovely." Our faces were close, and I could feel my attraction to him. It had been so sexy doing it for him, and I liked us cuddling together.

"You really do fancy her, don't you?" he said.

"Yeah, I do. She's lovely. It's funny, she's been a really good friend since we were small, and then like, I was suddenly thinking—I fancy you."

"She really likes you."

"And you as well. In fact, it looks like we're all getting the best of both worlds."

I took a tissue and began to mop up his stomach. "Anyway—look. I'm going to see her this morning. And I'm going to talk to her about—you know—stuff. You and me. Is that OK?" I threw the tissue in the bin.

He pulled a face. "I guess. Hope she's OK about it."

"I think she will be. She caused it, anyway. I think it's the way she wants it. Then we'll take it from there."

As soon as he was gone, I went back to my bedroom and got back into bed. Lying naked between the sheets, I felt so randy. I played with myself, going over in my mind what we had just been doing. I was so turned on by him. I knew I wanted to have full sex. I imagined it in my mind—him coming into me—that hot, hard shaft thrusting in and out of me. "Oh God, yeah, I want that," I whispered as I frigged myself. "Oh shit, yeah . . . yeah, yeah, OHHH FUUCKKK!"

I went round to Lou's midmorning. Her mother answered the door and gave me an odd look. "She's upstairs," she said. "Not feeling very well. She's going to miss church. She was in the shower a minute ago—I don't know whether she's finished yet." She called upstairs and I heard Lou come out of the bathroom. "It's Sally."

"Oh, OK. Come up, Sal."

"We're going to church, Louise, so you'll have to get yourself something to eat," her mother shouted, rather tetchily.

"Don't fancy it," I heard Lou say from inside her room.

When I went in, she was sitting in her dressing gown on the bed looking pale. I sat next to her, put my arm round her, and kissed her softly on the cheek. "Feeling a little off?"

"Oh shit . . . how much did I drink?"

"A lot more than me."

She turned to me and frowned comically. "You all right?"

"Fine."

"Smart-arse." She kissed me on the lips.

I felt a surge of attraction. *How weird,* I thought. *A couple of hours ago I was in bed with Jamie—and now I just want to make love to her.*

Her mother called up the stairs that they were leaving, and then there was the sound of the door closing. The house was silent.

"I wanted to have you, but I don't feel up to it," she said, smiling sheepishly.

"It's OK. Do you want a cuddle?"

"Yeah." She slipped her dressing gown off and got into the bed. She shifted to one side.

I hesitated.

"Come on," she said. "Take your kit off." She frowned. "What's the matter?"

I felt a lurch in my tummy. "You know, last night. When you made me snog Jamie?"

"Oh yeah, sorry about that."

"No. No—it was . . . well, look, don't hate me, but when we got into the house, we got it on."

Her face froze. "What—you and Jamie? I thought you were gay?"

"Yeah, so did I. I mean, Jamie and me, we're very close, so—I don't know."

"Did you have it off?" she said, sharply.

"Oh no. I said I wouldn't, not without you knowing."

"So you just snogged?" Her shocked eyes were scanning my face.

"Yeah—and I tossed him off."

"God," she said after a few seconds. "Making you snog was just a joke. I didn't mean it to have that effect."

"I know. I'm sorry, it just happened."

"And you didn't stop it."

"No."

"Did he get you off as well?"

"No. I was OK. Look, you don't hate me, do you?"

She pulled the duvet up to her chin and looked at me strangely. "No, of course I don't. I'm just shocked, that's all."

She looked away from me and didn't say anything for a moment. "Though he has said that he thought you were lovely looking in the past."

"Did he? I guess I didn't . . ." My voice trailed off. I didn't know what to say now.

She looked back at me and slowly a smile came to her face. "It's OK . . . I mean, I've had you, haven't I?" She looked at me for a minute—then she half smiled. "Come here."

I leant down and went to kiss her.

"Take your clothes off first."

I quickly undressed and slid into bed next to her. I wrapped myself around her gorgeous, warm body and we held each other close. "You're my best friend—and I really love you," I said, kissing her face and hair, "and I wouldn't want anyone to come between us."

"No, certainly not a fucking bloke, anyway." Her eyes were searching my face as though she was still thinking about what I had said. She kissed me softly. Her mouth tasted of toothpaste.

We kissed like that for a few minutes, just gently, tenderly.

"It's unbelievably sexy," she said, kissing me on the nose. "You and me, him and me, now him and you."

"Yeah." I felt the randiness rise up and kissed her hard, my hand squeezing her buttocks.

"Oh—careful—my head," she said, putting a hand to her forehead. "Oh shit . . ."

"Sorry," I whispered. "But you know what the best cure for a hangover is?"

"What?"

"A nice gentle orgasm."

She smiled wickedly. "OK."

"Just lay back." I kissed her neck, licking up into her hair and ears. I moved my hand round to her pussy and rubbed there slowly, moving my fingers in circles over the moist lips. She sighed as I took my time, tasting the smooth skin of her shoulders and chest.

Her tits were like little hillocks, topped by her puffy nipples. "I love your tits," I whispered. I licked round each one slowly, circling my tongue. She sighed softly, her eyes closed, her head lying back on the pillow. After a while, I took one of her nipples fully in my mouth and sucked very gently. Her pussy was slippery now, and I slid a finger easily inside.

"Oh, Sal. That's lovely."

Her skin was really nice, like a warm peach with the skin on, and she smelt lovely, clean and soapy. I kept going back to her nipples and kissing them. I could tell she loved it—and I just wanted to take my time with her, bring her off slowly.

I moved my finger around in her, gently rubbing around the fleshy walls inside. I drew it in and out, pushing farther inside every time. She had her head to one side, her eyes closed, and she was sighing softly. I felt such an incredible closeness to her. I had dryness in my throat and that wonderful throbbing lust in my stomach.

I kissed my way slowly and tenderly down her stomach until my mouth was hovering over her pussy. I breathed in the scent of her arousal—so amazing, that special smell a girl has when she is really turned on.

I adjusted my position on the bed and kissed her clitoris lightly.

"Oh, Sal, yeah, kiss me there."

I ran my tongue gently around it and covered it completely with my mouth. She moaned urgently and twisted against me, so that my finger slipped out. I could feel the little ridge between her pussy and bum with the tip of my finger, so I ran it down to her anus and circled it slowly.

"Oh, shit," she sighed.

"Do you like that?" I whispered, lifting my mouth away from her pussy, her juices covering my lips.

"Yeah, it's so nice."

Gently I pressed my finger against the opening. "And that?"

"Yeah . . . yeah—oh God . . ."

So I pushed, and my middle finger slid into her bum. Quickly, I put my index finger next to it and slid that into her pussy—then I began to pulse them both in and out, as tenderly as I could.

Her whole body writhed for a moment, and I could sense her muscles tightening all over her body. I licked her pussy more strongly now, curling my tongue round and round.

"Oh God . . . shit . . . SSSHHHITTTTTTTTTTTTTT!!!!"

Her orgasm seemed to come in little fits—and I pressed my fingers home, penetrating all the way, my mouth kissing her pussy, wet and running with juice.

She calmed and I moved up to lay beside her. "Nice?"

"Oh fuck—so amazing. You're incredible with that tongue of yours. And in my bum—God."

"I like that too—as you know," I said, kissing her face.

She hugged me and we kissed for a bit. "Do you want me to do you?" she said, after a while.

"No. You rest and nurse that hangover."

"OK. Tell Jamie I won't be up for it tonight, will you? My mum's really mad at me, and she won't let me go out."

"All right."

"You can look after him," she said, smiling knowingly.

We lay there cuddling for a bit—and after a few minutes she went to sleep.

I slid gently out of the bed and put my clothes back on, then I went over and kissed her lightly.

She seemed asleep—but just as I got to the door, she turned over. "Sal?"

"Yeah?"

"In the top drawer there." She pointed at the chest of drawers. "There are some condoms." She smiled at me. "Have fun."

I went to the drawer and found them.

"Take as many as you want—you randy bitch."

"Thanks," I said, going over to her again and kissing her lovingly.

Later, I had a bath. I was drying my hair when Jamie came in to my room.

"Hiya. All right?" I said, smiling at him.

"Yeah—you?"

"Yeah—good."

"How was Lou?"

"Hungover."

"I bet."

"She was in bed. So I joined her and we had a cuddle," I said casually. "She felt better after that."

"After what?" he said, flushing slightly.

I smiled at him provocatively. "After a nice lezzy orgasm. But she said that her mum won't let her come out tonight, I'm afraid, so you're just left with me."

"Oh. OK."

"She said maybe I could amuse you." I switched some music on my hi-fi. "What do you think?"

"Did you tell her what happened last night—you know, between us?"

"Yeah. I think she was a bit shocked at first. But she's cool with it."

"Really?"

"Yeah. She loves what she does with me—and what she does with you. And the thought of you and me together turns her on as well."

Looking at him, I slowly shifted my dressing gown off my shoulders, my hands across my tits, keeping the material in place. Then, when my shoulders were bare, I opened it down the front, again keeping my tits covered. I was gently rocking with the music, and as seductively as I could, I turned round, showing my back to him.

I let the dressing gown drop to the floor, still facing away from him, then slowly turned back, my hands still on my tits. I could see his eyes looking at them, willing me to take my hands away. I could see his cock was getting hard underneath his jeans. Slowly, I took my left hand and ran it through my hair, then the other, pushing my hair away from my face, my whole body, apart from my pussy, bare.

"God—you're so gorgeous," he said. He quickly undid his jeans, pushed them and his boxers down to his thighs, then put his hand on his penis and began to toss himself.

"You like the look of your little stepsister?"

Still keeping my eyes intently on his, I turned my back on him again slowly. I pushed my panties off my bum and wiggled it provocatively. Then I pushed them all the way to the floor and turned slowly, my hands covering my crotch.

"You want to see my pussy?" I said, stepping towards him.

"Yeah," he whispered.

I came right up to him and slowly took my hands away. My legs were touching his. I could feel my heart was beating quite fast, and I was getting really horny. "Do I live up to your expectations?"

"Yeah. Better."

"Let me do that for you," I said, looking at his cock. I sat down next to him and took his hand away from his cock. Instinctively, I put it on my breast. "I've had sex with your girlfriend already today—and now I'm going to have sex with you."

"Oh fuck," he said, looking at me intensely. Then he suddenly pulled me to him, kissing me full on the mouth. It felt electric, and I lay over him, kissing him deeply. His hands roamed my back and I could feel his cock hard against my stomach. I felt a surge of lust rush through me and a deep longing in my pussy. I shifted so that his cock was against my crotch and my clitoris tingled at the contact. Our tongues were wrestling together, and I knew my body was losing control.

"I want to do it with you," he said.

"Yes. Yes, I want you to. Fuck me, now." I was so wet I could feel my juice dribble down my leg as I lifted myself up and positioned myself above his rigid prick. I was about to have sex with a guy for the first time, and I could feel a slight bit of anxiety. Gingerly, I took it in my hand and guided it to my entry, then tentatively sank down on it.

I screamed out. I was no virgin—Maddie had seen to that—but whether it was from the pain of suddenly having him inside me, or from the intensity of the pleasure, I'm not sure—probably a bit of both. "Oh shit, it's so good." Anxiety flashed through my mind. I was unprotected and could get pregnant. "Wait," I said.

"What?"

I pulled myself off him and stepped over to my desk. I took one of the condoms I had put there and held it up. "Precautions."

"Oh right. Give it here," he said. He ripped the packet open and took out the rubber circle, then slowly unravelled it all the way down his cock.

I moved on top of him again and guided it back into me. I wanted him so much. This was my first straight sex, and I was loving it, sinking up and down on him, letting him fill me, feeling that incredible sensation inside me.

We kissed passionately, then I took his head in my hands and put his mouth onto my tits. "Suck them . . . oh yes, that's it . . ." An incredible wave of pleasure shot through me, and I felt the tension building in my groin. "Oh fuck, Jamie, I'm going to come. Oh God."

"Yeah . . . I'm going to come too . . . I can't hold it."

I hugged him to me and pounded myself up and down. He groaned and I could feel his cock swell inside me. He wasn't in my hand anymore, he was deep inside me, coming inside me, bringing me to the edge.

"OHHHHH YEAAA . . ." My whole body lit up with the most incredible orgasm. I was crying out at each wave of pleasure, crushing myself down on him, stars appearing in my eyes so I could hardly see . . .

I relaxed on top of him and kissed him tenderly. I could still feel him hard inside me amid the glow of my climax.

"Oh, Jamie, that was so incredible. So amazing, so quick."

"Yeah. Fantastic."

I smiled at him and kissed his nose. "Well, as soon as you walked into the room, I think I knew we were going to do it."

I raised myself off him. He took off the condom, and I could see all the spunk gathered in the end. I collected some of it left on his prick and tasted it. "Mmm . . . lovely."

"You've got a thing about my spunk."

"Maybe I have. Tastes so weird."

I knelt on the floor in front of him and took his prick in my hand. He was still hard, and I massaged him slowly. I looked at it. It was red and glistening and I knew I wanted to take it in my mouth. Looking at him, I lowered my head and engulfed it. It smelt of the condom, but the taste of his cum almost sort of fizzed in my mouth. The feel of his cock was amazing—so warm and strong and pulsing. I took it as far in as I could, but when it hit the back of my throat it made me want to gag. So I took him in and out, sort of fucking him with my mouth.

I raised my head and jerked him with my hand for a bit, feeling it grow even harder. He was sighing, but I didn't want him to come that way.

I stood up and pulled him to his feet, then I lay on the bed. I spread my legs. "Now fuck me again."

"Have you got another condom?"

"Yeah—in my draw there."

He got it, unwrapped it, and slid it on his prick.

He lay on top of me, and I guided it into me. As he pushed up inside, I gasped at how nice it felt.

"Lou was so lovely this morning," I said. I thought of her small, petite body, tiny tits, and pretty rosy face. I let the fantasy run and pictured myself sucking her tits, licking her pussy, kissing those sweet lips. Warmth spread from my pussy all over me. "Oh, I love sex," I said. I curled my legs round his body and sighed as he kissed my neck. He was pushing in and out of me and the feeling was so fantastic. We seemed to be a perfect fit. His prick was narrow, but really long, and when he was right in, it seemed to hit the end and make me shiver. He felt snug in my vagina. Maddie always used to say I had a tight little crack.

He was fucking me quite hard, pushing my legs out ever wider. We could both take longer now and had more control. I just loved the feeling of him slipping in and out of me. I'd had all sorts of things inside me when Maddie and I messed around—I'd even had a carrot that she had brought for her lunch—but this was the first penis, hard and hot, like the core of him, extending out. I pushed my clit up against him every time he thrust into me, and it sort of sparked, causing a lovely sensation. I gyrated my hips in tandem with getting him as deep as possible and getting his prick to move around inside me.

The walls of my vagina were getting hot with the friction, and I realised that sex with guys was such a different feeling. I could feel my nipples were really hard and the roughness of his face seemed to add to the pleasure. It was also his male strength, the fitness of his body, the lovely muscles in his arms and chest. He had such nice blue eyes, and I loved gazing into them as we panted and moaned, physically joined together.

"Do you like fucking your little sister?" I whispered.

"Yeah . . ."

"Because we are, in one way, aren't we? We've lived together for years, and our parents are married. I've always thought of you as my big brother, and you still are."

He started to come into me harder, grunting with the effort of each thrust.

"Yeah, I'm fucking my little sister, and I'm loving it."

I suddenly felt a spark from my clit and screamed out. "Yes . . . big brother, fuck me . . . FUCK MEEEE . . ." My orgasm rose like a violent muscular contraction, and I reared my back off the bed.

"Come on, sister, come . . . COME!" he groaned.

My body tightened all over as the climax burned through me, once, twice, and again. Even though my body was moving all over the bed, he was still coming into me, that long, hard prick sending convulsions through me. I grabbed his shoulders and clung to him, thinking the ecstasy would never end.

It suddenly died, and I flopped back onto the bed, my heart racing. "Ohhh God . . ." I whispered, hardly able to get my breath. "That was so amazing. This incest thing really does it for me." My pussy was hot and wet and I could feel I had ejaculated. I was wet all round my bum, and the sheet was soaked.

"Did you come?" I said.

"Not yet."

He was still moving in me, sending little aftershocks into my stomach.

"Can I fuck you from behind? I like that."

"Sure."

He pulled out, and his penis reared up, red and glistening, the condom stretched round it. "We're so wet," he said.

"Yeah. That's me. Sorry."

"It's OK."

I turned over onto my knees and crouched so that my face was on the pillow and my bum in the air. The wetness in my bum meant I could feel the air around my anus; it felt nice. I heard him reposition himself and then his cock probed me. I put a hand behind and guided him in.

"Oh shit . . ." he moaned as he thrust right into me.

"Oh fuck, so deep," I cried. It felt so good, and his moving in and out was lovely against my bum. I suddenly felt him swell in size and he fucked me sharply several times in and out before grunting loudly.

"Oh fuck—yeah. Yeah . . . YEAH . . ."

I squeezed my pussy muscles as tightly as I could—and he jerked into me a few times until I could tell he was spent.

We lay there for a few minutes, him on top of me. Eventually, he pulled out, got off the bed, and took off the condom. "Where shall I put it?"

"Just put them in the bin. I'll get rid of them later."

He came back and joined me on the bed.

"Well," I said. "Aren't you a lucky boy? Two girls to have when you want to."

On the Monday, I went back into school—and it was OK. There were a few odd looks, but nothing to speak of—and Lou and Jamie made a point of supporting me by hanging out and being really nice. I was so relieved. I knew that there might be some shit at some point, but I guess I was so taken up with what had happened to the three of us that it seemed less important.

"We did it," I whispered to Lou when I got her on her own.

"Did you?" she said, her face scanning mine.

"Yeah, it was fantastic."

"Yeah, well, he is a good screw."

"You sure you don't mind?"

She glanced around, checking no one could hear. "Course not—I told you. I gave you the condoms, didn't I?"

"Yeah. I'm going to the doctor tomorrow morning to get on the pill."

"Good. Well, I'm having him tonight," she said.

"Yeah, yeah, I know. No problem. He better not fuck me again until it's safe—you know."

"I love you," she whispered. Then, quickly glancing around, she kissed me lightly.

Sally's fingers were wet and sticky with her cum and she licked them slowly. She hadn't been able to stop touching herself as she sifted through those memories, and when she had thought about Jamie, she had climaxed sharply. She wondered what he was doing now. They had tried to keep in touch; she used to go to the Internet cafe and email him, but slowly they communicated less and less. *It's a long way,* she thought. *The other side of the world.*

She felt sad that she and Lou had fallen out so badly. They hadn't spoken for three years. Even when her mother was acutely ill, Lou hadn't bothered to get in touch.

But then that's what people are like.

Her mobile blared out next to her on the bed. She pressed the green button. "Hello?"

"Hi. Is that Sally?"

"Yes." The voice sounded strangely familiar, but Sally couldn't place it.

"It's Lou. Louise Maynard."

"Oh . . . my God." Sally felt a strong sense of shock—then a pang of anxiety in her stomach. "Hi."

"I tried this number, but wasn't sure whether it would still be the same."

"Yeah. I haven't changed it or anything."

"How are you?"

"Yeah . . . yeah, I'm fine."

"Good."

There was a silence.

"I just wanted to sort of make contact again. I know we, like, fell out at school, but I just thought I didn't want to leave things like that."

"Yeah. I see."

"I mean, I know it's been a bit of a long time, but, well, better late than never."

"Sure."

"Could I come and see you?"

"Well, I'm not in Birmingham anymore."

"Oh really?"

"No. I'm working on a farm near Stratford."

"Oh. That's nice."

"Yeah."

"Well, could I come there then?" she said brightly.

"Sure. I live in a cottage. I'd better explain how you get here. It's a bit out of the way."

She gave her the instructions, and they arranged to meet a few days later.

She went back into the kitchen and poured herself a glass of wine. That was totally weird. They hadn't spoken for three years. Then today, Sally had been getting herself off thinking about her—and it was almost as though she had conjured her up. Bizarre . . .

Chapter 10

Sophie chatted nonstop as they drove through the country-side to her parents' house. The weather was overcast, but warm, and Emma felt relaxed and happy.

"My father will just love you," she said.

"Why?"

"Because you are so beautiful. He loves lovely young girls. He will want to paint you."

"Naked?"

"Yes. Would that worry you?"

"Well, I don't know. Taking off my clothes in front of someone I don't know."

"He's an artist. It's not like anyone else. He does do paint-ings of people clothed, but most are naked."

"Well, I don't know."

"He has painted a lot of my friends. They said that after a while, they lost any inhibitions. He is very charming."

"Has he painted you naked?"

"Of course, hundreds of times—at all ages. I will show you." Sophie leaned across and kissed her cheek. "Don't worry. He's not a pervert or anything. But as a family, we are very open about these things."

Emma raised her eyebrows, and Sophie burst out laugh-ing. "You look so worried. Don't be. My family is lovely."

They drove on in silence for a bit, Sophie looking out of the window, watching the countryside go by. Emma turned briefly to look at her. She was at her most ebullient and lively and looked lovely. She had never met anyone like her before. She was outrageous and so extreme in some ways—espe-cially sexually—which in other people might have made her wary. She'd been so blatant in the way that she'd seduced

Emma—and what she was doing with the priest was in some ways very shocking. But it was all set off by her disarming innocence and loving nature, which Emma found so captivating. And now she was faced with the prospect of her father maybe wanting to paint her naked. *Well,* she thought, *I'd better try to go with the flow.*

"I know you are on the pill, but do you want Antoine to use a condom?" said Sophie suddenly.

"No. Without is fine."

"Good. I don't like condoms, which I know isn't very wise, but I like to feel the man's flesh against mine, sliding in and out of me." She slid her hand along the inside of Emma's thigh. "And I hate a man's penis smelling of rubber when I want to suck it."

"I'm sure none of us have got any horrible diseases, have we?"

"No, of course not. But he'll use one if you prefer it."

"Well, look. Can I see—you know—how I feel about it when I meet him? I mean, I did quite fancy him when we met, but . . ."

"Sure. But I will make love to him anyway."

"Oh yeah—yeah, of course."

Half an hour later, they drove up to a large, impressive-looking house. It had a long front, three stories high, punctuated with traditional French-style shuttered windows and covered in a rambling climber. The front door had ornate pilasters on either side and a small pediment, and at the far end, there was a round turret that looked much older than the rest of the building.

Sophie jumped out of the car. "Do you like it? It's lovely, isn't it?" she said excitedly. "Parts of it date back to the fifteenth century."

They took their bags from the car and walked through the entrance. A spacious, rather baroque-looking hall greeted them, the panelling painted yellow, with gilded arcading. Doors led off from either side, a large marble fireplace faced them, and the room was sparsely furnished, with two antique sofas and a gilded mirror above the fireplace. The floor was paved with two different colours of stone. The room was high, with a large central chandelier.

"Come through," said Sophie. "Let's find Mama." She took one of the doors to the right that led down a long, low, wood-panelled passage. At the end it opened onto a roomy kitchen with a low-beamed ceiling. It had a large fireplace with a heavy beam across it and a log fire was burning, even though it was hardly cold outside. A large wooden breakfast table stood in the middle of the room with chairs around. A tall dresser was on the right of the room, loaded with china, and a cooker and fridges on the left.

"Mama!" said Sophie as her mother entered.

"Sophie!"

Sophie ran up to her, kissed her on the mouth, and hugged her. "This is Emma."

Her immediate impression of Sophie's mother was a very attractive woman of about forty, dressed in jeans and what looked like a man's shirt. She smiled and came up to Emma, took both her hands, and kissed her on both cheeks. "Welcome," she said in English. "How lovely to have you here. Sophie has been telling me how pretty you are, and she is right."

"Thank you," said Emma. "It's lovely to be here." *She must have been very beautiful when she was young,* thought Emma. Her complexion was so like Sophie's—and though a little plump, she had aged so well.

"Would you like to take Emma up to your room? I have made up the bed next door as well, as Antoine is coming. I don't know what you want to do." She smiled at Emma in a warm, open way, as though saying she would not be so vulgar as to ask what the sleeping arrangement would be. "Maybe you would like something to eat now?" she said. "Dinner will not be until eight."

"Yes. Some bread or something," said Sophie. "I think we are both a bit hot after the journey. Maybe we'll go down to the river and have a swim. Emma, would you like that?"

"Yeah, why not? Sounds lovely. I'll get my bikini out of my bag."

"No, no. There's no need."

"It is very private," said Sophie's mother. "We own that part of the river."

"Oh, OK."

"Come, let's get some towels."

They stopped by a large cupboard in the corridor, formed from the wooden panelling that ran all along. Sophie pulled two towels from a shelf and shut the door, then she led them back the way they had come, only turning right down a passage to a side door at the back of the house.

It led onto a terrace with a stone balustrade that looked out over a formal garden. They walked to the end of the terrace, through the formal garden, and then down some steps to a rough lawn bordered by trees. Sophie took Emma's hand and kissed her on the cheek. "OK?"

"Yes, fine. Your mother is very nice. Lovely looking."

"Yes, she is, isn't she?"

As they entered the trees, Emma could see that a path led away and descended quite steeply. The path wound down the slope diagonally, and eventually Emma began to see glimpses of water through the gaps in the trees in the wood. When they reached the bottom a few minutes later, an expanse of a slowly moving, pale-green river spread out in front of them. It was quite wide, a good twenty metres to the other side, and to the right a line of stones broke the surface, and the river tumbled into rapids beyond.

"It is fairly deep here," said Sophie, "although my father had flat stones laid across the bottom at the side, so it is easy to get in." She slipped out of her clothes. "Come on."

"Are you sure no one can see?" Emma said.

"Don't be silly."

"OK."

Emma undressed, then slid her arms around Sophie and hugged her from behind. The touch of her warm, fragrant skin sent a shiver through her. "Thank you for bringing me here," she said, kissing her on the shoulder.

Sophie turned her head and kissed her lightly on the lips. "I love it, and I love my family. We're not like other people, but I hope that doesn't shock you too much."

"No, of course not."

Sophie turned and took her in her arms. "You've hardly seen anything yet." She kissed Emma again, deeply this time. Emma felt her press her groin against her, and she did the same, feeling a little spark from her clitoris. "I'm going to make love to you in my bed."

"Like you have with other girls?"

"Oh yes." They kissed again, more passionately. Their mouths and tongues moved and wrestled with each other and Emma felt her skin surge with lust.

"But first, we swim!" she said, suddenly breaking away and splashing into the water.

Emma laughed and followed her, stepping a little slower. The water was surprisingly warm and felt very soft on her skin. Sophie had swum a little distance away upstream, and when she caught up with her, Emma could see her eyes had that wild, mischievous look.

Emma rarely swam in river water, and she thought how delicious it felt. They swam to the other side, where a small shingle-covered beach came into view. Sophie walked onto it and sat on a log washed up at the side. Emma waded out and sat next to her.

"This is so lovely," she said, putting her arm around Sophie's shoulders.

"Yes, isn't it? I've been coming here as long as I can remember."

"The water is really quite warm."

"It always is in the summer." She looked up, then shrieked, looking across the river the way they had come. "Papa!" She leapt up and dived back into the water and began to swim back to the other side.

Emma looked across and saw someone standing by the water's edge. It was a tall man in an open-necked shirt. He was staring intently at her. Emma stood up, but immediately felt embarrassed that she had nothing on. She followed Sophie back into the water, quickly submersing herself.

Sophie reached the other side, ran out, and threw her arms around her father, kissing him. Emma reached the river's edge, but remained under the water.

Sophie turned to her. "Emma, come and meet my father."

Emma hesitated, but then saw there was nothing for it but to stand up. Self-consciously, she walked out of the water towards them.

His eyes devoured her body, and he seemed completely unembarrassed that he was looking at her in such a provocative way. He had Sophie's eyes—or rather she had his, she thought, which made his stare all the more penetrating. His face was good-looking, with a rugged air that seemed to suit his greying hair. He was dressed in dark trousers with a white shirt.

"My God. Where did you come from?" he said. His accent was very English, slightly posh.

Emma nervously ran her hands through her wet hair, but he continued to eye her up and down. Sophie in the meantime put her arm around Emma, and ostentatiously kissed her on the lips.

"Isn't she beautiful? I told you she was the loveliest girl I had ever seen."

"Sophie had raved to us about you, but I didn't believe her. Not until now, anyway."

"Hello," she said shyly.

"I must paint you."

His eyes were so penetrating. They seemed to sink into her, and she felt her tummy quiver. "Er . . . yes," she stammered.

"Good. Later on then." He began to undress, casting a smile at them.

"Is it warm?"

"Yes. It's lovely," said Sophie.

He pushed his trousers to the floor and stepped out of them. He was wearing nothing underneath. He smiled at them, completely unembarrassed at his nudity.

Emma couldn't help her eyes from flashing down to his penis, which hung limp and quite long. His body was a little plump, and his skin showed the slight sagging of age, but he was generally in good shape.

"Come, let's go," said Sophie.

"Right," said Emma. She picked up her clothes and went to put them on.

"Don't bother, we're going to have a shower now."

"Oh. OK."

Sophie began to walk away up the track, her clothes in her hand. Emma followed, but cast a glance back at the river. Sophie's father was swimming on his back, looking at her. For some reason, she hesitated for a moment, turned to face him, and ran her free hand through her hair. It felt like his eyes were gently stroking her body.

Back in the house, they went back down the central corridor—away from the kitchen—then up a wooden staircase that was old and slanted, lit by a large window with stained glass. The rest of the house didn't seem to live up to the grandeur of the entrance hall, and as they reached the top of the stairs, they came into a passage that was painted white but punctuated with timbers down the walls and across the ceiling.

Sophie's room was in the wing that ran off the main house. It was entered by a low doorway. It had a large antique bed with polished wood at the head and foot. To the left, the shutters were closed across the tall windows. Sophie ran across, opened the sash inwards, then threw the shutters open. The fading evening light poured in and revealed a view across fields of light green crops. Across the other side of the room, another window was already open, with the tinkling sound of a fountain drifting up from the courtyard below.

"This is lovely," said Emma.

"Yes, it is, isn't it? And it's only tidy because I've been away. Normally it's a pigsty. Do you like my bed?"

"Yeah—looks great."

Sophie put her arms around Emma's neck. "I'm so glad you're here." She kissed Emma sexily. "Let's have a shower."

As Emma put down her clothes on the bed, she suddenly noticed the wall behind her. On it was hanging a full-length painting. Whilst it was definitely a painting, it was of an almost photographic clarity, superbly finished. It was of two girls, lying together, naked on a bed. One of the girls seemed a bit older than the other, although both were obviously young when they were painted. The two were lying close, looking at each other, one girl's hand on the other's stomach, smiling as though they were talking.

Emma couldn't stop looking at it, it was so beautiful. The colours were so subtle, the expressions so telling.

"You like it?" said Sophie.

"Yes. It's lovely. Who are they?"

"They are friends of my father's. They're so beautiful, don't you think?"

"Yes, lovely. And this is the kind of thing he does all the time?"

"Yes. I told you—he paints people naked. That's what he does. He has always painted me naked, ever since I was a little girl."

"Isn't that a bit—you know—dangerous nowadays?"

"Why? He paints us as he sees us—as his daughters."

"Yes, of course."

"Come on. The bathroom is down the passageway."

She felt strange walking around the house naked, but assumed that nobody would think it odd in Sophie's family. The bathroom was very modern, with a large corner shower. They both got in, and Sophie turned on the water. The showerhead was very wide and cast an intense jet of water on them both. Emma pulled Sophie to her and hugged her, kissing her deeply.

Their showers together were always so sexy. Emma loved to rub soap all over Sophie, and they would wash each other's hair, massaging their scalps, kissing all the time. Frequently at the chateau, showering would end in them making love under the hot, invigorating water.

Emma felt Sophie's hand roam between her legs; her palm cupped her vagina and her fingers ran tantalisingly between her buttocks, softly grazing her anus. *I want to make love looking at that picture in the bedroom,* thought Emma—and she pulled Sophie's mouth to hers and kissed her hard. She ran her hands luxuriously over Sophie's soap-covered, slippery body. "Oh God," she whispered, as she felt Sophie's fingers slip inside her pussy and her skin surge with sensation. "You'll make me come like that."

"Come on," said Sophie. "Let's go back to the bedroom and make love on the bed."

They dried each other off and brushed their teeth, laughing, touching, kissing, then went back to Sophie's bedroom. Emma threw herself on the bed and lay looking up at the painting. It was so lovely. Two gorgeous, young, nubile bodies. Sophie lay next to her on the bed and leaned over and kissed her. "Let's do a *soixante-neuf*," she whispered in Sophie's ear.

"Yes," said Sophie excitedly, and she sat up and put her leg over Emma, turning herself round so that she was crouching the other way, the two round cheeks of her buttocks open to reveal the pink gash of her vagina and the little ribbon of flesh leading to her neat, puckered anus. Her thighs were slim and taut as they splayed across the bed, lowering the delicate sex to Emma's waiting mouth.

Emma sighed as she felt Sophie's hot mouth engulf her own pussy and her body suffuse with a warm gush of desire. She put her tongue up to Sophie's vaginal lips and licked the full length slowly and down again, slipping it around the nub of her clitoris. It tasted of soap, but as her tongue continued to caress the delicate skin, she began to taste the love juice seeping from her.

Only five weeks ago this would have seemed unthinkable, she thought. *To be having oral sex with another girl.* She loved this position, feasting her tongue on Sophie's sex, while feeling the hot pleasure of her lover's mouth on her own pussy. For several long, delectable minutes, they pleasured each other in ways they had so many times before in the past five weeks, their tongues exploring and teasing, loving each other in this most intimate of places.

Emma rested her head on the pillow for a moment and wrapped her arms around Sophie's legs, grasping her buttocks in either hand. They were smooth and voluptuous, and Emma fondled them, running her thumbs along the cleft.

She raised her head and slid her tongue into Sophie's vagina. She pushed it in as far as she could, then moved the tip around, caressing the inside of the hot sheath.

She felt Sophie's mouth lift off her pussy and heard a sigh. Emma pulled her tongue a little way out and then began to pump it slowly in and out. Her tongue began to ache, but she ignored it, pulling Sophie's buttocks closer to her, her nose grazing lightly against her anus.

Quickly, she licked one of her fingers and teased Sophie's sphincter, running rings around it and pressing in the centre.

"Ah yes, yes . . . it's so good . . . YESSSSS . . . AAAAH-HHHH!"

A flow of salty, sweet liquid inside her soaked Emma's tongue and her vagina opened, as if wanting her deeper in. Emma carried on loving her, her tongue hurting now, as she sensed Sophie's orgasm reach its height. Emma pushed in as far as she could, pressing her face against the wet lips. Sophie tensed for a moment, pushing her pussy down onto Emma's mouth. She tensed again, each time uttering a high-pitched cry.

She relaxed and Emma felt her head relax onto her thighs. "Oh . . . so good . . ."

Sophie lifted herself off Emma and lay beside her, her head still above her pussy. As the tender licking began again, Emma stretched her legs wide and sighed. She opened her eyes and realised that now that Sophie had moved, she could see the portrait.

The wonderful waves of pleasure seemed to bring out the eroticism in the picture. Emma could see that the two girls seemed to have an intimacy and ease with each other that made her wonder about their relationship. He had pictured them so at ease with their nudity, but at the same time there was a blush, a strange excited anticipation between them. The older girl's hand was spread out on the other's stomach as though relishing the seductive warmth of her friend's skin.

Emma felt Sophie's fingers pull her vagina open and her lively tongue delve inside her. She writhed on the bed, closing her eyes as delicious shimmerings scattered from head to foot. The soft fresh cotton of the duvet seemed to close round her like another lover and she moaned as the sensations coalesced in her groin.

She opened her eyes, and this time she studied the faces of the two girls: close, so loving, the hint of saliva glistening on the younger girl's lips that were slightly parted, a look of deep longing in the innocent eyes. She looked so young, and her hand was playing with the other's hair in the way that a young girl would.

Sophie's tongue snaked out of Emma's pussy and travelled down across the little line of skin to her anus. It played round her sphincter for a few seconds, causing her to tremble.

She cried out as it trailed to her clitoris, sucking on it, her tongue playing, teasing, torturing. "Oh God, Sophie . . . please . . . finger-fuck me . . ." She kept her eyes on the portrait, and it seemed to her that the two mouths must be closing together, the bodies about to touch, that hand inching its way lower.

She was torn away from it as Sophie's fingers entered her, pushing slowly inside, flexing inside her like some small loving creature, then drawing in and out in an irresistible rhythm. Her mind seemed to complete the story of the picture in front of two young girls finding each other in the joys of a deep sexual love. "OHHHH YESSS, I LOVE YOU!!!"

The tight ball of tension waiting in her abdomen burst hotly, exploding the orgasm across her, sending her body into every contortion of pleasure.

"I was looking at the painting as you made love to me," said Emma, as she put on a pair of white panties and a light, close-fitting summer dress—quite short, with no bra.

"Did it make you come harder?"

"Yes, it was so lovely."

Sophie, still naked, walked over to her and put her arms around her neck. She kissed Emma, and as her tongue played sexily in Emma's mouth, she could feel the incredible sexual hunger, the fathomless appetite that throbbed in that beautiful body.

"You're amazing," whispered Emma as their lips slowly parted.

"And you're so beautiful," said Sophie.

They kissed for a few seconds more, then continued getting dressed. Sophie pulled on a T-shirt and a short skirt, with nothing underneath. "I wear very little when I'm at home," she said.

"How did I guess?" said Emma.

They walked hand in hand back down to the kitchen, where Sophie's mother was busy cooking. A bottle of sparkling wine was open on the table.

"Do you want something to eat now, or are you happy to wait?" said her mother.

"I'm not that hungry," said Emma.

"We'll have some wine," said Sophie. She went to the dresser and took down two glasses, then poured the wine into them. She handed one to Emma.

"Sophie, could you lend me a hand with dinner?"

"Sure."

"Can I help?" said Emma.

"I'd rather you came to help me," said a voice behind them.

Emma recognized Sophie's father's voice and turned to see him leaning on the door. His shirt was now hanging open at the front. He had an odd, enigmatic smile that she had seen sometimes on Sophie's face. "Come with me."

"OK," said Emma, glancing at Sophie.

Sophie smiled and winked. "See you later, *cheri*."

She followed him back towards the entrance hall, then he took a door opposite down a corridor. It was decorated much like the entrance hall, only slightly less ornate. Off it led two doors: One was open, and she could see an elegant dining room with a large table. Sophie's father kept walking, however, and at the end of the corridor he opened another door that opened onto a vast space.

It was glazed at the top completely, and there were a series of French doors on the left-hand side. The whole room was painted white, and the evening light suddenly seemed much brighter. Everywhere there were paintings, hanging up or in racks. Emma found herself greeted by the naked human body. Some were single pictures. Others had two or even three figures in a sexual embrace of some kind.

"This is my studio."

"God. Incredible." Everywhere she turned, a nude form greeted her. She did a double take at one picture, suddenly realising it was of Sophie's mother, Therese. She was much younger and extremely beautiful. Slim, with a flawless complexion, her expression was of a purity of innocence mixed with a strange, almost wanton sexuality.

"That must be Sophie's mother."

"Yes. Isn't she gorgeous?"

"Yes. Beautiful. I can see Sophie in her."

"Some of them are my favourites that I like to keep here, but most of these are just waiting on collection—or I have to make some alteration at the client's request. I hate that. The finished painting is what I see, then that's that. But if they won't pay until it's changed, I just have to do it."

As they walked down the length of the room, Emma saw a platform with a bed, surrounded by curtains, a bit like a stage set.

"What's that?"

"People lie on that sometimes to pose. Or even make love on it. I had a couple in recently. Here, it's just been finished. During one session, they got off on fucking in front of me."

Emma turned and just to the side of the platform there was a tall painting, depicting two figures.

"Isn't that . . . ?"

"Yes. She's so lovely, I think. Mind you, so is he."

Emma instantly recognised a famous young British actress, presumably with her boyfriend. She stared at it. It was so incredibly lifelike, the resemblance perfect, and the detail and colouring uncanny in its reality. They were both on a bed, naked. There was a slight blush on her cheek, and she was looking up at him sexily. He was looking down in rapt anticipation.

"My God."

He laughed softly. "I'm doing more of them. So I did a film of them."

"A film?"

"Yeah. That way I can keep a record of what they look like and what shape they are."

"A film of them naked?"

"Yes. I don't keep them. As soon as the paintings are finished, I destroy them. Films are ultimately pornographic, voyeuristic. My paintings are erotic. That's a completely different thing. Here—sit there." He pointed to a large, softly upholstered white sofa that stood in front of an easel over by the French door.

Emma sat on it and lay back. Her short skirt ran up her thighs—and she immediately saw his eyes sweep over them. She felt a strange quivering in her stomach. What she had seen in the last few moments had left her in a kind of shock. "I don't know your name," she said.

"Gerald—and don't call me Gerry."

"Right."

"Your glass is empty. Here, let's get some more." He walked over to a large antique cabinet. When he opened it, there was a fridge inside. He took another bottle of sparkling wine out of it and began to undo the neck.

"That's a clever way to disguise a fridge."

"Yes. The cabinet's Louis the fourteenth, and the fridge, Jacques Chirac. I had them put together in Paris." He opened the bottle with a pop. "Here—*blanquette,* the most marvellous local wine. Its provenance is older than champagne." He took her glass and filled it.

She took a large mouthful, feeling the bubbles seemingly shoot straight to her head.

He put down the bottle and took up his pencil. He sketched on the pad on the easel, his eyes constantly flicking between the paper and her. "So you like my daughter?"

"Yes. She's lovely."

"You like having sex with her?"

Emma flushed slightly at the directness of the question. "Yes. She's a wonderful lover."

"It never ceases to amaze me how many gorgeous girls she manages to seduce."

"How do you know she seduced me?"

"She's normally very proactive."

Emma laughed. "Yes. She was. Mind you, it took her a couple of days before I let her into my knickers. Since then it's been five weeks of bliss." There was a pause. The wine was quickly going to her head, but it made her realize that she could just be shocked by all this—or she could try and relax and see where things led. "So—do I get to keep my clothes on in this session, Gerald?"

"For the moment. I am sketching your face."

She stretched on the chair and looked at him. His face was slightly sardonic, she thought. He rarely smiled, although his eyes smiled for him a lot of the time. His eyes were less green than a kind of dark grey, but were so vivid and penetrating, just like Sophie's. "I like the picture in Sophie's room," she said after a while.

"Yes. It's one of my favourites."

"The girls look lovely together."

"They're sisters."

"Sisters?"

"Yes. They're daughters of a friend of mine."

"How old were they when that painting was done?"

"Oh, I don't know. Sixteen and eighteen?"

"They seem so intimate, the way you have painted them."

"Well, that's the way they are. They always have been."

"If they're sisters, why did you paint them naked?"

"Why not? It emphasises their closeness—and their innocence. Anyway, that family are naturists."

Emma caught her breath—and felt a rash of shock shiver across her skin.

He looked at her provocatively. "We've always encouraged being natural in our family, too. We are used to being naked with each other, kissing on the mouth, that sort of thing."

"I noticed."

"Does it intimidate you?"

"No."

Emma took another long draught of her drink as she let the image of the two sisters sink in. She could feel shock and excitement competing in her mind. "So you must have a procession of beautiful young girls in here. Isn't that a temptation for you?" she said, letting her eyes rest on him.

"Yes, I love it."

"Do you ever succumb to their charms?"

"No, I never have sex with them. That would mean I couldn't paint them. I have to be excited internally. Sense what makes them so beautiful."

"Keep your spunk in your balls, you mean?"

"Yes, if you like." He looked at her, his eyes gleaming. "I allow myself to touch, to feel, but no more."

"Sounds like a bit of artistic bullshit to me. If you like touching up young girls, why don't you just say so?"

He smiled, looking at her in an old-fashioned way. "Think what you like. I can't paint a girl if I've fucked her. Anyway, Therese wouldn't like it."

She drained her glass and held it out to him. "So does that mean that I'm about to be touched up?"

"Not if you don't want to be." He reached for the bottle and leant over her and filled her glass.

"I certainly like the way your daughter touches me up." She held his gaze while taking another long drink from her glass. "So maybe being touched up by you is something I shouldn't miss."

He picked up the bottle and refilled her glass again, although it was still half full. "Could you take your dress off?" he said, casually. "I want to sketch your shoulders."

"I wondered when that would be coming. Can't you remember? You had a good look earlier."

She stared at him provocatively for a moment, then stood up slowly, her head slightly dizzy from the amount of wine she had drunk. Still staring at him, she pulled her dress over her head and dropped it behind her on the sofa. She then stepped out of her shoes and sat down again. She watched his eyes drift over her body and rest on her pubic mound sitting beneath the little slip of her panties. "Do you need to see my pussy to sketch my shoulders?"

"I want to feel your nakedness."

"Oh . . . I see. Sure." Lightly, she pushed the little slip of material down her legs, to the floor. Then she lay back, slowly opening her legs, still staring at him.

His eyes were smouldering, devouring her body. "You're exquisite."

"Thank you." She lay her head back, closed her eyes, and let her hands wander across her breasts and rest on her stomach. "I think I like posing for you."

She heard footsteps approaching and looked at the door. Sophie appeared.

"Hello," she said and walked over to Emma and sat next to her. "Supper is nearly ready." She put her arm around Emma's shoulders and kissed her on the cheek. She appeared totally unsurprised that Emma was naked.

Emma turned her head and kissed her on the mouth. He was watching them, and she felt it feed her lust.

As their mouths parted, Sophie smoothed the palm of her hand across Emma's breasts and stomach. "Are you enjoying posing for my father?"

Emma turned her gaze on Gerald. "Yes, I think I am."

He put his pencil down and picked up his glass. "If supper is ready, we can continue tomorrow."

"I'll look forward to it," she said. She put her hand on Sophie's face and kissed her again. The softness of her beautiful lips sent shivers down her spine. She heard Gerald leave the room.

"We'd better go and join the others," said Sophie, as she placed little kisses all over Emma's face.

"OK." Emma stood up and picked up her dress. She hesitated. "What is it about your father? I can't believe that I've just stripped off in front of him."

"Do you find him attractive?" said Sophie, as she helped Emma slide the dress back over her head.

"Yes, he's—I don't know—a bit compelling. Either that, or I'm really pissed."

Sophie chuckled. "All his models say the same. He has a kind of fascination for them. But he never makes any move on them."

"No . . . he told me that." She took Sophie's hand as they walked towards the door. "Doesn't your mother object to all this?"

"No, she knows what he needs to do. They both love each other very deeply."

"But don't you find it disturbing, your father ogling and touching young girls?"

Sophie looked at her and frowned, a look of incomprehension on her face. "Of course not. He's an artist. He treats them as models, not objects of lust."

The dinner was relaxed, the food and wine delicious. There was no doubt that Sophie's parents were wealthy, but they made no show of it. They ate in the dining room with the French doors open onto the garden, and Emma was struck by how quiet it was. They questioned her about her family, and she found herself talking a lot, accentuated by the amount of wine she was drinking. As the evening wore on, Gerald talked about how he had studied initially in Paris—where he had met Therese—then in England, but decided to go back to France. She found herself becoming more and more fascinated by him, and noticed that he spent a lot of the time looking at her. There was something magnetic about him—and his face seemed familiar, although she couldn't put her finger on it. She had probably seen his picture in a magazine.

When eventually they got up and cleared the table, it was gone midnight, and Emma could feel her head swaying.

"Is it OK if I take Emma into the family section?"

"Yes—of course, but remember to lock up," said Gerald.

"Yes, I know. Come, darling."

Emma felt a touch of anxiety in her stomach as Sophie led them through a sitting room, again quite ornate, with large sofas, which Emma thought looked rather out of place with the eighteenth-century feel of the architecture. It too had French doors that led onto the garden. They emerged at the back of the rambling house onto the terrace. Sophie led down the steps, then stopped at a door set lower in the wall. She took a key from her pocket and undid it. It creaked as it opened and there was a flight of stone steps down into darkness on the other side.

She flicked a switch and Emma could see rows and rows of wine racks, full of bottles.

"This is your wine cellar?"

"Yes, but not just that." She went down the steps, and they walked along beside the racks until they came to the end of the cellar. Sophie reached beside the final rack and Emma heard a click. Sophie pushed the side of the rack gently, and it swung away from them, revealing an entrance into another room. Again, Sophie clicked on a light and walked in. Emma followed and was greeted by a much larger room full of paintings, some on the wall, others stored in racks, or hinged on the side so that they could be swung open to view them.

This part of the cellar was whitewashed and the floor and lighting modern.

Emma stood openmouthed at the sheer number of paintings.

"These are of me," said Sophie, moving farther down the room.

At once Emma could see her, in picture after picture, portrayed at all ages, from the very young to her age now. Those when she was young were sweet, innocent, and beautiful in their way, mostly clothed. But as Emma walked down the row, she saw the transition from childhood to adolescence, and the provocative, sexy young girl whom she knew so well appeared.

At first they were clothed pictures, then, as she became teenaged, she was increasingly naked. Looking at some of them, she felt the hair rise on the back of her neck. They weren't sexually provocative—but she was clearly underage.

As she moved down the rack, there were quite a lot of Sophie and her sister, Anne-Marie. She was struck by one that showed them both outside in the sunlight, with skimpy summer dresses on, sitting on a garden sofa. Anne-Marie had her arm around Sophie, their faces were close, and they were looking lovingly at one another. It was a ravishing picture, thought Emma, superbly executed in its colour and attention to detail.

"You like this one?"

"It's gorgeous. You both look so lovely."

"There are others with Anne-Marie I like. I love posing for him."

"He paints you so beautifully," said Emma. "It's almost like a photograph—but has that magic, which only a painting can bring."

Sophie put her arms around Emma's waist and hugged her from behind. "He's so talented, isn't he? Here—come and look at this."

She moved on again to a larger picture of a pretty, nubile girl with a boy. He was kneeling behind her, his penis partly entering her. They were painted on a bed, their bodies so lithe and fluid somehow, she thought. The light was streaming in from the window, and it looked as though they had just woken up and were greeting the morning with their first act of love.

"He painted that from photographs."

"Really? So who took them?"

"A photographer friend."

Next to it was another picture of the boy lying back on the bed, his penis stiff in the girl's hand. Her mouth is poised just above it, but she is looking at him wickedly as though holding back.

"God—these are so explicit," said Emma.

"Yes—but they're beautiful, aren't they?"

"Yes, they are," said Emma. She grinned. "He's quite big."

"Antoine is quite big as well." Sophie nuzzled her head into Emma's shoulder and kissed her neck. "Do you still want to make love with both of us?"

Emma felt sensation flash through her. "I don't know—I'm a bit nervous. You know why."

"Antoine is a wonderful lover."

"I'm sure."

Sophie stretched her hands down Emma's body and ran them between her legs, rubbing over her mound.

"So you like his pictures?"

"Yes." She cast her eyes back down the row. "God, this is such an amazing collection. So erotic. How does he do it?"

Sophie turned Emma to face her and kissed her. Her mouth tasted luscious and Emma whimpered as their tongues played together. She felt Sophie's hand undo the zip at the back of her dress, and as their lips parted, she slid the dress down until it fell at her feet.

"I would love to have a painting of you and me," she said, as she kissed her way down to Emma's left breast.

Emma sighed as Sophie suckled her nipple, gently running her tongue teasingly around the areola.

As she looked across the room, she saw another picture, this time of a young girl with long fairish brown hair.

She was naked, looking directly out of the picture, one of her hands self-consciously covering the buds of her young breasts. "Who's that?" said Emma, stroking Sophie's hair.

Sophie lifted her head and turned to look. "Oh, that is Marianne. She lives just down the road. She is lovely, isn't she? We were school friends. She works in her father's business. She was sixteen when that was painted. My father likes to do lots of pictures of her."

"Yes, she is lovely. But she posed naked for him? When she was sixteen?"

"Yes. Why not?"

"But—isn't that illegal?"

"I don't know."

There was a painting next to that one, of Sophie with her, lying on a bed. Sophie was clothed, but Marianne just had a wispy skirt around her midriff and was naked from the waist up. It was set in what looked like the late afternoon, and they were holding hands, Sophie with her eyes closed and Marianne looking dreamily out of the window. Her eyes were large and slightly mournful. Her mouth was wide and sexy, and her skin pale, in contrast to Sophie's light olive-brown.

"My father asked us to pose like that."

"Did you have a relationship with her? I mean, you know, have sex together?"

"Yes."

"Do you still see her?"

"Yes, of course. She has a live-in boyfriend now, but she still likes to come round and see me. Would you like to meet her?"

"Er . . . yes—if you like."

Sophie smiled knowingly, knelt down in front of Emma, and began to kiss her stomach.

"Do you still make love to her?"

She looked up at Emma, her eyes bright as a child's who knows they have been naughty. "Yes."

"With her boyfriend?"

"No. She likes to keep it as our little secret. She says she would miss not making love with me as I was the first lover she ever had." Sophie kissed her way farther down Emma's stomach, then placed her mouth over Emma's panties.

Emma sighed at the touch of her hot breath on her vagina.

Her eyes strayed farther down the room, and at the rack at the end there was a full-length painting of a naked blonde girl. Emma judged she would be eighteen or nineteen. "Who's that?"

"Which?"

"The lovely blonde girl at the end there."

"I don't know. One of his old girlfriends, I think."

"She's so gorgeous. Sexy in a wistful kind of way."

"Yes. There are others of her."

Emma closed her eyes as she felt Sophie pull her panties down and her tongue trace her vaginal lips. It reminded her of the other blonde girl in her life—Sally—and for a few moments, images of her floated through Emma's mind. What was she doing—and what would happen when she got back?

There was a sting of pleasure from her pussy—she stroked the silky dark hair, sighing.

She looked up again, and against the wall at the back she saw a strange-looking small table with a semi-circular drum on the top. "What's that?" she said.

Sophie turned. "Oh—that's the Sybian horse."

"The what?"

"Sybian horse." Sophie stood up and took her hand. "It's wonderful. Let me show you."

They walked over to it. The drum was made of soft leather, and on the top there was a long plastic dildo. Just in front of that was a small pad that had bristles. A cable came from the drum, and what looked like some sort of controller was at the end.

"You sit on it, and then it vibrates, controlled by this." She pointed to the controller.

"What? You sit on it and have the dildo inside you?"

"Yes—it's amazing." She presented the box to Emma. "Do you want to try it?"

"What, now?"

"Why not? It bends and moves inside you as well," she said. "Look." She picked up the controller and turned the switch. The false penis began to slowly vibrate and the upper section moved in a circular motion. As she turned the switch farther round, it got faster and the vibrations more intense.

"Wow," said Emma.

Sophie turned the switch off, then leant down and took the dildo in her mouth. She licked up and down, coating it with saliva. "Get it wet and warm for you," she said, raising her head briefly, before sucking it again.

"Will anyone come?"

"Would it matter if they did?" said Sophie, standing up.

There were footpads either side of the table. Emma placed her foot on one side, then swung her leg over the drum, hanging on to Sophie as she did it. She took the penis in her hand, rubbed it along the lips of her vagina, then lowered herself onto it.

Gingerly, she let it move up inside her until her thighs were straddling the drum, pressing against the warm leather. "Oh . . ." she murmured, as a little shiver went through her. She could immediately feel the little bristles of the pad in front make contact with her clitoris.

"Does it feel nice?"

"Yes," said Emma, shifting herself. "It's lovely and deep."

"Are you ready?"

"Yes."

Sophie turned the dial on the switch and immediately Emma felt warmth spread from her vulva. The penis was rotating very gently inside her, and after a few moments, the vibrations seemed to make it feel as though she was melting inside. She spread her legs wider apart, lowering herself even farther. She sighed at the ripples of pleasure. She hung her head back and closed her eyes, her hair tumbling back and hanging down behind her. She ran her hands over her breasts. They were firm with arousal.

She felt Sophie come up behind her and cradle her head. With her eyes still closed, she felt the succulent mouth of her friend kiss her. Sophie's thick tongue explored her mouth and Emma suckled on it. A wave of intensity flashed through her, causing her to utter a little cry and break the kiss.

"Does it feel good?"

"Oh . . . amazing."

"Shall I turn it up?"

"Yes . . ."

She heard the note of the machine rise and cried out at the resultant throb of pleasure, her voice echoing down the long cavern. She gyrated herself on the dildo, feeling it move and buzz inside her as though it had a life of its own. Her thighs trembled and her knees grew weak as she suddenly realised that the little pad at the front was also moving, brushing against her clitoris, causing it to tingle. "Oh God . . . it's amazing."

She felt Sophie stroke her anus with a finger, sliding it up and down between her buttocks. It pressed against her sphincter, the nerve endings there suddenly coming alive.

"More?"

"Yes . . . yes . . . oh yes . . ."

The vibrations increased sharply, and suddenly it felt as though some wild animal was running riot inside her, tireless, stimulating every fibre, every nerve ending, while the pad at the front worked on her clitoris, the little bristles teasing it, making it swell and grow hard. "Oh fuck—I'm going to come!"

She felt her pussy grow hot—hot and ultra sensitive—and she responded to the relentless fucking of the machine by dancing on top of it, answering the tension building so rapidly all through her. "Oh fuck—fuck—fuck," she was shouting, her voice filling the cavern. "Sophie—Sophie—fuck—hold me."

Sophie put her arms around her and held her, cupping her breasts and kissing her neck.

Emma felt as though she was a volcano about to erupt. She could feel herself trembling inside, while her muscles and sinews tightened to prepare themselves for the incredible surge to come. She could only snatch deep, life-saving breaths before a spasm would take and hold her, her vision becoming blurred as the blood was forced into her head. Each time her body would tense again, as though resisting the relief she wanted, the climax she needed so badly.

Suddenly her whole frame turned to rock and she went into a silent scream, agonising for the release that would never come. Her eyes were tight shut, but they flashed open as the divine moment came. Liquid fire spurted through her veins and purged her with the white heat of pure pleasure as she heard a scream fight its way from her throat, her body heaving and shuddering, wracked from the tempest raging through it . . .

She felt herself relax into Sophie's arms, turn her head, and eat her sweet mouth. She had slowed the machine right down and only the slightest of warming vibrations now caressed her deep inside. She ran her hand across Emma's stomach, breasts, and down to her pussy, stroking her softly. She touched her clitoris, and Emma shivered at the little tremor that went through her.

"It can be very intense, an orgasm from the Sybian," a voice said from the back of the room. She flashed her eyes open and saw Gerald standing there. "Some girls find it too much."

He walked across and stood in front of her. Emma felt no embarrassment. It seemed as though this house was casting a strange sexual spell over her, and she wanted to give into it, a type of promiscuity that had no limits. "That was like a drug trip," she said. "Incredible."

Sophie switched it off and they both helped Emma step off the table. She felt quite wobbly, and her knees were trembling as she stood up. She leant against Gerald and he hugged her gently. She could smell the scent of his body. It had a strangely powerful pervasiveness and seemed to seep into her lungs. She felt Sophie close up behind her and hug her as well, and it was as if she had become their sexual creature.

"You had better go to bed and recover," said Gerald, gently letting her go. "Anyway, it's late."

"Yes, come on," said Sophie. She cuddled Emma for a few seconds, then she too let her go. She picked up Emma's clothes.

"I would like to do some sketches of you tomorrow—in the sunflower field," said Gerald.

"I have an idea for another painting."

"With both of us, Papa?"

"Maybe."

Emma smiled. "See you in the morning then, Gerald."

"Yes," he said, looking at her intently. "Sleep well."

Emma did not put her clothes back on as they walked back through the house. She felt wonderful: liberated and free.

In the bedroom, Emma washed, then got into bed. She watched Sophie undress, her beautiful olive body so languid and sexy.

"Are you too tired after that?" said Sophie as she took her in her arms.

Emma kissed her softly. She could easily have just fallen asleep, but she could sense the hunger in her friend's body. "I'm never too tired for you."

The next morning, Emma woke to see Sophie entering their room carrying two cups of coffee.

"Cafe, cheri?"

"Lovely—you angel. Didn't you put any clothes on to go downstairs?"

"No. Why?"

"Oh . . . no reason."

Sophie handed her the coffee. Emma sat up and sipped it. It slid down her throat, leaving a delicious, enervating sharpness in her mouth.

"Marianne called. I am going over to see her. She is very happy."

"Oh. I suppose I'd better stay here?"

Sophie put her coffee down on the side table. "No, of course not, my darling. She knows I have other lovers. Just as she does."

"Her live-in boyfriend, you mean?"

"Yes. He is nice."

"But he doesn't know you make love to her?"

"No."

Sophie got into bed and kissed Emma on the cheek. Emma put her cup down and cuddled up to her. As they kissed, she felt Sophie's hand stroke her thigh. "Has your pussy recovered from last night?"

"I think so."

Sophie smiled and pushed the covers off Emma's body. "Are you sure?" She kissed her way lightly over Emma's neck and breasts, taking time to gently suck and tease each nipple as her hand rose up her thigh and gently stroked her sex.

Emma could feel herself instantly secreting love juice as Sophie's fingers played with her. She was so relaxed now with what she thought of as her new sexuality. She smoothed Sophie's hair and kissed her, loving the sensuous feel of their mouths together. They had adjusted to the way each liked to kiss, and often in their lovemaking they would kiss for a long time. Emma's mouth often tingled with such arousal that she thought she might orgasm just from that.

She felt a gentle climax coming, and it was as though she was sucking it from Sophie's mouth. It was gentle, rich, and tender, a divine warmth seizing her for a moment, suspending her in paradise, then releasing her. At the height, she broke away from her lover's mouth only to cry out, to expel the enervating breath that had been feeding her with pleasure.

As they kissed again, she could sense the urgency within Sophie's body. Reluctantly, she left her mouth and suckled the small breasts, painfully hard with desire. She pushed her lover onto her back and knelt between her legs, lowering her mouth to drink from that sweetest of fruits . . .

They showered and dressed, then went down to the kitchen. After Therese had kissed Sophie, she hesitated for a moment before kissing Emma—lightly on the lips. It seemed slightly reluctant, as though she didn't want to presume too much. She asked them what they wanted for breakfast, and they sat down to coffee and almond croissants Therese had cooked that morning.

Gerald emerged a few minutes later. "So, do you fancy a walk in the sunflower fields?" he said. "They are just in bud, and the green of the crop is so special at this time of year."

"We were going to see Marianne," said Sophie.

"Oh. I wanted to get some sketches of Emma for the paintings."

"You go on your own to see Marianne," said Emma. "I'll stay with Gerald."

"OK," said Sophie. "What a pity. I'll see you later, *cheri*."

Emma went back up to their bathroom to brush her teeth. She looked out of the window over the fields beyond the house. The sun was shining—hazy with light cirrus clouds high in the pale-blue sky. She could see the sunflowers to her right. They were not tall yet, and the heads were a strange turquoise green, the leaves thick and lush.

Sophie and Marianne . . . Emma felt a slight twinge of jealousy. She dismissed it from her mind. She was leaving to go back to the chateau tomorrow in any case—so what did it matter? She didn't know when she would see Sophie again.

She tripped back down to the kitchen, but Gerald wasn't there.

"He has gone up to the field," said Therese. "It's easy to find. Just turn right out of the drive and through the first gate on your right. We own the field. He'll be somewhere there."

"Oh, OK."

"See you later." She sounded distant—slightly strange.

"Right . . ."

Emma followed the path along the edge of the field and saw Gerald standing at the top, diagonally across from her. By the time she reached him they were quite a way from the house and the road.

"Do I take my clothes off, Gerald?" she said, coyly.

"In a minute."

"Nobody can see us from the road, can they?"

"Why, are you bothered?"

"Well . . . no. I suppose I'm not really."

There was a bench at the top of the field, and he told her to sit down. He sat next to her with a small sketchpad. After a while he got her to stand and walk around. She felt nervous at first—but after a while she relaxed. He was coaxing her to show different emotions through a range of expressions and poses. Happy, sad, joyful . . . sultry, and sexy.

"Now take your clothes off."

Emma smiled. "Most girls who do this get paid," she said, undoing the buttons on her dress and slipping it off her shoulders.

"I'll give you one of the paintings," he said. "Though I say it myself, they're worth a lot of money."

"I doubt I'd want anyone to see it back in the UK—let alone sell it." She pushed the dress down her legs and took it off. She turned towards him and ran her hands through her hair.

"Anyway, now walk through the crop," he said, standing up. He had taken up a camera and was looking at her through the lens.

She wandered through the plants, looking back at him or away as he directed. She relished feeling free and sexy, naked apart from her slip-on shoes. The air was warm, and the countryside looked so green and fresh in the bright spring sunlight. The quality of the light was so beautiful, the colours so vital somehow.

She was constantly aware of him. It was as though he wasn't just photographing her, he was absorbing her, pulling her towards him in a strange kind of way. She had enjoyed flirting with him the day before, but now she was conscious of a strong sexual attraction, and if occasionally he would move her arm or readjust her hair, she would feel his touch like a small electric charge.

He remained aloof—professional—and detached when he made her stop and did a few sketches on a pad in pencil.

"So what happens to these photos and sketches, Gerald?" she said, smiling at him. "Do you sell them on?"

"No. They are destroyed immediately after I finish the paintings."

"I believe you—thousands wouldn't."

He gave her an old-fashioned look, and she laughed. She did believe him. He seemed to exude trust—that was why she knew she would do anything he asked. She felt so comfortable with him, so much so that she was disappointed when after about an hour, he decided he had enough. She put her dress back on, and it almost felt unnatural to be clothed.

They walked back around the side of the field.

"You don't think of yourself as a pornographer, then, Gerald?"

"No—I'm an erotic artist. It might sound bullshit, but there is a difference."

"I'm sure there are plenty of people who would say it is pornography."

"I'm sure there are. I don't give a fuck. I like photographing and painting young beauty."

"Marianne looks very nice—judging from the paintings you've done."

"She is very pretty—and has a nice body."

"But she's not a lesbian?"

"No. But she loves Sophie."

"Yes, Sophie said."

"Are you jealous?"

"No. Why should I be?"

"So are you a lesbian, or bisexual?"

Emma chuckled. "I'm not sure. Sophie is only my second girlfriend, but my last relationship with a man wasn't good."

"But you've had a lot of sex with men?"

"Oh yes. I love sex."

"Well, the randy young Antoine is coming tonight. You could try it with him."

"Sophie wants me to."

"I know—she said."

"Does she tell you everything about her sex life?"

"Mostly, yes. We're a very open family."

"I've noticed."

When they got back to the house, Gerald said he was going to his studio. He suggested she should come back with him, but she said she would rather sit in the sun for a few minutes.

She stood for a moment in the empty kitchen. It was neat and clean, and the sunshine shone warmly on the old French dresser that occupied nearly half the length of one side of the room. Therese was nowhere to be seen, and it was intensely quiet.

Sophie clearly wasn't back—and Emma felt the jealousy gnaw into her again. She dismissed it from her mind. She also knew that being jealous about Sophie was ridiculous—she was a free spirit.

"Would you like some coffee?"

She turned quickly. Therese was smiling at her, standing in the doorway. "Yes. That would be nice—thank you."

"Lunch will be soon."

"Oh, right." Emma looked at her. Her face was lovely, she thought—and she remembered that portrait of her looking so young. "Could I sit outside in the sun?"

"Of course. There are sun loungers out there. I'll bring you some coffee out."

"Thank you."

She walked out through the French doors and out onto a large paved area that stretched from the house to the lawn. There were attractive stone pots that had been planted with geraniums and other summer flowers, not flowering yet, but still in bud. She pulled her dress over her head and spread it out on one of the sun beds, then lay down on it. She was naked, but assumed that no one in this family would wear anything to sunbathe anyway. She took some sun cream from her bag and rubbed it into her arms, breasts, and stomach. She was just putting some on her thighs when Therese came out with a cup of coffee in her hand.

"Oh—that's lovely, thank you," said Emma.

"*Tien*," Therese replied. "Do you want me to rub some oil on your back?"

"Oh. Yes, that would be great."

"Lay on your stomach, then."

Emma turned over and lay flat on the bed on her front. She felt Therese smooth oil into her back, then massage her shoulders and neck. Her hands felt strong, and Emma felt her muscles warm under her touch. "Mmmm . . . that feels lovely."

"I was a professional masseuse before I was married. I don't do it now, only occasionally for friends and family."

Her hands progressed slowly down Emma's back. "Sun cream is not the best," she said. "It soaks into your skin too quickly. I have to use a lot. But that's probably just as well. The sun is hot today, even though it's still spring." Her hands found their way across Emma's buttocks. For a moment she gently stroked her palms over both mounds, spreading the cool cream all round them. It was strangely intimate.

"You have a very beautiful body."

"Thank you."

"But it's a little tense."

"Yes . . ."

"Let me try and relax you."

She pressed on down to her thighs. Emma moaned as Therese forced her fingers deeply into the muscles, then squeezed and manipulated them. It ached, but she could feel herself unwinding, and as Therese moved her fingers downwards again, the sinews felt hot and glowing.

For a few minutes, she lightly massaged the back of her knees with her thumbs. Emma sighed with delight. She found it such a surprise that this little area of her legs could be so sensitive. She felt more cream being applied as Therese moved down to her calves, stretching and probing the flesh as she had before. It was such a lovely sensation, being pressed and pummeled until it was painful, but then wonderful lightness and warmth followed.

Therese bent Emma's leg at the knee and took one of her feet in her hands. "Nice feet," she said. Emma felt the strong fingers caressing it softly, then weave in between her toes. She put that foot down, took up the other one, and did the same.

"That's so nice," said Emma. "It tickles a little."

"Feet are so sensitive. Much more than people think. They work so hard for us."

She put her foot down, then smoothed her hands along Emma's back. "There . . . now enjoy . . ."

Emma felt a shadow come across her face and then Therese's soft lips touch her cheek. She raised her head and opened her eyes. Therese's face was close to hers, her large brown eyes smiling at her. Emma immediately thought how like Sophie she was—that same innocence. They looked into one another's eyes momentarily, then Emma pressed her lips against Therese's mouth and kissed her. She didn't know why—she just wanted to. It was soft, sensuous, and sweet.

Therese quickly stood up. "I'll see you for lunch."

"Yes . . . thank you."

Emma closed her eyes again and lay her head down. Her head swam with an extraordinary sense of physical and spiritual peace. She felt the warmth of the sun caress her like another lover, and she luxuriated in it caressing her body.

Later, she turned over and drank her half-cold cup of coffee.

The next thing she knew was Sophie's face smiling down at her. "Hello, *cheri*."

"Hi. How was Marianne?"

"She's fine."

"Pleased to see you?"

"Of course."

"Did you make love?" said Emma, without being able to stop herself.

Sophie looked at her, as though she was slightly shocked. "No," she said, "I have you here. We kissed and cuddled, of course."

"But tomorrow you might?"

"Maybe . . ." She laughed out loud. "You know me so well."

It was suggested that she and Sophie go into Carcassonne in the afternoon, and Emma readily agreed. Sophie suggested that Antoine meet them there and asked Emma rather sheepishly if that was all right.

"Of course it's all right."

"But I don't think you're sure."

"Sophie—I want what you want."

"No, I don't think you do sometimes."

"I do, but we'll see how things go—you know, about later."

"OK."

Emma kissed her fondly.

As they drove down the motorway, Emma could definitely sense that Sophie was quieter than normal. Emma shrieked as she saw the fairytale sight of the medieval castellated city sitting majestically in the plain, but Sophie only glanced.

As they pulled into the car park and Emma prepared to get out of the car, Sophie pulled her back.

"Do you think I am superficial?" she said abruptly.

"No, I don't. You're just different. Different but wonderful."

"You don't think of me as some kind of cheap whore?"

"No!" said Emma, aghast. "Where's that come from?"

"I don't know." She paused. "What you said about Marianne. You're right. I will go there again after you have gone—and yes, we may make love. She wanted to, I know. I could tell she didn't like the fact that you were here."

"Oh, I'm sorry."

"She said she wouldn't come round to meet you. I was a bit hurt by that."

Emma put her arm around her. "Hey, I still think you're fantastic. Crazy, but fantastic."

Sophie looked up at her and smiled. Emma kissed the waiting lips. Gentle at first, she felt the hunger in her mouth. They flicked their tongues together and Emma felt her body shiver with delight. No one was around the car, so Emma didn't mind as Sophie's fingers undid the top buttons on her blouse and exposed her breast, and her mouth suckled the erect tit. Sophie's tongue circled round and round the nipple and the sensation tingled down Emma's stomach, glowing in her pussy. As though she sensed what was happening, Sophie's hand glided down between her legs and rubbed her panties. Emma sighed, opened her legs, and shifted down in the driving seat. She was on heat this weekend, she thought— permanently aroused—just waiting for the next sexual thrill. She lost her hands in the thick, dark locks of Sophie's hair as she felt Sophie's fingers find their way under her panties, through the little thicket of her pubic hair, and into the slippery valley of her sex . . .

Emma adored the old city. Every corner seemed to yield another stunning vista, and she insisted on exploring all the streets, the castle, the church, and all round the battlements. After a couple of hours, Sophie complained of being tired, and they looked for a cafe.

Weary and hot, they sat drinking beer under the large tree that sat in the courtyard of the restaurant they had chosen. Sophie phoned Antoine to tell him where they were.

"There's no pressure," she said as she put the phone on the table.

"How do you mean?"

"Having sex with him."

"No. OK."

"Only it would be fun."

Emma put her hand on Sophie's.

Sophie smiled, put her arm around Emma's shoulder, and kissed her on the mouth. Emma could feel eyes from the surrounding tables fixed on them, but only felt a thrill from being so blatant in public. She prolonged the kiss, and when their lips finally parted, kissed her lightly again.

"This has been wonderful."

"What has?"

"These five weeks with you."

"Hmm. I shall miss you," said Sophie. "We must meet up again."

"Oh yes."

"And when we do, will you want to make love with me?"

"I'll definitely *want* to. Whether I will allow myself is another matter."

Sophie laughed. "So English."

Antoine was exactly as she remembered him—only he was even better looking than before, she thought. He kissed her on both cheeks and seemed to look at her in a rather knowing way. Of course, she thought, Sophie would have told him that she had asked her to join them for sex.

He and Sophie talked animatedly in French. She was all over him, kissing him, and giggling. He occasionally stole a glance at Emma, who sat watching them, amused. He seemed more embarrassed by the way Sophie seemed to forget she was there.

Later, as they walked back through the city to the car park hand in hand, he kept looking behind at her. Emma said nothing, but returned his stares.

Sophie and he sat in the back of the car as Emma drove. Sophie wrapped herself around him and seemed to have her mouth permanently glued to his.

Back at the house, Gerald was in the kitchen. He shook Antoine's hand firmly. As they talked, Emma could tell they got on well. She felt Sophie's arm go round her waist.

"I've been neglecting you."

"Don't worry."

"No, I'm awful . . . poor darling." She kissed Emma softly on the mouth. "Shall we go and shower before dinner?"

"If you like."

"Antoine, we are going upstairs to have a shower. We'll see you later."

"Bon." He smiled at them both, but seemed unconcerned. Gerald was opening a bottle of *Blanquette.*

"Early drinks," said Sophie as they left the kitchen. "Papa always loves it when Antoine comes. Men's talk—all that stuff."

They shed their clothes quickly in the bedroom and made their way down the corridor to the shower. They washed each other, kissing and fondling under the refreshing jet of water.

"Have you thought any more about tonight?" said Sophie as they dried each other off.

"No, not really."

"I will want to make love with him, you know?"

"Yes. Of course."

"Maybe I'll make love to you first."

"You'd better. It's our last night together."

"Yes . . ."

"He's very good looking, but I feel very unsure, you know?"

"That's OK."

Emma pulled her close and hugged her. She snaked her tongue into Sophie's ear. "You can exhaust me with multiple orgasms, and only then will I let him have his wicked way with you," she whispered. Desire flooded her as she held the damp, beautiful body against hers. "I'm going to miss you."

"Me too. You and I will go to bed early—yes?"

"You bet."

"Come—let's go for a walk now." She walked to the cupboard against the wall and pulled out a dress. "Antoine always likes to drink with my father. I like that. Then he comes to bed a little bit drunk and very randy. He stays hard for a very long time."

Once they had finished dressing, they went back through the house and out into the drive at the front. Sophie took Emma's hand as they walked out onto the lane.

"I don't just think about sex all the time, you know. I will miss you—you know—as a friend," she said.

"Oh—so will I." Emma put her arm around her.

"When I suggested you have sex with Antoine as well as me, it was, well—when you feel for two people at the same time, and they are in the same house together, you wonder what it would be like."

"Mmm. I'm not sure about that. I think you're just sex mad."

"That's me," said Sophie, laughing.

They walked on in silence for a bit. The sun was still quite high, but there was a slight chill in the air. Emma felt relaxed and warm inside, as though she didn't want her stay here to come to an end. It was like being in bed in the morning, all snug and warm, knowing that you had to get out any minute.

"Tell me about Sally."

Emma was taken slightly aback. "Sally? She's lovely. But as I told you—we met the day before I came here, so I've only been to bed with her once. My first time with a girl."

"Just before you left?"

"Yes."

"And then you came to France and I appeared."

"Yes. I was so, you know, like, overwhelmed by what had just happened back in England that when you started coming on to me I was really confused. I didn't want to be unfaithful to Sally—even though we don't really have a relationship."

"But you finally gave in?"

"Yeah. I knew I fancied you, and . . . well, I'd had my first ever orgasms with her—I mean incredible. Eight years of having sexual feelings and then suddenly—kabam—you know, I suddenly got there. So when I met you I wanted to know whether it would happen again."

"And I satisfied your craving?"

"Mmm. Sex with you has been incredible."

"And how do you feel about Sally now?"

"Good. I mean, she said to me before I left that I should experiment with other girls to see if that's what I really like."

"And do you?" Sophie said, bringing her face close to Emma's.

"Yeah, I love it. I love being lesbian." She felt Sophie's arms stroke down her back and lift her dress. She was naked underneath, and Sophie's hands fondled her buttocks as they kissed deeply. Emma heard some cyclists approaching on the road, but she and Sophie stayed as they were, and as they passed, she heard wolf whistles.

"Men's ultimate fantasy," she said as the kiss broke.

"Yes . . . and Antoine's ultimate fantasy."

There was a sparkle in her eyes—and Emma smiled.

They skirted across a field that ran in front of the house. "Your mother gave me a massage," she said.

"Did she? It's wonderful when she does that. Did you enjoy it?"

"Yes. It was amazing."

"I know she thinks you are very beautiful." Sophie looked round at her with that same innocence.

They had reached the side entrance into the garden. When they got into the house, Antoine, Gerald, and Therese were gathered in the kitchen drinking *Blanquette.*

Sophie sat on Antoine's lap and gave him a long French kiss. His hand pushed her dress to within an inch of decency, but her parents seemed oblivious.

"Did you enjoy your walk?" said Gerald.

"Yes, it was lovely."

"He has been working hard on your painting," said Therese.

"Yes, but it won't be finished for weeks," he said.

"Will you need another sitting?" said Emma.

"Yes. Tomorrow morning, and then I will have enough sketches. I may do two or more pictures—I will see."

"Yes," said Sophie. "She is so beautiful, you will probably do lots." She got up from Antoine's lap and came over to

Emma. She put her arms around her neck and kissed her. "I am going to miss her so much, so I am going to make love to her all night."

By the time they sat down at table in the dining room, Emma had drunk two glasses of the sparkling wine and felt light-headed—but happy. To her surprise, Sophie sat next to her at the table and Antoine sat facing them on the other side. Therese and Gerald sat at either end.

The meal started with foie gras served with a sauterne, fragrant, sweet, and delicious. Then a large leg of lamb served with rosemary, accompanied by a deep, heavy red wine. Good local cheeses and a light soufflé pudding came and went, and Emma found herself floating, that wonderful sense that good food and wine can give you.

Sophie was very attentive to her and kept kissing her, sometimes turning her face so that she could kiss her on the mouth. Her hands constantly stroked Emma's thigh, and often she would take a deep sip of the excellent wine and feel, at the same time, Sophie's fingers stealing their way across her pussy. Sexual excitement would blend with the wine, perfuming her mind and taste buds.

As the evening wore on, she found herself becoming more and more aware of Antoine. His soft brown eyes and wavy reddish hair seemed to make him look even more attractive. He talked mostly to Gerald and Therese, but his eyes wandered constantly to hers. Inside she could feel an excitement building, and she was conscious that all round the table there was a strange kind of acknowledgment.

She remembered at one point taking a long sip of her wine, with Sophie's tongue snaking its way into her earlobe, and her eyes scanning Antoine's face. She extended her feet under the table and found his and Sophie's touching. She rubbed her bare feet against them, locking her eyes into a suggestive gaze.

Emma declined a cognac, but Gerald and Antoine had one each and remained at the table. Sophie, Emma, and Therese cleared away the dishes and took them to the kitchen, then

Sophie took Emma by the hand and led her out onto the terrace. There was a half moon casting a ghostly light across the garden, with the light from the dining room and kitchen spilling out across the lawn.

They began to kiss, and Sophie pushed her gently against the wall of the house. She pushed the straps of Emma's dress from her shoulders, then traced her kisses across her throat and chest, ending on the stiff nipple that had been exposed by the thin material slipping away. Emma gasped as goose pimples scattered across her skin, then her breathing began to hasten as Sophie kissed her way farther down across her stomach. She felt her dress being lifted, then, the next moment, a divine rush of feeling as Sophie's mouth kissed her pussy.

"Ohhhh . . . Sophie, darling . . . let's go to bed."

Sophie pecked urgently back up to her mouth, then kissed her passionately. Emma heard a step next to her. They broke the kiss and turned to see Antoine standing next to them.

"We're going to bed now," said Sophie, in French.

Quickly, Emma put her arm around him and brought her face close to his. "And you'll join us later?" she said.

"*Oui*," he whispered.

She kissed him, softly at first, but then immediately it became passionate and randy. Their mouths wrestled together as his hands explored her body. She felt her dress fall to her feet. Her pussy burned as their mouths parted. She took his head in her hands and kissed him again, then reached out and brought in Sophie, their tongues licking each other's faces.

"Are you going to give me a game before you spend the rest of the night servicing them?"

She heard Gerald's voice, and they parted to see him standing in the doorway. Antoine smiled enigmatically. "Sure," he said, in a heavy French accent.

He wandered to the door, then turned and waved at the girls.

Emma stepped out of her dress and picked it up from the floor. She looked at Gerald provocatively. "Sophie and I are going to bed now," she said. She walked over to him and placed a light kiss on his lips. "Goodnight, Gerald."

Sophie kissed her father and followed Emma into the kitchen. Therese was tidying the dishes.

"Goodnight, Therese," said Emma. She went up to her, and flushed with the alcohol, kissed her on the mouth as well.

She smiled, strangely impassively. "Good night, Emma— and you, Sophie."

Emma lay on her back, with the long, languid, naked Sophie on top of her. One of Emma's thighs was parting Sophie's legs, and she could feel her friend gently rubbing herself against it. Emma ran her hands down her back, smoothing the perfect, smooth skin against her palms.

They had been in bed for half an hour, kissing, talking, playing. At one point, Sophie had knelt above Emma's face and Emma had licked her pussy, savouring the sweet honey of her cum. Emma had brought her very near to orgasm, but then slipped her tongue away. Both of them seemed contented not to make love in earnest until Antoine arrived. They hadn't spoken about that, and Emma was randy and relaxed, ready for whatever came.

"I'll come and see you again," Emma said lightly.

"Are you going to miss me?" said Sophie, sexily pecking Emma's lips.

"Of course. Not that you'll miss me. You have Marianne." She stretched her tongue up and played it against Sophie's.

Sophie smiled sheepishly. "And you have Sally."

"Mmm. I don't know. It will be quite strange in a way. I mean, like, we met one day, made love in the evening and the following morning—and I haven't seen her since."

Sophie pressed her sex strongly against Emma's thigh and kissed her, rolling her tongue round Emma's mouth. "She would be mad not to want you again. You are so beautiful.

You could seduce any woman. There isn't a creature on this earth that wouldn't want to make love with you."

"I don't know about that."

"I do."

Emma kissed Sophie, drawing the full lips into her mouth and sucking them. Just then, she heard steps outside.

She looked across at the door, then back at Sophie. "I'm feeling a bit nervous."

"Why?"

"Antoine. I hope that I don't react badly—you know, find sex with him a turn-off."

The door opened. Sophie turned and Emma watched him come into the room. He smiled and began to take off his clothes.

"Of course you won't," whispered Sophie. "You like men—I can tell that. You have had one bad experience, that's all."

"Maybe."

"Enjoy . . ."

Emma was very aware of him watching them as Sophie slid down her body, kissing her neck, chest, both breasts, across her stomach, and then slowly to her pussy. Emma writhed at the shimmer of pleasure as Sophie's tongue snaked around her clitoris. She looked up at Antoine. He was standing behind Sophie, naked, staring at her. His penis was stiffly erect, long, and straight, and he was massaging it, pulling his foreskin back. She had a strange, anxious feeling mixed with excitement. She watched as his eyes scanned back down to his girlfriend's long back and buttocks, then settled on her pussy. He edged himself closer, and though she couldn't see, Emma knew he was pushing his penis inside her.

Sophie momentarily raised her head, a look of ecstasy on her face. Emma put her hands on her face and stroked her thick mass of hair. "Does it feel good, darling?"

"Oh yes . . . so good . . ." She lowered her head and Emma felt the point of her tongue search the folds of her vagina, then a hot rush of sensation as it slid inside. She looked up at Antoine, who was staring at her, his body pressed tightly against Sophie's buttocks, pushing firmly in and out. Sophie's body was moving with his rhythm, and she felt Sophie's tongue matching his motion inside her.

She could see the lust in his eyes, and she fixed his gaze, "Ohhh . . . you're both fucking me—and it feels so good," she murmured. She had turned to speaking in French without realising it, and knew that at this moment, she somehow couldn't express herself in any other way. She squirmed on the bed, taking deep enervating lungfuls of air, softly crying as each pulse of Sophie's tongue scattered delight through every muscle. It was almost as though Antoine was inside her as well—and she wanted it, wanted to be fucked by him. What was she afraid of? She felt that wonderful tension stir in her groin and felt it spread, her breath quickening, feeding the energy in her muscles, each exhalation bringing an increasingly high scream. . . ." Sophie, darling . . . I'm coming . . . .OHHHHHHH YESSSSSS . . ." She held it at bay for as long as she could, then felt it take her in a series of gentle spasms, bringing her into a paradise of sweet relief . . .

At its height, she had squeezed her eyes tight shut, and when she opened them again, she heard Sophie moaning, her head buried between Emma's legs. She shifted slightly forward, so that Sophie's head lay on her stomach, then cradled it in her hands. She looked up at Antoine. He was pounding Sophie's pussy sharply, and his eyes were roving over the long, elegant back of his girlfriend to Emma's breasts. She held his gaze as she stroked Sophie's hair and face. His groin slapped hard against her buttocks. Sophie cried out loudly, saliva dribbling from her mouth. "Antoine . . . I'm coming—yes, yes, OH YESSS!!!!" she cried, her snatched breath hot on Emma's stomach.

After a few moments, Sophie shifted upwards and they kissed long and deeply.

Emma became conscious that Antoine had gotten onto the bed beside them. When finally their mouths parted, they both turned and Sophie kissed him. Emma's hand drifted down from Sophie's back and she felt it come into contact with Antoine's penis. It was hard and slippery. Emma put her fingers around it and massaged it gently.

Sophie leaned down and Emma saw her mouth descend towards it. She let go of it and smiled at Antoine. He leaned across and kissed her hungrily. She was slightly taken aback by his passion and felt a twinge of anxiety in her stomach. But she told herself this was different, and she pushed her tongue into his mouth.

"Would you like Antoine to come inside you?"

Emma broke the kiss and looked at Sophie. She had that wild innocent look about her, and Emma felt a quiver of panic blend with the warm randiness that lingered with the sensation of his lips still on hers. She looked at Antoine's soft brown eyes, then down at his straining penis. "Yes . . ." she said.

Sophie shifted and lay down beside her, while Antoine knelt between her splayed legs. He put his arms out and suspended himself above her: Sophie reached over, took hold of his penis, and rubbed it up and down, searching Emma's vaginal lips. The next moment, Emma felt him push inside.

She cried out. It had been five weeks since that horrible experience with Charlie, and although she'd had Sophie's fingers inside her, his sharp thrust hurt. Instantly he began to move inside her in long, deep strokes—and she shuddered at the sudden memory of the last male invasion of her body.

He lowered himself onto her and kissed her, his tongue rubbing strongly around her mouth. He shoved his arms under her and grabbed her shoulders. Then holding her tightly, he began to fuck her urgently. His penis felt huge. She desperately tried to make herself relax and just let herself be taken, but his smothering of her mouth meant she couldn't get her breath, and she felt suddenly claustrophobic—but then he broke the kiss and raised himself above her. She could see his eyes were burning with intensity, scanning her body, drinking in every detail to feed his lust. She couldn't shake the image of Charlie, fucking her like a piece of meat, his thrusts, hard, sharp, deep, and getting quicker and quicker. She wanted to scream and was grasped by a rising sense of panic.

He was moaning now, and she felt him grow even bigger. His eyes were almost fierce, and his neck and torso were straining. At once his body seized, and his cock, huge inside her and painful, broke its rhythm and he jabbed in and out, groaning all the time . . .

Once he was spent, he collapsed on top of her and kissed her neck. She turned her head away. It was strange. The fear dispersed quickly, and she didn't feel revulsion as she feared she would, but instead a kind of detachment. She felt as she imagined a prostitute would. No involvement. Job done.

After a few moments, Antoine pulled out and lay next to her. Emma felt his semen dribble out of her. She closed her eyes. She had feared this might happen. She heard Sophie shift, and the next moment her hot mouth engulfed Emma's pussy. She looked down at the impish face.

"I'm going to lick his cum from your pussy."

The hot, insistent tongue entered her, and Emma felt the tension relax. She opened her legs wide and stroked Sophie's hair. "Oh yes . . . that's better. Lick me clean," she said. *I'm not going to let Charlie win,* she thought. *I want to love sex with men again. Why the fuck should I give in to that?* "Oh yeah . . . that's nice," she whispered. It was as though some tireless, furry animal was exploring inside her.

After a few moments, she lifted Sophie's head and kissed her. She could taste the semen on her tongue. "Let me watch you make love to Antoine," she said.

Sophie looked at her intensely for a moment. "Of course," she whispered. "Was it not good for you just now?"

"A bit too soon."

"Poor darling."

"I'll be fine. I'm loving it. I'll fuck him again in a minute." She glanced at him. She knew he didn't really understand what they were saying, but she could see a slight embarrassment in his eyes.

Emma edged off the bed. It wasn't that she didn't want what was happening—she just needed to be apart from it for a moment. She sat on the armchair nearby. It was made of cane, and the cushioned seat was wide. Stroking his now soft member, Antoine gave her a quizzical look, but Emma smiled back reassuringly. Relaxing back, she watched as Sophie put her head down and took Antoine's penis into her mouth. Her thick, glossy black hair fell around her face so that all Emma could see was her head lifting up and down and Antoine's face watching intently.

After a while, he began to moan softly. Sophie was an expert, thought Emma, and sure enough, when she lifted her head, his pole stuck up hard and stiff, glistening with her saliva. She moved forward, kissed him sexily, then positioned herself above it. She guided him into her with her fingers, then sank down, sighing softly.

Emma watched Sophie's beautiful hips gyrate sensuously over his groin. Her hands stroked his torso—and his constantly ran over her breasts, back, and buttocks. She was taken back all those weeks before when she had opened the door to their room at the chateau and come across them just as they were now.

Emma's hand drifted down to her vagina and began stroking the moist lips. Antoine had a lovely body. She wanted to watch them both until she felt herself desiring him—wanting him. Sophie had been so insistent about this, and Emma had never been comfortable with the suggestion—but she was right, she needed to do this.

Sophie leaned down and kissed him passionately, Antoine's hand running down her back, his fingers disappearing in the cleft of her buttocks. Sophie was moving slowly up and down on him and raising her head. She moaned softly.

Emma felt calmer now. She slipped her finger inside herself and moved it around slowly. She put another alongside it and pumped herself, and as she watched their hot rhythmic dance, she forced herself to imagine her fingers were Antoine's penis, pleasuring her, stretching her, and going deep inside her—but at her own pace, so that she was in control. "Ohhh, Sophie—you both look so sexy."

Sophie turned and smiled at her. "Make yourself come while looking at us . . . don't you want to?"

"Oh yes . . ."

Sophie leaned up, put one hand on his chest and the other behind her on his leg, then, steadying herself, flicked her pelvis back and forth quickly, her face a picture of concentration. Her movements were so erotic, so instinctive. Emma saw Antoine thrust gently up into her in turn, working himself deeper. She shivered as she watched. She could understand why people liked to watch others making love; it was such a natural and lovely thing. Their eyes were fixed on one another, and Emma could see a glint of saliva on Sophie's lips as she sighed, her breathing opening her ribcage and patterning that delicate and flawless covering of olive skin.

Emma put three fingers together now and pumped herself deeply, moving them in and out to the rhythm of the lovers in front of her. She spread her legs wider and shuddered as with each movement, her thumb grazed her clitoris tantalizingly. She could smell the scent of her vagina—the hint of sweat mixed with Antoine's semen. She had never made herself come before, never felt that amazing thrill that she had watched Susie enjoy one night in Turkey when she had thought Emma was asleep. It was very early morning. The dawn was filtering through their tent, and the soft, silvery sunlight had looked so gorgeous on Susie's young eighteen-year-old body lying naked on top of her sleeping bag, writhing gently as her fingers worked her pussy. At the time, Emma had felt guilty. She had closed her eyes and turned away from it, but could feel the excitement—her hunger for the sensation.

"Oh, Antoine . . . I'm coming again . . ." Sophie murmured. Emma watched the muscles in her thighs and groin tense and flex with the coming rush of pleasure. It was as though her skin took on a heightened sheen as her nipples stuck out like pinnacles and she gyrated on top of him with complete abandon. Then her little cries began to mount until she was screaming loudly, her face flushed and set.

Emma frigged herself faster with one hand, still pumping herself with the other, trying desperately to match Sophie's approaching climax. She watched entranced as Sophie froze at the peak, her body wracked with the intensity of her orgasm, then her own climax was coming, rising sharply, enriched by the gorgeous image of her lover in front of her, lost in sexual ecstasy. "Oh, Sophie . . . yes . . . I'm coming. Oh, I love you . . . YESSSSSSS . . ."

It was so sweet, different, a strange blend of the physical excitement she was giving herself and the sexy, natural loving in front of her. "Ohhhh, fuck . . . ohhhhhhhhhh fuckkk yeaaaah . . ."

"Ohhh . . ." she whispered. "I was never able to do that before."

Sophie turned and smiled dreamily. "And now you'll be able to do it whenever you want to. Again and again."

It is so amazing to be bisexual, thought Emma, as her body calmed, *and to be so open about it.* She got up from the chair and sat on the bed next to her, put her arm round her, and kissed her. "And I'll think about you—and this amazing, sexy moment." She ran her hands over the girl's body, smoothing her breasts, her back, and the taut stomach. Slowly Emma lowered her fingers to Sophie's clitoris, sitting just above Antoine's bush of public hair, and with her other hand, she pushed between Sophie's buttocks and found her anus, tickling it teasingly. She pushed her finger forward, finding the wetness oozing from Sophie's pussy, then worked her way back, smearing the cum around her sphincter.

"You'll make me come again," whispered Sophie.

"Good," said Emma. She licked the rich, olive skin, tasting the slight saltiness of perspiration. She suckled both nipples, gently biting and pressing with pursed lips.

She sensed Sophie pushing backwards and forwards, pressing her clitoris against Emma's fingers at the front, and pushing on to her other finger probing her anus. Sophie began to sigh again, and Emma could almost feel what she was feeling—the tremble of another climax gathering, just waiting for the triggers that Emma could press.

Emma was drawn down by the heady, tempting smell of sweat and sex. She licked in long strokes slowly downwards, until her mouth sat just above Sophie's neat, trimmed little bush. Lust burned sharply in her belly, and without hesitation, she lowered her tongue to the waiting little bud at the crown of Sophie's vagina. At the same time, she slid her finger from her anus into her pussy alongside Antoine's pulsing, rock hard penis, coated it with slippery juice, then moved it back and pressed it against her sphincter. The tip sank inwards, so she pressed farther—and felt the strong ring of muscle give and her finger slide right inside.

Sophie gasped. Emma flashed her tongue over Antoine's groin and up to Sophie's clitoris, then honed in on the little hillock, sucking on it strongly. She worked her finger in Sophie's bum, moving it around and pushing ever farther in.

Sophie began to cry out and ride herself up and down on Antoine's penis, and Emma felt her head being pressed downwards. She lashed her tongue over the base of his prick and then onto Sophie's vaginal lips as they moved together. Sophie's cries increased quickly and she pounded herself violently until she spasmed again as she came. Emma pressed her face harder onto Sophie's pussy, drinking in the strong-tasting cum trickling down the hard shaft of flesh. Sophie gasped in long tortured breaths, riding her orgasm, her pelvis still slowly moving back and forth . . .

Emma lifted her head, sat up, hugged Sophie, and devoured the girl's soft, limp mouth.

Sophie opened her eyes, and they seemed distant, lost for a moment. She smiled. "That was wonderful. You are such an amazing lover." She raised herself and moved off the top of Antoine. "Your turn."

Emma looked down at the hard, red pole sticking up towards her and felt the lust throb in her groin. She moved her leg over his body and squatted on top of him. She looked at him, his face alive with expectation. She lay down and kissed him, rubbing her clitoris along the wet shaft. She wanted to desire it inside her; she wanted to be crying out for it to fill her, to feel that old thrill she used to have with men—that longing to be taken. She slid herself up and down, her body gently trembling with the little eddies of sensation. She pushed her tongue strongly around his mouth. She wanted to enjoy his maleness, to absorb it, to revel in the breadth of her sexuality.

She felt Sophie part her buttocks and spit into her cleft—then her finger massaged her anus. The goose pimples coalesced in her groin and she shuddered. "Kiss me," she whispered to her.

The girl lay next to them, and Emma moved and kissed her—soft, feminine, tender. Then she switched back to Antoine—rough, strong, invasive—then back to Sophie until all three were licking and eating each other's mouths, saliva dribbling over their faces. She was switching so easily from one sex to the other, and both felt entirely natural. *Bisexuality is the ultimate gift*, she thought.

The familiar longing grew in her pussy, so she lifted herself and took his penis in her hand. She looked down at it for a moment. She could choose not to do this if she wanted—there were plenty of other ways all three of them could please each other—but this time she knew she was longing for it to be inside her. Tentatively she rubbed it over the folds of her vaginal lips and shivered at the little eddies of delight—then she lowered herself carefully, letting it enter her tunnel. There was no panic or pain this time, only a delicious surge as she felt herself stretch and give. She sat up more and began to move on top of him. The feeling was wonderful. He pushed up into her at the same time, and she uttered little cries as he penetrated farther and farther.

Emma's nipples were hard, almost painful with desire. She stroked Sophie's face and pulled it towards her breasts—and sighed as the wet warmth of the girl's tongue caressed them, soothing the tautness of their gorged, excited state.

Emma rode Antoine slowly. She was in control now and relished his slipping up and down inside her vaginal walls. The feeling was so different. "Sit on his face," she whispered to Sophie.

Sophie repositioned herself facing Emma, sitting across Antoine so that his mouth and tongue could pleasure her pussy.

Emma kissed the soft mouth of her friend while flexing her groin around the hard stalk moving inside her. She was liberated, hot and passionate, hungry.

"Does it feel better now?" Sophie whispered.

"Oh yes. I love the feel of him inside me."

Sophie looked down at Antoine's tongue running over her clitoris and sighed. "It's so good, the three of us making love," she whispered. "Promise me you'll come back and see us."

Emma kissed her, tracing her tongue around her mouth. "Of course I'll come back."

"Will you always want to make love to me?"

"Of course. I could never resist you. I'll always want you." They kissed again—wild and long.

Emma felt another orgasm kindling inside her—but she killed it by squeezing down hard on Antoine, his penis pressing deep inside her and a sharp, exquisite pain bringing her down, allowing her to wait for the tension to build again.

Sophie lifted herself off him and moved round behind Emma.

Emma lay down on Antoine and kissed him, pulling her knees up alongside her and rocking back on forth on his penis. She heard him moan beneath their kiss. The next moment, she felt Sophie's tongue trace around her anus. She lifted her head. "Oh . . . Sophie—yes, lick me there . . ." It was such a new and intimate sensation, and she shimmered all over and tingled. "Oh God . . . yes, OHHHHHH!!!" A chain reaction flashed around her groin, and this time she couldn't stop a mini orgasm sparking in her clitoris. She gasped and let it resonate round her body.

"Let me lick your pussy while Antoine is fucking you," said Sophie. "Turn round."

Emma lifted off him and turned round, then sank back down on his penis. There was a deep throb as it parted her vaginal walls, and it repeated each time as she lifted up and dropped down once more in the slow, gorgeous dance.

Sophie lowered her head, so Emma lifted herself slightly on her arms again. "Fuck me, Antoine." Antoine pumped in and out of her vigorously, and she felt her passage light up with the delicious friction. "Oh God, that's an amazing feeling. My pussy feels as though it will burn up—and my clit— Sophie, that's divine."

Sophie's tongue licked wickedly around her clitoris and she felt an orgasm coming so easily. She tried to hold it back, wanting to relish this feeling for longer, but the tension was gathering so quickly. For the first time, she was coming with a man inside her—and she gave herself to it, her stomach trembling, the burning sensation in her pussy, the muscles of her thighs and arms matching the rigidity in her stomach as the tissue ignited and her blood turned to liquid fire . . .

She collapsed back onto Antoine, laying across him. "Ohhh. Amazing. God—that was so intense." Her body felt heavy with tiredness and relaxation—and the effect of the wine seemed suddenly to return, making her feel drowsy.

Antoine shifted beneath her and she moved herself off him, the air cool on her hot pussy as his penis flopped out. She watched as Sophie repositioned herself above his groin and sank his penis into her mouth. She leaned across and kissed Antoine, this man she hardly knew, with his soft eyes. She looked down at Sophie, her thick dark hair falling onto his stomach as her mouth made love to him. She laid her head on Antoine's shoulder. "Oh, I'm feeling sleepy," she said.

Sophie looked up sharply, Antoine's penis popping out of her mouth. "Not yet." Her hand flew to Emma's pussy and rubbed her lips. It tickled, and Emma giggled, turning onto her stomach and laying flat. She felt Sophie pull her to her knees, but she carried on laughing, burying her head in the pillow.

"Fuck her awake," said Sophie.

She heard Antoine sit up, and a moment later his prick nudged her vagina. A second later, she felt it plunge inside.

She lifted her head and gasped. "Oh, Antoine—yeah . . . fuck me," she whispered. "Go deeper . . . right inside me." She could feel his hands stroking her, fondling her breasts, gently squeezing them. He pushed in hard and held his cock inside, pressing right up against her cervix. She cried out from the mixture of pleasure and pain, and each time he thrust in and out, little screams came from her throat.

Sophie shifted and positioned herself underneath Emma, edging into the sixty-nine position. Emma shivered as she felt her hot tongue lash her clitoris while Antoine pounded her pussy with increasing speed.

Emma lowered her mouth to Sophie's waiting vagina, closing her mouth around it, licking it strongly. The smell of sexual heat was intoxicating and Emma felt herself losing control; the burning of the friction in her pussy was topped by the playing of Sophie's tongue. "Sophie . . . FUCK . . . YESSSSSS!!!" she rubbed her face wildly in the juices pouring from Sophie's pussy, covering herself in it, finally raising her head and screaming as an orgasm ripped through her . . .

She collapsed forward, Antoine's prick flopping out. She rolled onto her back to see Sophie coming forward to hungrily suck on him, thrusting her head forward, his cock disappearing to the back of her throat.

Emma leaned forward and joined her, licking round his balls, gently sucking them, careful not to graze or hurt them. She could feel them getting firmer, filling with semen ready to explode. She felt that thirst she used to love, wanting a guy to squirt into her mouth.

"Let me suck him," she said to Sophie.

Sophie pulled off him, then kissed her softly. "OK, *cheri*. But share his spunk with me if he comes."

"Oh, don't worry—he's going to come."

Antoine lay on his back and smiled at her.

She looked at the long, straight penis lying taut, red, and wet along his stomach. She got on to her knees, took it in her hand and pulled the foreskin back a short way. It was slippery with cum, but the red, bulbous head seemed to grow larger as she pulled the delicate covering back beyond the ridge of his helmet. The glistening flesh was tight and straining with the tiny little hole at its centre. She worked her hand up and down the shaft, each time pulling his foreskin farther and farther back until it extended so much that the foreskin disappeared and it became a seamless pole of hard flesh.

She moved her other hand to his balls and felt the round globes tight in their sac. She massaged her fingers gently around them. "I can feel your balls have filled up again," she said, "full of that lovely juice, all warm and thick." Saliva gathered in her mouth as she worked him harder, up and down, the tumescent flesh hot in her hand. A large bead of clear fluid appeared at the eye and dribbled down the fine seam that ran under the head. Looking up at him again, she put out her tongue and carefully scooped it up. "Mmm . . . so sweet. I love the taste of men's juice . . . it's like a little aperitif." She leaned over to Sophie and put her tongue into her mouth.

She jerked him again, more vigorously this time—and more juice seeped out. She traced her tongue more fully round the head, anxious to catch all of the liquid. Looking at him, she savoured it for a moment, then leaned forward and took him partially into her mouth, licking all round the head, tasting the drying residue of Sophie's juice as well as his. She pulled it out again and looked at it swelling with anticipation.

"Fuck . . . that's good," he whispered.

She ran her fingers across the head, very tenderly squeezing and playing, teasing him, but not to the point where he would ejaculate. She began pumping him again, and each time she thought he was about to erupt, she would take her hand away and blow softly on it, letting him calm, before engulfing him briefly in her mouth to bring him back to the point of near ecstasy. Once or twice she ran both hands all over it from top to bottom, pulling at his foreskin, dropping spit onto the top to keep it slippery and wet.

She leant forward and licked his balls, curling her tongue around each one, before carefully sucking them individually into her mouth.

He moaned softly.

She raised her head to just over the end of his prick, then pulled his foreskin fully back and plunged it into her mouth. Suddenly she was overwhelmed by the feel and taste of it. She could sense the hot blood pulsing through the muscle—and uncontrollably, she pressed it to the back of her throat, taking it as deep as she could without gagging, letting it stretch and fill her mouth totally. She held it until she thought she might retch, then released it, gasping as she lifted off, saliva gushing from her lips. A few moments later, she plunged it in again, keeping it pressing farther into her throat and holding it for longer. She gasped again as she pulled it out—and long sticky strings of saliva covered it from top to bottom.

"Oh fuck," he moaned. "I want to fuck you . . . fuck your mouth."

She felt his hand at the back of her head pressing her forward towards it, and she could see the tip quivering with excitement, the little eye widening in anticipation.

She brought her mouth close to the tip and jerked him with her hand. She saw him swell deep purple and knew he couldn't wait. Quickly, she took a deep breath and held it, then let him thrust to the back of her mouth, fucking himself in and out, five or six times before he groaned.

She pushed him to the front of her mouth just as the first heavy spurt shot out of him. He pushed in again, and a second spurt spat onto her tongue. It was warm and heavy with that sharp tang of a living fluid—and it seemed to effervesce all round her mouth and down her throat. Still holding her head, he thrust sharply in and out a few times, still moaning

loudly, and she gave herself to it, gave herself to his pleasure, the semen gathering in her mouth and dribbling down
her chin.

He flopped out and she closed her eyes, rolling the fluid
around her mouth, feeling it melt and change . . .

Sophie sat up and put her arm around Emma's shoulders.
"Let me taste." Emma kept her mouth open as Sophie kissed
her, allowing his cum to flow onto her friend's tongue. She
felt suddenly wonderfully tired, satiated, and relaxed. She
pushed Sophie gently onto the bed next to Antoine, then lay
on top of her, kissing her for a long time . . .

She opened her eyes to see Sophie's face close to hers,
studying her. She kissed Emma softly.

"I am going to church with Mama," she said. "I will see
you later."

"Church? OK." Emma turned on her side, sleepily. It was
morning, and she couldn't remember falling asleep. She
watched as Sophie slid clothes over her sleek, sexy body. A
short skirt, no panties, and a silk blouse with no bra. "Where
is Antoine?"

"Next door. He likes a lot of room in bed when he sleeps."

"Did you sleep with me?"

"Yes—of course." She blew a kiss and left the room.

Emma dozed, tired from the exertions of the night before.

She didn't know how long it was when she came to, feeling a body lying behind her in the bed. She knew instantly it
was Antoine. She could feel his rough beard on her shoulder
and his hard penis pressing against her buttocks. His hand
smoothed her breast, then moved down between her legs.
His fingers explored her thatch of pubic hair and found her
clitoris.

He shifted his body downwards slightly, and she felt him
probe between her thighs. She moved her knees up to her
chest and she felt him slide his hand round so that he could

stroke her anus and pussy. His fingers opened her vagina slightly and his penis nudged her entrance. She gasped as the next second she felt him slide easily and deeply into her. She was relaxed and wet and she shivered with delight as he began to fuck her slowly.

He hugged closer to her, his hands moving to fondle her breasts and his mouth ravishing her neck and ear. She felt the sensation scatter across her body and pressed herself backwards to get him deeper. It was the first time she had been alone with a man since Charlie, but she quickly put that from her mind. Antoine was warm, considerate, and clever. Last night had been a revelation. She could easily slip from one side of her sexuality to the other, or enjoy both at the same time.

She turned her head and found his mouth. His hand had found her clitoris and she whimpered softly under their kiss at the gentle ripples of pleasure. The fact that they had hardly spoken last night and were not speaking now seemed to make it only more erotic. For a few minutes she lay in her near fetal position, letting him fuck her, the delicious peaks and troughs of pleasure coming and going. He was probing her deeply, and she could feel the walls of her vagina being stimulated with each thrust, parting as he came into her and closing behind with a lovely shimmer as he withdrew. It was slow and calculating sex. They were taking time to seek every avenue of stimulation, flexing their pelvic muscles to find every nuance.

She began to tense unconsciously and felt the stirrings of an orgasm grow in her belly. She smiled to herself. Ever since that horrible night with Charlie—then that strange and wonderful rebirth with Sally the next morning—she had almost assumed that she had become a lesbian, that she maybe didn't want straight sex anymore. Making love to Sophie had been so satisfying, so engrossing—why would she ever want to go back to the crude sex she'd had with men?

But last night had shown her that it could be different, and the strange attraction she had to Gerald told her that her sexuality was broad, all embracing, and that she could give herself in every way possible. She adored lesbian sex, but there was something about a man filling her, taking her, penetrating and probing her that was electric. She remembered his semen in her mouth, the urgency with which he came, the hot viscous taste.

She put her hand behind and stilled his thrusting—then eased herself off his penis. She could feel the cool air on the heat of her pussy as she turned herself round and pushed him gently onto his back. She smiled at him wickedly and took his cock in her hand. It was wet and slippery from her juice and she felt that familiar dryness gather in her throat as she slowly massaged her hand up and down its shaft. She squeezed it as she pulled up to the head—and a small bead of liquid appeared. She lowered her head, taking it into her mouth. She rolled her tongue around it, sucking gently. The strong, pungent smell of sweat drifted into her nostrils and the taste was salty. Last night's loving and today's warm mucus made a stringent cocktail that made her shiver and a huge longing build in her stomach.

She licked it clean, running her tongue all round it, sinking it in and out of her mouth. She heard him moan and raised herself to look at him. Keeping her eyes on him, she flicked her tongue all round the tip, teasing him as much as she could before she plunged it back into her mouth and sucked him strongly, pushing him as far back in her throat as she dared. Lust burning through her, she popped it out of her mouth and began to jerk it vigorously. She gripped it hard and pumped it up and down until her arm began to ache. It grew longer, harder, and hotter and she knew from the look in his eyes that he might come, so she let it go suddenly. It stood straight, straining, glistening, and red. She lay on the top of him and kissed him, taking his head in her hands. She wrestled her tongue with his as she felt his hardness press against her groin.

Unable to resist any longer, she rolled off him and lay with her legs open. "Fuck me," she whispered, and put her hands above her head and grasped the headboard.

He smiled at her, took his cock in his hand, and put it to the entrance of her pussy. He thrust quickly and strongly into her.

She cried out at the hot spasm of pleasure shooting up inside her. He held himself above her on his outstretched arms and was thrusting hard, slapping his pelvis against her. She looked down at where they were joined, watched as both their loins moved subtly and unconsciously to give and receive maximum pleasure.

His eyes were scanning and drinking in the contours of her body and face and she could see the concentrated lust. But he was a considerate lover, one who knew that the more pleasure he gave her, the more he would receive in return.

She ran her feet up the bed, tipping her pelvis more towards him to meet his penetration, allowing him in deeper. She shuddered as she felt her vaginal walls shimmer with sensation. She clenched herself tighter around him and immediately heard him groan softly. She wondered what it was like to have that hard shaft as part of you, burning with pent-up feeling and two tight balls desperate to release their precious nectar.

He began to move in a circular motion, which excited the walls of her pussy even more. She let go of the headboard and took his head in her hands, pulling him down into a passionate French kiss. She wanted to eat his mouth and pushed her tongue forcefully all round it. She loved the rough feel of his morning beard tingling on her skin and knew she could never do without sex with men. The strong muscles of his body, his lovely blue eyes flecked with grey, the sexy turn of his mouth, the sheer joy of lying back and being fucked.

She felt that delicious resistance form in her belly—the kindling of an orgasm. She would resist as long as she could, the pleasure heightening more and more, the inevitability of release becoming more intense. Why had she worried that she wouldn't be able to climax with a guy? She had been freed, allowed to flower, her body given the sweet secret, and she could allow herself to burn with whoever, whenever.

He broke from her mouth and lowered his head and ravaged one of her breasts. The pulsing from her vagina was suddenly joined by her nipple rejoicing at his teasing. The resistance spread from her stomach to her legs and arms, building to a glorious tension, the raging of a hopeless pitched battle where the forces of ecstasy would overwhelm her. "AHHHHHHHHHHHHH!!" she screamed. "YES—YES—FUCK ME . . . FUCK ME . . . FUCK MEEEEEEEEEEE!!!!" Her back arched off the bed and she threw her arms around his neck, crushing him to her as her orgasm cleansed every fibre, every muscle, every sinew . . .

He was still moving slowly in her, sending lovely ripples through her body, but she could tell that he hadn't come and that he needed to—as much as she had.

"You want to come?" she said to him in French.

"Yes," he said.

"Inside me—or in my mouth?"

"On your tits."

She smiled and raised her eyebrows. "Oh. OK."

He pulled out of her gently, then shifted up the bed slightly, kneeling. She took the slippery member in her hand, and squeezing it ever so slightly, massaged it up and down. She looked up into his eyes and could see him looking at her breasts intently. He began to moan, and she could see the hot shaft swelling in her hand. They shifted again so that it was pointing directly at her breasts, and in the next second, he groaned loudly, and long warm spurts of semen splashed across her, covering her chest, nipples, and breasts in thick, pearly drops. She pumped him, her hand flying up and down. "Oh yeah . . . lots and lots of lovely spunk." When he was finally spent, he sank back on his haunches, smiling at her.

"Good?" she said, putting her hands to her breasts and gently massaging the warm, slippery liquid into her skin.

"Fantastic," he whispered.

She sat up and kissed him. "That was lovely. I'm not going to wash it off. I want to keep it on my skin."

Antoine rolled onto his back, then turned on his side away from her.

She lay on her back, a gentle trembling still fluttering round her body. She looked up at the portrait of the two girls. Then for some reason Sally's face drifted into her mind. The girl who had led her into paradise. Emma wanted so much at that moment to see her again, hold her, kiss her, share this with her.

She got off the bed, went over to the door, and walked down the corridor to the bathroom. She peed, then brushed her teeth, but made no attempt to wash. When she returned to the room, she saw that Antoine was asleep. She took a short dress that she had brought with her and hung up last night for the creases to drop out, and put it on. She didn't bother with underwear.

She went down to the kitchen and helped herself to some coffee and croissant that had been left out. No one was around. Sophie and her mother were obviously still at church, and there was no sign of Gerald. She thought for a moment, then when she had finished breakfast, made her way through the house to the studio.

He was there, working on her portrait, using some sketches from their walk the previous day. He was dressed in jogging pants and a black shirt that was open down the front.

"Ah—good. I was hoping you would come down so that I could work some more with you."

"Are the others still at church?" she said nonchalantly.

"Yes. Wallowing in righteousness."

She stopped a few feet from him. "Sophie's Christianity fascinates me."

"It fascinates me. Still . . . the church loves sinners."

"Only she doesn't think of herself that way."

"Quite."

His eyes bored through her, and she had that same feeling of him undressing her, mentally.

She turned and wandered to the window, looking out at the sunny morning, bright on the lawn and fountain.

"Did you have a fun time last night?"

"In bed, you mean?" she said, looking back. "Yes . . . fantastic sex." She leant back against the window keeping her eyes on him.

"Antoine is a young stallion, isn't he?"

"Yes, wonderful."

"Did he have both of you?"

"Several times. All three of us made love. Then he had me on my own this morning. I've just got out of bed and left him asleep."

"Fresh from having sex with him?"

"Yes. I love it when you can still smell your lover on your body."

He hesitated for a moment, looking intently at her. "Come here."

As she walked over to him, she felt as if a magnet was pulling her. She stood in front of him and felt her pulse race. He put out his hands and pushed both of her dress straps from her shoulders. She felt the garment begin to slide and hang on her held only by her breasts. He gently ran his hands across her shoulders. They were surprisingly soft and supple and scattered goose pimples across her.

"So smooth, young, and perfect," he whispered. His hands drifted down to her breasts. He edged the dress off them and it fell to the floor. She kept her eyes glued to his as he fondled her breasts. She felt her nipples stiffen slightly as his fingers explored. Desire scattered across her skin like a cool morning breeze.

"What's this?"

She looked down. He was looking at the traces of white on her chest and breasts.

"Antoine wanted to come over my boobs. It felt lovely. So I rubbed it into my skin." She closed her eyes as his hands continued down her body, running down her stomach, the touch so gentle and profound. It was as though she had suddenly one less layer of skin and was naked in a way that she had never been before. She was conscious of her breathing and heart rate quickening. It was as though she was having her body explored for the first time, feeling that primeval excitement. "I love being naked for you," she said, opening her eyes. His gaze pierced deeply into her. She reached up and pushed his shirt from his shoulders and pressed her body against his. She ran her hands over his strong back, pressing her palms strongly against his flesh, as though wanting to sink into him. She tucked her head into his neck, licking and kissing his skin. He didn't have the fresh smell of all the young men she had made love to. It was darker, stronger, the scent of experience and knowledge.

She could feel his erection through his trousers. It was separated from her by just a thin layer of material. Instinctively, she pressed herself against it, gently and slowly at first, then as the arousal lit up her skin and pumped through her body, she rubbed herself more strongly, flexing her pelvis to crush her clitoris deliciously against his hardness. In seconds her sex was burning and she knew she would come. She ground herself wildly and uncontrollably against him, her orgasm rising like a fire held deep underground. As it burst out through her, she clasped his head. "Oh, Gerald . . . I want you . . . OHHH YESSSSSS!!!"

She clung to him, her gasping and whimpering echoing round the studio as the feeling subsided. She kissed his hair, his neck, his shoulders—and finally she brought her mouth to his and let his strong, thick tongue posses her.

He broke their kiss and pushed her gently from him. His penis was straining beneath his trousers: she put her hand on it—but he took it away sharply.

"Lie down," he said.

Still regaining her breath, she backed slowly to the sofa, keeping her eyes on him. She sat down on it and lay back, her hand drifting to her sex. She stroked it gently, feeling warm ripples of pleasure. "Don't you just want to come here and fuck me, Gerald? I'm offering myself to you. I want you to penetrate me. I'm wet and ready. I want to feel you come inside me—fill me."

"No, I'm not going to fuck you."

"Oh please." She writhed slowly, luxuriously. She knew she could make herself come again just by touching herself, but she wanted him—on top of her, taking her, hard inside her. "You don't have to let yourself come. Don't you just want to know what it would feel like to be inside me?"

He looked at her darkly for a moment, then looked down at his canvass without replying.

"I would come again instantly—I want you that much." Still staring at him, she pushed a finger slowly inside her vagina and sighed. "Maybe if I sucked you, you could let yourself come in my mouth?"

"I want to catch you in paint," he said sharply. "Haven't you been fucked enough?"

She was stung, and felt like a naughty schoolgirl who had been told off. She turned her head away and lay not looking at him, gazing out at the sun on the trees and the grass.

They didn't speak again until he told her the session was over. She got up, took her dress from the floor, and held it in her hand. Still naked, she looked at him. "I'll fuck you one day, Gerald," she said, then walked towards the door.

As she drove away, Emma felt the unbelievable sexual high of the weekend receding—like being pulled from the draw of a magnet with every kilometre she travelled.

When Sophie had come back, they went to her room and lay on the bed and chatted. They had kissed and hugged—but hadn't made love again. She had extracted a promise from Emma that they would meet soon.

They all had lunch and then they had kissed her good-bye—Sophie and Antoine passionately, Therese warmly on the lips, and Gerald casually on the cheek, as though it didn't matter to him at all.

Chapter 11

When Sally woke the next morning, the memories of the three of them—her, Lou, and Jamie—still lingered in her mind. Rain was pattering gently on the bedroom window. She rang the farm, and Emma's father told her not to bother to come over until the rain stopped. She made herself some tea and took it back to bed. She lay there and thought about Lou again.

It was funny being at home on my own that evening, knowing that Jamie was round at Lou's. I kept on thinking about them having sex. I wasn't jealous or anything, but I guess I sort of felt a bit left out. I was tired, but I made myself stay up quite late until he came back.

"Hi. Still up?" he said as he came in and saw me in the lounge.

"Yeah," I said. "Had some work to do." I was in my pyjamas: a little pair of shorts and a T-shirt. I could see him looking at my legs and tits.

"Oh . . . right."

I moved and made room for him on the sofa. "Come and sit down. How was Lou?"

"Yeah. Good."

"Good nookie?"

He looked awkward. "Yeah."

I looked at his crotch. His cock was there, still covered with her juice, probably. It sort of turned me on to think about it. I put my hand on his leg. "How many times did you do it?"

"Just once. Her folks came back."

"Did you shag her in her bed?"

"Yeah."

"With nothing on?"

"Yeah."

"Mmm, you lucky thing. She's got such a lovely body." I moved my hand up his leg and rubbed his cock under his jeans. "It's making me a bit horny just thinking about it."

"Really?" He smiled and looked at my tits.

I pulled my T-shirt over my head. "Yeah. I don't suppose you fancy another one?"

I saw the lust burn in his eyes. "OK. Here?"

"Yeah. Take your clothes off."

"Shouldn't we go to your room?"

"No. Mum's at work, and he's drunk. He won't hear."

I pushed my shorts down and lay back naked on the sofa. I watched as he quickly took off his shirt and jeans. He lay down naked on top of me and I felt an unbelievable rush of lust. I kissed him passionately and felt my clit spark at the contact with his body. "Your tongue has been in Lou's mouth and now it's in mine. Have you washed your prick?"

He looked crestfallen. "No—do you want me to?"

I smiled. "No. Let me look at it."

He raised himself and sat back, his legs dropping to the floor. I sat up next to him. His prick was standing hard and erect. I took it in my hand and jerked him slowly. "Only a few minutes ago, it was in Lou's pussy."

"Yeah." His voice was a little husky.

"With all her juice on it." I let go of it and brought my hand to my face. I smelt it, drawing in a long breath. "Mmmm. I can smell her." I leant down and took it in my mouth. It felt so unbelievably sexy running my tongue all round it, savouring the strong taste of sweat and cum, his and hers. It was though I went into overdrive. I pulled his foreskin back and licked it again, wanting to get all the smell and taste.

Then I couldn't wait any longer—I quickly lifted my head and put my leg over him and sat on him, taking his prick and guiding it into me.

The feeling of it stretching up into me was unbelievable. I cried out quite loudly and sank farther down, forcing it right up. "I want to fuck her and you together. I want all three of us to have sex. I want to lick her pussy and put my tongue inside her. I want to kiss her . . . ohhhh fuck . . . YEAAAH . . ."

"Shouldn't I put a condom on?" he said.

"Oh shit. Fuck. Yeah." I lifted myself off him. "I've got one upstairs. Wait a minute." I climbed off him and ran upstairs. I was completely naked. If Ray had come out of his room, he would have gotten a full view—but I just didn't care. My pussy was hot and throbbing and I felt so randy. I got the condom from my drawer, then tripped downstairs again. I opened the packet with my teeth, then put it onto his prick. He unrolled it all the way down.

I clambered back on top of him, then sank onto it, sighing at the gorgeous sensation.

"It'll be great when we don't have to use these bloody things," I said. "When you can just let yourself go and squirt all your cum inside me."

"Yeah—can't wait. It's a bit like sucking a toffee with the paper wrapping on."

I flexed my groin on top of him, grinding down, getting him all the way inside and my clit rubbing against him. I could feel his hard stalk stretching me, pushing up so deeply. "God, it feels so fucking good. I want to do this all the time," I said, my voice husky.

"Is it better than lesbian sex?"

I smiled at him. "It's different. Girl sex is more emotional—but this is pretty fucking good."

I was pounding myself up and down on him now and my orgasm was rising so strongly. For a moment I couldn't see, I was tensing so much. I didn't think it would ever burst, ever give me relief; I would always be on the edge, unable to breathe. "Yeah, yeah, YEAAAAH . . . FUCK . . . AHHHH-HHH!"

After what seemed like an eternity of gorgeous, draining sensation, I relaxed onto him, putting my arms round his neck, closing my eyes.

After a few minutes, I lifted my head. I smiled at him. "Did you come?"

"No. Didn't quite get there."

"Do you want to?"

"Yeah."

"Like this?"

"Can I fuck you from behind?"

"OK." I lifted myself off him. He was very wet from my cum, almost as though I had pissed on him. I knelt on the end of the sofa, sticking my bum in the air. I felt him come into me and heard him moan.

He fucked me strongly for a few long, luscious minutes. It felt nice, but I was too far gone to come again. Eventually, he grunted and jabbed into me in a random sort of way, and I knew he'd gotten there. He felt so big and hard, it was amazing.

Once he had finished, he pulled out and lay on top of me. We kissed for a few minutes, not speaking.

"You came quickly," he said finally.

"Yeah, well—I've been sitting here getting all hot thinking about you fucking Lou, haven't I?"

"Would have been amazing if you had been there as well."

"Yeah—well, I'm going to talk to her about that," I said casually. "I think we should organise it." I looked up at him. He looked so excited.

The next day, I went to the doctor's first thing and got my prescription for the pill. Then later, Lou and I walked home from school through the park. I glanced around to see if anyone was about, then I took her hand. "I've been thinking about the three of us—you know, getting it on and stuff."

"Yeah?"

"Well, don't you think it would be fun to do it together?"

"What? A threesome?"

"Yeah."

She smiled at me wickedly. "Yeah—do you think Jamie would be up for it?"

"Course he would. I've already suggested it."

She pulled me off the path into the wood, then pushed me up against a tree. "You're a really wicked girl—you know that?"

"Yeah—what am I like?"

"It'll probably be best at my place. I'll see what's going on and let you know."

We kissed, and I felt her fingers trace up my legs and onto my pussy. "Got time for a quickie?"

"You bet . . ."

That was on Friday, and that weekend, Jamie was away on a football course, and Lou had family staying for the weekend, so I didn't see either of them.

On Monday, Lou came up to me at school. "Got it sorted," she said. "My parents are going to a party, and there will be no one else in—this Saturday."

"OK—that will be fun," I said.

"Yeah, it will," she whispered, looking quickly around. "A lot of fun."

Jamie came back on the Wednesday, but I didn't get to see him alone until the following day. He sort of looked at me sheepishly and mentioned that Lou had told him about Saturday.

"Yeah . . ." I whispered, sexily. I went up and kissed him lightly. He was sitting on my bed in his football gear about to go out. "Do you fancy it before you go?" I said, undoing the buttons of my blouse.

"I haven't time."

"Sure?" I pushed the blouse from my shoulders and reached round and undid my bra.

"Yeah—I've got to go." He stared at my tits.

I put my hands on them and fondled them. "My nipples are really hard—and I'm on the pill now."

He smirked and got up off the bed, but I stepped in his way. Still keeping my eyes on him, I undid my skirt and let it fall to the ground. I put my hand into my panties. "God, I'm really wet. I'll come in a couple of minutes." I put my arms around his neck and rubbed myself against him. "Please fuck me. You can have me any way you want." I kissed him and felt his tongue shoot strongly into my mouth. His hands went to my panties and pushed them down. Laughing, I pushed his shorts down as well, and then I went and threw myself onto the bed.

I lay there with my legs open as he kicked his shorts off and pulled his football shirt over his head. I put my fingers to my pussy and pulled the lips apart. I was seeping with juice and couldn't believe how randy I felt. "My cunt is hot, wet, and ready for you. Just fuck it—now."

He climbed on top of me and I grabbed his cock, bringing it straight to my entrance. As he lay down on top of me, he pushed it in right to the hilt. The feeling was incredible. I cried out—I could already feel the onset of my climax, and as he thrust roughly in and out, it was like I was being pumped up with pleasure. "Oh fuck, I'm coming already. I just love your cock so much."

"Little sister wants a good hard fuck, does she?"

"Yes . . . yes, fuck me now . . . fuck me when you come back, fuck me tonight, just fuck me, fuck me . . . FUCK MEEE . . . AHHHHH YEAAAAH . . ." My body went rigid as the pressure rose. I didn't think I could bear it; he was pumping harder and faster and deeper every time. He was so deep inside me and fucking me so hard that it just overwhelmed me, the orgasm bursting right through—and I went mad, squirming on the bed underneath him.

"God, you're so fucking randy," he said, "I love fucking you . . . AHHHHHH!"

I knew he was coming, but still had such a head rush from my orgasm that I didn't feel his spunk squirting inside me.

"Oh . . . fuck, that was great," I said as my body calmed down. "Quick and so intense. Was it OK for you?"

"Brilliant. You're amazing."

"Mmm . . . so are you."

"Yeah. Shit—I better go." He still had his football socks on, but nothing else. He quickly got dressed and went to the door. "See you later."

"OK," I said, not feeling as if I wanted to get up. It was that fantastic feeling after really good and intense sex. As I heard him skip down the stairs, I turned my head onto the pillow and dozed.

When I finally came to, I had a nice, warm, randy feeling in my pussy. I put my finger down and could feel it was so wet between my legs, but also on the sheet. I had forgotten that if he wasn't wearing a condom, then it was going to dribble out of me. I ran it round my pussy, then pushed it down to my bum. My finger slithered around and it felt so nice. I loved having Lou's finger up my bum—and I thought about anal sex. What was it like? Did it hurt?

I noticed the new hairbrush I had bought myself. Getting out of bed, I washed the handle in the bathroom, then found the large jar of Vaseline my mum kept there. I put my finger in and scooped some up, then reached round to my bum and smeared round my sphincter. Then I pushed inside to lubricate more. Finally, I plunged the handle of the brush into the pot and covered it. I looked at it and smiled. I took it back to bed, lay back, and put the end on my anus. Gingerly, I pushed. The thin end slipped easily past my sphincter—it was cold, but felt good, and when I massaged my clit with my other hand, I began to feel that familiar stirring.

The circumference already inside me was about a finger size, but the thickness grew to about an inch and a half—about the size of an average guy's penis, I thought—before it tapered back off near to the bristles.

I frigged myself more vigorously, then pushed it a little farther in. I felt a surge of sensation from my sphincter—no pain yet, so I pushed again. There was a sudden hot stinging as I got it in to around an inch in diameter, but frigging my clit was making it easier to relax. I pushed again and felt a sharp pain, quickly followed by a ring of fiery pleasure.

"I can take it," I murmured to myself—and pushed it right into me. It hurt a lot for a minute, so I held it there, trying to get used to it. My clit was burning and I began to feel the pain and the pleasure merge. Slowly, I moved it gently back and forth, fucking myself. The pain was going now and I felt full and stretched—the nerve endings in my sphincter were sending lovely feelings scattering up my rectum, and I immediately knew I was coming, but coming in a different way. I was having an orgasm in my anus, my pelvis gyrating on the hard invading plastic, my sphincter relaxing totally, the large fat section sliding easily in and out of me, my whole abdomen being consumed in a rush of lovely pleasure . . .

My head swam and I just lay there in a daze. It had been so intense, so different, but so amazing.

I remember when we arrived at Lou's on the Saturday night, she seemed every excited—I think she'd had a couple of drinks already. She asked what we should do. I mean, it was a bit of a strange question, as we knew what we were going to do, but there was a slight nervousness between us.

"Let's play Trivial Pursuit," I said. "Instead of actually using the board, we should give each other forfeits if we get questions wrong."

"What—a bit like strip poker?" she said.

"Yeah."

Lou started, with Jamie asking the question. She didn't know the answer, so she took off the jogging bottoms she had on. I had a mini skirt on, so I remember feeling her warm bare legs against mine. Her eyes were bright with excitement, and I could see she was quite pissed.

She read the next question to me, and I got it wrong, so I took off my cardigan. I just had a T-shirt on with no bra underneath.

I read the next one to Jamie, and he got it right. We both giggled and booed, but Jamie just smirked. He read another one to Lou, and again she got it wrong.

"Shit!" she said—and kicked off her shoes.

I got mine wrong as well and began to feel quite excited. "If I'd known we were going to play this, I would have put a bra on," I said as I pulled my T-shirt over my head.

They both looked at my bare tits.

"Never mind," I said, "I do have knickers on." I leant my head down and put it on Lou's shoulder.

Jamie got the next one wrong and took off his shirt. "Mmm—nice torso," I said.

"Yeah—it's good, isn't it?" said Lou. She gave me a sexy smile, her eyes big and deep blue.

I knew the answer to the next one, but deliberately got it wrong—then I pushed my skirt down to the floor and sat just in my skimpy panties. They both cheered.

Jamie and Lou both got theirs wrong. Jamie ending up in his boxers and his socks, and Lou just in her bra and panties. They both got theirs wrong again after I got mine right. Jamie took off his socks, while I watched Lou unclip her bra, revealing her lovely, suckable tits, with their nice conical nipples.

I took her hand. "Hey," I said. "Who's going to be nude first?"

"Me, probably," said Lou. She kept my hand in hers and squeezed it gently.

Jamie asked her the question, and sure enough, she got it wrong. "Well, here goes," she said, and pushed her knickers down. I felt a little pang of lust as I looked at her.

Giggling, she asked me the next question, slightly slurring her words. I knew the answer, but said something different. "Hooray—there we go," I cried, as I pulled my knickers off and threw them across the room. I could feel the randy excitement build as I grabbed the box of questions. "Right, Jamie," I said, and asked him the question. He answered perfectly. "Shit!" I shouted.

He asked Lou the next one, and she got it right as well. I didn't know the answer to mine. "So—what do I have to do?"

"French kiss Lou," he said.

"Right."

She put her hand on my face and brought her lips to mine. I heard her moan softly and felt her mouth open so that we could French kiss. Her skin was so soft and sensuous, and we pulled each other together, kissing passionately. It felt so good that I couldn't stop myself putting my hand down to her pussy and feeling through the fuzz of hair to the moist slit. I ran my finger along and felt it ooze with cum.

"I think I got my next question wrong," said Jamie. We both looked, and he had pushed his boxers to the floor and was holding his rigid cock in his hand. "What's my penalty?" he said.

Lou looked at me wickedly and smiled. "Fuck your stepsister."

I kissed her hard, then told her to move up the sofa. She lay down lengthways, and I knelt with my knees either side of her. "Fuck me from behind," I said.

I kissed her lips, then made my way down to her neck and breasts. I felt his fingers probe me and then his long, slim prick eased its way in. I was in heaven as I sucked on her nipples, my bum thrust back towards him. He was slapping against me, and I felt little thrills of pleasure as he went in really deep. I could sense Lou rubbing her pussy on my stomach, and much as I loved kissing her tits, I wanted to lick her there and taste her.

I kissed down her tummy, and she shifted up farther so that I could get my head between her legs. She smelt really strongly, as though she was on heat, and when I took my first lick, I could tell she was really wet and excited.

She gasped. "Oh . . . fuck, that's great . . ."

She tasted nice. Her lips were not smooth like mine, but full and thick, and I ran my tongue up and down, easing them apart, and found her opening. As the tip of my tongue penetrated her, she drew in breath sharply.

Jamie was fucking me quite hard now and moaning loudly, and I knew he would come quite quickly. I pushed my tongue in as far as I could, and each time he thrust into me, my face was pushed up against her sex.

"Ohhh . . . fuck her, Jamie," whispered Lou. "This is so amazing . . . I feel so randy."

I lifted my head briefly and smiled at her, licking my lips. Her cum tasted so good in my mouth and his prick was sending shivers all over my body.

He groaned loudly. "Ohhh yeah . . . fuck yeah . . ." His thrusts became sharp and fast and a few seconds later I felt that tingle deep inside that told me he was ejaculating.

"Oh fuck, oh yeah . . . YEAAAH . . ." He pounded me more, fucking himself dry, then relaxed along my back.

"Good?" I said, turning my head towards him.

He pulled out his prick and collapsed back on the sofa. "Brilliant."

I adjusted myself, putting my knees on the floor, allowing me to get a better angle to go down on her. I felt a bit disappointed he had come so quickly, and could still feel the longing in my pussy, but I wanted to give Lou a good time. I concentrated on her clit now, putting my mouth right over her pussy and flicking it with my tongue. She seemed to like that.

"Oh, Sally . . . yeah . . . I'm going to come like that."

I reached my hand down to my pussy and collected some of his spunk that was already beginning to dribble out. I brought my fingers to my mouth and licked them. "Mmmm—I can taste his cum as well as yours," I said.

"Let me taste," she said.

I reached down and got some more on my fingers, then I reached up and put them to her mouth. She licked them sexily.

I felt an amazing throb of lust in my tummy—not just because my pussy was still hot from Jamie fucking me, but because I loved having her pussy in my mouth. I love cunnilingus. I love doing it and I love getting it. I suppose that should have told me something at the time, and it should tell me something now. I'm a lesbian. I like sex with blokes—I mean, I fell in love with Jamie, and in many ways I still love him—but nothing gives me the sexual thrill that making love with a girl does.

The lips of her pussy were so thick that I could suck them into my mouth. I knew she wanted me to make her come by playing with her clit, but I couldn't stop myself just sucking on the flesh of her lips, tasting it, exploring it with my tongue. She was getting more and more excited, and although I was keeping her climax at bay, I knew it would be all the more intense if I made her wait.

Every so often I would slip my tongue inside her, pushing as far in as I could—and every time I was rewarded by a little gush of her cum with its sweet, sharp taste.

"Sal . . . please, please . . . I'm so close."

I raised my head for a moment and looked sexily into her eyes, then I went back down and began to give her what she wanted, my tongue teasing the little hard nub of her clit. I lapped it with the flat of my tongue first, but then slowly I began to flick it from side to side, occasionally curling my tongue in circles round it, listening to her little cries to tell how close she was. When I thought she was just about to explode, I would hold off a little, then start again, building her higher and higher, bringing her to the point where I knew she wouldn't be able to stand it any longer.

She screamed with a mixture of frustration and ecstasy. I knew she was ready, so I brought my fingers to her pussy, pushing two in roughly, then brought my tongue to flick the underside of her clit fast this time and getting faster, until my tongue began to ache.

Her body lurched. She screamed again, and she clenched her thighs tightly around me, cry after cry, with her body contorting and shifting, my mouth still hard against her, kissing her, loving her, my fingers searching her inside, wanting to make the pleasure last as long as I could . . .

She lay for a long time, her head turned into the back of the sofa, breathing in fits and starts, almost as though she were sobbing, her rib cage jerking up and down.

I lay on top of her and stroked her hair. Eventually she turned her head to mine, a smile broadly extending across her mouth, her eyes half closed. I kissed her and she sighed, opening her mouth as though she wanted to eat me. We kissed again as she slowly calmed beneath me.

"I've never ever had an orgasm like that," she whispered.

I looked up, and Jamie was sitting in the chair opposite, stroking himself. He was hard again, his cock red and glistening.

"Let's have a taste of that," I said.

He moved across to us and dangled it in front of our mouths. I took it in my hand and put it towards Lou's mouth. She put out her tongue and licked it, so I put my mouth down to it and licked it as well. I wrapped my hand round the base and massaged it slowly as we played our tongues all round it. I heard him moan. I put it right into my mouth for a minute, letting him push to the back of my throat. It felt so horny having his hot, hard flesh stretching my mouth open and sitting on my tongue. I was the only one of us who hadn't come yet, and so I was even more randy than the other two.

I pulled it out and directed it into Lou's mouth. While she sucked on him, I kissed him, running my hands through his lovely fair hair. "Why don't you lie down and let Lou sit on your prick," I said, "then I will sit on your face. You can have your prick up her and your tongue up me."

She pulled his cock out of her mouth and laughed. "Better get on the floor."

Jamie lay down on the rug and Lou straddled him, sliding his prick into her until it disappeared completely. Then she began to rise and sink on him, her juice glistening on his shaft. It looked unbelievably horny. Her legs were splayed either side of him, the taut muscles of her thighs sticking out, her tits all pert, the nipples hard. I positioned myself above his head, then spread my legs until his tongue could make contact with my fanny. I was facing Lou, so I leant across and kissed her, rubbing my tongue sexily against hers.

We stayed like that for several minutes, our mouths locked together, our hands stroking and fondling each other's tits.

The feel of his mouth on my pussy was heavenly. His tongue was playing up and down my slit, and the fever inside me was building. Eventually, it felt so intense, I broke off from snogging Lou and I used my fingers to part my vaginal lips so that he could really get at my clit.

"Oh fuck . . . I'm going to come," I said. My heart was racing and the throbbing tension was pounding in my groin. My tits almost hurt with arousal and I was taking deep lungfuls of glorious air, sighing and crying at the amazing sensation.

Lou put her hands on my face and kissed me and that sent me over the edge. I screwed my eyes up tightly and yelled out, my whole body jerking with the shocks that were tearing through it. Lou still had hold of my head and was kissing my neck and shoulders and tits, sending hot shudders all round my torso. I wrapped my hands in her hair, pressing her to me. Jamie was working his tongue harder than ever, and I thought the orgasm would never end. Just when I thought I had reached the peak, another climax came, and I felt myself ejaculate several times. I gasped and relaxed, the shocks still shooting through me, but eventually felt myself calming.

"Fuck," he shouted, laughing. "You nearly choked me."

His mouth and neck were wet and I could see little splashes on the carpet. "Yeah—I cum a lot," I said. "You've got to learn to swallow it. You know, just like you want us to do." I raised myself off him and knelt next to Lou, kissing her. I put my fingers down to her pubic bush and gently rubbed her clitoris. Jamie was pushing up and down into her and she was sighing softly. "I'm going to sit behind you," I said, and I lifted my leg over his, straddling him as well, sitting close up to her, my tits pressing into her back. I put my finger back to her clit and fondled her boobs from behind with my other hand, then I began to kiss her neck and shoulders.

She moaned and turned her head to kiss me deeply. "Oh, this is fucking amazing," she said.

As I worked her clit with my fingers, I could feel Jamie's hard prick sliding in and out. I shuffled myself closer to her, spreading my legs, trying to rub my pussy against her bum.

"Oh God, Sal . . . I'm going to come again . . . hold me."

I rubbed her little bud harder and faster, bringing my other hand to hold her stomach.

She threw her head back and we were cheek to cheek. She was crying out now and I suddenly felt her body jerk and tense and a shrill scream come from her throat. I held her tightly, kissing her neck and cheek, and it was like she'd been struck by an electric current, wracking her body. I felt her spasm all over one last time and then make a long gasp. She seemed to not breathe for a long time before she relaxed into my arms. After a moment, she turned her head to me and smiled, with a lovely calmness all over her face. "I love you," she whispered.

I kissed her lovingly, rolling our tongues together. I heard Jamie murmur, and we both looked down at him. His face was concentrated, looking at us kissing, and his hips were thrusting sharply up into Lou's pussy.

"Oh fuck . . . fuck, that's so horny," he was murmuring, and I could see the blood pumping into his face. His torso was lovely and tense, exaggerating the muscles in his stomach, and I knew he was close to coming.

"Yeah, let it go," I said, and started kissing Lou again. His moans grew louder and then I felt his hand brush my leg. We broke the kiss and looked down and he was grasping Lou's thighs and pushing even harder and farther into her. She screamed a little as he pummelled into her pussy. She screwed her eyes tight shut. Finally, he groaned and thrust more slowly, grunting with each push, until he fell back. Lou fell forward onto him and kissed him.

"That was so deep," she said. "So deep it hurt a bit."

"Sorry."

"No—it was kind of nice. I've never felt you like that before."

I put my hand on Lou's bum and ran my fingers down the cleft, rubbing her anus gently, then traced it down farther to her pussy and felt his still-hard cock inside her, slippery from his cum that was beginning to seep out. I leant down and kissed her back. It was so smooth and the skin unblemished apart from the odd freckle. Her hips were splayed out, and I traced my tongue up the little bumps of her spine to the delicate shoulder blades.

I got off him and lay on the floor next to them and nuzzled my head into Lou's cheek as she was kissing Jamie.

All three of us kissed each other, then Lou lifted herself slightly and rolled off Jamie to the other side of him. As his prick slid out of her, I could see a large dribble of thick white semen drip out of her pussy. Quickly, I leant across Jamie and put my mouth between her legs. I scooped up his cum with my tongue and rolled it around my mouth, then plunged into her pussy, licking the inside as far as I could stretch, my tongue sizzling with the strong taste.

"Oh fuck, Sal—you're so good at that."

"I love it," I said. I moved my head to Jamie's softening cock and took it into my mouth. I sucked on it, drawing it as far back as I could, massaging it with my tongue. I felt the lust boiling up in me again and was determined to get him stiff.

Still sucking him, I put my hand onto his balls. They were sagging in their sac and it was more difficult to stroke them. I ran my fingers down to his bum and rubbed around the dry hole of his anus. He seemed to like that, and I thought I could feel his cock begin to harden. Quickly, I took my fingers away and put them into my pussy, soaking them in the juice that was still running down my thighs. Once they were well lubricated, I brought them back to his bum and rubbed there again. He sighed and moaned softly, and I could tell he was loving the feeling, so I pressed against his sphincter until my finger slid a little way inside.

"Oh fuck . . ." he gasped.

I put my other hand around the base of his cock and held it firmly, so I could pump my head up and down on him, bringing the tip of his cock to the back of my throat. At the same time, I pushed my finger into his bum right up to the knuckle. I remembered what it was like to fuck Maddie in the bum. It was such a randy feeling, and I could feel myself going into overdrive again. He moaned and I could feel his cock really begin to harden. I lifted my mouth off him and jerked him with my hand instead. I grinned down at him. "You like it up your arse?"

He just grinned back and went a bit red in the face.

I withdrew my finger slowly. "Well, now Lou and I want to be fucked—don't we, Lou?"

"Mmm," she murmured and kissed me.

I got on my knees and leant on the sofa cushions facing away from him. Lou crouched down next to me. "You know how I like it."

He came up behind me, kneeling on the carpet as well, and put his cock into me. It felt great as it pushed right up and I could feel the lust churn in my tummy. Then he began to fuck in and out quite fast and a delicious heat built up in my pussy. I pulled Lou's head down to me and kissed her sexily, our tongues playing and rubbing together. I felt her hand rub my back and run all over my bum cheeks. "Ohh yeah," I whispered to her, "finger my bum."

She smiled wickedly and put her finger on my anus. "What, there?"

"Oh yeah . . . fuck . . ."

"Naughty girl . . ." She ran it all round my sphincter and down that little sensitive bit of skin in between my bum and pussy.

"Oh shit, that's so fucking good," I said. Jamie was fucking me really hard now, and I could feel an orgasm coming. I buried my head in the sofa cushions and moaned. Lou's finger was sending fantastic vibrations up my bum and my pussy was getting red hot from Jamie's prick. I was in seventh heaven and didn't want to come just yet. I lifted my head and groaned as the pleasure just shattered all round me. I could hear them kissing and just thought how amazing this was, the three of us so relaxed with each other, trying new things, fucking each other in all sorts of ways. "Oh fuck, oh fuck, oh fuck . . ." I cried, feeling myself on the verge of coming. "Kiss me, Lou."

She leant down and plunged her tongue into my mouth, at the same time vibrating her finger on my anus. I was thrusting back on Jamie now, wanting him deeper and deeper, and faster and faster, and the combinations of all the sensations—her finger, his cock, our mouths entwined—sent a rush of heat through me that made me scream. The tension had risen so quickly that the pitch of the orgasm was almost too much. The blood rushed to my face and my breathing stopped as the explosion of relief suddenly pumped itself all through me, my pussy squirting so hard that it almost felt as if I was pissing myself . . .

I broke from Lou and dropped my head onto the cushions, my eyes tight shut. My body jerked as Jamie pulled out, and I concentrated on calming myself down. I heard them kissing and turned to look. Lou sat on the sofa, opening her legs, and Jamie moved in front of her, kneeling. His prick was still really stiff, wet from my pussy, and quite red. Lou took it in her hand and guided it into her. They both moaned as he pushed right up and Lou tensed for a moment. Then they slowly began to fuck again.

It was so lovely watching them. I had never watched any porn or anything like that at that time. I have since, but it's never been so horny as when I saw them. I suppose it's because in porn they are doing it for the camera at stupid angles, whereas this was just natural. The movement of Jamie's bum was so sexy, and Lou was gyrating her pelvis, just instinctively trying to get as much pleasure as she could. But also you could see they really liked each other. When they kissed deeply, or kissed each other's neck and chests, it was more than just lust. For one lonely moment, I wondered what they really thought, whether they just tolerated me, or loved me as well.

I needn't have worried, because the next second, Lou turned her head to me and smiled. I leaned over and she kissed me so sweetly, as though she knew what I had been thinking. Jamie put his arm around me and drew me to them and we all kissed together. We lay like that for a few minutes as Jamie went on fucking her, until I could tell that Lou was near to coming again. She was sighing loudly and kissing us hard, so I moved my head down to her breasts and started licking her left nipple. Her cries became more intense as she ran her hand through my hair. Jamie was fucking her harder now, and it was lovely to feel her body as the orgasm rose inside her—and when it took her, I moved my head to hers, kissing her all over her lovely face . . .

As her climax receded, she turned to me and kissed me on the mouth softly. Her eyes were closed, but she felt so loving. We lay like that for several minutes, and we curled round each other. Jamie had pulled out and was stroking our legs. When I finally looked up at him, he was tossing himself, his cock straining, glistening, and almost raw.

"Poor darling," I said. "We're ignoring you. Come here."

He came and knelt on the sofa beside me and I took his cock in my hand, then into my mouth. The taste was just like Lou's pussy as I pushed my mouth up and down it.

"Oh fuck . . . that's fantastic . . . oh, I'm going to come."

As soon as he said that, I sank my face onto him, letting him go deep, almost to the opening of my throat. I cushioned my tongue along it and pursed my lips so that they were quite tight on him, then with both my hand and my mouth, I fucked him for several strokes. I heard him moan, and the next instant felt my mouth fill with spunk. I almost choked because it squirted, but I managed to control it, swallowing a bit, and then grasping a breath, before more flooded out. I was quite surprised at how much there was given he had come twice already, but I loved it—and once I had taken most of it, I went on jerking him gently, wanting to give him all the pleasure I could.

When he had finished, he popped his cock out—and I turned to Lou, leant down and kissed her, letting it dribble into her mouth. She kissed me for a long time, out tongues playing with his juice . . .

I remember after that we lay together and chatted, drinking some more wine. It was amazing—three of us, naked, happy, and so relaxed.

Sally felt so relaxed as she lay on the bed. She had touched herself and made herself come twice reliving the memories. They had been just eighteen, all three of them—it was three years ago, but still so vivid. She licked her fingers, savouring the taste of herself, then looked at them. She had been so happy at that point, but had no idea then what was to come. Her mother getting ill, Jamie leaving, and her falling out with Lou.

She swung her legs off the bed and looked out of the window. Still, things weren't so bad now. But she was still intrigued about why Lou wanted to see her.

An hour had gone by, and the rain had stopped. She showered, then put on a blouse, a short skirt, and a cardigan. She didn't bother with a bra. She felt light and sexy as she drove to the house.

"Hi," she said to Emma's dad as she walked into the office. "What would you like me to do?"

His eyes flashed to her chest, as her cardigan was undone. "Er, I think you could probably catch up with some work in here," he said.

"OK," she said, and sat down at her desk. *Randy bugger,* she thought. She looked across at him and smiled. "Plenty to do."

"Good," he said, smiling knowingly.

She smiled back—and felt pleasantly amused.

Chapter 12

On the way back from Foix, Emma had taken a long detour to see her grandmother, who lived in a ramshackle farmhouse near the west coast. Emma had spent many happy holidays there when she was a child. It was nice spending the night there, catching up with the local gossip and being spoilt with delicious food. Her grandmother looked so much older than when she had last seen her. But she was so pleased to see her that Emma was glad that she'd gone—even though she had spent a lot of the time thinking about Sophie and her strange family.

Emma still couldn't quite believe what had happened, how she had fallen under the spell of Gerald—and how unbelievably promiscuous she'd felt. Not that she regretted it. Sex was so alive to her now, in a way it hadn't been before, and she wanted to enjoy what it could give her, catch up for lost time.

It was strange being at the chateau without Sophie, and on the first evening on her own, Emma felt listless. She looked at Sophie's bed across from hers. The cleaners had taken off the sheets and made it up with fresh ones. It was as though the past five weeks had been airbrushed out.

She'd heard some of the other students say that they were going down to the village, so she put on a light summer dress and walked to the square. She found a group of them at a bar: Hannah was there and one or two others that she knew.

During the evening, she became increasingly aware that Hannah kept looking at her. Initially, she smiled back and thought no more about it, but as the evening wore on, there was no doubt that Hannah kept meeting her eyes in a way that was unmistakable. Emma had been too wrapped up in

Sophie to really bother about anyone else, but looking at Hannah now, she was struck by her white blonde hair cascading over her golden brown shoulders and her clear, ice-blue eyes.

Emma looked at her again, holding her gaze until Hannah looked away. This happened several more times, and each time, Emma sent a message with her eyes: *If you're interested—I'm interested.*

Finally, Hannah got up to leave. Emma immediately stood up and went over to her. "Are you going back?"

Hannah looked slightly flustered. "Yes, I am a bit tired."

"Yes, so am I. I'll walk with you."

They walked in silence for a few moments before Emma thought she ought to say something. "Perhaps you are tired because the course is difficult?"

"No, I am OK. I have drunk too much wine. It is not good for me. For the health."

Emma smiled at her studied Swedish accent. "Oh, I think a little now and again is fine." She took Hannah's hand lightly in hers and felt a slight, shy resistance. They chatted for a while about their respective courses and how they had enjoyed being at the chateau. All the time, however, Emma sensed that there was something else behind the conversation.

"So, Sophie has gone, now?" said Hannah, as they turned into the chateau gates.

"Yes. She left at the weekend. Her course finished."

"Oh yes. Are you missing her?"

"Yes, I am rather. I feel a bit lonely."

"I didn't know you were . . . together."

"You mean lovers?" said Emma provocatively.

"Yes. I didn't realise that."

"Yes—we got together a few days after we arrived."

"That's nice. So—so you are a lesbian?"

"Yeah, well, bisexual." Emma squeezed her hand and felt a little press back. "I'm sorry if we embarrassed you that day at the pool."

"No, that was fine. I am sorry if I disturbed you."

"That's sweet. So, do you have a boyfriend or anything?"

"No. Not at the moment. I . . . I don't really have time."

"I'm surprised. You're such an attractive girl."

"Oh, I don't know about that."

Emma turned and faced her, taking her other hand. "I'm sure there are loads of boys who would love to hook up with you." The light from the chateau entrance cast a soft glow over them, and Emma could see the embarrassment in her eyes.

"I've never really got into that. Into the sex and boys."

"Well, you should."

"Yes . . ."

"You're really lovely." Emma pulled her forward by her hands and kissed her lightly on the mouth.

Hannah turned her head away. "I should go."

"Shall we play tennis in the morning? And then we could go to the pool for a swim."

Hannah looked at her again and said brightly. "Yes—that would be good."

"Good. That's a date, then."

They walked into the entrance hall and up the steps. At the landing, they both turned left as Hannah's room was a few doors before Emma's. At her door, they stopped.

"I'll see you tomorrow, then," said Emma.

"Yes. What time?"

"Oh, ten o'clock?"

"Good." Hannah hovered for a moment.

Emma smiled, then put her hands on her face and kissed her again. Her lips were passive, gossamer soft, and inexperienced. Emma increased the pressure, moving her lips over Hannah's, turning it from the affectionate peck of a minute ago, to the embrace of a would-be lover. When their lips finally parted, Hannah's eyes remained closed for a moment. When she opened them, she became immediately embarrassed. "Goodnight," she said, quickly turning and unlocking her door.

"Goodnight, Hannah."

Back in her room, Emma took off her clothes, pulled back the covers, and lay on the bed. She was feeling randy. Sophie had gone, but now she was alone on her bed, naked, with the touch of Hannah's kiss still on her lips.

She put her hand down to her pussy and frigged herself slowly, feeling the warmth build and the juice seep from her. Her fingers explored tenderly, peeling back the hood of her clitoris, teasing it gently, to the point that every caress seemed to echo round her body with shivers of delicious sensation.

Stimulating herself had never worked in the past. It was nice for a few minutes, but nothing ever came of it. It wasn't like now. She knew she could take herself to a climax quickly and easily, or long and slow, enjoying the journey, making her orgasm deeper and more satisfying.

She put a finger inside herself, closed her eyes, and remembered the weekend at Sophie's house, with Sophie and Antoine, watching them make love. "Watch us, Emma, and make yourself come. Come with me." She breathed in deeply and began to pump herself, adding two more fingers and feeling her vagina stretch, uncomfortably at first, then with a deep wave of pleasure. She paused, withdrew her fingers, and put them in her mouth. "Taste yourself and how nice your juices are." Sophie's voice echoed in her mind as she penetrated herself again, bringing herself ever closer. She wanted to make love to Hannah, to explore that athletic body, to release whatever hang-up she seemed to have about sex.

She thought of Hannah's breasts, imagined kissing them, taking each one in turn into her mouth, suckling each nipple. Then kissing her way up the delicate, sensitive neck to that lovely, anxious Swedish face, hovering for a moment above the fragrant mouth before their lips came together.

"Oh God . . ." she gasped and pumped herself quickly to an orgasm she knew she couldn't hold, her back lifting off the bed, the blood rushing to her face, and the whole of her body filled with the sweetest of relief.

She would seduce her tomorrow. Deep down, she knew that Hannah wanted her to.

The next morning, she went down to breakfast at about nine o'clock. Hannah wasn't there, so she sat with some other girls, ate her croissant and coffee, then wandered back to her room about forty minutes later. She stripped down to her panties, but as it was warm, delayed putting on her tennis things.

At exactly ten o'clock, there was a knock on her door. When she opened it, she held her T-shirt against her chest. As soon as she saw it was Hannah, she dropped it on the chair beside the door. "Come in, Hannah—sorry, I'm still getting dressed." She turned away and picked up her bra and tennis skirt. As she was dressing, she could feel the other girl's eyes on her. "Did you sleep well?"

"Yes . . . yes, thank you. I had the good sleep."

Emma sat on the bed and pulled on her trainers. She looked at Hannah. "I hope you will give me a chance at tennis today. You are much fitter than I am."

"You are a good player, I think."

"Hmm . . . we'll see."

"I have the hurting shoulder, so I think you may beat me."

"Oh? How did you do that?"

"I think that I hurt the shoulder playing yesterday."

They went down to the tennis courts. Emma chatted on the way down—but she thought Hannah was rather quiet. They played for about an hour. Emma did rather well, she thought, but Hannah still won practically every game, even though her shoulder was clearly hurting. Every so often, Emma would find herself admiring the other girl's young athletic body—her slightly muscular arms, her strong shoulders, and her long shapely legs. "OK—that's it—I'm really tired," said Emma finally. She walked towards the net. Hannah joined her and Emma put her arms around her neck and kissed her on the cheek. Sweat was dribbling down both their faces, and Emma could see the large wet patches under Hannah's arms. "Thank you. That was fun. Shall we go back to your room and have a shower—then we can decide what to do for the rest of the day."

The girl hesitated, her eyes wide. "Yes . . . OK."

"Good."

Emma could tell Hannah was nervous when she was opening the door to her room. She fumbled for her key, then couldn't get it into the lock for several seconds. Inside, Emma saw that it was a single room with a different layout.

"The shower is in there, if you want to go first," said Hannah.

There was a door to the left, and Emma could see that it was like a normal shower unit. "OK." She quickly undressed and laid her clothes on a chair.

"Here—a towel," said Hannah, her eyes sweeping Emma's naked body.

"Thanks."

As she showered, she felt a shiver of excitement. The water was hot and the jet strong, and she tingled with arousal. She dried herself thoroughly and let her damp hair hang down over her shoulders.

When she walked back into the room, Hannah had undressed and was standing with a towel held to her front. "Your turn," said Emma.

"Thank you."

Emma watched as she stepped into the bathroom. She had a long, beautiful back, full but taut buttocks, and strong thighs. Her skin was that rich, golden Scandinavian brown. Emma felt a little twinge of lust.

She brushed her hair with one of Hannah's brushes, then lay down on the bed. She could feel her damp hair tickle her neck and shoulders, and the coolness of the covers on her skin seemed to accentuate her sexy feelings.

When Hannah eventually emerged, she was holding a towel around her. She looked a little shocked at Emma lying naked on the bed.

"Come here. I'll massage your shoulders," said Emma.

Hannah nervously put a hand through her hair. "OK." She came to the bed and sat down with her back to Emma.

Emma ran her hands seductively up the bare, damp skin of her back. It had that sweet, clean smell of a newly washed body, and her hair wafted the scent of shampoo. "Tell me where it's tender," said Emma, putting her hands up to the slim, delicate shoulders and massaging them with her thumbs.

"Yes . . . there."

Emma moved both hands to Hannah's right shoulder blade and rubbed gently all round, occasionally pressing in on the muscles carefully.

"Oh yes . . . that is good."

She continued massaging the area for a couple of minutes, until her fingers and arms began to feel tired. She lightly kissed her there. "Is that better?"

"Yes. Thank you."

Emma put both her hands on either shoulder, then ran them down her front to her breasts. She pushed the damp towel away and cupped them, fondling them gently. She could feel the nipples were pronounced and firm. "You are so lovely," she said quietly. "Can I make love to you?"

"Yes," whispered Hannah—but she didn't look round.

Emma kissed her neck. It was long and elegant, with a soft blonde down close to the hairline. She could feel the muscles beneath the skin, and she moved her mouth over them, gently kissing her behind the ears. She put her tongue into her earlobe, pushing it in and circling it gently.

Hannah sighed. Emma massaged her breasts, taking the nipples between her fingers and pinching tenderly. Hannah turned her face, met Emma's mouth with her own, and they kissed. It was so soft and tender.

"Lie down," she said.

Hannah lay back on the bed, revealing her nakedness for the first time. She smiled up at Emma timidly. She wasn't actually a beautiful girl, thought Emma, but she had a lovely attractiveness about her. Her nose was quite pronounced, and her teeth were widely spaced, making her mouth wide. But her lips were full and sensuous, making it irresistible for Emma to lower her mouth to kiss her more fully this time, exploring her shyness, searching with her tongue.

Hannah responded slowly, whimpering quietly, her mouth gradually surrendering to Emma's insistence. After a few moments, Emma lifted her head, parting their lips. She wanted to take as much time as Hannah needed. She smiled down at her, and Hannah smiled back. Emma stroked her face and looked into her eyes—the pale blue pupils framed in the purest white. She pecked across her face with little kisses as her hand roamed down Hannah's body, stroking and caressing her breasts, her long, flat stomach, and the sensitive skin of her inner thighs.

Acute desire was building in Emma's groin. Only five weeks ago, she wouldn't have thought about being so attracted to another girl, but now her sexuality had broadened and deepened, and she could make love to either sex with a passion that had only grown. But as she looked at Hannah's naked form—her breasts with their conical, voluptuous nipples, the gentle ripples of her ribs giving way to her toned, flat stomach, and the full blonde bush that sat between her strong thighs—Emma wondered if she had always known somehow that she was bisexual.

Hannah's whole body jumped slightly as Emma touched the lips of her vagina. She was very wet, and Emma could sense that she was trembling. The look in her eyes was that of a frightened but excited child—there was an innocence about her, as though her sexual feelings had been suppressed for so long that she was now overwhelmed by what was happening to her. She eased her fingers delicately up and down, cupping her palm over the soft, wiry thatch of pubic hair.

Saliva gathered in her mouth as she looked down at the enticing peaks of Hannah's breasts. The nipples were a shade of pinkish brown, and they stood out in a conical shape as though they were offering themselves. Instinctively, Emma lowered her head and licked one gently, teasing it with her tongue, then opening her mouth to suckle more strongly . . .

Hannah gasped. "Oh . . . I . . ."

Emma probed carefully with her finger and slid it a little way inside. It felt very tight and confined, and she knew instantly that Hannah was a virgin, the confining ring of flesh gripping her as if forbidding her to go any farther. Emma eased it past her knuckle, but immediately felt Hannah grasp her hand.

"No . . . I don't think . . ." She was frowning, her eyes pleading.

"Why? Sex is very natural. Just let yourself relax." Emma moved her finger around inside. "That feels nice, doesn't it?"

"Yes."

"Good." She smiled at Hannah and lowered her head again, taking the other nipple into her mouth.

Hannah sighed and turned her head to one side, and Emma felt her hand loosen.

Slowly, Emma began to work her finger in and out, her thumb grazing Hannah's clitoris. She could hear Hannah's sighs become more audible, and the trembling had only increased. At the same time, she could still feel the pressure on her finger, as though her physical defences didn't want to yield. She took her time, sensing a kind of conflict deep within the girl, a deep-seated fear of letting herself go. She didn't want to hurt her, didn't want to cause her any pain, but somehow knew that Hannah wanted her to carry on, to bring her to the point where she wouldn't be able to resist any longer.

She kissed her way tenderly across her chest and slowly back to Hannah's face, still gently moving her finger in her pussy. Hannah's mouth was so enticing, so wide, the lips full and slightly curled upwards. As she kissed her, she thought the touch so soft and innocent, the kiss of a young girl still learning, still overwhelmed at the new world the caress of a lover's lips opened up. And suddenly Emma realised just how powerful the kiss of that older girl had been to her at the tender age of fifteen and how her own sexual development had been held back until released so wonderfully by Sally that night.

Emma felt the lust impatient in her own body, but resisted the urge to thrust her tongue deep into Hannah's mouth, to make love to her passionately like she had with Sophie. Instead, she gently pulled her finger out of her pussy and stroked her arms, her stomach, and breasts. She smiled at her lovingly, then kissed her lightly again. She pulled Hannah onto her side facing her, then put her arm around her, hugging them together. When she kissed her again, she brought her tongue forward and lightly brushed it over her lips. Hannah had her eyes closed, but she could feel her hands roaming her back.

Emma stroked her hair and looked at her. "Have you ever done this with anyone before?" she said.

"No . . . not really. I once kissed a boy at a dance—but he was rough with me. He just wanted to—you know."

"Did that put you off?"

"Yes. And anyway, my family is very strict. They are extra religious and say that sex must only come after marriage."

"Do you believe that?"

"Yes . . . but I have the strong feelings."

"Like now?"

"Yes."

"There's nothing wrong with this, is there? Just two friends being naked together? And touching each other?"

"No—I don't think so."

Emma kissed her nose and her forehead, then hugged her, pressing their bodies close together. "You feel so lovely."

"So do you."

Emma pushed her gently back down onto the bed, then sat up. She moved Hannah's legs apart and knelt between them. "Do you trust me?" she said.

"Yes," whispered Hannah.

"Do you desire me?"

"Yes."

She looked at Hannah intensely, then down at her golden bush, nestling at the top of her long thighs. She stroked her hands over the sensitive inner part of her thighs and was sure she could sense the trembling return. Slowly she stroked each time farther up her legs until she could graze her thumbs lightly over the thick, pink lips of Hannah's vagina. When she touched her there, she jumped again, as though it was almost hurting her.

"Sssh. What you're feeling is perfectly natural."

"Yes."

Emma ran the fingers of one hand so softly over her pussy. She wasn't going to penetrate her, she thought—maybe that had been too soon. Instead, she knelt down closer, and using both her hands, gently parted the lips and opened them out. A little trickle of pale white fluid came out. Emma looked up at her. "Your pussy looks beautiful. I want to kiss it."

"Yes," gasped Hannah quietly.

Emma lowered her head and put her mouth on the warm, wet opening. The taste of the juice on her tongue was sweet and sharp. She ran her tongue slowly between the lips and carefully sucked the little clitoris into her mouth.

Hannah cried out quite loudly, her thighs tightened, and Emma felt that incredible surge of lust inside her that made her just want to go on kissing the slippery, tender tissue, stimulating it lovingly. She longed to stretch her tongue inside Hannah's tight passage, but she knew that she had to excite her more first, bring her closer to the point where she would let go of her inhibitions. Emma ran her hands around the inside of her thighs, feeling the smooth skin taut over the straining muscles, hot with the blood pulsing through her. Hannah's vaginal lips felt so erotic in her mouth that Emma found herself stretching her body along the bed and rubbing herself against the sheet. She licked, kissed, and sucked with more intensity and could feel Hannah's excitement building. She slipped her hands down to her buttocks and cupped them, sliding her fingers along the cleft between the two cheeks. Saliva was flooding her mouth and dribbling down to Hannah's anus, so she rubbed it around the tightly closed sphincter with her fingertips.

She heard Hannah's moans grow louder and felt her pushing her pelvis against her mouth. Quickly, she positioned her tongue at the entrance to her vagina and pushed. She could sense the constriction and pressed gently against it. Slowly, she felt Hannah open herself, and she thrust her tongue right inside. Hannah screamed and her body seemed to seize, her thighs clamping Emma's head. She lurched one way and then another, finally gasping for breath and crying out again. Emma kept her tongue inside, pushing ever harder and farther until she sensed Hannah's orgasm receding . . .

Hannah's body relaxed. Gently, Emma lifted herself away then slid up and lay on top of her. As she kissed her, Emma could feel her mouth open and welcoming. "There. Now you can let yourself go . . . don't hold back anymore."

"Yes . . . yes, oh yes."

They kissed passionately now, and the pressure in Emma's groin became unbearable. Not being able to hold herself back, she lifted herself and slid her pussy along Hannah's stomach, sliding her legs to either side. The feel of Hannah's golden brown skin against her pussy and thighs was electric. It felt like warm velvet, and as she rubbed herself across it, she began to shiver.

"Oh, Hannah . . . your body is so beautiful . . . oh yes, I'm going to come . . ." She slid back down and found the sharp protrusion of Hannah's hipbone and crushed her clitoris against it. "OHHHHH YESSSS . . . YES . . . YES!" she cried, as she worked it furiously and the sharp, sweet climax took her. She thrust her groin round and round the hard little hillock, screwing her eyes tight as every muscle in her body seemed to spasm with ecstasy . . .

"Thank you. Thank you for that—it was so wonderful," whispered Hannah as they lay together.

"You see? It didn't feel wrong, did it?"

"No. No . . . it is foolish to say such things. I know that now." Hannah put her hand on Emma's face. "This has been so wonderful—but you go away tomorrow."

"Yes, but that's not important. Let's spend the time to-gether we have left. Will you sleep with me tonight?"

"Yes." Her wide, timid eyes looked curiously at her. "But don't you feel guilty about Sophie? Did not you love each other?"

Emma smiled. "Of course we were very fond of each other—but we knew that we had our own lives. Sometimes, people can be close for a short time, give each other a lot of pleasure, and then move on. That's how it was with us."

"Yes . . . I suppose so."

She could see sadness in Hannah's eyes. "Come on. We can go to the village and have a meal together. Yes?"

Hannah smiled. "I have classes this afternoon, but this evening would be nice."

Emma kissed her softly. "Good. Then we can come back to my room and make love all night."

With Hannah busy in her class, Emma felt at a loose end. It was a warm, sunny day, so she decided to go for a walk. She strolled through the formal garden and went up the steps to the fountain. The roses smelt as sweet as they had that first day. She smiled to herself as she recalled how brazen Sophie had been, making it so obvious that she fancied her.

She reached the top and looked out over the chateau and the woods beyond.

"It's a lovely view, isn't it?" a voice said.

She turned. It was Maurice, the chaplain. He was walking slowly towards her, a book in his hand. He was wearing his formal shirt and collar with a casual pair of trousers.

"Hello, Father," she said.

"Oh please—call me Maurice," he said, his eyes darting to her chest.

She was wearing a low-cut light summer dress with no bra—and she knew her breasts were quite visible. "OK. And yes, it's an amazing view. I'm going to miss it."

"Going soon?"

"Last couple of days."

"Ah. Has the course been good?"

"Yes, really good. I've learned a lot."

"You were doing the business French course?"

"Yes, that's right. How long are you staying here?"

"Another three weeks—until all the courses are finished."

"And then?"

"I'm moving to Carcassonne to do a bit more research, then going back to London."

"Research?"

"Yes, I'm looking into the Cathar period. I'm doing a report for the Vatican."

"Oh right. Yes, although it's centuries ago, it's still, like, very obvious—with all the castles and stuff. My grandmother often talks about it."

"Does she live around here?"

"Not close—a lot farther to the west."

"Yes, well. Not a time the church should be proud of."

"No, quite. Unbelievable slaughter."

"Yes." His eyes dropped to her chest again.

She suddenly had an image of him naked with Sophie in his room, her jerking him off. It felt strange, but quite amusing.

"Did you enjoy sharing a room with Sophie?"

"Oh yes. That was amazing."

"She's an intriguing girl."

"Mmm. Lovely."

"And she's left already."

"Yes—I went back to her parents' place for the weekend when she went back."

"You must miss her."

"Yes, I do. A lot." She couldn't stop a smile curling on her lips. "And of course, you must miss her too."

His eyes flashed to hers and he hesitated. "Yes, I do. She told you then."

"Yes."

"Were you shocked?"

"Nothing shocks me about Sophie. But I suppose I was a little shocked at you." She smiled at him, coyly.

"Well, I guess I'm not behaving strictly as a priest should, no."

"At least you're honest about it. And you're not a paedophile, as a lot of your colleagues seem to be."

"No."

"I think it's quite sensible, really."

"I gave up trying to resist it some time ago."

"Your sexuality?"

"Yes."

"Does it really haunt you?"

"Yes. I find it very difficult to concentrate sometimes. My work is very academic and dry, and after a while I find my mind drifts to thinking about all sorts of things."

"Sex?"

"Yes, particularly that."

"Have you ever had full sex?"

"Yes, when I was much younger. It was very hard giving it up."

"So what are you doing about it now Sophie's gone?"

"Making do."

"Oh dear. So you haven't managed to find another student to slip into your room and do the necessary?"

"Unfortunately, no. Sophie was quite unique. She knew there wasn't any possibility of any kind of relationship, but that didn't bother her."

"Poor you." She smiled at him coyly. Just then a breath of wind blew the top of her dress and partly exposed her breast.

His eyes flashed to her chest—then back to her face.

There was a sort of moment between them.

"Well, I must go," he said. "If I don't see you again, have a good journey back."

"Oh, I was just going for a short walk in the woods," she said quickly. "Do you really have to rush off?"

"Well . . . no, I guess not," he said, his eyes suddenly intense.

"Good."

She turned and strolled towards the edge of the wood. As she stepped under the cover of the trees, she turned and held out her hand. "It's quite warm today, isn't it? Quite makes you want to strip off."

He put his hand in hers and they continued walking into the woods along a grassy path.

"But then I couldn't possibly do that in front of a man of God," she said.

She looked at him, and his keen, intelligent face was suddenly like a young boy's—vulnerable and strangely preoccupied.

"I mean what an outrageous suggestion. Taking all your clothes off and wandering naked in the cool of the trees."

"I think it might be a bit risky," he said.

"Maybe. But I think that I might do it anyway." She let go of his hand and turned and looked at him—then she slowly undid the buttons on the front of her dress. She pushed it off her shoulders, let it slip down her body and drop to her feet, then she stepped out of it, naked apart from her panties.

His eyes devoured her body as she pushed her panties down and took those off as well. She stretched her arms above her head and ran her hands through her hair. "Oh, that feels good. You must be very hot with that collar on," she said, provocatively. She glanced about the woods. "There's no one around."

He reached behind his neck to undo the collar. He dropped it on the ground, then quickly unbuttoned his shirt, pulling it off his shoulders. She noticed his torso was fit and trained, and stripped of that fusty clerical dress, he looked so much younger.

He stood for a moment looking at her, then moved closer. Emma stood in front of him, unsure whether to touch him or not.

He undid the top of his trousers and pushed them and his boxers to his feet. His penis sprang out, stiff and hard—quite thick and a good eight inches long.

"Wow," she said, smiling at him wickedly.

"You're beautiful," he said. He wrapped his hand around it and began to massage it, slowly drawing the foreskin farther and farther back.

"Can't I do that for you?" she said.

Keeping her eyes on him, she put her hand on his, letting her thumb graze the swelling head of his cock.

She felt his hand slip from his penis, and she ran her fingers round it, feeling it so firm and smooth. She stroked it up and down and heard him breathe in deeply. She brought her other hand to his scrotum and gently fondled his balls. They were firm and compact.

"Don't you want to touch me?" she whispered.

"No. I would want more. Want too much."

"Please, I really want you to touch me. And I know you want to."

"Of course I do. But I mustn't."

"You just want me to make you come?" she said, eyeing him wryly. "Physical release?"

"Yes," he said, slightly breathlessly.

"Am I doing it all right?" she whispered. "Do you want me to pull your foreskin right back?"

He looked at her hand. "No—just as you are. It's amazing." His face was flushed.

"It's nice being naked for you." She quickened her pace rubbing him, and cupped his balls with her other hand, extending her middle finger along the little seam that led to his anus.

"Oh God . . ."

"Did you like Sophie being naked for you?"

"Yes, it was wonderful," he said, huskily.

"She has an amazing body. I adored making love to her." She felt his penis swell and grow harder in her hand—so she tightened her grip. "We had amazing lesbian sex, naked together in our room, day after day."

"Ohhh," he moaned.

"Yes, come over me. I want to rub your cum into my skin."

"Oh yes—oh God." He groaned and his face tensed and turned red. She looked down and saw long white spurts shoot out of his penis and spray her stomach.

"Oh yes. Come for me. That's so good." She kept up her rhythm, stroking him up and down, milking him, until the last drops were running down her hand.

Gently, she let go of him and licked her fingers. Her mouth fizzed with the strong taste. "It was so quick. Was it nice?"

He smiled, his face still flushed and his eyes bright. "Fantastic," he said. "Incredible."

Impulsively, she knelt down and, putting her hands on his thighs, took his penis in her mouth. She sucked on it gently, licking the last traces of his sperm from the head. "Mmm . . . lovely," she said, raising her head and licking her lips. "I'd like some more of that. I could make you come again if you want. In my mouth maybe?"

He sighed, hanging his head. "No—thank you. That was wonderful."

She stood up and spread the semen over her stomach and breasts, working it into her skin. "Lots of lovely holy spunk," she said. "Do I get a special blessing from the Pope?"

"I don't know about that, but you have made a very special contribution to my well-being."

She went closer and took his head in her hands—and kissed him tenderly. "What a pity I'm not staying longer."

"Never mind."

"Maybe in London?" she said, running her hands down his chest and smiling wickedly.

"Perhaps," he said—then he abruptly turned away and began to get dressed. He climbed back into his clothes hurriedly, almost guiltily, she thought.

She watched him. "You've got a lovely prick. I wouldn't mind that inside me," she said, lightly.

He fastened his collar. "I had better go."

"Sure."

When he had finished dressing, he hesitated and looked at her, slightly embarrassed. "Thank you."

"A bientot," she said.

"I hope so," he said, then strolled away down the path.

She stood with her eyes closed for a moment, feeling the cool air on her skin. She felt randy, but also rather shocked at herself. Her predilection for casual sex seemed to have grown over the past six weeks.

She decided she didn't care. She was feeling the best she ever had, and now she could look forward to the night with Hannah and then when she returned to the farm, hooking up with Sally—maybe.

She glanced around the woods, and up at the canopy of the trees—bright, fresh and so green. She was alone with her nakedness. There was something amazingly erotic about being nude in the open air. She put her fingers to her pussy and massaged herself. She could still feel the hot clamminess of Maurice's penis against her palm, remembered feeling it swell and get harder as she masturbated him, the intensity in his eyes, the way his stomach tensed as he came close, then the soft moan as he spurted and erupted all over her stomach.

She rubbed the still damp skin of her stomach with her other hand and increased the speed of her fingers exciting her clitoris. She closed her eyes and let the images of their brief encounter flit across her mind. Then as her pussy itched with her approaching climax, saliva still laced with the strong taste of semen gathered in her mouth, and a sweet, gentle orgasm took her. The soft summer air sent goose pimples across her flesh . . .

Maybe I'll fuck him when I get to London in the autumn, she thought, chuckling to herself as she ambled back down the hill. *If he'll let me.*

Emma laid back her head on the aircraft seat and closed her eyes. She had been late getting up, then had to rush to the airport to deposit her car and check in. Now she was deliciously tired.

Hannah had been a revelation. They had gone for walk, then eaten out in the village. Sitting opposite her, Emma had thought how lovely she looked. She had persuaded her not to wear a bra when they were dressing, and she had enjoyed the anticipation that the fullness of her breasts pressing against her blouse had given her as they sat eating. Her long blonde hair was cascading down her shoulders, and her eyes were such a pale sky-blue.

In bed she had been so unbelievably randy. She had done everything Emma had shown her and more. They had slept very little. It was as though now that her inhibitions were gone, she took to lovemaking like a science. Emma had lost count of how many times she had come.

She stretched out in her seat as the aircraft took to the air, the power of the engines pushing slightly into her back as the ground fell away.

Now there was Sally . . .

It had been at the back of her mind, but she couldn't let herself think about it. She had just assumed it would be all right somehow. But Sally was the one who had started this. She had flicked the switch, and now they had to face one another.

She took out her phone and brought up the pictures of her. She was better looking than Sophie, Hannah, or the girl at the airport. It was not only her amazing eyes, lovely complexion, and golden hair, it was the strange darkness behind that wicked sense of humour.

Her father met her at the airport. She threw her arms around him, much to his embarrassment, and talked at high speed as they found their way back to his car. The journey went quickly, and Emma found herself thinking more and more about Sally the nearer they got to home.

As they went up the drive, she couldn't resist asking about her.

"She's doing very well," said her father. "She knew a lot before she came—and she's a good worker. Never late, and always willing to work as many hours as we need."

"I knew she'd be good. It's going to be fun having her around this summer."

"Yes. I hope you're going to be available. I may need you occasionally as well."

"No trouble."

"Good. But—aren't you going away at some point?"

"No, I don't think so. Not with Charlie, anyway."

"Yes—your mother told me about that."

"I might find someone else to go with. I have paid for it, after all."

"Greece, wasn't it?"

"Yeah. A week."

As they pulled into the yard, she found herself looking around, expecting to see the slim figure with the blonde hair.

Chapter 13

Sally lay in the bath. She was expecting Lou to come round any time now, but somehow, she couldn't motivate herself to get out of the bath and dress. She didn't really want to see her again: she'd been such a bitch when the three of them split up, and somehow even now it was hard to think about forgiving her.

She stared at the ceiling.

Suddenly, out of the blue, Jamie had told me he was leaving. He was going to go back to Australia with his dad. His dad was leaving my mum, and Jamie was going back with him. It was all decided—their air tickets booked, and they were going in a week.

I froze. I was totally gutted. "You can't!" I said.

"I told you, I don't want to—course I don't. My dad just did it. And—I mean, I can't just stay here. What would he do? You know what he's like. He'd just piss himself into oblivion. I'm what he lives for."

"And what about me? Don't you live for me?"

"Yeah . . . but. Oh, I don't know."

I felt so hopeless. We just sat there on the bed. I stared at the floor. I felt so angry and bitter and resentful. In the end I told him to fuck off and go to bed.

The next day I rang Lou.

"Yeah. He told me," she said.

"But what do you think?"

"I dunno. I guess these things happen."

"But don't you feel angry?"

"I feel upset. But there's not much we can do about it."

"Can I come round?"

"Yeah . . . course."

We sat on her bed and talked about it. She was much more rational than me. But then, I had lived with him for eight years. It was like it was breaking up my family as well, even though I knew that my mum wanted to end the marriage. I started to cry, and Lou put her arm around me.

After a while I felt better—and I kissed her. "Good thing we've got each other," I said.

"Yeah," she said, with a half smile.

I put my hand on her thigh and slid it up to her pussy. She opened her legs and I played with her, but I sensed something was wrong. We kissed some more, I put my fingers inside her, and then she began to loosen up.

There wasn't anyone else in the house, so we took all our clothes off and made love on the bed. I went down on her and made her come, but she just seemed to lose interest after that.

"What's the matter?" I said.

"Nothing. I'm just a bit tired."

I felt so worked up I got myself off by rubbing myself against her thigh.

I went home feeling depressed. I thought about going to Jamie's room—but was still too angry. I went to sleep feeling miserable, wondering as well what the matter was with Lou. Then the next day I found out. I was walking through the park near the school—and I saw them. Lou and another guy. He'd always been keen on her, and I know she quite liked him—flirted with him, liked the attention. She had her arms round his neck, leaning against a tree. They were laughing and kissing.

I froze when I saw them. I saw red. I was so angry, I couldn't stop myself. I went up to them and I pushed him off her.

"You bitch—you fucking cow! You're a cheap tart—CUNT!"

"What? Get off! What's the matter with you?"

I turned away and walked off. Then I heard her behind me.

"Look, Sally," she said. "Jamie's leaving. He's going. Going to the other side of the earth. What do you think we should do? There's no point moping about it."

"Yeah, but what about me?" I shouted.

"What about you? Look—we had some fun, you, me, and Jamie. The sex was great—but what do you expect? You and me having some sort of dykey fucking relationship? The girly couple hanging around together? Get real— I'm not gay, and I don't want to be. Get on with your life, for fuck's sake." She turned and stormed off. Her twat of a guy stood looking at us—but I don't think he'd heard what we said.

I went home. I told my mum I wasn't feeling well and she rang the school. I cried and cried all day. I refused to come out of my room, and I missed supper. I knew my mum was upset about the break-up, but I was too selfish to think of her. I was too into myself.

Then I couldn't sleep. I just kept thinking about it. So, in the end, I went to Jamie's room.

I took off my dressing gown and got into bed with him. "Fuck me," I said.

"Sure?"

"Course I'm fucking sure."

"We'll have to be really quiet. My dad's back."

"Oh fuck him. I don't care if he hears. I want him to know you fuck me."

I pushed him onto his back and lay on top of him. I kissed him strongly. "You'll never find another lover like me. I'll do everything you ever want in bed," I whispered. I could feel his cock hard against my stomach. The lust burned in my pussy, so I raised myself, took it in my hand, and guided it into me, then I slid down onto him.

It felt amazing. I let him go right deep into me in one long gorgeous thrust. "You can have me every which way as often as you like. And you can bring other girls home—and fuck them. I don't care. If they don't want me to join in, I'll just watch." I was rising up and down gently on him, each time pressing him harder inside me.

"You're amazing. I know that. I know I'll never find anyone else like you."

"No, you won't. I'll do every sex fantasy you could ever want."

He grabbed my hips and began to push himself faster into me. "Oh, I love fucking you," he said.

"You like my cunt? You like fucking my cunt? Just think, if you stayed, you could fuck me whenever you wanted. Fuck my cunt, fuck my mouth, anywhere you liked." I felt an excited pulse in my stomach. "You can fuck me in the arse if you want." I wasn't scared—I wanted it. I wanted to do it especially now, just to show him I was a lover without any limits. But also, if I was going to have anal sex, it had to be with Jamie first, because I loved him—and would always love him.

But suddenly he was coming—pumping me and moaning. I could feel his spunk squirting in my pussy, and I squeezed him tightly, trying desperately to come as well.

But I couldn't. I was overwhelmed by a strange kind of lost feeling. I knew I could suck him and get him hard again—but I didn't want to. It was over, finished. He was going. And I suddenly knew that Lou had been right to cut him off—to reject him and go and hitch up with that twat who'd been fawning all over her for ages.

But I couldn't forgive her for what she'd said—never ever.

Sally stood up sharply in the bath and took the towel from its hanger. She felt a sense of panic. *But that's what always happens,* she thought. *They love you then cast you aside. Now she's come crawling back and can't help herself. It's all too fucking complicated. No relationships—I don't want that any more.*

Sally sat across from Lou in the lounge. She had just gotten out of the bath when the bell rang, so she had quickly pulled on a T-shirt, some pants, and jeans.

She was a bit surprised when she saw her. She was still very pretty, but looked different to the way she'd looked before. Lou had always been vivacious and sexy—but she wasn't this time.

When she arrived, she had given Sally a quick peck on the cheek, but ever since had not really made eye contact. She looked uncomfortable and rather serious.

They chatted about what Sally had done since they last met, and about why she had applied for the job on the farm. Sally kept it light, but she could feel the past and what had happened hovering awkwardly between them.

"So you didn't go to college or anything?" Sally had made some tea and was bringing it in on a tray.

"No. I just thought it wasn't for me," said Lou.

"Why? You always said that's what you wanted to do."

"Well . . . things changed in my life, and I went in a different direction."

"So what do you do?"

"I work for a Christian charity."

"Oh. Right." Sally poured a cup of tea. "Milk?"

"Yes, please. Anyway, one of the reasons I wanted to come and see you—to get in touch again—was to tell you that I'm getting married."

"Oh. Really—that's nice. Who to?" Sally passed it over to her. As Lou leaned forward, she got a quick glimpse of her breasts through the open neck of her blouse. She remembered kissing them and licking her way across the fine skin of her neck.

"His name's David. We met two years ago."

"Oh. Is he nice?"

"Yes. He's very good for me."

"Well—congratulations."

"Yeah. I'm so looking forward to it. I love him very much. He's been a real inspiration to me. It was really him that led me to changing my life."

"Changing your life?" Sally looked at the girl's face—her soft blue eyes and sweet lips.

"Yes. My Christian belief."

"Oh—sure. Well I know your family had always been religious, but I thought you didn't care much about it."

"No, but I really became a Christian when I met him, and it's completely changed me. I see things very differently now. And I know that you and I were, you know—close—before, and I now know that some of the things we did were wrong, but I still want so much for you to come to the wedding and be my bridesmaid."

"Wrong?" It had sounded sharp, she knew—but there was a self-righteousness about the girl that was beginning to infuriate her.

"Well, I've talked a lot to the minister of our church about the . . . the nature of our relationship, and he has said that of course what we did was sinful, but that God is all forgiving and that we could become friends again and put that behind us. But that we shouldn't leave anything we've done on this earth hanging unresolved, so to speak."

Sally took a deep breath. "I see. So that's why you came here?" She could just see Lou's knees sitting tightly together under the prim skirt. She remembered so vividly stroking them, then running her fingers up those silky thighs.

"Well—yes. I mean—I really want you to share the joy I feel now, and—I don't know—perhaps we can be friends again."

Sally thought there was a kind of ghastly false sincerity in the way she was talking. Where was the girl who was so randy—and such fun? "Friends again?" said Sally, forcefully.

"Yes."

"So I have to confess what a dreadful person I was having sex with you just to be accepted by you?"

"Well, I . . ."

"Look, we were kids and had a bit of fun, that's all."

"Well, I can't see it that way."

"So you don't like sex now?"

"Well, David and I have decided we won't have sex until we are married."

Sally wanted to laugh. "What? Really?"

"Yes."

"So the sex we had was wrong, was it?" Sally could feel herself getting angry, but at the same time she was conscious it was mixed with a raging attraction. She really wanted to rip the girl's clothes off and stick her tongue down her throat.

"That sort of . . . lustful activity is not right in the eyes of God."

"Well, I'm sorry, but I'm not on very good terms with your God. You see, he let my mother get cancer and die quickly in a horrible way. She was half the size she used to be when she died—did you know that?"

There was a stunned silence. Sally looked at her. In her mind's eye, she suddenly saw them both naked together, and the gleam in Lou's eyes as she'd shoved her finger up Sally's bum.

"Yes . . . yes. I often struggle with myself when I think how I didn't get in touch at that time . . ."

"Struggle with yourself? Try dying inside because your mother is in such pain!" Sally was furious now, standing up and staring down at her. "So tell me, what is so great about your God that he lets that happen?"

"I—I don't know . . . I'm sorry."

"And what was so bloody wrong about what we did?" she shouted. "You didn't seem to think it was so wrong when you were screaming your head off with my tongue up your pussy." Sally was resisting the urge to grab hold of her, slap her, strip her, and get to the real Lou.

"I'm sorry. This was a mistake. Perhaps I ought to go."

"Too bloody right. I wouldn't be your fucking bridesmaid even if you paid me."

"Right . . ." She got up, took her bag, and walked smartly to the lounge door without looking back.

Sally instantly felt remorse. "Look—Lou. I'm sorry." Lou went into the hall, then opened the outside door sharply.

Sally rushed up, took her hand, and pulled her back, pushing the door closed. "I'm sorry—I shouldn't have said all that." The touch of the soft hand made her glow.

"Don't worry—I'll just go."

"No." She put her hand to Lou's face.

Lou stared at her, her eyes wide. For a split second, Sally saw the scales fall away and a glimpse of the old friend she had known. Impulsively, she leant forward and kissed her.

Lou's lips were passive—but she didn't pull away. She shut her eyes tightly and frowned. "I'd better go."

"No, please," Sally said and kissed her again. Suddenly, she felt a response from the soft, sweet mouth, and they pulled together. Their lips parted only to close again as Lou pulled her into a hungry French kiss. Lou was breathing heavily as their tongues wrestled, whimpering softly.

Sally felt an incredible rush of lust. She broke from her mouth, kissing her neck, her shoulder blades, and down across the soft cotton over her chest, sensing the warm, firm flesh underneath. She pulled Lou's blouse out of her skirt, put her hands on her breasts, and pushed her bra away, cupping the familiar firm mounds. They were hot and the nipples stiff. Greedily, Sally took one, then the other into her mouth, sucking on them, tasting them with her lips and tongue.

Lou gasped. "Sally . . . oh, Sally . . . we can't do this."

Sally lifted her head, stood up, pulled her T-shirt over her head, and dropped it on the floor. "Why not? Do you really want me to stop?"

Lou stared at her, now naked from the waist up. They kissed again, and this time, Sally thrust her hand down between Lou's legs. She rubbed her mound through her panties, feeling the material become quickly damp.

Lou ran her hands up to Sally's hair, stroking it, pressing their mouths together. As their lips parted briefly, Sally could read the intense passion in Lou's eyes. She slid her fingers under the little white panty slip and into the sticky bush of pubic hair, running with fluid.

She broke the kiss sharply, keeping her face close to Lou's. "I remember what you always liked me to do," she whispered. She kissed her way down again, continuing this time until she was level with Lou's sex. She put her hands under her skirt and pulled her panties down over her creamy thighs until they dropped to the floor.

"Oh God," Lou whispered, as Sally pushed the skirt up out of the way and leaned in to the pink, waiting gash. *It smells intensely of sex,* thought Sally, as her nose lost itself in the little bush and her tongue snaked up and down the slippery flesh. Lou had always loved sex so much . . . and Sally could smell it, and taste it.

Sally sucked Lou's clitoris into her mouth. She pulled it between her lips, then licked it with the flat of her tongue. Lou screamed and pressed Sally's head firmly against her. Sally could feel her body shuddering and knew that she was on the verge of coming already, but she kept up her caresses, loving the tender flesh.

She slid two fingers inside her. Lou's body bucked again, and she went on uttering little cries, her hands clawing at Sally's hair. Sally pushed her fingers in and out, fucking her as her tongue continued relentlessly flicking all over her sex, never letting the hot, stiff nub of her clit relax.

"Sally—please . . . oh God—yes . . . YES, YES! AAAAAHHHHH . . ."

She held Sally's head in a vicelike grip, riding out her orgasm as though it would never end . . .

Sally finally felt her relax. She looked up and saw Lou's head was turned to one side, her eyes closed, her chest heaving, short gasps coming from her mouth.

Sally stood up, took her head in her hands, and kissed her softly. "Sex is so good—and you love it," she said, feeling Lou's panting breath on her face. "That's the only reason you came here. You wanted this to happen. Don't do this. Don't throw yourself away on this stupid guy. That's not what you want; you know that."

"I . . . I must go. I'm sorry," stammered Lou, pulling herself away. She pulled up her panties roughly and turned and opened the door, not looking back. She stumbled out, settling her skirt down, her blouse still hanging out and her bra tangled. Sally followed her. "Lou, look . . . don't leave like this. Stay for a bit. We can talk it through. Go to bed and make love properly." Suddenly she saw someone else was there—and froze.

"Emma . . ."

Emma stared at her bare chest, then smiled, obviously acutely embarrassed. "I'm sorry, Sal. I've come at a bad time." She looked over her shoulder at Lou, hurriedly getting into her car. "I'll come back some other time. Sorry, I only arrived this morning." She turned and walked down the path.

"No—wait."

Emma turned.

"Look—I'm really sorry . . . I . . ."

"It's OK—really."

Emma smiled and looked back quickly at Lou driving off. "I didn't mean to disturb you."

Sally put her hand across her breasts—she wasn't sure why—and walked down the path towards her. She was acutely conscious of the smell of Lou's pussy on her mouth. "It's really nice to see you. I'm sorry about that."

"Don't worry—really. I'll see you soon." Emma walked to a bike that was propped up against the fence. She half smiled at her, got on the bike, and cycled off.

Sally closed her eyes and sighed.

"Shit," she whispered.

Lightning Source UK Ltd.
Milton Keynes UK
UKOW03f0654160614

233491UK00001B/220/P

9 781628 579741